THE IMAGE OF CHRISTIAN

J. Crispin-Ripley

THE IMAGE OF CHRISTIAN

DOUBLE DRAGON

A DOUBLE DRAGON PAPERBACK

ISBN 978-1-78695-679-8

Double Dragon
is an imprint of
Fiction4All

Published 2021
Fiction4All
www.fiction4all.com

Cover Art by Deron Douglas

Chapter One

He might as well be comfortable waiting for Grace, presuming Grace existed. Christian chose a bench near the junction of two main paths, and sat. Although the park was alive with people, most were only passing through, journeying from one part of the widespread University of Noronto campus to another. He opened the cardboard cup of coffee he'd bought at the subway station and took a sip. It was dreadful but drinkable... just.

A cluster of students debating the logic of the registration process drifted past. One joked that getting properly enrolled was a secret test. If they got the right pieces of paper to the appropriate places within the time allotted, their academic success was guaranteed. That earned a collective, nervous laugh. Christian smiled to himself. In the ten years since he'd graduated, the jokes hadn't changed.

He put down his coffee and leaned back on the bench to enjoy the morning. It was warm for the middle of September--the smell of freshly mown grass mingled with the scent of the nearby flowers, neatly planted in rectangular beds. A black squirrel scuttled past, then stopped to see if Christian had any squirrel treats. It gave him a baleful look when none were forthcoming and continued on to investigate a garbage can. When Christian took the printout of the Internet job posting he'd replied to from his pocket, the squirrel looked back. Still seeing no food, it sat on its haunches and delivered a short squirrel curse before continuing about its business.

Christian read the ad again. "Generalist: DOS/Dostoevsky. Seeking adventure? If you know something about computers, literature and the social sciences, send me your resume. Also, explain what DOS and Dostoevsky have in common, and how they differ." The sender's name was purportedly Grace X Machina.

He wasn't looking for adventure, just a job, but he had the qualifications-¬such as they were. He had replied, "Dostoevsky wrote The Idiot and didn't make much of a living. I'm not sure what idiot wrote the original DOS, but someone who didn't made a fortune from it. Both DOS and Dostoevsky are now considered largely of historical interest, but do have their aficionados. My resume follows..."

Grace's response was that if he was in the park between eleven and twelve she would find, and interview him. Which sounded as unlikely as her name--Christian suspected a prank. However, since the alternative was to spend another day in his shoebox apartment, contacting companies at random to solicit work, he'd decided to chance being played for a sucker.

It was proving a good decision. Not only was it a lovely day, but the scenery was excellent. His eyes wandered to a rangy woman in white tights, sauntering along on the grass. That wasn't illegal, merely unusual--people normally kept to the paths. There wasn't anything ordinary about this woman though and from the way she moved, she knew it.

Luxuriant red hair spilled down her shoulders and over her halter-top. Her stride had the confidence of experience. Christian tore his eyes away to again admire the flowers. They looked as before.

Another glimpse of the woman would be far more interesting. It would make both of them happy. Only a few feet away now, she met his eyes, smiled, and stopped.

"Registering...?" Christian asked. He could have found a more inventive opening line.

"No, nice try though." The expression on her angular face put Christian in mind of a fox viewing a sea of unguarded chickens. "I'm not a student," she continued. "I have, however, done considerable research in postgraduate Biology."

To look up and meet her eyes (pale green, fading into nothing), he had to ignore the scanty top jutting into his field of vision. Quickly recognising the impossibility of that, he stood. She was even taller than he'd thought, barely less than his six foot four.

What to say to a goddess? "Sorry if I was staring. I'm waiting for someone I don't know. I don't know you, so I was checking to see if you were looking for someone." His words sounded lame. Christian felt a flush of embarrassment spread over his face. When he faced a beautiful woman his brain always tied itself in knots and his tongue went numb.

Her eyes met his and narrowed. He was at her mercy, and they both knew it. She put her snakeskin briefcase on the bench by his abandoned coffee. A flick of her head sent long hair swaying; it brushed Christian, making him shiver.

She grinned. Even her teeth were perfect. "Another feeble excuse. You don't think any better on your feet, do you? Well, while I'm tempted to take advantage, I must admit I'm not your blind date." She moved closer--a breath separated them.

"It's not a date. I answered a help-wanted ad..." He found himself babbling the story. This was the reticent Christian Plowman? He couldn't read her expression; he wasn't sure if she was interested or amused, and wasn't sure he cared.

"If you think it's a joke, come with me."

Christian shook his head. "No, I'll wait until noon. I made a commitment."

"Oh, how disappointing. I own several businesses myself, and I can always accommodate a strong, handsome man like you. Don't you want to come?" She touched Christian's arm. He gasped-- her hand felt like an iron, branding his flesh. Another headshake was the most articulate response he could manage.

She withdrew her hand, stepped back and bent to retrieve her briefcase, treating him to the depths her top contained. She hesitated, her other hand on his coffee. "You going to drink this?"

Another headshake. "No. It's probably cold by now." Hard as he tried, he couldn't keep his eyes on hers. Her breasts were magnificently full.

"Then throw it out." She kept the cup as she straightened. "Unless you feel obliged to drink it. You must have intended to when you bought it."

"That's different," he answered, taking the cup from her.

"I'm not so sure," she responded. "Well then, may I?" Her pale eyes flickered towards the garbage can and back.

"Be my guest." He offered her the unwanted coffee.

Her hand lingered on his as she took it. "But you're still sure you don't want to come with me instead of waiting around?"

"No, I'm not sure. I just know it's what I have to do."

"Very well then." After depositing the coffee in the garbage can, she took a business card from her case and gave it to Christian. "So be it. Some other time then. I must run."

She didn't quite run. Christian glanced at the card. "Lucille M. Firman, Subterranean Enterprises--Sole Proprietor". She had a toll-free phone number. The only address was for e-mail--interestingly, her address was at diluvia.org, as was that of the mysterious Grace.

"Lucille!" he called. "You didn't get my name."

She stopped and looked back. "I'm Lucy to my friends. Do get in touch, Christian. Soon." She hurried on.

She knew his name? He must have introduced himself and forgotten, befuddled by her head-clouding presence. Christian slipped the card into his shirt pocket and admired Lucy's rapid yet unhurried departure. She flowed effortlessly, red hair swinging. Her tights fit like skin, leaving little to the imagination. Christian imagined all the same.

As Lucy reached the road at the edge of the park a black limo pulled up in front of her and she got in, without looking back. Christian filed a salacious daydream in the corner of his mind, to be dealt with later. If the interview with this purported Grace turned out to be a joke now, he doubted he'd appreciate the humour. But if so, he could always contact Lucy. He suspected he would anyway, or if he didn't, she would contact him. She had the aura of someone who got what she wanted, or else. If she wanted him, however improbable that might seem, he was doomed.

But what a doom! Christian couldn't keep Lucy's image tucked away and got lost in a replay of her approach. This time he stood and took a step towards her. Without a word she melted into his arms and pressed against him, her body searing his...

"Christian?"

He wrenched himself away from Lucy. A short, dark woman in a brilliant red pantsuit stood in front of him, smiling. Slung over one shoulder was an immense purse.

"Yes? Oh! You must be Grace." It wasn't his day for making good first impressions.

"Indeed I must." She swung her bag onto the bench. "No, don't bother standing," she continued as she sat. Christian hadn't moved. "The weight of that darn thing on my shoulder gets to be too much after a while." She peered into it. "Here now, your resume's on top. Since you're sitting in front of me, I don't need it." She crumpled the paper into a ball and flipped it over her shoulder in the general direction of the trash bin. The wind caught it and deposited it dead centre. "The job's yours. Oh yes, my card." Her arm went elbow-deep into the bag.

Her card could have been from the same discount printer as Lucy's-¬"Grace X Machina, consultant", a local phone number, and the diluvia.org address he'd written to earlier. It didn't tell Christian anything he needed to know about his prospective employer but as Grace had said of him, she was here and he could ask.

Grace held up a hand. "Wait. I hope you were about to accept, but I do have reservations--for lunch. I don't want to pressure you, so I won't ask for your answer until after."

"Thank you." Christian took out his wallet and put Grace's card in where folding money was supposed to go. He considered transferring Lucy's card from his pocket and decided against. If Grace noticed he might have to tell her about his encounter with Lucy and he wasn't sure he could. He wasn't sure what had happened, if anything--or whether Lucy's proposition had been long term or short. He did know he needed gainful employment more than he needed sex and that Grace's offer was unequivocal. He couldn't afford to turn her down.

"Come along now." Grace stood, grabbed her purse and started to walk in one fluid motion.

"What sort of consultant are you, Grace?" Christian asked when he caught up.

"I've been called an efficiency expert, trend analyst, councillor, fortune-teller, business advisor... take your choice. Me, I don't call myself anything at all. People tell me their dreams and if I like them and they sound sure of themselves, I tell them to go ahead, and put them in touch with others I think can help. When things work out, I get a percentage." She gave a trilling laugh. "The better part of success is surrounding yourself with the right people." She smiled--teeth as perfect as Lucy's. "I also do personnel searches. I expect to be asked to start one today, but I'm going to be away from Noronto for a while so I need someone to stand in for me--you."

"What will I do as your stand-in?"

Grace grabbed his hand and pulled him to an abrupt halt. "How could I know? You'll be the one doing it." Her purse bumped him. "Trust to instinct and do what you feel is right. I'm hiring you because you have good sense and a good heart."

"But..." That wasn't on his resume. And she obviously didn't know him at all, didn't know what a mess he'd made of his life.

"And don't doubt yourself." Grace took his other hand. "Your decisions will have my blessing, whatever they are, okay?"

"Why?"

"Someday you'll be able to answer that question for yourself. Right now... I want my lunch. Chez Celeste awaits."

***

Christian thought he knew Noronto well but he'd never heard of Chez Celeste. It was close by in a large brownstone, on a side street. From the cars outside, the restaurant was upscale. Its sign was a small brass plaque on the door with lettering too fine to be seen from the sidewalk. Chez Celeste wasn't a place one would find by accident.

Grace was clearly known there, and well respected; she was greeted with a bow and they were immediately shown to an alcove, ahead of others who were waiting. The decor was simple and elegant, plain wood that didn't need ornamentation to show its quality. The patrons suited the establishment--Christian recognized a number of faces he'd seen on television or on the front pages of newspapers, although in many cases not recently. He felt underdressed and was, by a considerable margin, the youngest person in the room.

"Any time you want a table, call Uri and mention you work for me." Grace reached into her purse, took out another card and wrote a name and number at the bottom. "He'll find room for you, no matter what. Bring your friends."

She slid the card across the table. "And now, if you'll indulge me, I should check my messages." She extracted a small laptop from her luggage, pulled out its antenna, tapped a few keys, and waited. "Oh good, Cosmo says any time this afternoon is fine. I'll tell him we'll be there after lunch." After typing her reply she pushed in the antenna and closed the lid.

The food arrived, a small omelette and salad for Christian, and an immense Caesar for Grace. She lifted her fork and looked at him. "Okay. Tell me about yourself, things you wouldn't put on a resume like your life story or your philosophy. Or don't. But no business talk until lunch is over."

Christian wanted to ask if the "Cosmo" they were going to see was the one and only Cosmo Sharpe, Noronto's home-grown media mogul and self-proclaimed prophet. But that would be business, so instead he offered Grace part of the chronicles of Christian. That was much easier to relate than his philosophy--as far as he was aware, he didn't have one.

He glossed over his past jobs and how after he'd been laid off from the last, he hadn't been able to find another. The economy had gone into depression and from the viewpoint of many unemployed people, including Christian, had never recovered. He felt lucky though; his previous job had lasted seven years and he'd saved enough to see him through three lean ones. Many had been less fortunate.

Then he told Grace about Cleopatra Wong. He'd lost her soon after he lost his job. He'd met her at university when she'd been a business student and he an English major, drifting towards a degree. Cleo had given him direction, pushing him up a corporate ladder she found for him after graduation.

After the lay-off, she got him a position selling life insurance on commission. He discovered what he was expected to sell was fear and an expensive balm to assuage it--he walked away from that within the month. Cleo left him a week later, claiming she was moving in with a man she'd been maintaining an affair with for years. Christian didn't know if that had been the truth but hadn't seen or heard from Cleo since, or made any attempt to replace her.

Grace listened; making the socially accepted grunts and gestures that indicate one is paying attention. When the waiter asked if they would like dessert she ordered coffee and a double chocolate cheesecake for Christian, and a coffee for herself. When it arrived, Christian decided to give the treat his full and proper attention and quickly wound up his monologue.

He took a bite. The cheesecake was heavy and rich, cloying. He put his fork down. Grace looked at him over the rim of her full cup. "And so the past became the present, and then the future. What has been, always will be." She sipped and put the cup down. "To ensure this, when you meet someone new, you hand them a snapshot of Christian as the failure you know him to be, kindly saving them the trouble of creating their own Christian." She sighed. "It's time for a new image. You've presented me with the essence of the old. Now leave it behind. The waiter will put it out with the trash."

"I can't, Grace. You could fire up your computer and tap into databases that would tell you everything about me."

"Maybe, and yes maybe anyone could--if they bothered. But it wouldn't have sad music playing in the background. Besides, anything found there would need to be interpreted. Facts and figures are meaningless."

Christian shook his head. "You don't understand, Grace. This is the Information Age."

"Squawk! Information age--information age--Polly want a cracker-¬information age." Heads turned in their direction. Grace laughed, and lowered her voice. "Nonsense. This is an age of faith, just like any other. All that data gets shaped and moulded by the prophets of this so-called Information Age to create the reality they choose. These are the New Dark Ages, Christian. Ignorance rules, as always." She waved for the bill.

"But isn't that what you do, Grace?" She looked puzzled, so he elaborated. "Don't you analyse the available resources and the production and sales data when you make business plans for your clients?"

Grace laughed again, softly. "Bafflegab. No, I leave that sort of thing to others. My focus is on finding clients who know people are more than human resources and on finding people who won't contort into whatever shape they think is demanded. The best I hire for myself. You'll do well, Christian. Trust me."

She signed the cheque and stood. "But from now on let others decide for themselves who you are. Remember you left the old Christian behind, and see what happens. Let's go. Cosmo Sharpe awaits."

That answered Christian's earlier unvoiced question, although he'd been reasonably sure Cosmo Sharpe was the "Cosmo" Grace had meant. She'd said the name like it was a complete identification, like "Elvis" or "Madonna". In Noronto, Cosmo was probably as well known.

Outside, Grace walked to the curb and raised her hand. A taxi pulled up immediately and they got in. "The Factory," Grace told the driver. With a squeal of tires the taxi made a U-turn and sped down the street.

Grace turned to Christian. "Okay, let's hear what you think you know about Cosmo. The short version, please."

Christian closed his eyes, half to show he was thinking, and half to avoid watching as the taxi swung sharply around a slow-moving Volvo. "Cosmo started by buying a small radio station in the '60's. It was the first to play rock 24 hours a day and it took off. When I got to Noronto fifteen years ago, it was the country's leading station. Personally, I don't care for it anymore."

Grace cleared her throat. The cab lurched to the right. Christian reluctantly opened his eyes and tried to focus on Grace and ignore the cab's weaving path. "The short version," Grace said. "And not the Christian-centred version."

"Sorry. I'll stick to the facts. If they are facts. Cosmo's legend has been told by the stations he owns, so its accuracy is suspect."

Grace smiled. "Yes. He gives himself a positive spin, perhaps too much so, much like the old Christian gave himself a negative one. I'm glad you can see that. Continue."

"Okay, well, his is the basic rags-to-riches/man-with-a-vision-story." Grace's nod said she understood.

Christian took a tentative glance to see where they were--how long he'd have to sum up Cosmo. Not long--the driver was making excellent if reckless progress. "Cosmo owns the modestly named COSMO-TV, four or five cable channels,

17

some international satellite services, and dozens of radio stations. A few years ago he moved operations to the building we're going to, The Factory. It's a converted shoe-assembly plant on the self-declared avant-garde part of The Street. Cosmo will put anything on the air, as long as it gets an audience. Short enough?"

"Not bad. Judgmental." The cab screeched to a halt in front of a grey-brick building with large, smoked-glass windows. "I've known Cosmo since before his beginnings. He's not his legend." Grace dropped a bill onto the front seat as they got out. "Few of us are." The taxi disappeared in a cloud of exhaust. Grace stopped outside The Factory's door and waited for Christian to catch up. "And do remember to let people make their own decisions about you. Follow the flow, and you'll be fine." She hurried into the building.

Chapter Two

The lobby of The Factory was the size of a small park. The prim couches and chairs scattered along the walls and the promotional magazines neatly placed on the attendant tables gave the space the feel of an unused waiting room, or a living room reserved for "company". It was a long walk to the reception desk, located on the back wall.

Christian didn't mind--it gave him an excuse to keep his eyes on the woman behind the desk. Her black T-shirt fit like a second skin. She reminded Christian of Lucille Firman, although she was blonde, not redheaded and her face a study in planes rather than angles. The two women shared a certain poised sensuality; a calm self-assurance bordering on smugness people would find them not only attractive, but compelling. Which Christian did.

"Christian Plowman and Grace to see Cosmo." Grace said, all business now. "He's expecting us."

The woman flipped a switch on the electronic console and murmured into her headset. "He'll be here in a minute, Mr. Plowman." Blue eyes explored Christian then met his with an unvoiced question. He opened his mouth to answer, then closed it without doing so. One corner of the blonde's mouth twitched with amusement as she looked away.

"Remember what you're forgetting, Christian." He turned to look at Grace. She shook her head and smiled. "Or perhaps you should forget what you're remembering."

"Pardon me?"

"I most certainly will. But don't expect that of everyone."

A door behind Grace opened as he was puzzling over her remarks. It took Christian a moment to recognize Cosmo Sharpe. He was much shorter than Christian had expected from seeing him on television.

Cosmo paused, squared his shoulders and strode into the lobby.

"Christian. Good of you to find time to see me." His voice boomed, filling the lobby. In a much quieter voice he added, "Grace. I am honoured."

A woman in high heels clattered through the still-open door. She bore down on them as quickly as her outfit allowed--a tight short skirt had her hobbled. Her dark wavy hair bounced with every step, then swung when she teetered to a stop beside Cosmo. With an impatient flick she swept her hair onto her back.

Dark jade-green eyes looked up and penetrated Christian. With a start, he realized he was in the presence of the one-and-only Aurora Medici; those piercing eyes were her trademark. Like Cosmo, she was far different in person than on TV--there she seemed silky smooth and voluptuous. The woman in front of him was a polished gemstone, all dazzling edges. Like Cosmo, she was much shorter than the image of her Christian held in his mind. She might be five three, at most... not including five inches of spiked heel. She cleared her throat.

Cosmo flinched, just a little. "Oh yes. Pardon me. Christian... Aurora."

"He knows." Aurora reached for Christian's hand, took a firm grip and didn't let go.

Christian glanced at Grace, and found no guidance. He looked back at Aurora. "I think I may find it impossible to keep my mind on business this afternoon."

Aurora squeezed harder.

"I doubt that." Cosmo gave a chuckling cough. "You're too smart to let her fool you. Under her frills, Aurora's a pirate. After all, she is my niece."

Frills? Hardly. Christian hadn't known the two were related. Now he did, he could see it. The physical similarities were few. Cosmo's eyes and thinning hair were nondescript brown, his face and body sagging while Aurora was trim and flamboyant. They held themselves the same way though. Christian had a fleeting image of them both dressed as Napoleon, and had to stifle a grin. He didn't quite manage.

Aurora smiled back politely, like a royal accepting public esteem. The glint in her eyes suggested something far different, a warning he wasn't displaying proper reverence for the anointed.

Cosmo offered Grace his arm. "Grace, since Aurora seems determined to join our meeting, I'll escort you and allow these two to become better acquainted. Don't tease him, dear." He took Grace's arm and led her away. Christian saw them exchange a few words as they disappeared through a door. Then his eyes and Aurora's locked, absolutely and completely. He saw her, and only her.

"I don't tease." As she let go of Christian's hand, Aurora moved to his left side, hooked her arm through his and pressed against him. Her body felt like rock, except for the breast moulded around his forearm. "You don't mind me being forward?"

Grace had said to follow the flow; Christian was more than willing to do so¬-this was Aurora Medici at his side, pressing into him. "No, but why? Why me?"

He felt rather than saw her shrug. "Power attracts me. Cosmo doesn't rush out to meet just anyone. You're going to do things for me. Life's been dull lately. You're going to change that."

They started moving. "I can't imagine your life ever being dull." He knew Aurora had started in broadcasting in her late teens, about fifteen years previously. Since then her name had been continuously and intimately linked with those of rock-and-roll and movie stars, the popular elite of entertainment. According to the rumour mills she'd left few sheets unturned. She was a mainstay of COSMO-TV and VideoView, Cosmo's rock video outlet.

"I'm sure you're too smart to believe all the shit you've heard about me."

"Can I believe some of it?" Christian asked as they came to an elevator.

Aurora pushed the button. "You're going to be some of it. Scratch my back, and I'll scratch yours. Cosmo's been steering me out of the limelight and into petty administration. That's going to change now."

***

22

A small smile appeared on Cosmo's face as Christian and Aurora walked into Cosmo's office. "You're getting along well, I see. However, we do have business to discuss so, Aurora, you behave yourself and sit over there. Christian can sit beside Grace on the couch."

Aurora pouted her way to the chair Cosmo had indicated. She sat and crossed her legs, displaying an expanse of well-toned thigh.

"Yes, well, maybe that wasn't such a good idea either." Cosmo shook his head, then shrugged. "But this should be quick. I have an appointment five minutes ago."

If so, he wasn't in any hurry. He talked at length about Ovation, a fine-arts channel he was launching on cable in January. It would feature an eclectic and aesthetic mix of music, the visual arts and critically acclaimed movies. Most of the programming was set but he needed a host for the flagship show, a person who would become the public and on-air face of the venture. It was already late September so time was running out.

"I can't see who would be right for this," Cosmo said to Grace and Christian. "You've done this sort of thing before. I'm counting on your fresh eyes to see things more clearly. I suppose Aurora feels she should sit in because she knows as much about my organization as I do."

"More." Aurora crossed her legs in the other direction. Christian almost completely forgot Cosmo. "I know where all the bodies are."

"You should. You've buried enough of them." Cosmo didn't sound like he was joking.

Aurora's faint smile denied nothing.

"As I was saying, Christian. Christian?" Christian looked at Cosmo. "As I was saying, if you're agreeable, I suppose Aurora can act as your liaison and answer questions about our staff and operations."

Aurora didn't look happy. This wasn't a task one asked a star to perform. Christian didn't think Cosmo was telling the entire truth about why he was hiring outside help either. Maybe he did want a fresh perspective on hiring a new host, but more than that, Cosmo wanted Christian to act as a buffer between him and Aurora. That might prove to be an uncomfortable, perhaps even dangerous role--family fights could get ugly. A surreptitious glance at Grace told him nothing; she was doing a fine imitation of a graven idol. He decided to put the conflict into the open. If he didn't he could become a one-man no-man's-land in an undeclared war.

"Are you comfortable with that, Aurora?" Christian tried to look at her as if she was just another meeting participant. No bra? No... none. "Or do you want the position, and think you might be in a conflict of interest situation?"

Aurora shot a quick look in her uncle's direction, licked her lips, and turned narrow green eyes on Christian. "Of course I want it. Ovation will be on satellite, so this is high profile with international exposure. But I guess Cosmo thinks the public sees me as too shallow, too rock-and-roll--or maybe just too old. Even if I convinced you to tell Cosmo I was the best person for it, he'd just tell you to quit thinking with your dick. What about it Unc?"

Cosmo doubled over on his desk, laughing. Aurora didn't appear to think she'd said anything funny. With a visible effort, she held her anger to a glower while Cosmo composed himself.

"Well I did know Aurora wanted the job." That chuckling cough would quickly get annoying. "But as she seems to sense, it isn't a person like her I'm looking for..."

Cosmo let his comment drift off. Grace rummaged in her purse. Aurora contemplated her nails. Christian felt Cosmo was prompting him to say something like, "Oh, and what sort of person are you looking for Cosmo?"

Which would undoubtedly set off another prepared speech. Christian didn't appreciate being cast in such a limited and predictable part. He would ask the question, but he would give it a twist.

"Yes, I can tell she isn't the person you're looking for." He tried to sound worldly and wise, almost bored. "But I'm afraid I can't see why. Maybe it would help me understand what you are looking for if you'd explain why Aurora is unsuitable."

Aurora looked up from her nails. Green eyes flashed on him and then to Cosmo. Until then, Christian had thought green a warm, friendly colour. Not always, it seemed. Cosmo twitched, and tried to avoid his niece's eyes. Christian sat back.

"That request, sir, puts me in an uncomfortable position." Cosmo twisted in his chair.

Christian didn't respond.

Cosmo glanced at Aurora and grabbing the edge of his desk with both hands, continued. "Christian, you're a man, and men are fascinated by Aurora. Teenagers of both sexes like her--they see her as a rebel, a rule-breaker. Unfortunately, Ovation's primary audience will be female and over thirty. Women don't like Aurora. They think everything about her screams 'slut'."

Aurora's eyes flickered. Cosmo pushed his chair back and sped up his delivery. "The rock thing doesn't matter. I'm looking for a host, not an expert. Experts we buy. Yes, I suspect the host will be a woman. But it must be someone other women could feel safe leaving alone with their men."

There was a short silence. "Am I still your favourite uncle, Aurora?"

"You never have been." Aurora stretched languidly. Her skirt hiked further up her thighs. "You're saying it's a matter of image, and mine isn't right. You're wrong, as usual." Hooded eyes moved to Christian. "Right now, I'm more interested in talking to a man who doesn't understand the rules of the game."

Cosmo made a show of wiping his brow. "Good. You did put me on the spot, Christian. The spot's yours now, and I do have that appointment." He looked at his watch. "Aurora dear, would you take Christian downstairs and get him an ID card? Don't bruise his face until after the picture's been taken. Grace and I will wrap up the details here, and then I'll see about that other business."

"Well done," Grace said quietly to Christian. "Enjoy your evening. Check your e-mail later. If you take her anywhere, it's on expenses."

Christian stood and went to shake Cosmo's hand. "Yes, that covers it. I'm sure Aurora will take good care of me."

"You bet!" Aurora hooked her arm back into his, as before but with more authority. "I'll close the door on the way out." Almost dragging Christian, she spiked the door with a heel and closed it as firmly as she could without actually slamming.

She hauled Christian halfway down the hall, came to an abrupt halt and pivoted on one heel to face him. Her hands shifted to his waist. "Okay, you knew I wanted that gig." She squeezed. Her mouth was slightly open, showing pointed teeth.

"And, like you said yourself, I also knew you weren't going to get it."

"Why?" She improved her grip. "Cosmo might have gone for it if you'd recommended me, told him I could do a look women would accept."

"No, he has his mind made up about you."

He felt Aurora's grasp lessen. Her eyes searched his face. Christian hoped she would find what she was looking for. "You're probably right. So you think I should strike out on my own."

Christian didn't believe he'd suggested any such thing.

Aurora moved a hand down from his waist. "And you're going to help me. And in return, I'll make all your dreams come true as well."

"Can I take you out for dinner and dancing first?"

27

She shrugged. "It might not hurt. There may actually be some people in Noronto who don't remember who I am. Let's get that picture taken first."

***

They weren't ready to go for some time. To Christian's eyes, the photo for his ID card was perfect, but Aurora said it wouldn't do. It didn't capture the real Christian, the one she saw and wanted to be seen with. She ushered him into the Wardrobe department.

"Hi, June. This guy is supposed to take me to that thing tonight, and look how he comes dressed."

"Yeah, sure." The woman Aurora had addressed raised her eyes from her magazine. "There ain't no 'thing' anywhere tonight, honey. I seen the schedule." She stood and considered Christian top to bottom, her eyes coming to rest squarely on his groin. "Then again, yeah, I know the 'thing' you're talking about. What'cha want him to look like?"

"Like he can afford me."

"Like anyone couldn't, the way you dress like some cheap hooker."

Aurora laughed. "I love you too, June. I'm going to change."

"Bitch," June muttered... after Aurora left. "Okay, mister, let's see what we can do. You're pretty conservative, so let's stick to grey. One of the newscasters is about your size, I think." She wandered away, riffled a rack of suits and pulled one out. "Perfect. It was made in Italy and you'll be unmade in Noronto. My condolences. Changing room's over there. I'm going for a smoke."

Christian put the suit on, folded his clothing neatly and took a long look in the floor-to-ceiling mirror. This certainly wasn't the old Christian Plowman, the one Grace was urging him to leave behind. June had said he seemed conservative but even in grey, this suit was ostentatious... and obviously expensive. In a corner, he noticed an abandoned shopping bag with the logo of Ray Mentor, Noronto's most exclusive and expensive men's store. He put his own clothes in it and went back into the main area to wait for Aurora.

She arrived wearing a tiny, clinging cream-white dress that covered less than her "working clothes" had. "So, what do you think?" She pirouetted slowly.

"Even in this suit, you have me outclassed."

Aurora turned to face him. "Bullshit." He'd said the right thing. She came up to him and draped her arms over his shoulders. "We're a perfect match." Christian bent to kiss her.

She pulled back. "If you start that now, we'll end up doing it right here on the floor. We should at least take your picture again first. After that, I'm yours. Sure you want to take me to dinner?"

"I think we should." June had offered condolences? Was that just spite? He pulled away and picked up the bag containing his old clothing. They went to have his picture taken again. The second ID card didn't look at all like Christian. Aurora pronounced it perfect.

"Dinner?" she asked again.

"I suppose so."

"Okay, let's go then!" Aurora grabbed his hand, and led him upstairs and into the lobby. "I'm out of here, Kathy!" she shouted to the receptionist

They burst out into hot, late September sunshine. Christian scanned The Street for a taxi. There were plenty of other vehicles: automobiles, trucks and even three streetcars jamming the two narrow lanes between all the parked cars, but no taxis. It figured.

A clutch of teenagers who had been peering through a smoked glass window into The Factory spotted Aurora and rushed over. "Ms Medici, can I have your autograph? Is he anyone? What's Madonna really like? Aurora, can my friend take a picture of me with you? Please?"

Aurora looked at Christian and shrugged. She signed books while denying she had slept with any of the Rolling Stones, let alone all five at the same time. "Look, guys," she finally said. "Our limo isn't here, but we're supposed to be somewhere else. No, I can't tell you where, it's a secret. You'll have to keep watching VideoView. Right now I've got to find out where that damn limo got to, okay?" Her fans parted as Aurora swept back into The Factory.

Inside, she sighed heavily. "It's the price of having touched fame, Christian." She sounded resigned but her cheeks were flushed and her eyes sparkling. "Let's rethink this. It's only four. If we wait for dinner and dancing we won't get down to business for hours. Seems a waste of time. What do you think?"

Whatever she thought. "That I don't want to wait that long."

"Good boy." Aurora strode to the reception desk. "Kathy, would you call a taxi?"

Kathy's smile was treacle. She didn't look at Christian. "I already did, Ms Medici. Usual cab, usual door."

Chapter Three

Aurora whisked Christian through a warren of corridors, and out a fire door to the cab. They made one stop--for a bottle of wine. "Red." Aurora licked her lips. "We'll be eating meat." They arrived at her building. She lived nearby, in an elegant refurbished low-rise.

Once inside her apartment, Aurora took the package with Christian's old clothes. "I'll hang these. Take that suit off. Get comfortable. Corkscrew and glasses are on the bar."

It was a complicated set of instructions but Christian did his best. With the wine in one hand he managed to undo the pants as he walked to the bar. He put the wine down, let the pants fall to the floor and then picked them up and draped them on a stool. Taking a firm hold on the bottle he plunged in the corkscrew and spread its arms. The cork rose with a satisfying pop.

He shrugged out of the jacket, put it on top of his pants, snatched two glasses, put them down and started to unbutton his shirt.

"Now, this is interesting." Aurora's tone of voice wasn't quite right for the situation. He grabbed the bottle in one hand and glasses in the other, and turned to face her.

She was by the door and still in her dress. In hand one hand she had a business card. "This fell out of your pocket. Were you intending to mention you know Lucille Firman, or keep that to yourself?"

Her voice rose a little as she started towards him. "Exactly how well do you know her?" she asked.

He wasn't sure what Aurora was really asking. Complete honesty would be the best policy. "I met her this morning. All I know about her is that she's tall, has long red hair and talks to strangers. Oh, and I suppose she may be almost as sexy as you." Well, not compete honesty. Aurora would pale beside Lucy.

He paused. He couldn't read Aurora's expression. Did she know Lucy?

Was she jealous? "And I promise I'll never get in touch with her if you don't want me to," he added, crossing his fingers.

Aurora laughed. "No, I guess you don't know her well. All I've ever heard of her are whispers and rumours. One is that she's bald. If that's true, the hair would be a wig. Another is that she gets what she wants. If she asked you to get in touch with her, you'd better." She undid her dress. It fell, but was too tight to make it past her hips. And no, she wasn't wearing a bra... and probably should. "You don't know me very well either," she continued in a voice full of big-screen steam. "Any woman you could still want after having me, I'd want too."

She dropped the card on a coffee table as she passed. "But she's not here, and I do see something interesting poking over your waistband."

Aurora tore off his shirt and slid down. "Put the wine down," she said to his navel. "It would be a shame to waste a drop."

**

33

When Christian was next fully aware of the everyday world, he was in a large four-poster. Aurora's head was nestled on his chest, her long dark hair splayed to either side. Her eyes were open. In the subdued light their jade-green seemed almost black.

"Hi. You're back." Her voice was a whisper. "I just returned to earth myself." She licked her lips, exactly as she had earlier, in the taxi. "Hmm... I don't remember much, but it was great. I don't think I was careful though." She slithered up.

"It's been a while for me." That was a decided understatement. "And I've had a blood test come back negative since. You don't have anything to worry about." He might though. This was how AIDS was spread.

"Damn!" Aurora wiggled her way back down his body and sat on his ankles to remove the condom that hung limply between his legs. "For me, putting one on is automatic when I'm with a man, part of the act. Now, I wish I'd forgotten. My last test came back negative too and like I said, life's been dull lately. We don't need these."

She pitched the condom in the general direction of a large chest of drawers. Christian lifted his head in time to see it disappear into a wastebasket. "Years of practice." Aurora's leer seemed calculated--it went with the words. "And some luck. Let's do it again. Now. Without." She moved back up.

Christian put his hands on her waist. His fingers almost met on her back. He squeezed to see if he could force their tips together.

"Oh damn again." Aurora said. "I need to pee. Better let go--unless that turns you on."

He quickly removed his hands. "No thanks. It's never appealed."

Aurora vaulted off the bed. "Whatever... be a good boy and get me a wrap from the toy closet?" she asked as she disappeared into the en-suite bathroom.

Christian wasn't sure he'd heard properly. He looked around. Near the window, he saw a closet with a sign in dark Gothic script, "The Toy Closet". He eased himself off the bed, almost stepping on another used condom beside the bed. Impressive. He hadn't known he had it in him.

He tried to remember the past couple of hours. It had been like they weren't even in the bed, the room, or even on the planet, but instead floating in space, fused into one orgasmic being. He walked the condom over to the garbage, dropped it in, and went to the closet.

As he reached it, he saw a small note on the door. "Abandon no hope, ye who enter her." And he'd thought Aurora didn't have a sense of humour.

The choice of garments ranged from white fluffy nothings to studded black leather armour. On the floor a wine rack had been converted to hold vibrators and dildos. Assorted whips, chains, ropes and straps hung inside the door, and on the ends of the closets.

"What, you haven't decided?" He'd been so fascinated he hadn't heard Aurora return. She delicately raked his side with her nails. "The red silk at the end will do."

Christian handed it to her. "I feel out of my depth."

"Funny, I was thinking the same thing. I don't like losing control like that. What happened?"

"Want to find out? It may happen again." Christian was ready.

"Later. I need a drink, and the wine's certainly had time to breathe." Aurora went to another closet and pulled out a large light-blue terry-cloth robe. "Here. It matches your eyes." She tossed it to him.

Christian caught it. "Thanks. Be with you in a minute." He headed for the bathroom.

Aurora wasn't in the bedroom when he finished. The hall seemed longer than he remembered. Actually, he didn't remember it at all. From a certain moment in the living room until he focused on Aurora lying on him on the bed was lost time. Well, not entirely lost, but without form, unstructured. Maybe that was the way sex was supposed to be. He walked towards the living room. There was another door along the way, obviously a second bedroom.

As he reached the living room, Aurora was hanging up the phone. "I ordered pizza. Get me some wine?"

"Certainly." He poured and delivered her glass to where she was sitting in the middle of a white leather couch and then sat across from her in an overstuffed chair, the glass coffee table between them. He wanted to talk and knew if he sat beside her, they wouldn't. "This is a two-bedroom apartment?"

36

She sipped her wine and looked at him over the edge of the glass. "Yes."

"Do you share it with someone?"

"Yes." She drained her wine and put the glass on the table. "I suppose you want to know who?"

"Well, I thought that since we're..." He couldn't find the right word.

Aurora supplied it. "Fucking? Don't get mushy, Christian. I'm not about to marry you and have babies."

He hadn't had time to think about it, but from the way her words hit Christian knew subconsciously he'd been hoping for something more than a one-night stand. Better not press the matter though. "So you're not going to tell me about your roommate?"

"Didn't say that, and don't sound so sulky. I'm being nice. You're so straight and middle-class I figured I'd better warn you. I'm not a woman you take home to mother."

"My mother's dead. Father too. Car accident."

"Oh. I'm sorry. I didn't mean it literally. Recently?"

Christian shook his head. "When I was eighteen. I'm over it."

"I doubt it. Anyway, about me. Patrick isn't really my 'roommate'. He gets mail here, and his name is on the lease. He has another place."

"But his name is on the lease."

Aurora leaned back on the couch and put her legs on the table. "He's never fucked me, if that's what you're asking--not that it's any of your business. He has other uses. Patrick works for

Cosmo as a part-time video director and full-time behind-the-scenes fixer. Around The Factory, he's known as Patsy. Any more questions?"

"No." None he should ask. Aurora's world was different from his. Until he understood it, he should be cautious.

"Good, then I have one. Anything you need to do before tomorrow? Other than me, that is?"

Christian checked the time. Seven in the evening. Was that all? "Well, I should check my e-mail."

"No problem." Aurora pointed to her computer. "Cosmo insists we be on¬line, the little techno-freak. I should check in too, and see if I have anything in particular scheduled for tomorrow. Oh, and one other thing." She twisted one leg on the table and picked up Lucille Firman's card between her toes. "You should write her." She lifted the leg with the card high in the air.

Christian stood and took it. "You want to meet her?"

"Damn right." Aurora lowered her leg, took her other off the table and stood. "I wasn't even sure she was real. If she is, and even half what people say is true, she influences or controls a good bit of entertainment and fashion. If you arrange for me to meet her, I'll owe you."

"I wonder if it's the same person. The Lucy I met doesn't look much over twenty."

Aurora shrugged. "I'd like to find out. The real Lucille Firman, if there is one, isn't anyone many would dare impersonate."

"Okay, fire up your computer."

As she did, Christian realized he was facing a new problem. He didn't know his password. His computer was set up to log in automatically and he'd only typed it the once. He needed to go home and call his Internet provider from there. He couldn't invite Aurora over either. She thought he was a big wheel. If she saw his building, she'd know he wasn't--it was one step up from the street.

It didn't take long for Aurora to check with The Factory. She had an interview scheduled for mid-afternoon and wouldn't go in until then. "There's a message for you here too," she said, a grin on her face. "Guess Cosmo figured out where you'd be tonight."

The message was from Grace. Christian gave silent thanks she'd thought to send it to Aurora's address. How he could have told Aurora he had to go out, but would be back? Exactly like that, he supposed, but it certainly wouldn't have gone over well.

Grace wanted to see him "sometime before noon", and gave a suite number in the Casa del Carlos, along with its address. Christian knew where the building was--it was one of the most prestigious buildings in Noronto. Cleo had wanted them to move there. Then he'd been laid off, and she'd moved out. Instead of Casa del Carlos, he'd moved into a building Cleo wouldn't be seen dead entering.

Christian wrote Grace, confirming he'd received her message.

Then he sent a note to Lucy. "Hi. Remember me? My name is Christian. We met in Queens Park this morning. I got the job, but would like to see you again." He thought for a minute and added, "Oh, and may I bring someone? She's not sure if you're the Lucille Firman she's heard of, but she'd like to meet you."

He looked over what he'd written. It sounded awkward, but asking to bring another woman on what amounted to a date, was. He had to ask. The worst Lucy could do was say no.

The door buzzer sounded. Christian sent the message and signed off. Aurora wasn't dressed in a way suited to answering the door.

He had barely enough to pay for the pizza but told the driver to keep the change. He'd get it back. Grace had told him to put everything on expenses.

They ate sitting across from each other at her small dining table, without talking but with a good bit of eye contact, much like in a movie he remembered seeing on late-night TV. And he discovered Aurora was every bit as talented with her feet as she'd shown by picking up the card with her toes, and that her legs were just long enough to reach his lap. It was a small pizza but by the time it was finished, Christian was ready to burst.

Aurora got up and went back to the couch. "Bring the rest of the wine." He'd have done anything she asked. Bringing the wine was easy, even if walking wasn't.

He emptied the bottle into their glasses. Aurora patted the couch beside her. Yes, that's where he'd been intending to sit.

Aurora drained her glass. When Christian didn't reach for his immediately, she drank it too.

She swung a leg over, moved to straddle him and leaned forward. Her nose touched his. "Ready to have some fun?"

"You have to ask?"

Her laugh was deep in her throat. "I mean real fun." She moved back and stood. "Follow me." She led him to the bedroom, and the "Toy Closet".

"Stand here." She took four straps from the door and handed them to him. "Go lie down and wait. I'll be a minute."

Christian went to the four-poster and examined it more closely than he had the first time. There were eyelets in each post, and at various places in the head- and footboards. He tested a post--it was solid, he couldn't move it.

"I said 'lie down'. Then close your eyes," Aurora ordered. "I want to surprise you."

She already had. Christian obeyed.

He heard rustling. His body tensed. Aurora quickly and expertly strapped him down, face up. "Relax. You'll like this, a lot. If you start to cramp yell 'Red' so I can let you loose." She cupped him gently. "But don't unless it's serious or you'll miss out." She let go, drifted down his body and sat on his ankles. "My, you are a big one. Tall too. Okay, you can open your eyes."

Sheer black stockings came to her thighs, and a black shimmering something pushed up her breasts, making them seem fuller. The 'something' hung from there to just above the flare of her hips. "You were expecting leather? It's such a cliché, not to mention uncomfortable." She slid up again and suspended herself above his mouth. "Greedy,

greedy--my, what a long tongue you have. I'm in no hurry. Savour the experience. Think about how lucky you are. Every night, thousands upon thousands of viewers fantasize about being with me."

It wasn't what Christian would have chosen to reflect on, but he could tell the thought inflamed Aurora. If anything, it brought him crashing back to earth. Once there, he watched her stage a professional performance--writhing, moaning and making the most of her props, of which he was one. Aurora played the scene to wrench every gasp and every cry from both of them until finally, despite his best effort to delay, Christian shot into her, again and again.

When he was finished, she got off and released his feet and hands. "So?"

She wanted a review, Christian thought. It hadn't been magical like the first time, but "two thumbs up" might be taken the wrong way.

"You're the sexiest woman I've ever been with." It was the truth. The truth also was that her competition was limited.

"Thank you," she said, running her fingers through her hair and fluffing it. "I'm afraid you'll need to do a lot more before I can return the compliment."

Christian did his best. He kept going until he was raw, and every nerve yelped. Aurora seemed insatiable.

Finally, as the first light of dawn showed at the window Aurora rasped. "Enough. Congratulations, Christian. You're the first man who's ever outlasted

42

me solo. Set my alarm for noon." She closed her eyes and began to snore.

Christian staggered to his feet. If he was going to meet Grace later that morning, he didn't dare sleep. He stepped into the shower. He felt used up, but more alive than he had in years.

Chapter Four

After leaving Aurora's apartment, Christian went directly to Casa del Carlos. Grace had said to see her before noon. He hoped eight wasn't too early. For once he'd been glad to travel on the transit system at rush hour, when there weren't any seats. If he'd sat, he would have dozed off.

The guard in the lobby kept an eye on him and called to see if Christian was indeed welcome. He covered the mouthpiece. "Go ahead. Top floor. Turn right."

Christian considered his hands, remembered his right was the one he didn't write with and went to the elevator. He wasn't in good shape. As the door closed, he saw the guard speaking into the telephone again.

When the door opened, Grace was there "Fred was concerned you might get lost. I can see why. It was an interesting night?"

Her apartment was steps from the elevator. He could have found it.

Grace ushered him in. "Sit down. Then again, no--upstairs."

They walked through the living room to a flight of stairs. Christian had enough left to follow, but not enough to argue.

Grace opened a door, closed it and opened another. "Here, I think. The other room gets morning sun. Bathroom at the end of the hall. We'll talk later."

Christian nodded. This was the strangest job he'd ever held. He fell asleep wondering how much longer he'd have it.

He woke to the smell of bacon. After visiting the bathroom, he went downstairs.

"Sit." Grace appeared from the kitchen with a large mug of coffee, black and strong, the way he drank it. "Your brunch will be ready soon."

"Sorry. I don't think I've made a good second impression."

"Oh, I'm not so sure," Grace said. "I was looking for someone who gets into his work."

Christian wasn't sure he'd heard that right until Grace broke out laughing. "Don't worry about it, and don't look so shocked. I'm not that old and I'm certainly not dead."

"I'm not shocked, just slow. And I don't think you're old." In her late forties? From her face, perhaps. Her trim figure seemed at least twenty years younger.

"Bless you for that, my child. We'll fix you up."

The bacon, with eggs and a pile of toast, arrived before he finished. "We'll talk when you're ready." She swept out of the room, leaving her words hanging in the air.

When he was finished, he took the plates to the kitchen, got a second cup of coffee, and went to find Grace.

She was in a small room at the end of the hall, in front of a computer. "Better?" she asked. "Good. See if I got this right. I set up an account for you with diluvia.org. I'm not impressed by your

45

provider." She stood, patted the monitor and moved to a desk with a second computer and a scanner.

Christian sent a test message to his usual account. Then, without thinking, he logged on there to check. Hold it! He'd remembered his password? When he'd sat in front of Aurora's computer, he'd blanked. It must have come to him while he was sleeping--sometimes things did.

He checked his mail. The message he'd sent had arrived, and there also was one from Lucy Firman. He deleted his, called up Lucy's and without reading it, decided to test Grace's system by printing it on the laser. With a whirr and a puff of black it spat out a sheet of paper.

Christian signed off. "Everything seems fine, except maybe your printer. I could swear it smoked."

"Do you mind?" Grace got up and walked to the printer.

"No, not at all."

She glanced at the printout. "I think my system may be too sensitive. The printer is fine." She paused. "You've already met Lucy?"

"Yesterday. In the park. She came along just before you did. It might have been more than coincidence? You know her?"

Grace nodded. "We go way back. She used to work for me." She returned to the chair at the other desk.

"She quit?" Christian finally asked.

"We parted company. She thought she could manage my business better than I could. I told her

46

set up her own operation and see. She did. She's been quite successful, in her way."

"She doesn't look old enough to have done all that."

"She's older than she looks. We're of an age." Grace paused again. "By the way, what does she look like these days?"

"Good... like she's in her early twenties." It seemed an odd question. If Grace knew Lucy, she'd know what Lucy looked like, wouldn't she?

"Other than that."

"Healthy? Happy?"

That wasn't what Grace wanted either. "She's about six feet tall, maybe a hundred and thirty pounds, and has green eyes and long red hair. Aurora said the hair is probably a wig."

"Probably," Grace said. "Same old Lucy-- everything in excess. Aurora met her too?"

"No, but she wants to."

"She would. Oh, here--I read your mail and you didn't." Grace handed him the printout. It did smell singed.

Lucy suggested they meet at The Second Circle the next evening. Christian had never been there, but he knew where it was--after all, it was the largest nightclub on The Street. Lucy would leave his name at the door--bring anyone, the more the merrier.

"You don't mind?"

"Not at all! If Lucy is interested in you, it makes me even more certain you're the right person for me. Write and tell her you'll be there."

47

"Good," Grace said when he'd sent his reply. "Now. Since I'm leaving Noronto tomorrow, we'd better get down to business. Anything you want to ask about our meeting with Cosmo?"

There was a lot he wanted to ask about Lucy-- and Grace, but clearly those subjects were closed. "Not really. It seems straightforward. He's looking for a TV personality, and I'm to find one. You do realise, Grace, that I don't know anything about broadcasting?"

"What's to know?" She shrugged. "TV is two-dimensional. You're an English major--you understand ideas and archetypes. If someone looks like a host and sounds like a host, they're a host. You'll find the right person without any problem, Christian--just don't do it too quickly or Cosmo will think you didn't give the search enough effort. December would be fine. He really doesn't need anyone before then."

Grace's answer almost made sense. He needed to find someone who could play the role of host, in essence, an actor. In the flesh Aurora certainly wasn't what she seemed on the small screen. Aurora... flesh... next question. "Okay, there's just one other thing. Why did you set me up with Aurora?"

Grace's face lit. "Now that's a question worth asking! You assume I did?"

"Well, yes--at any rate I get the feeling the condition I showed up in this morning was what you intended."

"Pretty much. If Aurora hadn't gone after you there was Kathy, the receptionist. I'm sure you

48

noticed she was interested, and she'd have probably been better for you--she seems more your type. But that's not how it worked out. Aurora made sure of that."

"I don't understand." That was an understatement. His type? He didn't have one. Cleo, maybe--but not anymore. He tried to find the appropriate question. "Why?"

"You needed to get laid. Complaining?"

"No, guess I can't." He tried again to find the right words. "But, but I consider it mighty arrogant of you." 'Arrogant' wasn't quite right either, but it would do.

Grace grinned. "Sure, I'm overbearing--what some call 'controlling'--I admit that failing. But I had nothing to do with you and Aurora. Okay, I could have managed things so you'd leave with me and nothing would have happened--at least, not between you and Aurora, but why? After tomorrow I'm not going to be around and able look out for you, so I looked out for you by letting nature follow its course with her. You do attract women, Christian. You can't help it."

"Can't say I ever noticed it before."

"That was the old Christian Plowman. Remember him? Good! Now forget him."

"So that was how you look out for me? Gee, thanks, Mom."

"No problem. Mom? Not necessarily what I had in mind but it's been a long time since anyone called me that. Consider yourself adopted."

"Well, you can't replace the one I had, but--consider yourself adopted too." He was an adult; it only seemed fair to adopt in both directions.

"Thank you. Now--to business."

Grace explained her computer set-up. The first computer, the one she'd used set up his new email account, was on the Internet--with the complete works of Shakespeare and various religious texts available to be read or downloaded. She could set up an unlimited number of email addresses with her provider. At the moment only Grace and Christian had accounts there, but he was free to set up others.

The other computer stayed off-line but was also an answering machine. The phone never rang; that computer took a message instead. It held files on clients and contacts, and was used for off-line work and games. A couple of older laptops were available, but Grace would be taking the one she'd used at Chez Celeste.

"How well is this computer protected against being hacked?" Christian asked.

"Good question. I suspect Lucy found out about you by intercepting my e-mail. My machine is undoubtedly secure, but unless you encrypt, anyone can snag and read mail. I can't be bothered fighting that sort of nonsense. If you get something from me that doesn't make sense, assume it really isn't from me. I ignore all the foolishness I'm sent--and boy, some days there's a lot."

She opened a drawer, and pulled out some documents. "Oh well, I suppose I've avoided the paperwork as long as I can."

It took next to no time. Christian signed on the dotted lines, confirming he was employed by Grace X Machina and would pay tax. Then they went to the bank next door to Casa del Carlos. With a solicitous manager hovering, Christian again scribbled his name as instructed. A credit card was issued on the spot, for expenses, and arrangements were made for Christian's pay to be transferred to his personal account every month.

Outside the bank Christian patted the pocket containing his wallet, and new credit card. "Did I misunderstand, or could I bleed you dry with this?"

Grace shrugged. "Either I can trust you like a newly adopted son, or not. I'll be disappointed if you cut corners, Christian. Cosmo's contract is minor. Your main task, for now, is to establish yourself as a public figure so you can go on to bigger things. That's a matter of image. You need to be seen and become recognised as a man of consequence." She pulled a watch out of her purse and shook her head. "I'm running late. Go shopping--get a couple of expensive business suits, and whatever it is you need to be taken seriously on The Street. Spend."

Grace lifted a hand in the air. A cab screeched to a halt in front of them. "I'm off see my lawyer and hand over all this paper."

Christian opened the door for her. "Come by tomorrow," she said with a slight bow to acknowledge the courtesy. "About the same time-- I'll be leaving before noon." She closed the door. The taxi leapt into action, careened around a corner and disappeared.

Christian headed south on foot. Bay and Bloor, the first shopping area he should visit, was about fifteen minutes from Grace's apartment. He still felt groggy and the walk might help him wake up. He wasn't sure he wanted to though--this might all be a dream: Grace, the job, Lucy, the credit card, Aurora-¬things like this didn't happen, or if they did, they didn't happen to Christian Plowman.

Chapter Five

"I'm not sure our clothing is for you," the salesman in Ray Mentor Tailors said with a sniff. "You might prefer to shop elsewhere."

Christian hadn't gone to his interview prepared for a night away from home, so this was the second day for his clothes. Even when new, they would have cost less than any tie in the store.

"Yes, I might prefer to, but I'll try you first." He handed the man his new credit card. "I'll be paying with this."

"I'll return in a minute... sir." The salesman disappeared into the back of the store.

He reappeared, smiling. "Mr. Plowman. Sir! What can we do for you today, sir?"

Evidently the card was good. "I need two business suits, shirts, ties and shoes. I'll rely on your good taste. Oh, and something for formal occasions. To be delivered this evening."

"Our policy, sir, is that quality takes time."

"Then perhaps I should go elsewhere. My card, please?"

In an hour he was on his way, thoroughly measured and still in yesterday's clothing. His order would be delivered to Grace's before nine. Christian wanted her to have an opportunity to send everything back. Besides, it was the only address he could use--anything sent to his building would be stolen unless he was there to receive it.

He needed to go to The Street next. No store in the carriage trade district would have anything that would be acceptable in The Second Circle. The level of snobbery was probably about the same, but they were different worlds. Christian stood on the curb for five minutes trying to attract a taxi. He gave up and took the bus.

He got to The Street around four-thirty. The stores were busy. He went into one at random, The Black Whole.

This clerk didn't sniff. However, like her upscale cousin, she did call to check the card. When she came back, her eyes had a similar glow, and more. "Maybe you'd like to come to the back and see what I can do for you?" she asked. In case that wasn't obvious enough, she slowly licked her lips in as suggestive a manner as Aurora had the day before. They knew each other? It was possible, but more likely they just watched the same TV programs.

"Unfortunately, I'm in a bit of a hurry today." And not the least bit interested. The night before was taking its toll. "I'm going to be working around The Factory, and need something to help me blend in. Also, an outfit for The Second Circle, not too much leather, something understated." He had intended to use Aurora's line about leather being a cliché but faced with someone dressed entirely in black cowhide, he didn't.

"Sure. But looking like you do and wearing our clothes, you'll be noticed. That's what it's all about. Okay?"

"Guess it'll have to be." He didn't believe her. She was in sales--lying was her job.

54

He walked out the door dressed in black. Again he'd arranged to have everything delivered to Grace, his old clothing along with what he would wear the next night. First The Factory to see Aurora, and then home.

The receptionist greeted him with a brilliant blonde smile "Mr. Plowman!"

"Good afternoon, Kathy, and please, it's Christian. Is Aurora around?"

Kathy had puffed up as he came in, and then deflated at his question. She had a talented, expressive chest. "Oh. Somewhere. Try the usual places."

"Which are? I'm new around here."

"You sure are." Kathy looked behind him. "Hey, Judy! Got a minute?"

The woman who did the weather reports on COSMO-TV's morning show was named Judy. Christian got up early every morning at least in part to see her bubble as animated weather symbols cavorted in front of her. She was a morning person, and he wasn't--seeing her helped get him started on his day.

He turned around. It was that Judy. Unlike Aurora she seemed the same in person as on television--except Christian hadn't known her hair was red, like Lucy's--like Lucy's wig. He also hadn't known or guessed Judy's eyes were deep, soft, and blue. His TV was an old black-and-white he'd bought second-hand when the big-screen he'd owned with Cleo proved too large for a one-room apartment. Judy had started with COSMO-TV since he'd moved.

"A minute? At least." She didn't walk, she bounced. "I was only heading home. What's up? Hi, I'm Judy."

The sound had failed on his TV the previous Christmas, and he hadn't bothered fixing it. Judy's voice was as remembered, except live instead of through a tinny speaker, it sang rather than crackled.

"I'm Christian. Very pleased to meet you." Very. They shook hands.

Kathy cleared her throat. "Christian is looking for Aurora."

Judy dropped Christian's hand. "You're her latest?"

"I suppose you could say that--I'm not sure she would. I'm going to be around here, off and on, trying to find someone to host Ovation's flagship show." He wasn't sure that would be generally known, and thought it should be. "Cosmo assigned Aurora as my liaison."

"I was going to tell you that this evening Judy," Kathy said.

"It's public knowledge?" Christian asked.

"I'm sure it is," Judy said with a smile big enough for Christian and Kathy to share. "The roomie is always the last to know. If you want to know what's happening around The Factory, ask Kathy."

"So if you want the job, Judy, Christian's the one to screw." Kathy tone was matter-of-fact. "Of course, you could do that for fun too. You said the other night you needed a good fuck."

"I did not!" Judy blushed a red not far off the colour of her hair. "You did!"

"Oh yeah, sorry." Kathy didn't look particularly contrite. "Well, either way it's true. I'll leave him for you."

"Come on, Christian, I'll help you find Aurora, and then I'm going home." Judy took two steps and turned back. "Except you'll be there, won't you, Kathy?

Maybe I'll go apartment shopping instead!" She resumed her exit.

Christian caught up with her. "Kathy certainly speaks her mind. Really, you'd be perfect for Ovation. I'm a big fan. I get up early just to see you."

"Kathy is 100 percent bitch. I don't know why I put up with her." Judy stopped and turned to face him. "But thank you. And keep that idea to yourself, please? Aurora and I are on okay terms. I'd like to keep it that way."

"What difference would it make?"

"You don't know Aurora, do you? She wants that job and what's more... you're hers. If it looked like I was after either, she'd make my life miserable. Come on, let's find her."

Judy commenced a scientific search by asking everyone they met if they'd seen Aurora. Christian probably could have managed that himself, but then he wouldn't have had such delightful company. The technique proved effective. The fifth or sixth person Judy asked said Aurora was around the next corner, finishing an interview.

"I'm out of here," Judy whispered. "By the way, I think you're sexy too." She scurried away.

Aurora and a man with a three-day beard were sitting on shipping crates in an open area, in front of two cameras. The setting suited the man's scruffy jeans and wrinkled shirt, but Christian thought Aurora looked incongruous in her designer suit. She asked a question, and the light on the camera facing her winked out. She grimaced, squirmed on the box, rearranged her dark curls, and glancing around, noticed Christian. Just before her camera turned on, she held up two fingers and returned her attention to the interview, once again perfectly composed.

Christian couldn't hear what they were saying, and didn't want to get closer in case he interfered. Only two minutes left anyway, if he'd interpreted properly. The man being interviewed looked familiar, but Christian couldn't place him. That he was at least mildly famous seemed likely from Aurora's on-camera smile.

Both lights went out. Aurora and the man stood. She hugged him, and whispered something in his ear before leading him over to one of the camera operators, an exotic woman in jean shorts and a tank top. The three exchanged a few more smiles before Aurora came over to Christian. The other camera operator, a bearded male in his twenties, had already packed up and gone.

"Hi. What gives? I'm working, you know." She gave him a once-over look. "Nice outfit, I suppose. The Black Whole? That slime-bucket, Eunice? Looks like her taste."

So they did know each other. "You don't like it?"

"You should have asked me to recommend somewhere. I wouldn't have suggested The Black Whole."

"I gathered. You're free for dinner?" The Street was evidently a small world, with local in-fighting

"No, I'm live on Bull's-Eye News, at six and eleven. So... why are you here?"

"To see you. And take you for dinner if you had time. Oh, and to tell you we have a date with Lucy tomorrow, at The Second Circle at eight. I hope you'll manage to be free then."

"I'll be there." Aurora moved closer. "Can't make it before nine though--I'll bring someone with me. Can't have people see me go anywhere alone." She rose on her toes to kiss him. "I'm excited about meeting Ms Firman. Tell her that. Now, go and get some rest. You'll need it."

Christian made it back to the lobby by retracing the path Judy and he had taken. Kathy was on the other side of the reception desk, chatting with the person now behind it. She saw Christian, and came over. "Judy left, and I knew Aurora was busy. I figured you'd be back. I'm off work, and free for the evening. Feel like company?"

"You want the Ovation job too?"

"Hell no." She laughed. "Just sex. Judy said you sort-of hit on her, but she's too chickenshit to steal a man from Aurora." Kathy's gaze was blue-grey steel. "I've done it before and survived."

"I didn't hit on Judy." That seemed the safest statement to respond to.

59

"She's still talking to you?"

"Sure. Typical redhead--heats up and cools down fast. And you certainly did. It's okay, she didn't mind, and I don't blame you--unlike Aurora, Judy likes men. I do too. Treat yourself, Christian, and me. You'll never lust after dear Ms Medici again."

Like Aurora, Kathy believed in getting to the point. They didn't have much else in common. Five foot eight to Aurora's five three, Kathy seemed the same height only because she didn't wear heels. She didn't bother with any of the other feminine touches Aurora favoured either: lacy frills, scent or cosmetics. As she had the previous day, Kathy wore a plain T-shirt and jeans that showed off a full figure, and had her thick blonde hair in a simple ponytail.

"So, what do you think?" She'd been watching him examine her.

That she was stunning. "That it wouldn't be a good idea."

"You think too much." She wheeled away without waiting for the explanations he'd been preparing: that alienating Aurora would complicate his assignment, that he had to be at work early, that he was tired and certain Kathy would find him disappointing. He'd half-hoped she'd press the matter and force him to give in.

After three or four steps she stopped and looked back. "In case you were wondering, I don't give rain-checks."

Her eyes were cold. Kathy seemed like Aurora in one respect. "No" wasn't an answer she accepted good-naturedly. Christian doubted she'd hear it often. Her body was the lush North American ideal--everything a man could want.

She stalked out the door onto The Street. Christian almost rushed after her, but thought better of it, deciding their misunderstanding could be dealt with better some other day. He was dead on his feet.

He went home, pulled out his sofa bed and fell asleep immediately.

Chapter Six

The grumbling of his stomach woke Christian at six Wednesday morning-¬half an hour before the alarm would have gone off. He'd been so exhausted the previous evening he had fallen into bed without eating. He put it off a little longer. The building's hot water always ran out around six-thirty. If he ate first, he'd have to shower in cold.

By the time he got to the table his stomach had started to scream. Still, before he poured the milk onto his cereal, he sniffed it. Sour again. His refrigerator could be set to either freeze everything or leave it too warm, the option Christian usually chose. He ate his cereal with tap water. It was better than no cereal at all.

The COSMO-TV morning show didn't start until seven, so Christian read instead of setting up his television. To be at Grace's on time, he would have to leave right after the show started. The few minutes he'd watch weren't worth the time he'd spend fiddling with the rabbit-ear antenna. As for the weather, he could tell by looking out the window it was going to be another fine day. He didn't need a cartoon sun dancing on Judy to tell him that.

He breezed up to the security booth at Casa del Carlos just before eight, fed and rested, in total contrast to his condition the previous day. "Good morning, Fred. Ms Machina is expecting me."

"Yeah Plowman, she is. What's more, she insists you be issued a pass." The guard levered himself from his chair. "Might as well do that now."

The picture was even worse than the one on Christian's ID card for The Factory. The flash camera had given him an oversized nose, beady red eyes and washed out his hair. "I look like a lemur."

"Yeah, you do. Blame your ancestors."

Grace wasn't waiting at the elevators again, but did open her door before Christian knocked. "Good morning, Christian." Judging from the filmy nightgown either he was early or she was running late. Adopted mothers shouldn't wear such things. He averted his eyes.

"Morning, Grace. I gather I'm moving in?" He immediately hoped she wouldn't take that wrong, considering. He still didn't look at her.

"I thought you'd decided that when you sent your fancy clothes here." She turned and went into the kitchen. Her figure did remind him of Cleo. No, it couldn't! Didn't. Did.

Christian started to explain why he had sent the clothing there, but she waved him off.

"Calm down. I'm teasing." How did she mean that? "I'm glad to see you spent a little, but don't stop now. Can't have you seen in the same thing too often. And by all means, keep everything here if you want." She looked around the kitchen. "Now why did I come in here?"

"I have no idea," Christian said. "To get a coffee?" So she could stand in front of the window, showing her considerable all?

"No, no... oh well." She bustled into the living room, nightie streaming after her like wind-blown cloud. "As I think I was going to tell you, Christian, I'll out of town for three months, until at least Christmas. It simplifies matters to have you on record as living here. After all, it is your office. Sleep over if you want, have people in, and do live here. What's mine is yours." She picked up a pillow from the couch, fluffed it, and suddenly smiled. "Oh yes, now I remember. I was going to pack my bag." She dropped the pillow and started for the stairs. "Get a coffee. I suppose I might as well change too. My plane takes off at noon."

Grace returned dressed more appropriately in a severe brown suit, carrying her oversized purse and a suitcase that would handily fit into it. "I have clothes at the other end too," she said in answer to his look. "The climate there is quite different. Now... I do need to leave within the hour, so I'd appreciate if you not ask questions. I'm easy to side-track, and there is much I must tell you." She poured a coffee and sat with him at the table.

"Okay. Like I said, treat this place like your own. Which means take care of it too. You'll find the number of my maid service on the computer." Grace lifted her coffee, and put it down. "Still too hot. In the living room, we have books." She leapt to her feet and poked each of the three bookcases in turn. "Take time to read some. You never know what you may find helpful."

She crossed the carpet to the entertainment centre, and opening and closing doors rapidly, continued. "TV and VCR--including a feed from a private satellite. CDs and tapes, and in this drawer the remote controls, and manuals. But I'm sure you can figure it out." She returned for her coffee and took it into the kitchen. Christian followed.

"Let's look in on the computers," Grace put down the cup and swooshed down the hall, snagging her purse along the way. In the office she sat and rummaged through. "Just want to make sure I have everything. Any questions about the set-up here?"

"I can manage, but I do have other questions."

"Let me get through this first, okay? Now, anyone I do business with knows to use e-mail. Check yours frequently. Look for phone messages if and when you remember, or never."

She put down her purse, stood and started pacing. "Keep in mind that you work for me. No one else can tell you what to do. Other than for Cosmo you won't need to concern yourself with existing clients. They contact me directly. Feel free to take on new business though. Oh yes! Here--I printed cards for you."

They identified him as Christian P. Plowman, Associate of Grace X Machina, consultant. "If you don't mind me saying, Grace, I think you're paying me too much." That had been all Christian had noticed on the contract. Eight thousand a month was far more than he'd been making before he got laid-off.

"I don't. You'll be worth every penny. Give some away if you want. Complain about it again and --well--I'll double it."

Christian laughed. "I'm just not sure how I'm going to earn it."

"Neither am I. If I did, I wouldn't have needed to hire you, would I?"

She'd said that before. It was beginning to make sense to Christian, almost. "Can you give me any hints?"

"No, but I can give you 'motherly' advice." She stopped pacing.

"Yes, please." Better that than nothing.

"Very well. I'm sure you already know these things, but--listen more than you talk, and make sure you understand a question fully before you answer. Don't guess, or lie--not knowing is no shame, and neither is not telling all you do know-- the whole truth confuses people most times. Let's see, what else? You remember what I told you before we met with Cosmo yesterday?"

"To follow the flow? Let people make their own decisions about me?"

"Right. It worked, didn't it? Of course you nudged the flow the direction you wanted, and didn't let yourself get pushed around. Any time you can't manipulate right back, get out of a situation as best and soon as you can."

Grace picked up her purse and pulled out a watch. "If I go now, I'll have time to get everything done. Any quick questions?"

"That you would answer?" They walked towards the door. "If you won't tell me anything about Lucy, could you tell me if it's safe to get involved with her?"

66

"Safe? What a strange idea. Life isn't safe, Christian--never. If you're really asking whether you should have sex with the woman, all I can say to use your judgement--like you would with anybody else. But don't be intimidated by her, or anyone. Fear is the greatest adversary."

Grace opened the door. "Grab my bag and escort me downstairs. Oh, I almost forgot these." She pulled a ring of keys from her purse. "It would be horrible if you couldn't get back in."

A taxi was waiting at the curb. "This one I ordered in advance." Grace hugged him. The purse and the bag made it awkward, but they managed. "You'll do fine, son. Don't worry about a thing." She opened the door, took the bag, and was gone. Christian watched the cab cartwheel around the corner.

**

His second full day and the boss had left town, with him in charge. What would a dutiful employee do? Find out what he was in charge of? Snoop?

The clothing he had ordered was in the closet of the room where he had collapsed yesterday. He went across the hall to check the other guest bedroom--a window facing east and only a light set of curtains. Grace had been right about which suited him better. If he used either, he would use the first, the one without any windows at all.

At the door of Grace's room, Christian reached for the knob, paused, and changed his mind. Grace hadn't told him her room was out of bounds, but going in only to satisfy his curiosity didn't seem right.

67

Back in the living room, Christian turned on the big-screen TV. Unlike his tiny black-and-white, it worked perfectly. He turned it off and examined Grace's compact discs and tapes. She had an extensive collection: classical, blues, folk, rock-and-roll, and a fair bit he couldn't categorise, all mixed together--eclectic taste and a haphazard system of organisation. Somehow, that was what he had expected.

Christian grabbed a disc at random. The Rolling Stones--"Sympathy for the Devil"? No. He took the next, Bach's Brandenburg concertos. His mother had liked Bach. He put it on.

The books matched the music collection in spirit. The shelves were neat, but science fiction and fantasy were mixed with books on religion, philosophy and the arts. As far as Christian could tell Grace had every book written by Castaneda, with a number of duplicates.

Don Juan's teachings not being what he fancied, Christian took a copy of Robert Heinlein's "Glory Road" from between a book on Hindu temple art and Sartre's "Being and Nothingness." He put his selection on the dining table, and went into the kitchen. Lunchtime. Now what could he find?

Almost anything. The refrigerator brimmed with perishables--Grace evidently did intend him to stay there. He made ham sandwiches, reheated the cup of coffee she had poured but not touched, and sat to eat and read his book.

After lunch Christian went to the office to check Grace's files. In addition to the usual office software, the off-line computer was loaded with the latest games. It made him feel virtuous to ignore those and start the database. He had a job; these were working hours.

There were two files, "Clients" and "Other". "Other" proved short: Grace's lawyer, accountant, maid service and the like. He opened "Clients". Grace had numerous clients, thousands, but the data was limited to contact people, meeting dates, and a category called "Current". In this the answer was "yes", "no", and occasionally "never again". Most of the dates were from long before computers were used, some so far back as to make no sense at all.

Without contacting these people Christian wasn't going to learn much about Grace's business. While she hadn't told him not to, she'd certainly implied he had no need. He closed the database and checked the word processor. It had never been used. No letters had been saved, no notes, no nothing. After checking for phone messages and finding none, Christian gave up on that computer.

The filing cabinets were crammed--with books. That was all they contained--no papers, no records, no files--books. From the way they weren't organised, Christian assumed them to be overflow from the living room.

That left the computers. He found a message from Grace on the first. "I'm at the airport. Please remember to water the plants. Don't forget the ones in my bedroom. And if you ever have occasion to use my bed, feel free. It's big enough for orgies. Just remember to change the sheets, okay?" It was signed "Mom."

Christian decided she was teasing again. He checked to see if there was a record of e-mail she'd sent. Of course not. He logged off. Now he could satisfy his curiosity about her bedroom without feeling guilty. After all, the plants might need watering.

He found a small cactus on Grace's dressing table, a plant his mother had called a prayer plant sitting by the door to the en-suite bathroom, and a large tropical tree by the window. The soil in the cactus felt dry, while in the other two it was moist. Christian assumed that was the way things were supposed to be.

Grace had understated the size of her bed. It was huge--the sheets would need to be custom made, probably by a sail-maker. It was a four-poster, like Aurora's, but without eyelets for restraints. He felt ashamed for having checked.

In the large closet, clothing. Like the red pantsuit Grace had worn when he met her, it all looked expensive. Half, perhaps more, was bedroom wear. He didn't examine that. About fifty pairs of shoes sat along the bottom. Christian carefully checked for plants in the corners and on the shelf. After all, that was the only reason he'd looked in the closet. He didn't find any, or anything that resembled a skeleton.

The bathroom was large, but otherwise unremarkable.

The dresser had the cactus and an array of cosmetics on top. Searching for plants in its drawers would be unseemly, so with a glance to see if he'd missed anything, Christian left the bedroom.

He went back to the computer and started the Web browser. The connection Grace had was amazingly fast. He leapt from page to page, never staying anywhere long. The speed made a difference in how quickly pages loaded, but it didn't improve their content. Still, when he lifted his eyes from the screen, it was dark outside. He signed off and went to find out the time. Neither of Grace's computers had their clock set properly. He'd change that, when he remembered.

The only timepiece downstairs was on the microwave. It showed a few minutes after seven. Christian had told Lucy he would be at The Second Circle at eight. He dashed up the stairs, yanked the eveningwear from The Black Whole from the closet and changed.

He checked in the mirror. Yes, he still looked like Christian Plowman, dressed in black, shiny regalia. It didn't suit him, but would have to do.

A search for the telephone delayed him. He found it by starting at the jack and following the cord. Grace kept it in a kitchen cupboard, between the sugar and the flour. Christian suspected the phone was the least used item on the shelf. He called for a taxi, sprinted upstairs to get Grace's keys from his other pants and hurried down to the lobby.

Outside, he waited twenty minutes. Fred, the security guard, came out after ten. "Oh, it's you, Plowman. We don't get many people dressed like that hanging around."

"I'm waiting for a taxi."

"Who'd you call?" When Christian told him, Fred laughed. "They're a lowlife outfit--they don't get calls in this part of town too often."

"Thanks for telling me."

"You being sarcastic, Plowman?"

"No, not at all. I didn't know."

Fred went back inside, muttering to himself. Why he'd taken such a dislike to Christian was as inexplicable as why Lucy and Aurora had... and far less interesting. What was going to happen on his double date? Aurora'd made it clear she was open to just about anything imaginable, and probably a good bit that wasn't.

Chapter Seven

The line-up outside The Second Circle was a black snake winding down The Street. Christian hadn't gone to a big club since he and Cleo split, but thought this unusual for Wednesday. Large men cruised up and down, watching for trouble and checking those who appeared to be under the drinking age. As Christian reached the end, one bruiser told a girl who didn't look a day over fourteen she might as well leave. She burst into tears. The man noticed Christian and waved him over.

"Mr. Plowman? Percy. Follow me, please. The boss said to keep an eye out for you." He led Christian inside. The doormen were frisking a couple wearing jackets festooned with chains. "At the end of the bar, on your left. Have an interesting night."

Christian hiked across the room. As he approached the fenced-off dais Percy had pointed to, a tall figure on it stood. In the murky red light he couldn't make out much detail. He walked up the steps, and stopped. It was Lucy Firman, but not as he remembered her. The rumour Aurora had heard was probably true¬-the lady wore wigs. The face was the angular one burned into his memory, but other than that, looking at her was like looking into a mirror more perverse than the one he'd checked in before leaving Grace's.

Lucy's clothing was the same as his, although it followed far different curves. Her hair was short, light brown, and like his, slightly unruly. As he moved towards her again, he saw her eyes were also different. No longer green, tonight they were the same pale blue as his own.

"Good evening, Lucille." He felt like establishing a formal distance.

"Good evening, Christian, and please, it's Lucy." She came around the table. "I hope my little joke isn't too upsetting." She stopped in front of him. Tonight's slight heels made her exactly his height. Her lips brushed his cheek.

Christian managed to gulp a response. "It's an interesting effect. But how did you know what I'd be wearing?"

"My spies are everywhere," she answered with a hint of laughter. She looked to her left and down. Eunice, the woman who had sold him his clothing in The Black Whole, stood there, dressed in a black leather body suit. A zipper ran from below the grin on her face to between her legs.

"You have two jobs, Eunice?" Christian asked her.

"Not anymore." Her grin widened. "Lucy put out word on The Street to keep an eye open for you, you know? Right after you left, I called her. Overnight I've gone from being a part-time waitress here to manager. Maybe we should go somewhere so I can thank you properly." She ran her zipper down much further than could be considered decent.

Lucy reached over and jerked it back up. "He'll let you know if he's interested."

"Right, boss. Sorry." Eunice looked back at Christian. "Hey, how come you know my name? I didn't tell you."

"Aurora Medici recognised your taste in clothing." He looked around The Second Circle, and then at Lucy. "She said she'd be here around nine and might bring someone. I didn't think you'd be so busy."

Eunice exploded. "Aurora? Aurora will be here? I love it! I'll tell the boys to look for her." She started away and then stopped. "If that's okay, boss?"

"That's fine." Eunice scuttled away. Lucy smiled and took Christian by the arm. "Do sit. I expected your guest would be Ms Medici. This evening should be entertaining."

"I emailed you from her account, didn't I?" He knew he had. Since he'd forgotten his own password, he hadn't had much choice. He'd changed the return address to his own, but the originating account would have been Aurora's.

"You did." Lucy's smile grew. "When Eunice started working here part-time, Aurora was listed as the person to contact in case of emergency. That changed six months ago."

"And is the real reason you made Eunice manager?"

"Didn't you know success in this world depends entirely on who you know, and sleep with?" Lucy laughed softly. "If Eunice can't do the job, I'll dismiss her, like I did her predecessor, a man who put his hand in the till once too often. I doubt Eunice will make that mistake. Money won't be her downfall."

"You have an odd sense of humour, Lucy."

She acknowledged his comment with a slight nod.

Time to change the topic. "Grace said to say hello. You missed her in the park the other day. She couldn't have been much behind you."

"She never is. Sneaking you away would have been amusing, but you turned me down, you rat. I have a message for her too. Tell her I'm ready to resume our long-distance chess match."

"You can tell her yourself." Christian didn't want to assume the role of go-between. He dug in his wallet and found the first business card Grace had given him. He didn't need it anymore. "Here, this is her current email address. She's out of town right now."

"Out of town--what a surprise. I suppose she left you in charge. Be careful. I'm not the only one who terminates employees. Of course if she dumps you, you can work for me."

"Did she fire you, Lucy?" Christian was still curious about what had happened, and how long ago. Tonight, looking at Lucy and listening to her, he'd upped his estimate of her age from twenty to perhaps a year or so younger than him, say about thirty. How old was she? How old was Grace?

"Fire?" Her laugh echoed off the ceiling. "I wouldn't say 'fire', but it's a matter of opinion--she and I went our separate ways. Over the years I've proven I understand people better than she does.

76

My business is booming. Grace, well Grace is holding on."

That didn't help. One more try. "What business are you in anyway, Lucy?"

"What business?" She straightened in her chair. "Thanks for reminding me. Tonight I'm supposed to be in the hospitality business, as your personal host. I've been doing a lousy job so far. I haven't even offered you a drink. Have you eaten?"

"Actually, no. I was cruising the Web and lost track of the time."

"Seductive, isn't it? I love it. How about a steak? Say yes, and I'll have an excuse to have one too. How do you like it? Rare, almost bleeding? A man after my own heart. Look, I need to make a phone call. I'll send a waiter over. Eunice should be back soon. She can keep you entertained." With a whirl, Lucy was gone.

Christian ordered beer. He wasn't much of a drinker, and knew better than to put anything stronger into an empty stomach. Eunice returned as it arrived.

"I left Aurora's name at the door." She sat next to him. Her zipper had been lowered again. Her outfit suited her better with it up, holding her fast-food figure in. "Then I arranged an interview with the band. I know she'll want that. Of course, she'll need to be nice to me."

"Maybe you should be nice first."

"Huh?"

"I think Lucy hired you because you know people in the media, Aurora in particular." Well, it wasn't a lie, not quite. "If I were Lucy, I wouldn't be happy if you made an enemy of Aurora."

"Hey, the bitch dumped me, you know? Be nice? Boy, that would confuse the shit out of her."

Eunice had her mind made up regarding her ex. Time to change the topic. "Why would she be so interested in the band? Who's playing?"

Eunice gave the band's name. Christian had never heard of them.

"We leaked word to The Street this afternoon," Eunice said. "This is a warm-up gig for the tour of the year--sold out everywhere. They play retro-punk-rap-jazz fusion. They're the biggest, all famous before they got together." She named the musicians and their former groups.

Christian only knew one name, a guitarist from a '60s trio. The band Eunice cited as his previous claim to fame was another Christian didn't know. He felt out of touch.

"Yeah, anyway, they all owe Lucy--so when she found out they were rehearsing in Noronto, she suggested they play here tonight. Suggested," she repeated with a cackle. "I'd say it's a command performance. Lucy said I could set up one interview, my choice. Be nice to Aurora? Shit no. If she wants that interview, she'll have to kiss more than my ass."

There wasn't any point arguing. "I'd clear it with Lucy first if I were you."

"Oh yeah, I'll do that, for sure. Here she is now. With steaks? Boy, you do rate."

His steak was great, rare and oozing. Lucy sat beside Christian, but like him she didn't want to talk, she wanted to eat. Eunice moved to Lucy's other side to harangue her. Out of the corner of his eye, Christian could see the discussion was intense, on Eunice's part. Occasionally Lucy would turn her head, say a couple of quiet words and return her attention to her meal. Eunice yammered on. Finally Lucy put down her fork.

"I said 'no'." And everyone in The Second Circle heard her say it. Eunice sat frozen as Lucy resumed eating. Finally Eunice stood and went away. Lucy and Christian finished at almost the same time.

"That was about the interview?"

"What else? Frankly, Christian, if Aurora wasn't with you, I'd have allowed Eunice to play her little game. I don't owe Aurora any favours."

"I don't think I do either." He wasn't as sure of that as he tried to sound.

"I'm sure Aurora feels differently."

"She should consider an introduction to you sufficient payment."

Lucy laughed. "Good point." She leaned forward. Her copy of his shirt was unbuttoned halfway down now and she wasn't wearing a bra. Her, it suited. "I'll do my best to ensure it. I don't want you to feel beholden to anyone."

"Except you?"

Lucy sat back again, removing the wide-open vista from view. "My my... Grace chose a cynic this time around. She's learning--I'll give her that." She put a hand gently on his arm. "No, like dear Grace all I offer is freely given, no strings. Whether or not you feel obliged is up to you. I'm not at all like sweet Aurora."

Aurora, Kathy, Lucy... women like these didn't make moves on just anyone, let alone Christian Plowman. Christian knew that, but couldn't deny what was happening. Lucy had made herself every bit as clear as the other two, or had she? A shiver ran up his spine, one completely independent of the effect Lucy's body had on his. This was no time to make a mistake. He tried to put together a response.

Lucy patted his arm and removed her hand. "We can talk later. Aurora's making her entrance. Again, I must play host."

Chapter Eight

All eyes were on Aurora and, from the slinky prance in her step, she loved it. Her tiny black velvet dress shimmered in the dim red light. Lucy hugged her as if they were best friends, not people meeting for the first time. In Lucy's arms Aurora looked petite. Dressed as a man, Lucy made Aurora seem more feminine, almost fragile.

The embrace ended. Lucy took Aurora's hand and led her towards the table. Christian stood. As they got closer Christian noticed Aurora had brought someone with her, as promised. A short, balding man wearing an outfit that might have suited him if he were forty pounds lighter and ten years younger jiggled along beside Lucy, mouth flapping. As they came up the stairs to the dais Christian could make out some of what he was saying.

"Baby... oh Mama... so hot... babe... make you feel so good..."

Neither Aurora nor Lucy seemed to be paying any attention to him. Lucy's focus was on Aurora, and Aurora was glowing, gazing up at Lucy with adoration and lust.

Lucy brought Aurora to Christian and ceremoniously handed her to him. A "baby, baby" drifted over her shoulder.

With Aurora transferred, Lucy wheeled to face the babbler. "You. You will sit and be quiet. There." She pointed to a chair on the other side of the large, round table. "If you're a good little man, I may find treats you can beg for later. Sit." The man flew backwards as if hit by a truck, and scrambled to get to the indicated spot.

"Christian?" Aurora said. "I don't think you've met Patsy. I'm ashamed to say he was all I could find to bring at last minute. I don't think it was a good idea." She pulled away from Christian and went to Lucy. "I apologise. If he's too annoying, I'll take him away."

Lucy hugged Aurora again. Aurora melted into her arms. "Oh don't worry," Lucy said. "Everyone understands. Actually, I find the little chap amusing."

She released Aurora, walked to Patsy, and ran a long red fingernail down his nose. "He'll do anything I tell him to. Won't you?"

Patsy's head bobbed in frantic agreement.

"I know exactly what to do with his sort. I suspect you're far too gentle, Aurora. I won't be. He knows that--don't you, worm?"

His eyes glazed and Patsy's head bobbed even faster.

"Good. Now sit. Stay. And play dead." With Lucy's last command, his head snapped to an immediate halt, frozen.

Aurora hadn't moved. "The chair beside Christian is yours, Aurora." With a gentle touch Lucy returned Aurora to Christian. "Now, if you'll pardon me, I must desert you. Duty calls."

Aurora stood beside Christian and watched Lucy evaporate into the shadows behind the bar. Then she watched the shadows. As Christian guided her into her chair, he could feel her quivering. He waved to a waiter.

"What would you like to drink, Aurora?"

"What? Drink? Oh, tequila. A beer for Patsy I guess." Finally, she looked at Christian. "After all, I guess I am responsible for him. Until now I didn't appreciate how disgusting he is. Don't worry about him, Christian. He'll be in his glory, being seen at the owner's table on a night like this."

Christian hadn't been worried about Patsy--the man had dug his own grave. "She's quite something, isn't she?"

"Who? Lucy?"

"No, Madonna." It slipped out before he could stop it. Whether he or Aurora was more surprised would have been debatable. At least it got her attention. She fixed a green glare on him.

The drinks arrived. Aurora emptied hers, put her glass back on the tray and ordered another. "You're quite something yourself. How dare you talk to me like that? Who do you think you are? And why are you dressed like her? Is this your idea of a joke?"

All good questions. Christian could answer the last. "I think it's Lucy's idea of a joke."

Aurora stared at him until her second drink arrived. As she knocked it back, Christian tried to change the flow of the conversation. "You might be interested to know an interview with the band has been arranged for you. I understand it's an exclusive."

Aurora handed her glass back to the waiting waiter. Christian signalled that he should continue to wait. "Oh, well, thank-you," Aurora said. "I apologise. I guess I owe you."

"Don't thank me. I didn't arrange it. I don't think you'll be thrilled when you find out who did. Waiter, would you bring her another drink please? A double?"

Aurora smiled. "Why, Christian? If it's Lucy, that's fine. Shit, I'd crawl over broken glass to get into her bed. Didn't you notice? Don't you know I swing both ways?"

"I'd gathered."

"Then what's the fucking problem?"

The waiter had reached the bar, and Aurora's drink was being poured. "You didn't know Lucy owned The Second Circle, did you?"

"No. I knew it'd been sold. I didn't know who'd bought it. What's your point?"

The waiter was on his way back. "Then I'd guess you don't know who she's hired to manage it, the person who set up the interview for you."

"No, and I repeat. What's your fucking point?"

"I'm sure you remember Eunice? Your ex?"

"I didn't tell you that about her."

"No, she did." Christian found the glimmer of realisation trickling into Aurora's eyes more enjoyable than he should. "Eunice is the manager here now. She set up the interview."

The waiter put Aurora's drink in front of her. She drained it. "Bring me another."

The waiter left. Aurora lifted her eyes again to meet Christian's. "Then I guess tonight I'll be doing something I swore I'd never do again, won't I?"

Like her eyes, her voice had gone flat. Aurora and Eunice apparently played by the same rules.

"That's up to you."

"No. I have to have this interview. It's big."

"I told Eunice I didn't approve, and Lucy backed me up." That was close enough to the truth.

"Why? Why would you do that, Christian?"

"Because you're my girlfriend?"

Aurora's laughter started quietly, but grew. Her drink arrived. She tossed it down, and regaining control, gasped for air. "You think that? I screwed you so you'd recommend me for the Ovation job. Now you've introduced me to Lucy, got me an exclusive, and saved me from Eunice. You want to come home with me tonight? Okay, I'd say you've earned it."

She looked around to see if people were watching. They were. She flicked back her hair, leaned forward and gave him a quick kiss. "Besides. It's probably time I was seen having a hot time with a man. Better you than Patsy."

"Gee, thanks. So, for you sex with men is business, with women it's pleasure, and Patsy's never been more than camouflage."

"Oh quite often it's business with women too, and I've found an occasional man who gets me off--like you."

"I'll choose to believe that," Christian answered.

"Oh, it's true. The first time was incredible."

"People can't believe you and Patsy were ever..."

"Fucking, Christian? You've got to learn to say the word. The public buys the story. Folks in the business know better, but that doesn't matter. It's a common arrangement."

Christian wanted to continue the conversation, but Lucy and Eunice were approaching. Aurora hadn't noticed. Christian touched her arm and flicked his eyes in their direction.

"Oh. Thank-you," Aurora said.

Eunice took Aurora's hands to pull her to her feet. Aurora didn't budge.

"Aurora! Good to see you! You look great!" she said in a voice that would carry, and then continued softly. "Look, I know I screwed up. Those guys didn't mean anything. I just wanted to throw you a surprise party."

"You thought I was in Vancouver, slut," Aurora answered, every bit as quietly. Then, "Eunice! Sweetheart! I love your outfit!" She finally stood to hug Eunice. "It suits you. Makes you look like trash," she hissed, loudly enough for Christian to hear, but only just.

She let go of Eunice and turned to Christian. "I walked in on her and four of the dumbest security goons from The Second Circle, going at it hot and heavy. Laugh like I just said something witty, Christian."

Christian complied as best he could.

"And here I'd thought we had a committed relationship. I went for blood tests--if she'd given me anything, I'd have killed her."

Christian believed Aurora might have.

86

From her face, Eunice did too. "Would an exclusive interview with the band be enough apology?"

Aurora knew the interview was already hers. Christian had told her. He waited to see how she would play out the scene.

She verged towards the high road. "It might. Take me to meet them and I'll think it over." She took Eunice's hand. Together they strolled in the direction of the stage, superficially two old friends who hadn't seen each other for a while.

"Aurora puts on a good show." Christian's concentration on the melodrama had been so complete he hadn't heard Lucy return. She smiled at him before going to Patsy and petting his head. "Has he been any trouble?"

"I forgot he was here."

"Good. Very well, Patsy, you may go and use the little eunuch's room. Be back in five minutes." Patsy bobbed his head once and left.

Lucy came back to Christian. "The DJ will start in a minute. The music will be too loud for us to talk. Let's go to my office for a drink."

She led him around the end of the bar, through a door that blended into the wall. A short hall led to stairs at the end. There were two doors. Lucy opened the first and ushered him into an office. As he stepped inside, Christian heard the music in The Second Circle begin. It was faint, but clear. When he closed the door all that remained was a throb in the floor.

"You don't have to have a drink of course. You can have anything." Lucy unbuttoned her shirt

87

further. "Maybe on the couch? Or I can clear the desk."

"Anything?" Grace had said he should use his judgement. He judged Lucy was taking control, and he didn't like it.

"Yes," Lucy answered. She pulled the shirt open. Her skin was creamy, her figure extraordinary. From breasts so full they should sag but didn't, her body tapered to an improbably slight waist. Lucy was no pin-up. On paper no one would believe she was real.

"No silicone." She tweaked a nipple, hard. "You'll want to test that, of course."

Christian moved towards Lucy. "I've decided," he said. He cupped her head with his hands and gazed into pale blue eyes, eyes that had been green when he met her. Then he carefully removed her wig. "I want this." He stepped back.

"I like the red one better, but you're rather attractive au naturale." He handed her hair back. "I'd be interested in seeing your real eyes too. I also want a beer." He went to the refrigerator opposite the couch. "Anything for you?"

Lucy's chuckle was low. "No thanks, but go ahead. Yes, Grace has done well for herself this time around. I don't think you're ready for my eyes though, not yet." She went to a door to one side of her desk. "I'll be back."

When she re-emerged, she had not only the long red hair and green eyes, but also the white tights and halter-top from the first time they met. "I thought I'd present you with the original package."

Christian put down his beer, went to her and softly kissed her forehead. Her now pale green eyes met his always-pale blue ones.

"I make the score Christian Plowman two, Lucy Firman nothing. Believe me, I'll even it up. Now, let's make an entrance."

In black mannish clothing, Lucy had blended in. In white, figure fully displayed, that was no longer the case. They entered the maelstrom that The Second Circle had become. Instead of returning directly to their table, Lucy took Christian on a parade route. They strolled down the long bar and along the edge of the dance floor where customers were displaying their charms in time to loud, pre-recorded music.

Heads turned. Eyes followed. The pulsing thunder of the music swelled and shook the walls. A growing murmur began to threaten the music's dominance. In response, the music got louder. The room was at boiling point.

Christian felt calm. The attention was for Lucy; he was only her shadowy attendant. None of the so-called supermodels of the world could have stood naked beside her and been noticed.

As they walked up the three steps to the dais, the room and everyone in it seemed to slow. Only he, Lucy and the music were moving at normal speed. All others were swimming in molasses.

"This is fun," Lucy whispered. "I must remember to do this more often." In the din her words were clear.

"You'll be the talk of the town tomorrow."

"No, Christian. Few will remember me."

"I don't see how that's possible." How could anyone forget her?

"Wanna bet?" she asked. Her grin almost escaped from her thin face.

Christian looked at the people at the owner's table. Aurora, Eunice and Patsy had all returned. They seemed dazed, as if reaching a point of sensory overload they had shut down before burning out. He turned to consider the entire scene. Everyone looked that way.

"No."

"Smart man." She clapped once, and the world returned to normal. Aurora jumped as if she'd seen them appear from nowhere. The waiter delivered another double tequila. Aurora drained it and smiled a belated greeting to Lucy and Christian. It was far too noisy to talk.

With Lucy on his left and Aurora on his right Christian sat sipping his beer, and thinking. Had Lucy hypnotised him, or everyone else? Aurora kept looking past him, at Lucy. Aurora would remember Lucy tomorrow--Christian had no doubt about that.

The band started to play. They were even louder than the recorded music, too loud for Christian to make out more than a beat. He danced with Aurora and then stood by as she autographed books, paper coasters and the backs of peoples' hands. He danced with Lucy. Lucy danced with Aurora. Patsy's head wobbled in time to the music.

The band took a break. Eunice disappeared backstage and didn't reappear. The band returned and played a slow song. Christian danced with

Aurora pressed close. Lucy cut in. The slow song ended. Aurora returned to the table and ordered more tequila.

The night continued with the collected flesh whirling ever faster. On the floor Lucy, ghost-like in white, looked like a stork surrounded by crows. The crows gave her space. Another slow song--this time Lucy danced with Aurora, and Christian cut in. Aurora was flushed, hot to the touch. She leaned in as if resting. The song ended and Christian took her back to the table. One more fast song and the band left the stage. The house lights turned up; quiet music drifted from the speakers. People started moving towards the door. Closing time.

Christian helped Aurora to her feet. Lucy signalled to Patsy, who snapped to attention. Christian had forgotten him again. Lucy led them to the end of the bar and beyond, out a back exit. A black stretch limousine sat there, engine throbbing.

Lucy opened the front passenger door. "You sit up front with Dicky," she said to Patsy.

A man in a black uniform hurriedly limped around from the driver's door, mumbling apologies. As he held the door for them, Christian saw piggy eyes hidden in folds of flesh. Dicky seemed familiar, but Christian couldn't think why. He asked Lucy.

"You may have seen his picture," she answered. "Dicky was president of a large concern. They ran him out for being corrupt, and dumb as a sack of hammers. He's loyal, to me. Always has been." She waved a hand, dismissing Dicky. "So,

91

how did I do at the hospitality business, once I got started?"

Christian looked at Aurora. She was by the window, staring out through black smoked glass. Lucy's eyes flickered between him and Aurora.

"Quite well. The steak was excellent and the drink flowed freely, maybe too freely." He shifted over and put an arm around Aurora. She remained oblivious. "And Eunice and Patsy behaved. Wouldn't they make a handsome couple?"

"Wouldn't they just? Two birds with one stone." Lucy closed her eyes, and laughed softly. "Yes, I see it. And I like it."

"It may have been too much hospitality for Aurora to handle," Christian continued. Eunice and Patsy weren't worth the thought Lucy seemed to be giving them. "She enjoyed herself, maybe to excess. It'll be interesting to see how she feels in the morning."

"You're spending the night with her? Think she'll notice? We can drop her off."

"She's expecting me to." Aurora hadn't been enthusiastic, but had said he could.

Christian wasn't thrilled either but better Aurora than Lucy. He didn't think Lucy would believe that, but it was more true than not. On one level, the physical, he wanted her more than he'd ever wanted a woman. On another, she terrified him. Whether she'd mesmerised him or the assembled multitude at The Second Circle didn't matter. If she could do that, what else could she do? Tonight wasn't the night he wanted that question answered.

92

Lucy studied Christian. "I see," she finally said. "Very well. Let me bring her back." She slipped between Christian and Aurora, separating them effortlessly.

Lucy turned Aurora's head and kissed her. Aurora moaned and snuggled into Lucy.

Suddenly, Lucy bit Aurora's lip. Aurora yanked her head back. Lucy's tongue shot out to capture the drop of blood that appeared. "There. All heated up, and all yours." Lucy licked her lips--Aurora and Eunice could both take lessons for her on exactly how to do that in the most lewd way possible. Next to her, they were amateurs. Lucy returned to the facing seat.

Aurora looked at Lucy wide-eyed, and slid over beside Christian. The limo glided to a stop.

"Don't worry about the little guy," Lucy told them. "I'll make sure he's properly taken care of." Her eyes gleamed. Flickers of red escaped from the edges of her contacts. Christian shook his head in denial--it was late, he was tired, he hadn't seen that. And again, he'd forgotten Patsy.

"You can keep him forever for all I care." Aurora's voice was unadorned emotion.

"Why thank you, Aurora. I'll do that."

Aurora got out. Christian followed. The street was deserted. He swung the door closed. Without a sound the limousine glided away.

Chapter Nine

Inside, Aurora shot the deadbolt into place, shed her dress, unhooked her bra and peeled down her pantyhose, ripping it. "Fuck me. Now. Hard."

When he didn't immediately react, she turned and headed down the hall to her bedroom. By the time Christian got there she was on the bed, waiting. He stripped and slipped between her legs.

Aurora wailed like a banshee as he entered her. She came with a wild buck and muffled her scream by sinking her teeth into his shoulder, then went rigid, and suddenly limp as, with a gasp, her jaw released its grip. Her head fell to the pillow. Ten seconds--maybe less.

Christian propped himself on his elbows. Relaxed, Aurora looked different: softer, cherubic. Blood from his shoulder dripped onto her, mixed with her sweat, and ran in a slow trickle between her breasts and down her concave stomach. At last, he recovered enough to push himself off, turn off the light, roll over and fall asleep.

He woke in darkness. On the other side of the bed, Aurora was restless. Deep in her throat she moaned. "Lucy."

Christian called to her, but she didn't seem to hear. The bed rocked as she thrashed about. He didn't go any nearer--once bitten, twice shy.

"Lucy, oh... oh... yes... Lucy." The bed shook. "Oh... Yes... Yes! Lucy!" The sheet lifted and fell with a final thud of a body hitting the mattress.

Then silence. Christian went back to sleep.

The next time he woke the bedroom was lit by light from the open bathroom door. Aurora came out, dripping in a thick terry-cloth robe. "Hi! Look, I've got to get to The Factory. Have a quick shower while I get dressed and put coffee on."

Christian took no more than five minutes. When he got out, Aurora was in a smart yellow pantsuit, towelling her hair dry. "Coffee should be ready soon. Get dressed and get a cup. I need to do my make-up."

As he was taking his second sip, Aurora bustled in. "You might as well go home. I'll be tied up all day." She poured a cup, and knocked it back.

"We need to talk," Christian blew on his coffee.

"About how to handle the Ovation situation. Sure. Give me a call. Today I've got a million things that need doing." She headed for the door. "Aren't you finished?" She opened it.

Christian pushed himself to his feet and walked out into the hall.

"Bye." Aurora rushed down the hall to the stairs and disappeared.

When Christian reached street level, there was no sign of her. He assumed she must have had a taxi waiting. There wasn't another in sight. He looked around: parked cars, apartment buildings with isolated lit units, a chilly early morning fog that wafted and swirled, and chilled his bones.

He flexed his tender shoulder and started walking. He should have it looked at, but not now. Now he wanted to go back to bed, alone.

A few taxis sat outside a marginal downtown hotel, engines off, drivers on the sidewalk talking. He patted a pocket. Wallet? Yes. He patted the other side. Keys. He pulled them out. Grace's keys. His were at her place. He took a taxi. It was easy to flag one when it wasn't moving.

At Grace's he went to his room, stripped and tossed everything into a corner. It all needed to be cleaned. He turned out the light.

Again Christian woke in the dark. He fumbled around, remembered he was at Grace's and found the light switch. His shoulder throbbed. He looked balefully at the heap of clothing in the corner. He needed something to wear. The daytime clothing from The Black Whole? No way. He tossed it on the heap and walked into the hall, naked.

In the other bedroom he found two robes, both large, both white. He put one on and went downstairs. Off the hall between the kitchen and the computer room there were two doors he hadn't opened. The first was a bathroom. The second contained a washing machine and dryer. He went back upstairs for his dirty clothing. Phew--it had been a rough couple of days. He put his in the washing machine, and everything from The Black Whole into a garbage bag to be dropped off at a drycleaner, when and if he remembered. That expense he would claim back from Grace as a matter of principle.

By the microwave clock it was three in the afternoon. While early morning fog still clouded the insides of his head, he felt better--except for the shoulder. He heated a cup of coffee, looked in the refrigerator and decided he would eat later. Coffee in hand, he went to check his e-mail.

There was a note from Grace. "See Cosmo before the weekend". Once again she signed as "Mom". Forwarded through a series of remailers, the path the message had followed to her machine gave no clue as to her whereabouts.

"Will do. Lucy returns your greetings and wants to arrange a chess game?" It made as much sense as anything, he supposed. "Life is interesting," he added and sent the message to Grace's local account.

A message from Cosmo had also arrived. He had Grace's tickets for a charity ball for the following Tuesday. Would Christian please pick them up? Christian sent a quick reply, confirming he would.

Then he sent Lucy a thank-you for the hospitality shown him and his guests. His mother had taught him to be polite. He didn't suggest another meeting--he had no idea how to handle Lucy. His mother hadn't given him much advice about women--the car accident had happened about the time she might have started.

Christian suspected he wouldn't have listened anyway. His grandmother and Aster, his kid sister, had tried--especially with respect to Cleo. He hadn't paid any mind to them, so why would his mother have fared better? After all, he hadn't realised she wouldn't be around forever until she was gone.

He stared at the now blank screen. He hadn't thought about his family in some time, but didn't feel he could contact the remnants now, in a time of crisis. Except for his shoulder, he felt numb. He needed to talk things over with someone but was alone.

He left the computer, transferred his clothing from the washer to the dryer and prepared brunch. As he ate, he continued reading "Glory Road". He did the dishes and then finished the book. If only things could work out as well for him. It was a fantasy; real life never worked that way.

He checked the time again--six o'clock, news time. He turned on Grace's big-screen and tuned in COSMO-TV, leaving the sound turned down. All seemed normal in the world: murders, accidents, wars, weather (the man on in the evenings wasn't as cute as Judy, at least not to Christian's eyes), entertainment.

Aurora appeared, decked head to toe in black leather. If she truly considered leather a cliché, as she'd said, tonight she was either adjusting her beliefs or striving for a "common touch". Christian turned up the volume.

"Before I show you highlights from the exclusive interview airing tonight at nine on VideoView, I'll tell you the most exciting news," Aurora informed the camera, and the world. "Tomorrow night I'll be live, backstage, for the opening-night concert in New York City. You'll only see me on VideoView, so tune in."

Christian turned her off and went to collect his clothing from the dryer. Apparently he wouldn't see Aurora in person for a day or two unless he went to New York. That didn't bother him. Aurora and he were obviously finished with each other.

Christian went home. Still tired, he went to bed immediately.

He slept well, and got up early Friday morning. His cereal had to be eaten with tap water again. He hadn't picked up milk. The fridge was almost empty, and even its minimal contents were spoiled. He put everything into a garbage bag and set up the TV to watch Judy. This morning, he had time.

Judy was on The Street outside The Factory, wearing a raincoat. Black cartoon clouds appeared on her front. She laughed and smiled as lightning shot down her body. Christian promised himself he would buy a new set--he wanted to hear Judy, and see her in colour. Then again, Grace had a perfectly good television.

He turned off his and looked around. His apartment was cramped and dingy. He took his briefcase from under the table, dumped the papers and filled it with clean underwear. More clothing went into his backpack. He put the pack on and with briefcase and garbage in hand, left.

At Grace's he put on one of his new suits and a tie, and looked in the mirror. He still looked like Christian Plowman--overdressed. He checked his e-mail. Another Grace note had arrived, longer this time.

"Tell Lucy the game is on. On second thought, don't bother--I'll contact her directly. After you visit Cosmo, take the weekend off. Take in a concert, and put it on expenses as research. And do enjoy the formal next Tuesday. You doubt you will? Well, take someone congenial and with tone, and there won't be any problem. My lawyer is forwarding a sizeable cheque to the organisers with your name noted as my representative, so you'll be more than welcome. Expect me to be out of touch for a week or so. Going hiking. Mom."

Christian printed the message and considered it over coffee. Grace was telling him something more than what the words said, or at least he hoped so. Christian needed guidance. Trying to read between the lines was an affliction common to all English majors. Grace knew he was one--Christian hoped she had intended to write between hers.

The message for Lucy was straightforward and the instructions to take the weekend off clear-cut-- even though he wasn't sure what he was taking time off from. He'd need to see what concerts were in town. For some it would be too late to get tickets, but surely something would be available.

Other than the part about the cheque, Grace's advice concerning the formal was puzzling. Christian wasn't sure he knew anyone "congenial and with tone". Of the many words he could think of to describe Aurora, "congenial" wasn't one. And while she had tone--as did everyone, at least of some variety--Grace probably meant the sort of tone that would seamlessly blend in to a society gathering. If Aurora had that, she'd hidden it from him.

As far as Christian could tell, Grace was telling him to not take Aurora. Fine. He didn't want to, not after last night and this morning. Christian flexed his shoulder. Ouch! The bite might be infected.

Was there anyone else? Lucy? He couldn't see it; "congenial" wasn't her either. He had no doubt she could carry off the "tone" part. Lucy seemed capable of being whatever and whoever she wanted to be. Still--no.

Christian put the printout aside. He could worry about his date later. If worst came to worst, he would go on his own. That might be best, even if Grace had said to take someone. He checked the time on the microwave. Might as well go to see Cosmo, and then start the weekend early.

Christian walked to The Factory. It took over an hour, but he needed time to himself, time to think. He didn't, merely churned previous thoughts over and over again.

Kathy glanced at Christian as he entered the lobby and then returned her attention to a seemingly busy switchboard console. He walked to the desk and waited. Grace had said Kathy was more his type than Aurora--perhaps he should ask her.

After several minutes, Kathy looked up. "Yes, Mr. Plowman?"

"I'm here to see Cosmo--to pick up tickets for the fund-raiser next Tuesday."

"How nice for you." A couple of lights flashed, and she returned her attention to her work. The ice in her grey-blue eyes was so hard that Christian continued on his way.

Cosmo hung up the phone as Christian appeared in his doorway. "You've come for these." He grabbed an envelope from his desk and rushed around to shake Christian's hand. "I can't tell you how much I appreciate everything you've already done. With those rock-and-roll exclusives, Aurora's back on top. She won't want Ovation now. Oh, and you'll be pleased to know she'll be covering Tuesday's event for Bull's Eye News." He gave Christian a meaningful wink.

"Then I guess I'll see her there."

"I assumed you would take her."

"Grace instructed me to invite someone else. You won't have any problem getting Aurora in, will you?"

"Of course not, but does Aurora know? When she left for New York, she thought you'd ask her." Cosmo sighed. "She won't be happy." He sighed again.

Christian decided Cosmo wasn't as good an actor as Aurora. She sold her lines; he merely said them.

"Did Grace really tell you to take someone else?" Cosmo asked when his histrionics didn't get the desired reaction.

"Ask her if you don't believe me." Grace wasn't anywhere she could be reached. He thought she'd told him to not take Aurora and trusted she would back him up in any case. However, he felt more secure knowing his beliefs couldn't be tested.

"Then I guess I'll see you Tuesday, Mr. Plowman. I look forward to meeting whomsoever Grace might prefer to my niece." Cosmo glanced at his watch. "Damn, I'm late for an appointment again." He rushed out.

Christian followed at a more leisurely pace. This was a fine mess. Now he couldn't go to the ball alone.

Chapter Ten

Saturday morning the sun was hidden behind a curtain of smog. Christian sat at Grace's table, sipped coffee and gazed out over some of Noronto's most expensive real-estate. He had a problem.

He'd had one Monday morning too--how to find the job he needed to keep from ending up on the street. But that had been an uncertainty he'd learned to live with. He hadn't expected to find a job; his failure was the next logical step in his progress down society's ladder.

Instead he'd moved in the opposite direction, at least temporarily. Now, he needed a date for a society fund-raiser. Grace had told him to take the weekend off, but before Tuesday Christian had to find a woman who would dazzle Cosmo, and maybe Aurora. No, that was asking too much, but he had to find someone plausible.

Christian reread the printout of Grace's message. He was to treat himself to a concert this weekend, and take "someone congenial and with tone" to the ball. Okay, who? He rummaged through his mind. Cleo? Probably not. Even if he could find her, Christian didn't think Cleo would meet Grace's criteria, or his.

The sun finally broke through. Light streamed into Grace's apartment, and Christian's eyes. He moved into the living room, and for the first time took a good look at it. All the furniture was natural wood with grey cushions or upholstery, but ranged from antique to ultra-modern. Any one piece would be worth more than the contents of his one-room apartment. The woven rug added colour, as did the painting of flowers hanging on the back wall. Nothing matched, but everything fit.

Grace's approach to her employees seemed equally offhand. Christian hoped it proved as effective. Apart from finding a host for Cosmo's new channel, Grace had told him his objective was to establish himself as a public figure, a man of consequence. As with everything else, she'd left the details up to him, except to say he should feel free to spend money.

Okay, he would. Monday morning he would call the escort agencies and hire a high-price call-girl to accompany him. Not only would that solve his problem, it seemed the ultimate test of whether or not Grace meant what she said.

He didn't see how she could object. After all, he had no intention of paying for sex, only company. Besides, the difference between Aurora and a professional seemed slight, hardly worth mentioning. Aurora had only slept with him because she thought he could advance her career. Christian tested his wounded shoulder. It wasn't as sore. On the way back from The Factory the previous evening he'd stopped at a walk-in clinic. The doctor had said she'd seen worse, prescribed an antibiotic cream and suggested a muzzle to prevent any recurrence. Avoidance would be as effective.

Christian went out for the papers. Back upstairs, he leafed through the entertainment sections. There were a number of rock concerts, but after The Second Circle, he felt rocked out.

Besides, if he were going to feel right about putting it on expenses as research, he should check out performances in what were considered the finer arts, culture of the nature Ovation might broadcast.

A tenor was performing at Roy Thompson Hall. That didn't appeal. Ballet downtown--possible. He didn't understand ballet either, but it was more scenic; he appreciated the tights on the ballerina in the advertisement far more than the opera singer's girth. Sunday afternoon in a concert hall up near the end of the subway, a group was playing Bach's Brandenburg concertos on authentic baroque instruments. A recording of that Bach, his mother's favourite, had been the first thing Christian had played from Grace's collection. It seemed destined.

He extracted the telephone from the cupboard and called to see if tickets were available--yes, a single, close to the stage. He could pick it up at the door. The clock on the microwave indicated a touch after noon, and the concert wasn't until two the next afternoon. After checking for e-mail and phone messages and finding none, Christian settled in for an unproductive weekend off, as instructed. He had a bookshelf half-filled with fantasy to read, and games on the off-line computer to play.

***

Christian arrived early for the concert. He'd allowed extra time for subway delays and hadn't needed it. After picking up his ticket, he stood outside and watched the people. Many were dressed formally, in rigid suits and dresses. To them culture was a serious matter, even on a sunny Sunday afternoon. A few others were in tattered jeans, adherents of an alternative conformity. Some, like him, had selected something in-between. When almost everyone else had entered the hall, Christian straggled in.

His seat was on the aisle, third row from the front. Christian smiled a greeting to the woman next to him. She gathered her flowing skirt and tucked it underneath her, pushed her thick-rimmed glasses up her long nose and returned to studying the program. The musicians were on stage, tuning up.

Christian had forgotten how much he enjoyed concerts. Even the best sound system couldn't reproduce the tones of live performance. He joined in enthusiastic applause as the first half ended.

The woman stood. "Excuse me. I like to beat the crowd."

Christian thought that an excellent idea. He stood aside, and then accompanied her up the aisle. Tall and graceful, she walked with a powerful, effortless stride. They reached the top before most people had moved from their seats.

She glanced at him and moved to one side of the door. He followed. She stopped and raised an eyebrow.

"Can I buy you a drink?" Christian asked. "Would anyone object?"

"I wouldn't." Her voice was deep and full, resonant without being loud. "Scotch, please. If you want to get served before the intermission ends you'd better go now."

Christian rushed to the bar, but it still took him ten minutes. "Scotch, single malt. Two." Plastic cups? How tacky.

The woman accepted her drink, sniffed and tasted it, and with narrowed eyes looked at Christian over the rim. "So... the good stuff. Thank-you. Trying to pick me up?"

He searched for a clue in her deep brown eyes. "Would you mind?"

"That depends. Hoping to get laid?"

She'd asked in a matter-of-fact tone, one Christian tried to copy for his answer. "No. It just felt natural to fall in beside you. When you stepped over here and waited, I assumed you were interested. Was I wrong?"

"Not necessarily." She sipped her drink. "I just want to make it clear if you're in the market for a quickie, you're wasting your time."

"Believe me, that's the last thing I'd want."

Her eyebrow went up.

"No offence intended. But after this week..." The bell signalling the end of the intermission started to ring. "I can't explain now. It's a long story, and if we don't want to miss the last three concertos, we'd better get moving."

Her mouth twitched in a half-smile. "Yes, we should. I came to hear a great man's music, not a common man's tales of tail."

That stung. Christian didn't answer until they were seated. "I may be run¬of-the-mill, but my yarn is twisted."

That earned another eyebrow.

In the second half Christian attention was split between the music and his new acquaintance. She seemed so self-assured. Her brownish-blond hair was in a severe bun, displaying a high forehead. The glasses didn't suit her at all--the rims were oversized and rested on her high cheekbones. The baggy blouse and skirt were neat, but showed nothing beyond, or below, remarkably broad shoulders. In sum, her appearance seemed an artful effort to appear artless. She sat absorbed by Bach, motionless except for fingers that flickered as if playing an instrument.

As the applause following the second encore dwindled, Christian moved into the aisle. She joined him and they left the hall together.

Outside, she shifted out of the flow. "You were studying me." Her eyes stayed level with his. "What did you decide?"

Caught. "You're gorgeous. You're a musician. You could be a nun."

Her smile made her look ten years younger, perhaps twenty-five. "Gorgeous is a matter of opinion. Thanks for yours. Yes, I am a musician, among other things. And no, I'm not a nun, but if you promise you'll treat me like one, I'd like to hear you unravel your twisted yarn."

"Do nuns eat dinner?" Christian asked.

"We should talk before we make so serious a commitment. We might find we're not that interested in each other."

Christian responded with what he hoped was a suitably nonchalant, yet sophisticated smile and shrug. From her faint smile, she was amused by his effort. They walked to the small park beside the auditorium and she sat on the first available bench.

Christian handed her a business card and bowed. "Madame, my card. Know what? I've always wanted to use that line."

"And now you have, and shouldn't ever again." A grin took any sting from her words, this time. She read the card. "Do sit down, Christian. You prefer Christian to Chris? My name is Marci. And please, don't ever call me Madame again."

He told Marci about his week. He started with Grace's ad on the Internet, and continued on to his meeting Lucy and then Grace in Queen's Park. Marci listened attentively, so he gave a detailed account, with as much as he could remember of the conversations. Her only reactions came from her brows.

Christian noted she used both equally well. He took the account through lunch at Chez Celeste up to the point he left Cosmo's office and Aurora kicked the door shut. "Dinner now?" he asked, attempting an eyebrow lift of his own. An image of Groucho Marx immediately came to mind.

"Certainly. As long as you remember you're to treat me as if I were a nun."

"Agreed. Shall we then, Sister?"

At a pay phone Christian found the card Grace had given him at Chez Celeste, the one with Uri's name and number. He called, mentioned Grace's name as instructed, and asked if it would be possible to get a dinner reservation on such short notice.

Uri assured him it would be no problem, although all that was left was a small private room-- if Christian found that satisfactory, it was his.

Marci had been listening. "I'm not sure this is a good idea," she said, but only after he had hung up. "They probably won't let me in. I've heard of Chez Celeste. People like me don't go there."

"Why not? I saw your eyes flicker when I said where Grace took me. I don't know what you're worried about." He scanned Yonge Street for a taxi.

"I'm not dressed well enough."

"You're dressed as well as I was the time I went. Better. I'd say you're dressed perfectly, considering you're a nun."

"It's too expensive."

"Nonsense. You're a great audience and I need to talk to someone. This is on Grace. I'm sure she'd insist." He waved at a passing cab. It ignored him. "How are nuns at hailing cabs?"

Marci walked to the curb and beckoned. A taxi that had been speeding by on the other side made a screeching U-turn and stopped in front of her, engine pulsing. They got in. Christian didn't want to continue his story with the driver listening, and waited for Marci to say something. She didn't. They rode downtown in silence.

At Chez Celeste they were whisked through the busy main dining area to a small room at the back. Marci remained ill at ease until the waiter took their order, and the sommelier brought the wine. She tasted it and nibbled on a breadstick. "Okay, so I was wrong. You got me in. Continue. Aurora slammed the door..."

"I'm not sure the story is suitable dinner conversation."

"Let's see if you can disgust me enough to put me off my feed." She settled back in her chair. "Make it raunchy."

With breaks as food arrived and plates were taken, Christian continued, picking at his meal. Marci helped herself to what he left on his plate and again paid close-lipped attention. Even her eyebrows remained silent. Christian didn't leave anything out: Aurora's toy closet, the scene with Lucy in her office, his second night with Aurora, the bite.

By the time after-dinner coffee arrived, Christian was back to the present--needing a date for the ball. He told Marci he'd first considered trying to find Cleo and then decided to hire an escort for the charity fund-raiser.

"And now you won't. I'm here and you'll take me." She refilled her cup, took off her glasses and put them on the table.

"I will? Thanks for listening, Marci--but I'm not asking you to get involved."

"No, and since you're not, I'm offering. You'd be a fool to take anyone else." She put the glasses away.

Christian raised an eyebrow, knowing he didn't do it as eloquently as Marci. "Why?"

"Because Grace told you to take someone who suited you. One of the first things you said to me was it felt natural to walk beside me." Marci leaned forward. "I'm not going to trade my story for yours, not tonight, but by bringing me here and talking to

111

me, you've asked me to be your friend. I accept." She reached across and squeezed his arm.

"I'm certainly a better bet than your ex," she continued. Her hand was strong, her grip painful. "That idea was stupid. The escort services were a thought. Trouble is, anyone who would do, would also be known in those circles. And I would like very much to go with you Tuesday. Please?"

Christian's mind whirred. Without the glasses, and with open excitement in her eyes, Marci didn't look like the person he'd met in the concert hall. He couldn't have even joked the woman in front of him might be a nun.

"I don't understand. At first you were aloof-- now you're throwing yourself at me..."

"Idiot!" Marci lunged forward and slammed into the oak table between them. It moved to within an inch of Christian's chest. After a couple of deep breaths, Marci sat back. "Get. This. Clear. I'm not throwing myself at you. No way, no how. Okay?"

"Okay. It was a bad choice of words, but..." Christian put his hands on the table and tried to shift it away. It didn't budge.

The corner of Marci's mouth curled. "Sorry, I'm tired. Temper got the better of me." She yanked the table back towards her. "All I said was I would like to be your friend, and go with you Tuesday. You're a man, so I suppose I can't blame you for not understanding the difference between friendship and sex. After all, it's well known men do most of their thinking with their pricks."

Now she'd mentioned it, Christian could see Marci was exhausted. The amazing amount of food

112

she'd put away probably hadn't helped, but it was more than that. "I think Aurora has made a start on teaching me that difference. It's okay, Marci, you can go with me."

"That sounds like pity. It may be a charity ball, but I won't put up with yours. Your guess I'm a musician was good--I'm classically trained and accomplished enough to help concert musicians prepare for concerts. I'm also an artist--that's my real calling, and how I intend to eventually make my living. In Canada, I work as a cocktail waitress at times--not because I need the money, but to help explain where I get it."

"You make a lot in tips?"

"You could say that. You also guessed I'm not the person I tried to appear to be, and made it into a joke about me being a nun. I'm far from that. You couldn't have met a better person to wade with in the society cesspool." Marci's head drooped.

"It's okay, I'm convinced." She was in no shape to continue. He'd take his chances. She was right about Cleo--but he'd known that. Now, he could also see any call-girl who could move in society might know quite a few of the people at the fund-raiser, intimately. Marci probably was his best bet. "Here's Grace's address." He wrote it on one of his business cards and handed it to her.

"Condescending bastard." She put the card into her purse and stood. "Maybe I'll finish the lesson Aurora started." Christian took her arm to steady her.

"I called a taxi for you, Mr. Plowman," the maitre d' said as Christian used Grace's card to pay at the door.

"Thank you."

"Would you call a second one?" Marci asked.

"It's okay, I'd rather walk," Christian answered. "I could use the exercise." He needed to unwind. As Marci had stripped off the layers of her disguise, Christian had begun to wonder whether in trying to solve one problem, he'd created another. He'd been hoping to find someone who would impress Cosmo and Aurora. Marci was more likely to intimidate them. "Congenial and with tone?" Christian didn't think so, no matter how one defined those terms.

Chapter Eleven

While Christian was playing computer games Monday, an icon started flashing in the corner of the screen. The computer was answering the phone. He changed the configuration so that wouldn't happen again and then decided he might as well see who had called.

Aurora. "I called your place six times. Where are you?" Click.

He phoned his apartment. Sure enough, there were six calls on his machine, all from Aurora. They started quietly. In the last she shouted that he was an "ungrateful asshole" before slamming down the receiver.

He called The Factory. Aurora eventually came to the phone. "Your timing is lousy; I'm busy editing the tape from New York. You saw the special on VideoView of course? No? Your loss. So, what's this about Tuesday? Who's the bitch?"

"It's business, nothing personal."

"Of course it's fucking personal! And business. You'll be meeting the morons who will sponsor Ovation. I'm your liaison, remember? We have to impress the pants off them so we can steal their wallets. Your bimbo better be hot stuff, Plowman. I looked real stupid when Cosmo told me I wasn't going with you. So don't tell me it fucking isn't personal!"

She took a breath, and Christian broke in. "Well, the way you left me on Thursday morning, what did you expect? And I had to hear on TV that you were leaving town. Besides, my job is to find a host. I wonder if Marci might be interested." He hadn't thought that until he said it, but it was an idea.

"Your job is what I tell you it is, mister. You and this Marci better look out for me." Slam.

It should be another interesting night. He put the phone back in its cupboard and returned to his game.

Early to bed, early to rise, Christian muttered as he dragged downstairs Tuesday morning. The clock on the microwave read nine o'clock. Okay, it wasn't all that early, but he wished he'd been able to sleep later.

Something started to ring. He checked Grace's phone. Turned off, as always. The ringing continued. He traced the sound to a receiver by the door, one he'd noticed the first day and then forgotten after deciding it must be connected to the guard station.

"Hello?"

"Ms Michaels is here. She says you're expecting her." It was an accusation. "You didn't leave her name with us." True--he hadn't. Ms Michaels?

He was only expecting one person, Marci, and not at this time of day--the fund-raiser didn't start for eleven hours. Still... "Yes, I am," he said. "Sorry, I did forget to tell you. Please ask her to come up."

Slam! Fred, Christian assumed. He went to wait by the elevators.

The door opened. "Don't fold them." Marci handed him two clothing bags. She was dressed in a pair of paint-speckled overalls and her hair was flopping in a half-hearted ponytail. On her back was an old pack and in her hands an equally well used suitcase. She had more with her than Christian had brought when he moved in and looked as tired as when he'd seen her into the cab outside Chez Celeste. If she was in better shape than he had been the first time he came to Grace's apartment, it wasn't by much.

"I'm surprised Security called instead of turfing you." Christian made his question a joke. "Did they at least look disapproving?"

"Only about you. For not mentioning I was coming."

He hung her bags in the closet by the door. "Sorry, I forgot. Of course, I also didn't know your last name. Besides, I wasn't expecting you this early."

"No need to apologize." Marci dropped her suitcase and shucked off the pack. "Nice place your boss has here."

She wandered into the kitchen and then out again. "You'll have to excuse me. I've been up all night. I got involved with a canvas and lost track of time. Thought I'd better come over, or I'd fall asleep and not make it at all." She collapsed into a chair in the living room. "Matter of fact, I'd better sleep now or I'll be useless later."

"Can you sleep in a well-lit room?"

"I can sleep anywhere. Here is fine."

"A bed would be better."

117

He showed her to the room across from his.

"Wake me at four." She fell face first on the bed.

Christian heard the shower turn on at three-thirty. Marci stumbled down the stairs twenty minutes later. "Coffee," she said. "Black." She plopped into a chair at the dining table.

"Thank you," was her only response when he brought the cup.

Christian sat down and tried not to stare. In an old tracksuit, wet hair plastered in wild disarray, she looked different. He'd been right when he'd told her she was gorgeous, or perhaps not-- no, not gorgeous: stunning, magnificent, idiosyncratic, imposing--he searched for the right word.

He was still shuffling through his vocabulary when Marci finished her coffee and turned to see him scrutinising her. "Yeah, and I'm sure I look as rough as I feel." She tried to shift a strand of hair off her face, and failed. "Order the biggest pizza you can. Two if you intend to eat. Then leave me alone until they show up. I can't handle your gawking. This is me. Get used to it."

After ordering the pizzas, Christian went to play computer games. When they arrived, he paid and took them to the table. Marci put the book of Hindu temple art down and dug in. She finished hers and the half of his he left.

She finally broke the silence. "Much better. Thank you--for feeding me again, and for putting up with me." She turned on a smile.

The apartment suddenly felt too warm. "You're welcome. And if I was staring earlier, I apologize."

118

Christian knew perfectly well he had been. He hoped he wasn't again; he was trying not to.

"I overreacted. I do. Now, anything I need to know about tonight you haven't told me?"

Christian told her about Aurora's messages, and their conversation.

"You finished with her? It's all the same to me if you aren't, but I need to know before we see her."

"I'd like to stay on good terms, if possible. I thought she was finished with me."

"Don't understand women, do you? Or show business? And you want to keep your options open. I'll see what I can do. Now, where can I do my make-up? The mirror and lighting are wrong in that room."

"Grace's room maybe. I'll show you."

Marci approved. "Much better."

"Can I help you with anything?"

"Like what? I can dress myself." She went to Grace's closet and pulled out a dress. "Excellent taste. Too bad I'm not her size."

Christian thought that an understatement. In Marci's hands, Grace's dress looked like doll clothing.

After struggling into his new tuxedo, he went downstairs and waited. And waited. He opened the book of temple art and leafed through. A sex manual for contortionists. He turned the TV on, and then off. He searched through the CDs. Nothing seemed appropriate. He waited.

Shortly after seven, Marci came down. He knew it was her because she had been the only person upstairs. Her face had acquired an incorporeal glow. Makeup? Not entirely. The hair remained wild, but now its chaos seemed calculated as it cascaded over bare shoulders and arms. As Christian had known, her figure wasn't that of a high-fashion model--two of them, maybe. Her muscles rippled without bulging, quite.

Christian kept his eyes moving. The dress, blood red, flowed out in an inverted V from a strip around her neck, barely making it around the sides of her ample breasts in time. She pirouetted on her heels. The back was almost all skin; the rich fabric met below the waist, just above the limit of decency, maybe. She was sculpted, milky marble. Imposing. Christian settled on that as the word to describe her, if he could only use one.

"So Christian, will I fit in?"

"Never. You'll stand out." Christian moved a step closer. He wanted to take her into his arms and let nature follow its course.

Nature had more than one course she could follow. "Thank-you, but this is still me. And if you don't back off, stick your eyes back into your head and tighten up that slack jaw, I'll do it for you."

Christian retreated. "You can't tell me you don't expect men to lose control."

"Most men, yes. That's the idea. I expected better from you though. I thought you could see past surfaces. Guess I was wrong. You're a man, just a man." She collapsed onto the couch.

"I'm sorry." Christian crouched beside her, then knelt. "It's not superficial. I feel a connection with you; your presence overwhelms me. It has from the first."

120

"You're so full of shit you should explode." Marci lifted her head and met his eyes. Hers were deep, brown and hurt. She took his hands and stood, pulling him to his feet. "We'll settle this later. For now, just keep that silver-plated tongue from dragging on the ground. Okay?"

"Or else?"

"No, not or else," Marci sighed. "Look Christian, this is an act, one I do well. I'm no great beauty but I have my role down pat. You're about to go on stage with me. Play your part. For tonight we're friends from way back, yes and maybe lovers but comfortable with each other. Got it?"

Christian had it; he just wasn't sure he could pull it off.

Chapter Twelve

They were among the first to arrive, but not the very first. Cosmo was by the door, lying in wait. "Christian! I hoped you would be here early so I could meet your guest. This must be..."

"Marci Michaels, Mr. Sharpe." She extended her hand for Cosmo to kiss in the approved manner. He did, eyes bugging. Christian hoped he hadn't been that transparent when Marci first came downstairs. Probably.

Marci went to work. She professed it an utter thrill to meet such a renowned media mogul and insisted Cosmo tell her all about Ovation, the venture that had poor Christian working so hard on his behalf. Cosmo gave the speech he'd made in the meeting with Grace and Christian.

"Sounds first rate." A woman Marci's size shouldn't be able to fluff her voice so. "You must have a fair bit of programming lined up."

"Of course." Cosmo rattled on, mentioning artists and musicians. Christian had heard a couple of the names previously. Marci made what were apparently insightful comments, and complimented Cosmo on how solid the line-up sounded.

"Solid yes, but I still need something spectacular to launch Ovation."

"For instance?"

"Oh say if Anne-Sophie Mutter or Yuka would drop by for an interview and play some solo fiddle or a sonata or two," Cosmo answered with a laugh.

"Without relieving me of an arm and a leg of course."

"Well, Mutter's not in North America until next April. But Yuka's coming later this year. I heard her in Paris last spring. Her playing is even more exceptional than ever."

"She didn't tour last year." Cosmo looked up at Marci with narrowed eyes. "She took it off to rest and record."

"Oh, it wasn't a concert. She was there to shop. We both ended up at a boring party at some Count's estate. They convinced her to play." Marci waved a casual hand. "I did hear Bartoli at the Opera House."

The conversation drifted on, with neither Marci nor Cosmo paying any attention to Christian. The room began to fill. Everyone noticed them, or rather, noticed Marci. Christian didn't doubt she would have drawn attention even in the darkest corner but in front of the entrance, it was a given.

At long last Cosmo surfaced. "Much as I regret leaving your company, I must circulate and ingratiate. It's been a pleasure, Ms Michaels."

"Marci." Again she offered her hand and again Cosmo kissed it.

Cosmo nudged Christian as he passed. "Aurora's going to hate her."

Marci took Christian's arm and moved them away from the door. "We lost you, didn't we? My mouth outran my brain, but I think it went okay. We'll mix for a while and then dance."

While Marci didn't seem to know any of the people, she effortlessly inserted herself into conversations, introduced herself and Christian, made a few knowledgeable, witty remarks and passed on to other people, other groups. Christian played strong and silent, and stood reverently by her side.

They approached another cluster. "Damn. Fritz does know me." She took a deep breath and fluttered up to the man she had indicated. Christian's estimation of Marci's acting talent went up another notch. That firm a body couldn't flutter but hers did, somehow. "Fritz! Fritz Weber. Marci Michaels."

"Ah, yes. Yes, yes! Marci, what a surprise." Fritz's mouth said "surprise"; his eyes said "shock". "It's been a long time... Marci. Too long. You must drop by the gallery sometime soon."

After a few phrases of no consequence, Marci moved on. "Let's dance. Fritz owns the place I hang my paintings. He didn't know I was in Noronto, and might have called me by the name I paint under. It's the only way he knew me, until now. I don't want that name linked with Marci's."

Christian filed another question, and they danced. Marci filled his arms but felt lissom, like an over-size sylph. She floated across the floor and led beautifully, subtly enough that Christian suspected few people would notice. He felt the eyes of the room on them, and didn't have any trouble controlling his desires despite having both hands on the naked expanse of her back. They were the main act. He couldn't let Marci down.

"Not much of a dancer either, eh?" she whispered into his ear after some time. "I've got a lot of work to do with you. Now... Aurora is glaring from the sidelines, and her video-cam operator is off doing background shots. Shall we get it over with?" She moved him off the dance floor and then allowed him to lead her to Aurora.

Aurora's scowl darkened. To Christian's amazement she looked cultivated and cultured in a slinky black frock. If Marci hadn't been there, Aurora might well have been the belle of the ball. Christian noticed Cosmo lurking nearby, presumably for the anticipated spectacle of Aurora with claws unsheathed. She restrained herself as Christian made the introductions, her eyes flickering from Marci to Christian and back.

Marci pre-empted her. "Aurora. Good to meet you. You're so much more attractive in person than on TV. Christian told me all about you, of course. You certainly made an impression on him." Marci put her hand gently on his injured shoulder. Christian winced and pulled away. It wasn't that painful now--the infection had gone, and the bite was healing, but he thought a little over-acting called for.

Marci had presented herself as the primary target. Aurora didn't say anything, but gave her hair a contemplative caress.

"You should be furious with me, my dear." Marci smiled. Was she flirting? With Aurora? "But you'll have to forgive poor Christian."

Okay, why? Aurora had enough anger for both of them.

"I hadn't seen him in such a long time," Marci went on. Christian allowed she was telling no lie.

125

Forever was a long time indeed. "But on the weekend I ambushed him. He didn't have a chance. You know how pathetic men are."

That Christian didn't like one little bit, but he could see it had been a winner. Aurora nodded agreement, and almost smiled.

"Of course I wouldn't blame you if you tried to take him back." Marci crossed her arms, indicating her lines were finished.

Aurora surveyed Marci top to bottom, without favouring Christian with so much as a blink. "Oh hell! He's yours if you want him. I was about done anyway." She stalked away.

"How gracious." Marci smiled at Christian, her mouth twisted at one edge. "Of course from one of her class I expect nothing less. Dance?"

Marci's last word wasn't a question, but a cue or stage direction. The light she had cast him in was hardly flattering but Christian could hardly complain. As promised, Marci had dealt with Aurora--skilfully, as far as he could tell. He didn't understand how she'd done it, and wanted to ask what she meant by "Aurora's class", but this wasn't the time, or the place.

Christian began to get the feel of dancing with Marci and gradually she handed over the privilege of leading. She rested her head on his shoulder. "You're a fast learner. There may be hope for you after all."

A short time later Christian noticed a man peering at Marci, dancing his partner closer to get a better look. It went beyond general fascination. Christian used his new control to swing Marci around. "The grey suit with the red-head in yellow. He thinks he knows you."

Marci kept the circle he had started going so she only faced the man in question for a moment. "He does. If he comes over, expect him to call me Freyja." Command transferred back to her, Marci moved them to the edge of the dance floor.

"He thinks you're a Norse goddess?" Christian asked, showing off some of his literary background.

"Very much so. Don't you? We'd better get out of here. I think you've had enough, and I didn't think this appearance through properly. I should have known."

"Known what?"

"Later. Pumpkin time, Christian. If we stay, the magic will fail."

They made it to the door with a series of nods and smiles to people they had talked with earlier. "I need to powder my nose." Marci added an eyebrow that spoke of consuming a bit too much wine. "Wait for me here."

"But..." But Marci was on her way to the ladies' room. He'd been about to ask if she could hold it; Aurora was nearby, in front of a camera with the distinctive Bull's-Eye News logo, interviewing Cosmo and a bejewelled society matron. Christian knew Aurora would finish soon--on-the-spot interviews for Bull's-Eye seldom exceeded thirty seconds.

The camera blinked off. Aurora cruised towards him, leaving Cosmo, companion and camera-operator behind. Christian prepared himself for the onslaught. Aurora looked composed, ominously so.

"That's some woman you've got there, Christian. Or should I say who's got you?" Her voice soft, the silk of a strangler's cord, Aurora smiled with her lips. Her jade-green eyes sent a different message.

"Say whatever you want. You going to shred me now she's not here?"

A grin appeared. "My, you are paranoid. No, this evening is a fait accompli. I understand. We all have our price, Christian; you must find her money irresistible. Shit, that dress is a Paris original, and in her size it must be custom made. If she gets tired of you, tell her I'm available. Drop by The Factory-- we still have business to discuss. Oh, and congratulations on the catch--she's coming--I'm gone."

Marci materialised on his arm. "My explanations and stories should wait until we get back, but what was that about?"

On the way to the lobby, Christian told Marci what Aurora had said. Marci shook her head. "I never considered she'd think you'd been bought. Doubt she believes it; she's playing for time until she gets the goods on me. I should have known it was risky showing up here--Noronto's not that much of a backwater. And I made a mistake while talking with Cosmo. It's probably won't do any good, but I'll make a call when we get back and try to cover at least that." She gripped Christian's arm more firmly. "Let me work out my plan of action. I'll explain later. Promise."

Chapter Thirteen

At Casa del Carlos, Marci kicked off her heels, searched Grace's cupboards, found a supply of Scotch and as a bonus, the phone. "Grace can stand me to a few more drinks. I'll call from her room. I saw a jack there."

Christian got out of the tux, put on a tracksuit and went back downstairs. It was only a bit after midnight and he didn't feel tired. He found an open bottle Marci had passed over in favour of a full one, sat down at the table and stared out over the city. As he waited, he replayed the evening in his mind and tried to sort his questions and put them into logical order. Who--what--when--who?

After about twenty minutes, soft footsteps came down the stairs, and stopped behind him. "All taken care of, maybe. Yuka will tell Cosmo Marci's a crazy Canadian she met through a mutual acquaintance, if he asks. First she'll agree to do a special for him, so he probably won't delve too deep. He knows how it's played. Don't know if it will help though--I'm likely only delaying the inevitable." She moved around the table to face him and put her bottle on the table between them, beside his. She had taken off her make-up and changed into a tracksuit. Her hair remained wild and free. "If I didn't know better, Christian, I'd say you're sulking. Sorry, but that couldn't wait. You had a few questions?"

"A few?" He had dozens, hundreds, all crushed together. The one that came out was, "Who are you, Marci?"

She poured a tumbler of Scotch. "Yes. Marci. With you I'm trying to be Marci." She drank a quarter of the glass. "Earlier, you were in the company of Freyja Van Deer. She's a whore. Oh, she'd call herself a courtesan or something of the sort, but she's a tramp for hire, nothing more. There's a third woman in this body as well, a painter who wants to be set free. But me, I'm Marci."

"Now I'm really confused. Let's see if this helps." Christian tried to copy Marci by downing his quarter-glass of Scotch but choked before he finished half.

Marci laughed, took his glass, and emptied it. "It's not a competition, Christian. I guess I do need to tell you my story after all. You told me about a week in your life--I need to go back much further. But we've got all night, I guess, and tomorrow."

"And tomorrow, and tomorrow," Christian agreed as he recovered. He refilled his glass and topped up hers. "As long as I don't try to keep up with you in the Scotch department."

"Don't. If I'm going to tell you the story of my life, I want you to remember it in the morning." She had another drink, and started.

***

Her mother had died giving birth to her. "My father always said he could see a fair bit of her in me, but nothing of himself. He didn't think I was his." She took another drink. "I pray he was right."

His family had money and social position. He didn't remarry and brought Marci up to replace her mother as his hostess. From the time she could remember, her days were filled with lessons: riding, languages, ballet, art, music. She didn't go to school. Instead, she had tutors. No friends--there were no other children in her world. Even if there had been, she wouldn't have had the time.

On her tenth birthday, her father started coming to her room at night. "I accepted it of course. What else could I have done? He explained it was a duty my mother had performed, something everyone did but no one talked about. He didn't do anything that hurt me physically, I'll give him that."

She put her glass down and put her hand on Christian's. "Of course, my name wasn't Marci Michaels then. I left my name behind, with everything else... but I'm getting ahead of myself." She removed her hand, emptied her glass, refilled it and resumed.

When she was fifteen, things changed. People came to talk to her father, and to her. She didn't tell them anything. Strangers couldn't be trusted. They moved immediately, and she was put in a boarding school, her father seeing her only on weekends and holidays. Since she'd never had a friend in her life, she didn't make any--but from listening she learned her situation wasn't normal. Eventually she discovered just talking about it to an adult could end it.

"It gets difficult to justify what I did then. Maybe I truly am his child. I can't tell you that... I can only tell you what I did." She planned for her future, while letting things remain the same. When she wasn't in school she spent time with him in the isolated villas he rented, or hotels--booked in under assumed names. She never met anyone he knew. The time she didn't spend in bed with him, she spent alone. She read, painted, played music... and plotted.

"I could have escaped any number of times, but I wasn't ready. I waited for my eighteenth birthday, and then graduation. I finished with school and him on the same day."

Her father had pleaded, screamed and threatened when she announced she was leaving. Then, for the first time, he tried to beat her. It had been the last mistake he made with Marci. She was as big as him, younger, and convinced she was fighting for her life.

"I came close to killing him, but knew I couldn't--that would have spoiled everything. When he recovered enough, I told him I'd been his whore for eight years, and wanted payment. If he didn't agree, I'd geld him."

"He agreed?"

"He knew I was serious." Marci shrugged. "I should have done it anyway-¬looking back, that's my biggest regret. I told him if he ever made any attempt to follow or contact me, I would. Guess he believed me, and maybe even thought I'd change my mind, come back and do it anyway. I found out later he sold everything and disappeared. I have no idea where he is, or if he's still alive. Can't say I care."

Marci moved to Noronto, and applied to change her name. When that became official, she flew to Switzerland, had her tubes tied, and underwent some expensive plastic surgery. "They did excellent work. I've met people from the boarding school, and no one has ever recognized me. While I recuperated, I spent my days in psychotherapy. My therapist agreed that, for me, leaving everything behind had been the right choice. It all cost more than I'd allowed for but I wasn't broke so I kept to my plan. When I'd healed, on the outside at any rate, I came back to Canada and enrolled in university. I did enough class work to pass, painted, and thought about what to do with the rest of my life."

By the end of the academic year she'd made rough plans. She went to the Rockies, to Banff, and became a room-service waitress. For a price hotel security not only ignored her extra activities, but also aided the bell captains in making contacts for her. "Too damn many freebies." Marci refilled her glass. "Still, what I made that summer financed my school-year, and more."

The next summer she took a job serving cocktails in an up-scale bar in downtown Vancouver. Her customers tipped generously in public and gave her expensive gifts in return for what she did for them in private. "I sold the trinkets and made far more than I had the previous year. Never had a pimp since then. No one knew me as Marci either--like I had in Banff I used a nametag another waitress had left behind. I've always been careful--until I met you."

"Where did you tell them you were from? And what did you say about your family?"

"Whatever they wanted to hear." Marci's smile twisted around her words. "Men crave fantasy. I deliver."

"Didn't anyone try to hang on to you?"

"Not seriously. I'm good at managing men."

"I've noticed."

Marci laughed and resumed her narrative. When she returned to Noronto for her third year of university she invested the remainder of what she'd got from her father in a house. Her success that summer had convinced her she'd never need to worry about money again. She enrolled but completely ignored her classes. She fixed up her house, furnishing it lavishly with a music room, a small gym and an art studio. Her days were then spent playing music, working out and painting.

She emptied the remainder of the bottle she'd opened earlier into her glass. "Then I went to Europe in the spring, and Freyja emerged."

"Emerged?"

"That's certainly how it felt. In Banff and Vancouver I'd discovered European men were the most appreciative. Especially the old money--they didn't seem as intimidated by my tough Teutonic look, or by an intelligent woman. I decided to play it up, and went to England first, to ease my way in to the Continent. The first month I didn't work, just checked out my surroundings and acclimatised." She drank deeply. "I did the tourist thing, including Stonehenge. That's where Freyja showed up."

"But Freyja is Norse. Isn't Stonehenge a Druidic ruin?" Christian enjoyed showing off, but seldom got the opportunity.

This would have been a good time to forgo the pleasure. "No, pre-Druidic. Besides which, I'm telling you what happened, Christian--don't tell me it isn't logical. And don't try to squeeze my reality into yours--it won't fit." She took a minute to finish her glass and then refill it from Christian's bottle, topping off his glass as well.

"As I was saying, Freyja emerged--full-blown and ready for action. If you insist on an explanation, say she was the synthesis of all I'd learned about what attracted men to me. Say whatever you damn well please. She manifested."

Over the winter Marci had worked out extensively in her gym and her already robust body had acquired a tone seldom obtained by any but elite athletes. "I'd wondered about my new-found obsession with fitness, but only in an offhand manner. If I figured anything at all about what was happening to my body, it was that as I moved into my prime, I was filling out. Then I discovered the truth. Freyja had been laying the groundwork for her take-over."

Upon returning to London from Stonehenge, Freyja acquired a new wardrobe, one featuring shimmering silvers and golds. Marci's hair was made lighter, flaxen-blonde rather than the mid-range colour she had maintained since parting company with her father. Money didn't matter anymore--Freyja soon commanded prices Marci

135

never would have considered, and Marci had never sold herself cheap.

Freyja became the legend she already considered herself. Each day with her cost more than the previous, although occasionally, on a whim, she'd stay with a favourite for free. It was a rare client who didn't propose marriage. Freyja wasn't interested. Marriage, she said, was something she'd done once, or rather, had done to her once, and she had no interest in doing it again. What's more, Odin was an asshole. A free spirit, she intended to remain free.

Marci emptied the last of Christian's bottle into her glass. "So, who am I, you ask? You tell me, Christian, you tell me." She drank. "I said that with you I'm trying to be Marci, but Freyja slipped out and took over. And earlier in the day, I was the painter." She paused, lifted her glass, and put it down again. "Who am I? I ask myself. In many ways, Freyja was the first me, the person my father moulded and who later destroyed him. She overpowers me. You've seen her do it."

Christian took her glass from her hand and drained it, forcing himself to not gag. "I didn't notice Freyja until you pointed her out. In truth, I still don't. There's no such person. Or rather--there is, and you're her."

Marci took his glass, which was still full. She looked at him through the Scotch. Her deep brown eyes faded in its amber. She didn't drink.

"I may be naive, but I think you're as sane as anyone I've ever met. Yes, you're a goddess--you are Freyja. To me the only way you're in the least crazy is in thinking that your life should make more sense than it does. Life doesn't."

Marci drained Christian's glass. "On that profound note, I'll declare I've had enough for tonight," she stood, swaying a little.

Christian got up to steady her. A bottle and a half of Scotch would have put him in the hospital with alcohol poisoning, or more likely, in the morgue. Marci probably didn't even need him to help her navigate, but he would anyway. That's what friends were really for, whatever the sappy song might say.

He manoeuvred her up the stairs. She leaned on him more than he thought she needed to. And no, she wasn't wearing anything under the tracksuit. Christian conducted her to the room she'd slept in earlier. When they reached the bed, she pulled away.

"So? Want to spend a few hours you'll never forget?" she asked, a two-eyebrow question although both had drunken lilts.

"Just did. All I want to do now is pass out."

"If you say so." Marci turned and pitched forward onto the bed, much as she had earlier. Christian slipped a pillow under her head, covered her, and went to his own bed. He left both doors open.

Chapter Fourteen

When Christian woke up, his door was closed and his head throbbing. He wondered what shape Marci would be in. She'd consumed ten times the Scotch he had.

He stumbled to the bathroom. There were fresh towels hung beside damp ones. A long shower, warm at first and then cold, failed to activate his brain. He did feel better though... weary rather than woozy. He dressed in a fresh tracksuit and went downstairs. Marci was in the living room, leafing through the book of temple art.

"Coffee's hot." She followed him to the kitchen. "Wasn't sure if you'd feel up to eating." From the evidence, she had been.

He grunted a response.

"I'll take that as a 'yes'," she said. "Guess you're not much of a morning person. Neither am I, but I've been up for hours." If she'd felt the effect of her over-indulgence, she'd recovered. She looked and sounded chipper, frisky--light danced in her eyes.

Christian managed a smile and moved around her to the table.

She sat across from him. "You do remember me, don't you? Marci?"

"Freyja. Yes, I remember."

"Darn, and I was hoping you'd blacked out before that. Oh well... could you eat if I cooked? Pancakes?"

The thought didn't turn his stomach. "Yes, thank-you, that might be just what I need."

Marci snorted. "You need a lot more than that--we'll start with pancakes. Is there any chance I could use a computer while you're eating? I should check Freyja's e-mail."

"I'll set up an account for you," Christian pushed himself to his feet. "In Freyja's name?"

"Please, that is... if it's not too much trouble, if you're up to it, if Grace wouldn't mind."

He returned from the computer room just as she put the food on the table. "Freyja's temporary password is 'Marci'." Christian slumped back into a chair.

She raised an eyebrow that questioned his sense of humour and left the room.

When Christian finished eating, he visited her in the computer room. Intent on the screen, Marci said she was doing fine and would be with him in fifteen minutes.

Christian went back to the kitchen, did the dishes, and made another pot of coffee. He went into the living room and browsed the bookshelf. Nothing caught his eye. He went back into the kitchen and watched the coffee drip into the pot. It was as intellectual an activity as he felt capable of. He didn't feel hung over any more, just sluggish.

Marci returned from the computer room and stood in the doorway, watching Christian, not the coffee. He waited for her to say something.

He gave up. "A fair bit of mail?"

"Freyja could work 365 days a year, if she wanted. No offers she couldn't refuse, although fifty thou' for a week in Monte Carlo tempts. She has to drop by there once in a while anyway, to keep her resident status."

Christian didn't know what to say. He hadn't expected details.

"So, should I leave now?"

"Only if you want to. Why do you ask?"

"Well, in part because you seem rather distant today, and also because I don't fit in here. If dear little Grace were around right now, I probably would wring her scrawny neck." She advanced on Christian and put her hands on his shoulders. Her touch tingled. The eyes he'd previously seen as soft, flashed bolts.

"Should I remind you I'm not her?"

"I know. I wouldn't do this with her." She held his head steady, and kissed him. The lightning shot into him and down as her tongue teased his teeth. He tried to pull her to him, with no success. She was too big, too strong--she couldn't be moved anywhere she didn't plan to go.

Marci broke it off. "Well, at least you're back in the same room as I am now. We need to talk."

"Talk?"

"Yes, about what a pushover you are--how you've let Grace sucker you spreading your legs on her behalf while she buggers off and hides." Marci conducted him to the couch, and explained.

From Marci's perspective, Grace had sent Christian as a lamb to the slaughter. Marci had been hooked by Christian's story from the time he first mentioned Lucille Firman. She wasn't personally acquainted, but their worlds touched and what she knew of Lucy, Marci didn't like.

"Freyja may be a whore, but she has standards and a sense of propriety. The depravity surrounding Firman is beyond your imagining, I hope." She explored his face carefully. "You're out of your depth, Christian. If Grace honestly wants you to succeed, her theory of on-the-job-training makes me want to puke. If I hadn't been there last night, that pit of vipers would have eaten you alive."

Christian didn't think it would be smart to point out that Marci was mixing metaphors. One smart aleck remark and he might find himself sailing through the window, head first. "I don't think I'm quite as hopeless as that. Besides, you were with me."

"But the old bat couldn't have predicted that. She evidently can't read you. You're right, you're not hopeless--you do have some self-respect, and you didn't like the way things were developing. But Grace evidently couldn't see that. She assumed Aurora would continue to be your guide. It would have worked--if you enjoyed kissing Aurora's butt. Aurora wouldn't have let anyone embarrass you, except herself of course. She'll take care of her dependants. She's an aristocrat, after all... old blood."

"She is? I didn't get that impression."

"And of course, you asked her all about herself. Hah!" She shifted away from him on the couch. "Anyway, since you'd dumped Aurora, I figured it was up to me to help you survive. I'm willing to keep on doing that, if you don't decide my company is equally demeaning."

"You're not like Aurora. When she doesn't have any immediate use for me, she acts like I'm not even around."

"Which is how a gigolo deserves to be treated. Act like meat and you get treated like meat. If you can't get Aurora to accept you as a person worth knowing, you might as well give up. I'm exactly like Aurora that way, Christian--except I'm voicing my contempt."

"And why are you bothering with me?"

Marci's sigh filled Grace's living room and spilled into the hallway. "Don't think I'm not asking myself that. Probably because you're a challenge, and I think Grace was right about one thing--you do have potential. She wants you to sell yourself to the world? Well, who better to teach you how than another whore?"

Christian hadn't thought of his job in those terms. He didn't agree. He wasn't... that. Or, if he was, then so were a lot of other people: actors, models, politicians. But they weren't and he wasn't. Prostitution wasn't a profession anyone with any self-respect would admit to. He couldn't say that to Marci. "So, what do you think I should do?"

Marci smiled. "That evasion wasn't a bad start. More than anything, you need to learn to look at yourself realistically, but that will take time. For now, you desperately need a remedial course in Western culture, so you don't feel and sound like a complete moron when you're in the circles Grace wants you to move in. Okay, you're a hunk, but knowing the names of all four of the Monkees won't get you far. What the hell was she thinking of?"

Christian didn't answer the rhetorical question. Since no voice from the ether did either, Marci outlined what she wanted Christian to do. First, he was to listen to the classical selections in Grace's CD collection, read the liner notes, and look up the composers in a music encyclopaedia Marci pulled off Grace's book shelf. She put it and three other volumes in a pile on the table. "You can read--educate yourself. I'll come over on Sunday and see how you're doing."

Marci walked to the bottom of the staircase. "I'll leave some of my things here, if that's okay."

"That's fine." Christian got up from the couch. "You don't have to leave."

"Yes, I do."

She went upstairs. Christian stood at the bottom, unsure whether he should follow. He wanted to talk to Marci, to convince her he wasn't as big a loser as she thought, to defend Grace and say she also had suggested he educate himself--she just hadn't been as forceful. He didn't want Marci to leave. But he couldn't think of a thing he could say to get her to change her mind. What could he offer Marci to convince her to stay? He waited for inspiration to strike.

Marci took her time. When she came back down, Christian was frozen in the same position. All Marci had with her was her backpack. She definitely did intend to come back. Considering all she'd brought over, she now had more in Grace's apartment than he did. He'd have another chance.

She stopped halfway down. "Indecisive, aren't you? Who knows what would have happened if you'd come upstairs and into that bedroom with me."

Christian turned away from her and led the way to the door. He heard her soft steps behind him. "I doubt much would have happened."

"Most of the time you don't think. Then you try to make up for it by thinking too much. Oh well, don't worry about it, Christian--but I'm warning you--if you come on to me and then change your mind like you did with Aurora, you'll discover another difference between us. She's civilised--I don't walk away from my mistakes--I obliterate them." She grabbed him by the shoulders, turned him around, and kissed him. This time her tongue didn't tease; it pinned his and then rammed into the back of his mouth, investigating where his wisdom teeth had been.

She released him, and was halfway to the elevator before Christian reacted. He moved into the doorway. That hadn't been a friendly kiss. Yes, she was a goddess: exciting, imposing, overwhelming. The elevator arrived. Marci held the door, turned, lifted an eyebrow and paused for a heartbeat. Christian couldn't think of anything to say. Marci shrugged, got in and was gone.

***

He'd disappointed Marci, and didn't know why, or how. He wished he'd been able to live up to her expectations, whatever they were. She needed him, needed someone to understand her. She needed him in a way no one ever had before.

144

And he needed her, to goad him. She was right. He was too accepting of his failings. Yes, in order to find the right host for Ovation, he should know more about art, classical music and also brush up on his social graces. He had more background than Marci might realize; his parents had given him a good grounding, despite themselves. When they'd died, he'd buried the world they'd shared. If they could see him now, he knew they'd be as disappointed by him as Marci. More.

Marci reminded him of his mother then? No, hardly--Grace did a little--her attitude was to show Christian the world, and expect he'd be interested enough to explore it. Marci had rubbed his face in his ignorance. If she resembled anyone in his family, it was his sister, Aster. Aster had tried, but it was hard to take a sister eleven years younger seriously. Mind you, she was twenty-three now, hardly a "kid" sister any more. Christian wondered how she was doing. When the confusion cleared, he'd look her up.

Christian wandered into the kitchen to check the time. Just after four in the afternoon. He checked for messages before he got down to the tasks Marci had set. There wasn't any email, and no phone calls to answer. He couldn't put it off any longer. He went back to the living room, put on a CD, and laying aside the liner notes, glanced at the top book. Curiously, it was the book of Hindu temple art. Why had she put that out? It must have been a mistake. He looked at the next. "Movements in Western Art"--that looked more like it. He'd tackle that, right after he read up on Beethoven, and his third symphony.

Chapter Fifteen

Thursday morning Christian put on one his new business suits. Grace had given him only one client and if he was going to continue pretending to earn his eight thousand a month, he should make an appearance at The Factory. Aurora hadn't seemed angry Tuesday night; he expected she would have changed her mind. No, she didn't have much respect for him, but as she put so much stock in appearance, she might respect the suit. It wouldn't be out of place in the executive wing of any of the movers, shakers and arm-breakers of the Bay Street financial district a few short blocks from The Factory.

Christian checked in the mirror. No, hiding behind the suit wouldn't work, at least not until he learned to wear it, rather than vice versa. He left it on--¬everything he'd bought at The Black Whole was in the garbage bag he'd put it in after his night at The Second Circle. Today, he would drop it off at a dry-cleaner.

When he stepped outside he was met by light rain. If he had thought to tune in the COSMO-TV morning show he probably would have seen animated raindrops falling from Judy's breasts to her stomach, and been prepared. He went back into Casa del Carlos and politely asked Fred, the security guard, to call a taxi.

"Not my job, Plowman. But you don't have to take your own garbage out. We have a garbage chute--all the modern conveniences."

"It's my dry-cleaning," Christian answered.

"Probably the trash I saw you wearing last week. Okay, since you've got such a nice suit on today, I'll call a cab for you--there's a cleaner two doors down. I'll tell them to pick you up there."

"Thank-you, Fred." The suit had paid off after all. "Oh, and would you put a note on the visitors' list that Ms Michaels is welcome any time."

"I should damn well hope so. Don't know what a respectable woman like that sees in you, Plowman."

***

Kathy spotted Christian the instant he walked into The Factory. "Hail the conquering hero," she said, breaking off the conversation she'd been having with Judy. She stood and gave an exaggerated bow. "Hear you made the bitch look bad the other night. Guess there's more to you than I'd figured."

"That wasn't what I intended."

"Who cares? You're here to rub it in?" Kathy's eyes were as warm as grey-blue steel could be.

"No, but I am here to see Aurora."

"Oh goody! This time I do know where she is." Judy came over and took his hand. "I'll fill you in on what happens, Kathy," she added over her shoulder as she led Christian away.

"You're not worried any more that Aurora might think you're trying to move in on me?"

They rounded a corner, losing sight of Kathy. Judy squeezed his hand before she let go. "I think someone has already done that. Besides, a chance to get a shot in at Kathy doesn't come up every day.

She'll be pissed I took you away before she could grill you about your new girlfriend. So, tell me, is it true Marci is connected the Swedish royal family?"

"I don't think so, but I wouldn't be surprised to discover she knows them." He tried to find a titbit he could safely offer Judy. "I'd gather in Europe Marci frequents the same circles as Aurora's family." That was a guess.

"Her mother's side. Yes, that fits."

Judy's satisfied tone made Christian suspect he'd said too much. "So, how is Aurora?" he asked.

"Quiet. It's got people scared." Judy led him through a door into a large room. Aurora's back was to the door they entered by. A ring of unoccupied desks surrounded her.

"Thanks. I'll better take it from here. You might want to make yourself scarce."

"No way. You think I'd miss the next episode of this soap opera? Not a chance." Judy perched on the corner of the desk nearest the exit. The room quietened as Christian made his way across.

"Hello, Aurora."

She spun in her chair. "Well hi. I'm surprised to see you so soon. And so alone." She stood. "You look great. Love the suit."

"You're looking good yourself." That wasn't true. There were dark circles under her eyes, and the one button done up on her jacket was in the wrong opening. Christian went over and undid it. "You do seem a bit tired though."

She slipped into his arms. His went around her in a comforting hug. "To tell the truth, I feel like crap," she said in a whisper. "Having you come to see me makes me feel better." She pulled back and looked past him. "Hi, Judy. Thanks for bringing him by. You're a sweetheart."

Judy blushed, mumbled a response, slipped off the desk and made a hasty exit. A phone rang. As if that were a signal, normal office noises resumed.

"What's with her?"

"You noticed her. She'd prefer you didn't."

"Really? But she's the sexiest woman in The Factory. Wouldn't you agree?"

"Present company excluded, yes."

Aurora laughed and let go of Christian. "Come on, I'll buy you lunch and you can tell me more lies." She hooked an arm though one of Christian's and they exited by a different door. "Might as well stop by Cosmo's office," she added once they were out of the range of enquiring ears. "He has something he wants to ask."

Cosmo hung up the phone as Christian and Aurora walked in. "Glad to see you two have made up." He rushed over to shake Christian's free hand.

"Like you give a shit, Unc. Mind if I steal your umbrella?"

"I have a choice? Christian, would you and Ms Michaels be able to attend our Halloween bash on the 31st?"

"I'll have to ask her. Costumes?"

"Of course. I hope she can fit us in to her schedule. And do thank her for me. Her friend, Yuka, called the day after the ball--Yuka herself, not her agent. Not everyone has contacts like that. If I thought we could afford your Marci, I'd offer her the hostess job, but I'm afraid she'd be out of

150

my price range. A woman like her certainly wouldn't work cheap, would she?"

"I couldn't tell you that, but no, I'm sure she wouldn't want the job." It sounded like Cosmo knew Marci was Freyja Van Deer. But he hadn't asked and Christian wasn't about to offer anything. "I'll ask her about Halloween."

Aurora tugged on Christian's arm. "Come on-- I'm hungry. Thanks for the loan of the umbrella, uncle dear."

"I'll never see it again." Cosmo's grumble followed them into the hall.

In the lobby, Kathy once again had Judy for company. Aurora walked over to them. Since he was attached, Christian went along.

"Hi ladies," Aurora said, with a smile. "I have a two o'clock interview so if anyone calls, tell them I'll be back by then. Say, you two doing anything tomorrow night? I've got front-row tickets for the Knight Move male strippers I'm not intending to use. Interested? Judy, I can see you are--Kathy? Well, I'll give Judy the tickets, and maybe you'll change your mind. See you both later." She moved towards the door without giving either of her victims a chance to respond further.

"I've decided I need to pay more attention to the little people. Especially the cute ones," Aurora said quietly to Christian as they left the building. Outside, she opened the umbrella. "Here, we can share. My usual dining spot is just down The Street, in the Westshire. Order something expensive. There is such a thing as a free lunch--I get them for feeding celebrity business to the hotel."

Christian felt almost as bewildered as Judy and Kathy had looked. This wasn't the Aurora any of them knew, the one he had slept with. "You're sure you're feeling okay?"

Even her smile was different, softer. "Don't seem like myself? Well, being a bitch hasn't got me anywhere lately. Meeting Marci reminded me there are other ways to get what you want. Remember, Christian, Machiavelli was an advisor to the Medici family way back when."

If this was merely a different type of manipulation, it was, at least, a pleasant change of tactics. "You really are a Medici?" Marci had implied that he should find out more about Aurora, although she had phrased it more bluntly. Aurora had given him an opening; he'd take it.

"It's my mother's last name. She didn't fancy becoming Cecilia Carpentier, so she kept Medici when she got married."

"Can't say I blame her. Which side of your family is Cosmo on?"

"My father's kid brother. He didn't think anyone named Claude Carpentier would make it in the Anglo business world--Cosmo Sharpe indeed-- he'll always be a clod to me." Water sprinkled off the edges of the umbrella as Aurora shook with laughter. Christian took it from her. He should have earlier--better late than never.

"So..." Aurora moved closer. "Think I can get Judy over being scared by me?"

"You have plans for her?" She had plans for him?

"It's a thought--mind you, I'd keep her a bit scared. She wouldn't run around on me then."

The hotel doorman nodded a greeting to Aurora. For the next few minutes she kept busy saying hello to people they met. Most seemed pleased to trade casual words about family or business with her, although Christian did notice a few who gave her a wide berth. Some he recognized from the charity ball greeted him as well. Aurora discreetly supplied the names he couldn't remember through her own salutations. Perhaps Marci had been right, Aurora would take care of him socially, if he let her.

"You're quite a politician," he said once they were seated in the dining room.

"Gee, thanks loads. Okay, let's get this out of the way. Yes, you made me look bad, but I've had some time to think about it, and figure I had it coming. I underestimated you and it cost me."

A waiter delivered a seafood plate. Christian gave it a questioning look. They hadn't ordered.

"My usual appetiser. The entree you can choose for yourself."

Christian felt it was time for him to say something. He opened his mouth; Aurora deftly inserted the shrimp on a toothpick he'd thought was on the way to hers. "I'm not finished. Okay, from here, Christian, I figure you and Marci can either be my friends, or my enemies. I don't think there's a middle ground."

Christian swallowed. "I opt for friends. I expect Marci will too."

"Good. She reminds me of some of the girls I went to boarding school with. Except none of them were built like she is. There can't be many like her in the world."

Aurora was asking him to tell her what he hadn't told Cosmo. He couldn't, not unless she asked directly. It would be violating a confidence. If she asked, he could confirm. "No, there can't be. You went to boarding school?"

"And you don't want to talk about her? Yes, I went to several. My father died in an accident when I was seven, and Mother, not being particularly maternal, farmed me out. In my time, I've been expelled by most of the leading girls' schools in North American and Europe."

Aurora filled the rest of lunch with ribald tales, some from her own past, and others about socialites he had met at the gathering Tuesday night. Christian had a hard time matching the peccadilloes with the people, and didn't believe half of what Aurora said but it didn't particularly matter. She was witty and entertaining. He suspected she was also driving a point home, with a gossip-heavy hammer. He'd underestimated her every bit as much as she had him. Certainly, she was avaricious, scheming and self-centred, but he'd thought her shallow and that she wasn't. He'd never said as much, so he made a mental apology and left it at that.

The waiter refilled their coffees and cleared the dessert plates. Aurora finished her latest story and sat back. "So, Christian--I'd gather you haven't bothered to watch me on TV lately?" That, he couldn't deny. "Why don't I mail a tape to you? Where should I send it?"

Aurora wanted to know where she could find him. That seemed fair enough. "Here, I'll give you my current address, and leave your name at the guard station in case you decide to drop over."

"It's not likely I would. Isn't Marci there, at least once in a while? She might not appreciate my company--any more than I relish the guests I've had at my place the last few days."

"Guests?"

"Rhymes with pests. Patsy decided he lives with me after all. Hard to boot him when his name is on the lease. I never should have given him a key. Someone convinced him he has a right to sleep there, with Eunice. If only they would sleep. I think Lucy has been with them a couple of times. I didn't hear her, but I felt her presence."

"You didn't check to see if she was there?"

"Enter a room where Patsy and Eunice are going at it? Please, give me credit for having some standards."

"But you said you were willing to sleep with Eunice for the interview. And that you'd crawl over broken glass to sleep with Lucy."

"And you said you wanted us to be friends." Aurora's fingers curled around her coffee cup.

Christian tried to meet her eyes but her focus was on his forehead. He prepared to duck. "Do friends lie to each other?"

"If they're smart." Her eyes shifted down and fixed him with piercing jade. "A friend might think I would have changed my mind about Eunice at the

155

last minute. A friend might give me the benefit of the doubt. As for Lucy, okay, she's hot. I can't keep her out of my dreams, and maybe I'd do anything she asks, but she hasn't asked. Aurora Medici doesn't beg for anything, from anyone." She put the cup down, stood and headed for the door.

Christian caught up with her in the hall, but only because she'd stopped to talk with two men who looked like they had been born in their thousand dollar suits. He waited to one side for Aurora to finish. After a couple of minutes, she deigned to notice him. "Yes, Mr. Plowman? There was something you wanted to say?"

"I think I owe you an apology."

"If you think about it, you'll realize you owe me a fuck of lot more than that. Gentlemen, I'll be in touch." She strode away.

One of the suits laughed. "Don't worry, friend. Her bark is worse than her bite."

"Don't bet on it," Christian answered. "Her bite is infectious." That earned him polite laughter he hadn't been seeking.

156

Chapter Sixteen

The rain had progressed from a sprinkle to a downpour, and Aurora had taken Cosmo's umbrella. Christian stood under the awning, waiting for it to let up. A featureless black limousine with heavily smoked glass slithered to a stop in front of the hotel. Dicky, Lucy's driver, got out and hobbled around to the back door. He stood there, his uniform getting soaked.

Christian went over. "You're limping, Dicky, you okay?"

"Only my phlebitis acting up, thank you, sir. The weather I expect. The lady would like to offer you a ride, sir."

"You're here for me?"

Dicky opened the door. Lucy was wearing a light pink cocktail dress that made her wig seem a deeper red. "How did you know where I was?" Christian sat as far from her as he could, on the other side of the facing bench.

"And a very good afternoon to you too, Christian. My word, you do look handsome in that exquisite suit. In answer to your rude and abrupt question, I told you my spies are everywhere. I always know where anyone I care about is. Especially those I suspect are avoiding me."

"Sorry. You do look lovely, Lucy, as always. But you know that."

She picked up the phone to the front. "Just drive around, Dicky. And turn up the heat. My guest seems chilly."

Warm air spilled from the vents. Lucy swivelled to face him. Christian realized he'd never seen her in anything other than pants before. The long legs that stretched towards him were shapely and supple. She spread them slightly and slipped off her shoes. "So, I hear you've made a move up in the world. Aurora's an amateur, but Freyja, she's the consummate pro." Lucy shifted closer and rested a bare foot on one of Christian's ankles. "She's never appeared in Noronto as herself before. Must be costing Grace a pretty penny."

"Oh yes, Grace. She said to say hello and tell you the game is on. She meant the chess game you suggested, I suppose."

"Naughty boy. Not only are you trying to change the topic, you're late with that news. We opened a private channel on the Internet and got the opening moves out of the way. We know each other's game well--we've played before. Now we will continue by email. It's so much faster than the old days; I so love science." She ran her foot up his leg. "But I don't want to talk about her, or even the pricey plaything she's provided you. It's time we had an intimate dinner and talked about us."

Christian's clothes felt as damp as they would have been in the rain, from the inside instead of the out. "Could you turn down the heat, Lucy? And drop me at Yonge and Bloor. Or anywhere. I just ate, and I don't think a discussion about us warrants a dinner. I'm not ready to make that serious a commitment." He made a mental note to thank Marci for the loan of a line.

Lucy moved back to where she'd started from, and gave Dicky his instructions. The heat turned off. "Going shopping? Tell me what you want, and it's yours. You can have three like Freyja, if you like. Or, in case I haven't been obvious enough, you can have me. I'll be Freyja for you, or anyone. I'll make you, very happy."

"Like you make Patsy happy?"

"Oh no." The red glint was back in her eyes. "You, I'll permit to touch me. And I'll touch you--everywhere. You may have taken a step up with Freyja, but compared to me, she's nothing. I'll prove it, if you'll permit. I can tell you're interested."

His interest was indeed visible, and growing. She might not even need to touch him again, merely continue stroking him with her eyes. Christian was close to losing control of himself--controlling the situation was out of the question. Time to run, or at least, waddle away from Lucy as best he could. "If you'll have Dicky stop, I'd like to get out now."

Lucy sighed and turned her head away. "Oh, put up with my company a few minutes more and I'll drop you where you want. And I do have a message I'd like you to pass on to Freyja."

Christian's groin started recover. "Couldn't you email her or something?"

"Don't be silly, dear boy. I want you to hear this as well. I've known Freyja Van Deer and Marci Michaels are one and the same for years. I admire the woman--she's intelligent and talented. A terrible liar though, the stories she tells about herself are quite unbelievable. Which did she tell you? Sold by poor parents into white slavery? No? How about the

159

orphan waif adopted by rich paedophiles and dumped when she turned sixteen? No again? Pity, I've always thought that was the most inventive. Don't tell me she still using the poor little rich girl, born with a silver spoon and Daddy in her mouth? Oh my, I am disappointed. Tell her she can do much better than that old fable. It's so prosaic."

"Is that the message, Lucy?"

"Oh hardly. Until now, Freyja has hidden in the shadows. She's about to become public property. Tell her I'll take care of her, and keep her from harm. All she has to do is ask."

"So I should tell her that you're threatening to tell the world about her?"

"No. I don't know who's been poisoning your mind about me. I like to do things for people, give them their heart's desire. I mean Freyja no evil. She outed herself, I didn't. She'll never be able to hide as Marci Michaels again, and she's going to be closely watched. I can shield her from all that."

The limo glided to a stop. "And here you are, where you wanted to be, all safe and sound. If you find you regret not letting me take you somewhere more exciting, give me a call, any time--the offer's open. I'll see you on Halloween, if not sooner."

"You've been invited to the party at The Factory?"

"Just try to keep me away from it."

"I'll look forward to seeing you then," Christian answered. Lucy's laughter followed him back to Grace's apartment. Marci was right; he was an inept liar.

Chapter Seventeen

First thing Friday morning, Christian washed his sheets. The previous afternoon he'd returned to Grace's and worked--reading and listening to classical music, studying Western culture as directed by Marci.

He hadn't thought about Lucy, or rather, had tried not to--quite a different matter. The image of her in the limo kept filtering into his mind. Also, Lucy in the park, as he'd first seen her--and in her office, stripping off her shirt. In daydreams, she proved more difficult to rebuff than in the flesh.

Later, Christian had become involved with her--in his dreams. She teased him to full tumescence and presented her backside. Just before accepting her invitation, he woke up, twisted in sweaty sheets. He'd been about to accept--no question.

Eventually, he slipped back into sleep. Again Lucy was with him, in the same position. Christian poised himself, closed his dream-eyes and thought of Marci. Marci!

In the morning Christian felt mortified. Usually he took care of matters before it got to that point. He tried to be philosophic; the sheets had needed doing anyway. As penance, Friday would be a day of domestic chores. He hadn't visited his own apartment in a week. He should, if only to check his mail.

The machine did the real work of washing; Christian checked his email. Grace had written again.

"Cut my climbing expedition short--sitting on top of a mountain isn't as much fun as I'd remembered. Guess I am getting old. Came back to find several notes from Cosmo. He wouldn't agree but it sounds like you've done well--for yourself, your new companion, and me. Congratulations. Lucy seems determined to win our latest match, but I've discovered a new gambit. Love to you both-¬Mom."

Christian made a printout to show Marci when she visited. Perhaps Grace's praise would soften Marci's attitude towards his boss.

By noon he'd remade his bed and the one Marci had used with freshly laundered sheets. After a quick bite to eat, he was ready to leave for home, to check in and see what had been happening in his old life. He didn't expect much would have--it hadn't when he was there, why would it when he wasn't?

***

Christian didn't care if he ripped his mail trying to get it out of the overstuffed box. Junk and bills, that's all he got. Gone a week and the thing was crammed. As usual, the nearby garbage can was overflowing. Management emptied it once a month, maybe. At least no one had tried to burn it again, yet. Christian took everything upstairs. He'd take it back to Grace's. Her building had recycling.

His apartment looked smaller than he'd remembered and didn't feel like home. A week at Grace's had spoiled him. He wrote the cheques necessary to keep his old world intact, then he stripped the sheets from his sofa bed, and took them

162

and his dirty clothes to the common laundry area in the sub-basement. For a Saturday afternoon, it wasn't busy. He got the last two functioning machines. While he waited, he finished the novel he'd been reading before he met Grace, if only because he'd started and paid for it. Uninspiring drivel. He left it behind.

After he'd remade and refolded the sofa bed, Christian tidied his room. When he cleared the paper off the answering machine, he saw the light was flashing. He hadn't checked it since erasing Aurora's messages Monday.

"Christian? Hello, stranger, it's Horatio. I know I haven't called for ages, but neither have you." Horatio's booming laugh crackled through the speaker. "Anyway, I'm on to something that might interest you. Give me a call, okay?" Horatio gave two phone numbers and hung up. The message had been left Tuesday.

Horatio? Christian hadn't heard from Horatio Beeble for a year and a half.

Not long after Christian was laid-off, Horatio talked his real-estate office into hiring Christian to set up a small local network. The last day they went to dinner, talked about their university days, and parted--making the usual sounds about how they must keep in touch. For a while they had, by phone, but Horatio was always on the go, and Christian embarrassed by his newfound poverty. The calls dwindled, and then stopped. Until now. Christian wondered what Horatio wanted.

He called both numbers. The first was a cellular service that informed him the subscriber's phone was turned off. A machine answered the second. Christian told Horatio he hadn't checked for messages until Friday, and would call again Monday. The man had always been impossible to find on weekends, and Christian had plans of his own. Marci had said she would visit Sunday, and before then he had a lot of reading to do. He was determined to impress her.

Chapter Eighteen

Sunday morning Christian was up at seven in anticipation of Marci's arrival. Around two he heard a tap on the door. Marci skipped in, brushing his cheek with her lips in passing. "Hi. Hope you weren't expecting me earlier."

Christian gave a plausible denial and a standard inquiry as to how things were with her.

"Great, thanks. Can't you tell? Picked up a couple of Brazilian kids eager to spend their inheritance. They were so damn good, I gave them the night for free. Want details?"

He didn't. Marci sprawled on the couch. "So, how's your reading coming?" she asked. "Anything happen in your life since Wednesday?"

"Oh, I chatted with Aurora and Cosmo--I'll fill you in on that later. Heard from Grace--there's a printout on the table. Went for a spin with Lucy, and turned down a night like you just had--except she offered me three, not just two companions. Not to mention herself. She dared me to compare her talents to yours. Since I couldn't, I had to turn her down."

Marci sat up. "Glad to hear that, but not as glad as I am to have you bite back. That whipped puppy thing you do gets on my nerves. Now, tell me what happened."

Christian did, leaving out a few minor details he didn't think mattered--like the wet-dream Lucy he'd overcome by changing her into Marci. That, Marci didn't need to know. Her eyebrows flickered as she listened and he tried to read her reaction from them. All he could get was that she was going to have plenty to say when he was done. He was surprised by what she dealt with first.

"I'm glad you gave Aurora this address. I think you blew her off far too soon. And yes, I'm sure she and Cosmo have figured out who I am. Firman is right. I've shown myself in Noronto in a way I never had before. I've decided you were right the other night too--like it or not, I am Freyja Van Deer. That's one reason I went for a romp. No use trying to hide any more. But as for Firman's offer-- she can stick it where the sun doesn't shine."

"She might enjoy that."

An eyebrow went up, slowly. "She probably would. Would you enjoy sticking it there?"

"I'm afraid I probably would."

"If you ever do, make sure you use a strong condom." Marci rose from the couch and came to sit on the carpet beside Christian's chair. "Or, you can use me instead, if you want." She rested her head on his thigh. "I'm available." A hand started up his leg.

"You've changed your mind?"

Marci looked up to meet his eyes. "No, you came on to me like a jerk before. I'd have said yes, if you'd asked nicely. I'm a whore. What's another cock to me after the thousands I've known? Sex wouldn't make any difference to our relationship." The hand kept moving.

Lucy had said Marci was a terrible liar. Right then, Christian believed Lucy. Marci wasn't telling the truth about what had happened, or what

166

accepting her offer would mean. He pinned her hand an inch from its target.

"No."

An eyebrow asked for an explanation.

"The day we met, you said I'd asked you to be my friend. I'd like that. If we have sex, I don't think the friendship will last. When you feel as comfortable with me as you do with other friends, like Yuka for instance, maybe then."

Marci extracted her hand from under his, and stood. "Yuka and I have never made it."

"Maybe we won't either. It's not like either of us will lack for partners."

Marci laughed. "I won't, but you? The way you talked about Aurora you sounded like a jilted virgin. From what you've told me, I say you're yet to have the first great sexual experience of your life. You could have it with me." She wandered in the direction of the table.

"But I couldn't keep you. Then I'd spend the rest of my life pining."

She laughed again. "What lovely bullshit. Okay, let's see what the twit you work for has to say." She read the printout of Grace's message. "Full of herself, isn't she? And she sends her love. How touching." She put down the paper. "I'll tell you what really annoyed me about what Firman said, Christian. It's that she'd think I'd work for Grace X Machina any sooner than I'd work for her. Far as I'm concerned, they're two sides of the same coin. Say, have you screwed Machina?"

"What?" Christian sat up straight. "No. Didn't you see? She signed herself as 'Mom'."

"And your point is?"

"That I haven't, won't, and she doesn't want me to." He stood and walked over to Marci. He hadn't meant to challenge the story she'd told him the other night, but she'd pushed him. "Did you really have sex with your father, Marci?"

"No," she whispered. "He had sex with me. I made love to him." She dropped her eyes.

If it was a line, it was convincing. Christian couldn't find an appropriate response. He waited.

After a minute Marci looked up and spoke in a normal voice. "Okay, now I'd like to hear all about Christian Plowman--before he met Grace. I've told you my lies, let's hear yours. In your way, you're as mucked up as I am. Why?"

For a moment, Christian considered inventing a patchwork that would rival Marci's autobiography, as told. He decided against it. Hers was artful, seamless-¬she'd had years to perfect it. He'd tell her the truth.

"I had a normal childhood in the suburbs of Vancouver."

Marci broke in. "Let me decide how normal it was. Start with how your parents met."

"My father was a mechanic in a small town in the B.C. interior. Mom was a local girl, ten years younger. She got pregnant and they moved to Vancouver." His father's family had strict religious beliefs, a rigid creed he rejected by marrying out of their faith. They closed the door behind him. If he had gone to visit his former home, they would have refused to acknowledge his presence. To them, he had died.

His mother's background was everything his father's wasn't. Her own mother had been born out of wedlock in the bohemian expatriate community that flourished in Europe prior to World War Two. Orphaned of her single parent in her teens, Christian's grandmother moved to North America and gravitated to the counterculture worlds of the west coast. She found a living under a variety of pseudonyms, writing paperback novels: westerns, romances, and science-fiction. She also produced two daughters--one in California, the other in British Columbia. Christian's mother was the second, the one born in Canada.

"Grandma Weeks would have preferred my mother to have me on the commune, but her first daughter had already run away and disappeared. She didn't want to lose another. She was the only family present at the wedding. Afterwards, she made sure they could pay their bills."

Christian's mother had completed her high school through correspondence and gone on to attend university. Grandma Weeks moved to Vancouver, buying a small house nearby where she wrote, and baby-sat Christian when her daughter was in class. Christian's mother graduated with a doctorate in philosophy when he was eight. Then she freed her mother and stayed home, writing papers and books of her own--an absentee at-home mother. One became a best seller... in the world of philosophy. It made far less money than any of her mother's potboilers, but got her known in her field.

Marci's eyebrows had been dancing for some time. Finally, she interrupted. "A normal childhood? What did your father do all this time?"

"Work. He didn't understand Mom, but he adored her. He took me to hockey games and stuff, but I'm afraid we didn't have much in common. A couple of times he tried to interest me in working on cars. Boy, was that a disaster!"

"You were your mother's child from the sound of it. Don't take it wrong, Christian, but the way you phrased it, it sounded like you weren't sure you were your father's."

"I gather he was a candidate. Mom grew up in a free-love environment. Once they married, she was totally loyal to him, I think. I always wondered why he asked, and why she accepted."

"Because they loved each other."

Christian thought there was more to it than that… or less, but continued his story. Eleven years after Christian, his sister Aster came along. Although no one said anything, Christian was certain her arrival put his mother's career plans back years.

"But when Aster was seven, and I was eighteen, Mom got a job offer here in Noronto. Dad decided he would retire and go back to school himself. We moved here right after I graduated from high school."

His mother never started her new job. A month after moving, Christian's parents were killed in a head-on collision. "I was devastated. For all that they had been distant--both Aster and I were errors

170

in contraception--they were good people. They loved me, and I loved them."

Christian had stayed in Noronto, and used insurance money to pay for an intense electronics technician course at a private college. He wanted to be busy, to not have time to think.

Aster returned to B.C., to live with Grandma Weeks.

Christian's other grandmother, his father's mother, was still alive. Although she had never seen Aster or Christian, she applied to the courts for custody of Aster. A seven-year-old girl should have a stable family environment. She and Aster's God-fearing aunts and uncles were the ones who could provide it.

To keep Aster, Grandma Weeks again sacrificed her lifestyle. She bought a rambling farmhouse on the outskirts of Victoria and hired a battery of high-priced lawyers. On the court date, the other side didn't show up. Neither Christian nor Aster had heard of them since.

"Oh yeah, all completely normal. What's next? Grandma and Aster get abducted by aliens?"

"No, they lived a quiet life together until Aster went to university."

"I'll just bet they did. Okay, let's keep this about you. You took the electronics course. Did you have a girlfriend?"

"I wasn't interested. I graduated after a year and a half, and went looking for a job."

He had found one that wasn't challenging. For the first time since his parents' death, he wasn't busy every waking hour. He was twenty and had money left over from the insurance. He soon discovered women. "Or maybe I should say, they discovered me--a naive kid with lots of cash."

"I know the type. At least you finally started getting laid."

"Occasionally. That only lasted a few months, and I was usually too drunk by the end of the night."

The eyebrows spoke scorn.

"Yeah, yeah, I know. When I went to Victoria for Christmas, Grandma Weeks set me straight. Was this what I wanted to do with my life?"

His grandmother had helped Christian get his finances in order. He had enough insurance money to pay four years' tuition at university, including living expenses, if he was careful. When he returned to Noronto, he had quit his job to spend six months touring Europe, staying in youth hostels-- Grandma's treat.

"So then you started getting properly laid."

"No, I avoided women like the plague. I'd learned my lesson."

"No, and you still haven't. Okay, back from being a wandering monk and off to university. There you met Cleo? From the little you said, it sounds like she was a real prize, or to be honest, you were still a prize sucker."

"I didn't meet her until my third year."

In the first two years, Christian had reverted to the pattern established in his electronics course. He spent his time in class, in the library, and sleeping. That changed after he met Horatio Beeble.

On his way back to his room from the library one evening, Christian heard gospel singers. He stopped to listen, and then followed the sound to its source, a small theatre. He stood in the doorway until a man in the back row got up and insisted Christian sit if he intended to stay.

That had been Christian's introduction to Horatio. He looked like a football player, but was a business student instead, originally from a small town outside Atlanta. Since his family couldn't afford to pay for his education, Horatio supported himself by hustling women.

At the time Christian met him, he was keeping company with Lydia, a woman from one of Noronto's leading families. She was in her last year of business and when she graduated, intended to get married--not to Horatio, but to a New York City stockbroker who was a family friend. While at university Horatio was a status symbol but a very big, very black man wasn't acceptable husband material.

Horatio had thought it a curious morality, but the gifts she gave him more than made up for any slight. He told Christian, privately, that he was just as glad. Lydia was a dull conversationalist and a lousy lover. Next time, Horatio said, he'd do better. In the meantime, her generosity paid the bills.

Marci had been making choking sounds and at that point couldn't hold it in any longer. Christian didn't think giggling suited her. "Okay, what's so funny?"

She struggled to get herself under control. "No wonder my profession didn't shock you. Your best friend's a hooker too."

"He just did that to get through university. He's a successful businessman now."

"So he changed careers, if he did--I'm intending to do the same. Anyway, let me help cut a long story short. You and Horatio became friends, and good old Lydia got tired of you taking up time she'd paid for. So she introduced you to Cleo. And finally, you started getting laid. Okay, describe Cleo--in ten words or less."

"Another business student. Chinese-Canadian. Flexible beyond belief."

"Lucky you. She knew her way around a bed?"

"Until I met Aurora, I thought so. Cleo certainly knew her way around the business world. After I graduated, she found me a job with a big electronics company, shuffling paper and attending meetings."

"Which you hated."

"It wasn't that bad. I had a comfortable apartment, a lover and a good income. What more could a man want?"

"What more indeed? But it fell apart."

"Not all that soon. It lasted seven years. I wanted to get married, but Cleo wasn't ready. She had her career to think of. She was a business consultant, and worked a lot of nights. And she travelled."

Marci rolled her eyes to the heavens. "Right. Then you weren't actually living together."

"No, not until the end."

Christian had received a promotion that year, which meant the papers and meetings he was responsible for became much more important to the company. As was his custom, he made plans to visit Aster and Grandma Weeks over the Christmas holidays. In early December, Cleo announced she would accompany him. It was time she finally met his family.

Aster and Cleo hated each other on sight. At seventeen, Aster was in her first year at university and, in her opinion, knew everything about the world worth knowing. The second day they were in Vancouver, she took Christian aside and told him he had to make a decision, then and there. Choose her or the tramp; he couldn't have them both in his life. With Cleo around Christian didn't have a mind of his own. She offered to introduce him to some of her friends. He could do better than Cleo, much better.

Aster left the next day. Grandma Weeks remained polite but distant for the remainder of the holidays. At the airport she suggested that the next year Christian should visit alone.

"And of course, you haven't been back since."

"No, you're wrong. I went again the next year. Cleo was gone. She had moved in with me in January and then out again in April after I was laid-off. I'd given up my apartment and moved to where I am now, but I could still afford to travel. It was tense over Christmas. The third day Aster said I should either shoot myself and put them out of my misery, or smarten up. That time, I left."

"I think I like Aster. Have you seen her since?"

"Last Christmas she and Grandma Weeks passed through Noronto, on their way to spend the holidays in Europe with one of Aster's friends. I saw them at the airport. Aster said she could get me on the flight, but I wasn't packed or anything. I turned her down." Christian's voice cracked.

"You should have gone."

"I know." Christian couldn't remember having cried in years, not since his parents' funeral. Marci's shoulder was solid comfort.

Later, she cooked dinner. Afterwards, Christian couldn't remember what they'd eaten. Marci left around eight. "I'm going to England for a week. Work. Tell Cosmo we'll be there for Halloween. Wouldn't miss it. I'll supply the costumes."

Christian thought that best. Marci was the expert in being someone she wasn't. "So I'll see you next Sunday?"

"I can't sleep on planes. My flight comes in early that morning. I'll probably go home and see you whenever."

"You could sleep here." Christian took a spare key off Grace's key ring. Grace wouldn't mind. "Here. If I'm still asleep, let yourself in." He expected he'd be up, waiting.

Marci took the key. "Okay. Thanks. I'll think about it."

176

Chapter Nineteen

When Christian called Horatio Beeble Monday morning, the man himself answered. Christian agreed to meet him at his new address, not too far from the foot of Yonge Street, near Lake Ontario. He knew the area. It was an area undergoing a process the papers referred to as urban renewal, in which pretentious new buildings replaced older serviceable ones. Since it sounded like Horatio had a business proposal for him, Christian put on a suit.

The windows of Horatio's building were boarded up. On the door a faded sign that read "Washboard Sound" hung by one corner. Below it was another, "Loading dock in rear". Christian knew Horatio as a big-time realtor. This wasn't a realtor's office.

The small waiting room didn't have any chairs, and there was no sign of life other than footprints in the dust, leading to a door. Christian opened it and found himself at the edge of an expanse of empty desks. The floor was slightly cleaner. "Hello? Anyone here? Horatio?"

He heard the scrape of a chair and then Horatio was rushing down a hall towards him. "Christian, my man! It's been far too long." He skidded to a stop. "But is that you in that suit? I didn't hear you arrive. I was fighting with my accursed computer."

Horatio stepped forward and enveloped Christian in a massive hug. He was one of the only people Christian knew who could make him feel small. The hug done, Horatio held Christian at arms' length and inspected him again.

"It really is a very fine suit, Christian. Where did you steal it?" His laughter echoed off the walls.

Horatio's own suit might have come off the same rack. Some said clothes made the man, but in Horatio's case, Christian had always thought it the other way around. The man could look well turned-out in a T-shirt and jeans. Dressed for business, he was sartorial perfection.

"It's a long story, Horatio." One Christian suspected he wouldn't have a chance to tell for some time. Horatio had that look. He wanted to talk about Horatio.

"Christian, you won't believe what this fool has done. I hope you're not still angry with me, because I need your help. I've made a glorious mistake."

"Why would I be angry with you, Horatio? But I won't be much use around here. This is a recording studio. You own it?"

"It was a fantastic deal, far too fine to pass on. It took the last of my remaining fortune, but what are fortunes for if not to spend?" Horatio took a deep breath. "But why do you say you cannot help? And if you are not angry, why do you never call? I thought it was because of Cleo."

"Because your girlfriend introduced me to her? I'd be a small man if I held that against you, Horatio."

"Yes... well... but then why would you refuse to help? You studied electronics. This place is nothing but."

"You need a sound engineer, Horatio, not an electronics technician. I'll bet I'm as lost here as you are. Come on, let's take a look at that computer and then you can show me around."

Horatio hadn't plugged in the monitor. That was a technical problem Christian could handle. As for the studio, it was far more sophisticated than Christian would have guessed from the dilapidated building exterior. There were rooms behind glass walls, with banks and consoles of knobs, levers and dials in front. Christian felt confident he could power everything up but that was about it.

"Even if I had studied sound, Horatio, my diploma is over ten years old. Most of this is new. It wouldn't have existed then. What possessed you to buy this? I hope you haven't given up your real-estate career."

"Selling land and buildings has no soul, Christian. When I saw this, I saw a way to recapture joy. Which I will, whether or not you share my vision. But even if you think yourself useless, it's good to know you still consider yourself my friend. I'll buy you lunch and we can catch up. Anything happening in your life? Any interesting women come your way? Of course not. Why would I ask?"

"You'd ask so you can boast about yours. Lucky for you did. Now that you mention women, I see I may be able to help you after all. Where's your phone?"

Horatio handed over his cellular. Christian called The Factory and asked for Aurora. She was pleased to hear from him, particularly when he told her the reason he had called was to introduce her to the new owner of Washboard Sound.

"I knew you'd come through with more contacts, Christian," Aurora said. She agreed to meet them for lunch at the Westshire in an hour.

On the way, Christian told Horatio a little about his new job and how he had met Aurora. In return he got a shopping list of Horatio's women. The man hadn't changed; he knew their vital statistics--measurements and personal wealth.

Aurora got to the restaurant fifteen minutes late. Christian thought she looked faded; her eyes had lost their sparkle, and her entire body seemed to be sagging instead of just her breasts. His was probably a minority opinion. When she entered, most of the eyes in the room went to her and followed her to their table. After all, she was Aurora Medici.

She hugged Christian, and when he introduced her to Horatio, shook Horatio's hand. "Sorry I'm late."

"No problem." Horatio bowed. To kiss her hand? No, not quite. "I'm very pleased to meet you. I see our Christian hasn't lost his power over women, and remains as oblivious as always. It's a blessing--he'd be insufferable were he aware." He pulled out a chair to seat her.

"Thank you, Horatio. Since you bring it up, tell me about his other women. I'm fascinated."

"And fascinating, of course. I'm afraid I did exaggerate a little." Horatio had exaggerated a lot. Power over women? Him? That was Horatio's stock in trade. "Truly, only one woman from his past is worth mentioning. Once upon a time, he and Mistress Cleopatra were an item."

"The infamous Ms Wong? That is interesting. Do tell more." Aurora leaned forward.

"She tried her usual, but couldn't control him. Because I like you, I thought I should give you fair warning. Christian is easy to underestimate. Don't make that mistake."

Aurora's eyes slowly shifted from Horatio to Christian. "Thank you. I appreciate the advice, even if it does come too late."

Christian didn't like the direction the conversation was taking. It was like listening to a bad soap opera. "Excuse me? I brought you two together to talk business, not tell lies about me and gossip."

"Ah, but all business is based on gossip. But lies? I don't think so. You don't know what the truth is, my friend--especially regarding yourself, and Cleo."

"What's so special about Cleo?"

Horatio lowered his voice. "She eats men's souls."

"Oh come off it, Horatio," Aurora turned to Christian. "Cleo likes to think of herself as a power broker, but really, she's nothing more than a small-time con artist. Only a fool would fall for her act, so I'm not surprised you didn't. She married one, Irving Spratt, an up-and-coming city councillor. There have been others." She let her remark trail off.

The waiter brought Aurora's usual complimentary seafood appetiser and took their orders. Aurora ordered rack of lamb, and Horatio, shepherds' pie. Christian didn't feel hungry--a Caesar salad would do for him.

"So, Horatio," Aurora continued. "I gather you're the sucker who bought Washboard. Know anything about the recording business?"

"Business is business. If you work hard, you're bound to succeed."

Aurora almost choked on a shrimp. "You're kidding, right? If not, sell it. Now."

Horatio pushed his chair back and stood. "I was led to understand you might help me. If not, I might as well leave."

Aurora speared a scallop. "Without my help, Horatio, Washboard will not only go under, it won't produce a note. I have the contacts, and you don't. From what I learned about your financial situation, you won't be able to make them in time no matter how hard you try. You can sit or leave. It's all the same to me." She popped the crustacean into her mouth. Horatio slowly sat.

The remainder of lunch was Aurora's show. She barely touched her food as she entertained them, and a good bit of the room, with anecdotes about show business and celebrities she knew. Christian could see Horatio's mood start to lift. By the end of the meal, his friend seemed almost his old self. The waiter cleared their plates and brought after-dinner coffees. Aurora excused herself to visit the ladies' room.

"She's rough, but she's all woman," Horatio said to Christian. "I think I can work with her."

"That's good. Okay, what happened to you in real-estate? It sounded like Aurora found out something you didn't tell me about."

Horatio fiddled with his coffee, putting in sugar and a precise amount of cream. He spoke to the cup. "I overreached and invested in a development Cleo recommended. All I was left with was Washboard." He raised his eyes. "It will be enough. You know me; I can't help but succeed."

"I'll help you all I can, Horatio." Christian got out his wallet and handed his friend one of his business cards. "Here. Grace said I could take on new clients. You can be the first. And I'll pick up the bill. I can put it on expenses."

"You're a better friend than I deserve."

Aurora had made a couple of phone calls while she was away, and said they should go back to The Factory. One of the technicians there had been with Washboard. They could talk to him, a few other people, and make plans. "You don't need to stick around, Christian, but would you please walk over with us?"

On the way, Aurora chatted brightly to Horatio, discovering what other people they knew in common. Christian suspected she already knew, and had talked to most of the people mentioned while she was away. She ignored him, except for the hand she held and intermittently squeezed. As they walked into the lobby of The Factory she moved closer and wrapped an arm around his waist. At the reception desk, Kathy glanced up and then quickly returned her attention to the switchboard.

"Horatio, that's Kathy." Aurora's voice filled the lobby. "You might not guess it, but she's one of the most important people around here, in charge of rumour control, among other things. I'd suggest you introduce yourself to her." Kathy looked up again.

"My pleasure."

"Don't bet on it," Aurora said, quietly… when Horatio got out of earshot. "Okay, what do you really want me to do, Christian? Finish him off?"

"Why would I want you to do that? He's my friend. You're not interested in Washboard?"

"Oh, I am. I tried to get Cosmo to buy it, but he went chickenshit and said he didn't want to compete in that business. Too dirty for him, he said. Now you've handed it to me. I owe you again."

"Then pay me back by being nice to Horatio." He escaped from her and went over to Horatio and Kathy. "I'd better be going. Keep an eye on him, Kathy. He thinks he's irresistible, and will probably try to hit on Aurora."

Kathy's blue-grey eyes examined Christian before moving back to Horatio. She smiled. "Don't worry, he won't. He asked me for a date, and I accepted. Frankly, he seems to be much smarter than you."

184

Chapter Twenty

When Christian arrived back at Grace's apartment, he wrote a long, detailed report to her, including everything that had happened. He was confused. He considered Horatio a decent human being, despite his failings, and as he'd tried to make clear to Aurora, a friend.

He thought Aurora had accepted that, finally, but only because he'd insisted, and he still wasn't sure Aurora wouldn't take advantage of Horatio. Christian didn't understand Aurora at all. Grace had introduced them, and said she had known Cosmo, Aurora's uncle, forever. He wanted Grace's view on how he should deal with Aurora.

He wrote thousands of words, trying to capture not only exactly what had happened and what everyone had said, but also what he'd thought at the time, and why he had reacted as he had. If he was going to find a hostess for Cosmo's new cable station, he had to know more. Aurora clearly wanted the position, along with whatever else she could get. Or at least, Christian thought that was clear. Marci seemed to believe he'd misjudged Aurora. After seeing Aurora with Horatio, Christian was back to his original opinion. She was not what he'd term a "good" person.

It was night by the time he finished. He emailed the report to Grace. He needed some answers.

The week passed. Christian read, played computer games, and checked his email a dozen times a day. Nothing arrived until early Friday morning. Then two messages did, one from Grace and the other from Horatio. He opened Grace's first.

She said she'd be back in Noronto on the 31st, in time for Cosmo's party. She'd read his report with interest. Two lines, signed "Mom".

Horatio was more straightforward. "I've been trying to call, but Aurora tells me this is the only way to contact you. Why do you bother having a phone?

Come and see me at the studio. It's important."

After he checked his answering machine and Grace's, Christian felt guilty. Horatio had called each number once on Tuesday, and several times on Wednesday and Thursday. The message was always a variation on "Please call." By Thursday he was no longer saying "Please".

It was too early in the morning to respond. Even if Horatio was already at the studio, the subway didn't start running for an hour. Christian went upstairs and looked at himself in the mirror. The person who stared back was unshaven, and his eyes shifted and tried to avoid making contact. He cleaned himself up and went out for the first time since Monday. On the way through the lobby, he looked to see if Grace had received any mail. It was all junk except for a small package addressed to him, from Aurora. He hadn't been expecting anything from her. He opened it to see if she'd included a note.

It was written in red. "Dear Christian. Since you missed seeing my reports on VideoView, I decided I would mail you a tape. Enjoy. Hope to see you soon." She signed with her initial, A.

Christian put it back in the mailbox after throwing out the junk. He'd pick it up when he got back.

Horatio's building had been painted, and the boards removed from the windows. A new sign hung on the door, "Beeble Productions." The waiting room was spotless, but still empty. In the office area boxes of equipment were piled high on the desks.

As had been the case the previous time, no one was in sight, but there was music coming from the back. He went towards it and found Horatio watching a man operate the control board. Aurora was in one of the glass booths with several musicians, including the scruffy man Christian had seen her interview. She waved.

Horatio turned. "Oh, it's you. Come to my office. I'd hate to upset the talent."

"It looks like things are going well," Christian trotted to keep up as Horatio headed down the hall to an office.

Horatio closed the door. "Things are not going too badly, no. I have a partner now. Aurora convinced Cosmo to invest but I made sure I kept control. Aurora brought her people in. I gather they know what they're doing. God knows, I don't. A recording of hers will be my first release. I can live with that. She's a decent singer. With VideoView behind us, it should be a success."

"Then what's the problem? What's so urgent?" Christian asked.

Horatio hadn't moved since closing the door. He stepped forward. Christian tried to shift away, but there was nowhere to go. "I said I can live with Aurora being my first artist. I can even live with her being the one who is really running things, for now. I can take charge later, when I'm ready. Yes, I could live with all this, if it weren't for one small thing." He punched the door above Christian's head, turned away, and mumbled something Christian couldn't make out.

Against his better judgement, Christian moved closer. "Pardon me? I couldn't hear that. Except for one small thing?"

Horatio wheeled. "You asshole. You've screwed up my whole life."

Christian retreated, back towards the door. "Pardon me?" He couldn't think of anything else to say. "I'm sorry, but I can't see what the problem is. I found you the help you needed to get this place going, and as a bonus you got an introduction to one of the sexiest blondes I've ever seen."

"Son-of-a-bitch!" Christian heard rather than saw Horatio's fist. It whizzed past his ear to hit the wall, just wide of the door. Silence, then a sigh. "Aw, shit-¬just when I had the place fixed up."

Horatio's hand was in wrist deep. He pulled it out. Christian could see into the hall through the hole. "You okay?" he asked.

"No. What a fucking stupid question. Weren't you listening?" Horatio turned, and lumbered to his desk.

"I meant your hand."

"Oh. Yeah. It's okay. Thanks." He sat. "Sorry."

Christian sat in the chair on the other side. Time to try again. "Okay, what's the problem?"

"Everything. I lied. I can't stand the way Aurora's taken over. No one pays any attention to me. And I've been out every night this week with Kathy, and she won't let me touch her. I'm losing it, Christian. Worse. I've lost it."

Christian stifled a sigh--this was pathetic. "I'll talk to Aurora, okay?" He stood. "And maybe you should quit seeing Kathy? Look up someone from your little black book instead."

Horatio shook his head. "No way. She's got me hooked, but good. Have you seen that body?"

No, and you haven't either. Christian didn't say it. That would have been cruel.

Aurora met Christian in the hall. "Is there something wrong?" She peered past him at the hole. "I'm just on my way out, back to The Factory. Got an interview to do, but I thought I'd better check this out. The boys told me it sounded like Horatio went off the rails. Looks like it too. You okay?"

"I'm fine. How about you?" The circles under Aurora's eyes had been joined by red lines throughout. Her clothes were wrinkled and hung on her like they were too large.

"Can't complain," she answered. "Busy, busy, busy. And Patsy has had Eunice over every night this week, the toad. He walked out on his job at The Factory, so I don't have that over him anymore. Lucy got him a contract producing anti-drug spots for the government. What a howl!" Her laugh was forced. "Anyway, I've got to get going."

"When can I see you? We need to talk."

189

"Not tonight I've got this interview, and then Bull's Eye at six and eleven. Tomorrow's pretty busy too. Up first thing in the morning to be here, assuming I sleep, and then the afternoon at The Factory. Maybe after the six o'clock newscast tomorrow--if you're not going to be busy with Marci on a Saturday night."

"Marci's been out of town all week. She's in Europe."

"Earning a living? And you're all alone and horny? Is that what this is about, Christian? What do you really have in mind? Talking or fucking?"

"Talking."

"Why don't I believe you?" Even bloodshot, Aurora's eyes could pierce. "I'm better in bed than she is, I bet, and you want me back. That's it, isn't it?"

"I wouldn't know. I haven't slept with her. Marci and I are just friends."

Horatio had missed. Aurora connected. Fortunately, she was under half Horatio's size, but her slap still rocked Christian. "Lying bastard!" She stalked away. At the end of the hall she stopped. "If you're really interested in seeing me, come by The Factory around seven tomorrow evening. Maybe I'll let you try to make amends. I'll think about it."

Christian managed to sneak out of Beeble Productions without talking to anyone else. He felt embarrassed. In her way, Aurora had been right. He hadn't admitted it to himself, but yes, he did want to sleep with her again.

In another way Aurora was wrong. He couldn't imagine sustaining an intimate relationship with

190

her. Then again, he couldn't imagine anyone doing that with Aurora. She wasn't likeable. She did, however, have a sense of humour, and--where other people were concerned--a fair bit of insight, if no compassion. And the first time he'd had sex with her had been incredible.

It came back to that. How shallow.

On the way in to Casa del Carlos, Christian retrieved the videotape Aurora had sent him. He'd watch it in the evening, after dinner. For the rest of the morning and the afternoon he planned to study Mozart, in keeping with Marci's cultural awareness plan. He ended up immersed in a spy thriller instead. Grace's bookshelf contained too many temptations. Mozart played in the background as Christian read.

At six o'clock, he watched Bull's Eye. Aurora's segment was short. The camera flickered to her face and then away to a long shot before going to her subject, an actor. They agreed his latest film was brilliant, his best work to date. When Aurora mentioned a possible Academy Award, he sounded convincingly modest. Christian knew they said that about every film and every actor. If they didn't, COSMO-TV would be blacklisted by the studios and not sent film clips. Aurora did a good, if uninspired, job. It was fluff, standard COSMO-TV fare.

The tape she had sent proved fascinating. The Aurora on it wasn't one he'd ever met. In the longer interviews, she listened to her subjects and drew them out, making them talk about themselves. The interviews were about them, not her. She treated the camera as if it were a third person, a silent one, and was warm, smooth and friendly. Christian had seen her do interviews previously, but only before he'd met her. Knowing her made a difference. This was an Aurora he had yet to meet in person. Did cameras need to be rolling before she appeared?

192

Chapter Twenty-One

Saturday, Christian arrived at The Factory a few minutes before seven. He showed his ID card to the woman behind what he thought of as Kathy's desk and said he was there to meet Aurora. "If you can tell me roughly where she is, I'll go find her."

She looked up from filing her nails. "She said you should wait out here." Message delivered, she went back about her business.

Aurora appeared almost as he sat. "Should I change?"

He'd fussed over what to wear for hours, and settled on a suit. Aurora had made a different choice. If there were natural circles around her eyes, they'd been covered by heavy black make-up. Her shiny, low-slung pants hung tenuously and her top, knotted below her breasts, left no doubt she wasn't wearing a bra. Someone should tell her she needed to, but it wasn't going to be him. Her hair looked like it hadn't been combed in weeks... the latest style.

"I like the contrast. Let's go. I've got a busy evening planned."

They sauntered down The Street, Aurora's hand in his pants pocket and his arm around her. People looked. Everyone recognized Aurora, but no one said hello or asked for an autograph. Hers wasn't an approachable look. They went to the Westshire, to the stodgiest and most formal of the dining rooms. Christian was dressed for it. Aurora wasn't. They didn't have any trouble getting in.

The eyes of the room followed them to their table. Christian recognized almost everyone from the charity ball. They'd seen him with Marci. Now they were seeing him with Aurora in her post-apocalyptic costume.

"You're making a statement?"

"Shut-up and kiss me." She didn't tilt her head up, so he had to bend awkwardly. The maitre de waited, and seated Aurora when they were finished. "Wipe yourself." She handed him the napkin from her wine glass. Her black lip-gloss was smudged. She took a mirror from her thin purse and repaired it.

"This is revenge?"

"Not at all. This is theatre, and face-saving."

"It won't do much for your chances of getting the position at Ovation."

"Fuck Ovation, and fuck Cosmo--as if anyone could without barfing. You were right--it is time for Aurora Medici to move on."

Christian still didn't remember suggesting any such thing. It probably didn't matter. Aurora thought he had. "Glad I've been able to help."

"That sounded like irony, Christian. Didn't think you were capable of it. You've done more for me than you realize. You've forced me to examine my life, and pointed out my next lover to me."

"Judy?" It certainly wouldn't be Horatio.

"Yeah, I'm working on her. She's interested, just shy. She'll love me before I'm through with her."

"Are you sure you're okay, Aurora?"

"You think I'm going crazy? Deluding myself?"

"It's possible."

"Well, fuck you too, Christian. Oh, I forgot. You want me to, don't you?"

What Christian had wanted was to talk with her about Horatio, and how the way she was acting made Horatio feel. It didn't seem like a good idea, considering. He deflected the conversation to Aurora's favourite topic, Aurora, by saying he'd watched the tape she'd sent and greatly admired her interviewing skills. That led to a series of anecdotes about other interviews she'd done. Dinner passed without any further damage.

After dinner, she told him their next stop would be The Second Circle.

"Are you sure that's a good idea?"

"No, but it's something I need to do. You're right, Christian. I'm losing it, and know it, and know why--since the last time we were there, I haven't had an hour's sleep that hasn't been broken into by dreams of Lucy Firman, or the sounds of her lackeys humping in the room next to me. I need to confront her--to put an end to it--and I need you to help me. Please?"

Outside The Second Circle was what Christian supposed the normal Saturday night line-up. Aurora stopped to sign autographs and talk. She seemed more relaxed than she had in the Westshire. Again, Aurora was asked about her connection with the Rolling Stones.

She had a new answer. "I've always liked to think I might have been the inspiration for that line... what is it? 'I'm ever so hot for her, and she's so damn cold?' Sorry folks, got to go now." She took Christian's arm and added quietly. "Amazing what one can sell people who want to believe, isn't it?"

"Maybe you do know what you're doing tonight after all."

"Don't count on it, and please, don't desert me."

Percy was at the door. He they should go to the owner's table.

"Perfect." Aurora sounded like she meant it. "Thank you."

Lucy rose to meet them. She was wearing the red hair and a black body suit that followed her form perfectly. She might as well have been naked. Her contacts gleamed like cat's eyes. Behind her Christian saw two small shadows he assumed were Patsy and Eunice.

"Christian! I see you're slumming tonight. Couldn't afford Freyja's fee, or is this a trip down memory lane--to remind you what sex was like before it got good?"

Aurora's open hand flashed towards Lucy's cheek, but Christian caught and held her arm before Aurora connected. Her arm went limp and fell by her side. Christian held her hand.

"It's a good thing you were able to control your plaything, Christian." Lucy's eyes flashed red.

"You're just upset because I won't be yours," Aurora answered.

"Oh, but you are, my dear. When you accept that, it will make your life so much more pleasant."

196

Lucy caressed Aurora's face and softly kissed her forehead.

"Hell will freeze over first." Said with a hiss and a spit.

"Indeed. Christian, are you staying?"

"I don't think so. We'll just thank you for your hospitality and be on our way."

"Yes, and thanks for taking care of my trash for me, Ms Firman." Aurora smiled past Lucy, at the shadows. "Throw it out when you're finished. See you around, Eunice, Patsy." She squeezed Christian's hand. As they exited, Aurora was again smiling and chatting to her fans. She had another appointment, she explained. She'd just dropped in.

They walked down The Street, towards The Factory. "Was that what you had in mind?" Christian asked.

"More or less. I intended to get things into the open, but didn't think she'd co-operate by starting it. Thanks for stopping me from hitting her. A girl could cut her hand on that pointy jaw."

"What's in the open?"

"Well, for one thing, you supported me. I learned that was what she expected and know you're on my side now. Lucy didn't get where she is by being a poor judge of character. For another, maybe I did take a swing at her, but on the way out I didn't tell everyone I was leaving because the place is a dump, passé, history. If I'd trashed The Second Circle, lots of people would quit going there. There's still room for reconciliation." They reached The Factory and stood in front of one of the

197

smoked glass windows. "I'm yours, if you want me. Do you?"

"Let's go somewhere and talk about it."

"Fuck talking-- kiss me." It started as a kiss. It ended with Christian pressed against the window, fumbling with Aurora's belt.

Aurora broke free. "Better leave it there, for now. VideoView is broadcasting live from behind this window tonight. With luck, we just went nationwide." She looked into the window and smiled.

With luck he'd had his back to the window the entire time. "There's a cab," Christian waved a hand behind her back. For once, it worked. The cab pulled up in front of the window.

Christian held the door for her. With a last flutter of her hand to the window, she got in.

"Were there really cameras on us?"

"You never know. You just never know, do you?" Aurora crumpled against him and started to tremble. Christian gave the driver Grace's address, took off his jacket, put it around Aurora's shoulders and held her. Her skin felt like ice. It had been fever hot a minute earlier.

At Casa del Carlos, Aurora regained her poise for long enough to strut past Fred at the guard station, and make a loud, obscene suggestion concerning what Christian should do with her in the elevator. The door closed and she sagged against him, again quivering. He had to almost carry her into Grace's apartment.

Once inside, she pulled away from him again. "Okay, I know this isn't your place. I had you checked out. You live in a dump. We do need to talk. Is there somewhere I can freshen up first?"

"Second door on the right if it's a small job. Upstairs at the end if it's major." He wasn't surprised Aurora had investigated him. As he'd told Grace the day he met her, it was easy enough to do.

Aurora went upstairs.

Christian hung his suit jacket and put some soft Bach on the stereo. He heard the shower start, and went to make fresh coffee. The shower stopped. After a few minutes he went upstairs to see if anything was wrong.

Aurora came out of the bathroom, wearing a towel. "I can't put that stuff back on. Is there something else I could wear?"

"Well, my robe would be too big, and anything Marci left in her room would be too. Grace is closer to your size. Let's see what she has."

"Marci's room. I like the sound of that. You really haven't slept with her, have you?"

"No, I told you that. She's offered."

"Then you're a fool. If she asked me, I'd be all over her."

Aurora decided that while Grace's robes might fit, they were all too frilly, frivolous and delicate. She pointed at the top shelf. "Looks like track suits up there. Grab me a black one. And when you go downstairs, could you turn the Bach up a notch? Good choice, I've always liked Gould's take on the old man. I'll be down in a minute."

"You seem to have recovered."

"I'm faking it, okay? Or, I was faking it before. Or maybe I'm a complete schizo. Take your choice.

Now, beat it. If I strip in front of you, you'll be too turned on to talk."

Christian barely had time to turn up the music before Aurora came downstairs. Grace's tracksuit fit snugly and left her midriff bare. Christian found that more exciting than if she'd been naked. "Coffee?"

"Wimp. I need a drink. Scotch, I suppose. Tequila makes me too wild."

Christian fetched the remainder of the bottle Marci had started, poured Aurora a glass and sat. "I'd gather you've figured out Marci's other identity." Might as well get that out of the way first.

"Firman just confirmed it for me. Cosmo won't be happy. He's in denial. He said there was no way a woman like Freyja Van Deer would hang out with a hireling like you when there are better prospects available--himself, for instance."

"He told you I work for Grace."

"After our first night together, when I was sounding off about all you were going to do for me. I decided it didn't matter, and that, as usual, I had better people sense than him. You're on your way up, and I'm along for the ride. Cheers." She drained her glass. "Good stuff. So, how long you known Freyja?"

"Just met her a few weeks ago."

"Figured as much. I plan to stick close to you, and her. You're what's happening. So, what did you want to talk to me about?" Her green eyes sucked him in. In interview mode, Aurora was compelling. She poured herself another drink.

"Horatio."

"Boring. Next topic." She smiled. The other, more familiar Aurora--almost.

"Maybe, but he's my friend from way back, and feels like you're running roughshod over him."

"And you want me to cut it out. Okay. Done. Next topic?"

"That was about it."

Aurora drained her glass again. "I don't think so." She stood. "What about us? We almost did it on the sidewalk. The floor here is carpeted."

Christian went to her and kissed her. It lacked something. Cameras? A sense of adventure--of doing something forbidden?

Aurora became heavy in his arms and her lips went slack. Christian pulled his head away. Her jaw fell open, and her eyes remained closed. That's what it lacked--a partner who was awake. It was time to put her to bed, not take her.

He carried her upstairs, being careful to not bump her head. If Marci returned on schedule and did come over, she might be less than thrilled to find Aurora in her bed. On the other hand, Grace's room was available and he didn't expect her back any time soon. He wasn't going to put Aurora in his bed, with him. While he didn't think Aurora would object, it didn't feel right.

He arranged Aurora's head on Grace's pillow, covered her, and brought the chair to beside the bed. She'd been having bad dreams, and her behaviour awake had been erratic, so he thought he should keep an eye on her. But if crawling in with her in his room felt wrong, here it was out of the

question. This was Grace's bed. Some things were
sacred.

Chapter Twenty-Two

Christian stayed by the bedside, slumbering, waking occasionally to see Aurora still sleeping peacefully, then nodding off again. Alert in half-sleep for sounds from Aurora, his nap was disturbed by sounds from downstairs instead--the door opening--Marci. He heard her thank someone for helping her with her luggage.

He stood, stretched, tried to work a cramp out of his leg, and went downstairs. Marci came out of the kitchen. She was in jeans and a t-shirt, her normal casual mode.

"You're a sad sight. How's Aurora? Better than you, I hope?"

"Sleeping like an angel. You knew she was here?"

"Two glasses on the table told me it was someone. Other than that, I guessed."

"How was Europe?"

"Fine. You're still dressed, and I don't smell sex. What's going on?"

"It's a long story. How was your flight?"

"Okay, as it turned out. Halfway here, the pilot said we might not be able to land because there was freezing rain in the Noronto forecast. It's a hell of a storm, but it hasn't started freezing yet."

Christian went to the window. It was indeed raining. Below, he could see trees, bent in a high wind. It had been warm the night before. "Quite a change in the weather."

"Quite. Now. What happened last night?" Marci had come up behind him. She put her hands on his shoulders and turned him around.

"Is there any coffee?"

"A whole pot. You left it on. I was about to throw it out."

"I'll drink it."

The coffee was bitter. Christian told Marci about the previous night, and filled her in on the relevant details of what had happened in the week she had been gone. Without the background, his latest adventures with Aurora would have made no sense. Even in context, they didn't--at least not to him.

Marci seemed to have a better grasp on matters. "Sounds like Aurora's having a nervous breakdown. Erratic behaviour, personality switches, lack of inhibition--it all points to that."

"I thought that was just the normal Aurora."

Marci smiled. "If it wasn't overdone, even for her. And she does know I'm Freyja. Good. I can use that." She stood up. "Okay, I'm taking over. You're going to bed."

When Christian woke up later, he heard voices from down the hall, then laughter. He went back to sleep.

When he got up, it was early afternoon. Aurora and Marci were in the living room. He stood at the top of the stairs to listen. Their conversation concerned the career of Freyja Van Deer. Marci was debunking rumours about her alter ego.

The conversation dwindled. "Come down, Christian. We've been waiting for you," Marci called.

Aurora was wearing the bright-red pant suit Grace had worn the day he met her. Considering it hadn't looked large on Grace, it was a surprisingly good fit. The colour did make Aurora look washed-out. Marci had changed into a black power suit that made her look like a successful executive. It was an aspect of her Christian had never seen before.

"You look better." Marci got to her feet. "The weather has let up, so Aurora and I are going out to kick some butt. It should take a couple of hours. Clean yourself up and get something to eat. You'll have things to do when we get back."

Aurora came over to him. "Sorry about last night."

"Quit flirting, Aurora. If you want to screw him later, fine. You'd better use the bathroom before we go. I don't want to stop anywhere for that."

"Yes, Freyja."

Christian was amazed. "You've got Aurora eating out of your hand."

"I've got her doing anything I want. So do you. You'd better figure out what that is. You've got about two hours."

It took a little longer than that but when Marci returned, Christian hadn't decided anything. Marci was alone. "Aurora's in a cab downstairs. She's going to stay at your place for a while. She'll explain." Matters had been decided for him, again.

Marci handed Christian a roll of bills. "Here. Pay the driver, and give him a good tip. We've had him since we left, and it's a lousy day to be driving. Still slippery."

As Christian started past her, Marci stopped him. "Don't hurry back on my account. I'll be here when you do, probably asleep." She pecked his cheek. "You did well last night." She handed him his jacket. "Don't mess up now."

Aurora was in the back seat of the taxi, a suitcase beside her. Her eyes gleamed like they had at times the night before. She smiled a greeting, but didn't say anything. Christian gave the driver his home address. Aurora nestled in beside him. It felt comfortable.

Arriving at his building, Christian found there was another, larger, suitcase in the trunk. It didn't look like she was there for a short stay. They went upstairs.

Aurora sat on his sofa bed. "So, you probably want to know what's going on."

"It would be a nice change."

"I'm on vacation. Marci says I should hide out and recoup."

Aurora told him that when they had left Grace's apartment, they'd gone to her place, packed, and left. While Patsy had keys, she wouldn't sleep there. Then they'd visited The Factory where Marci laid out the facts as she saw them to Cosmo--Aurora was on the verge of a burnout--if he'd had a brain in his head, he'd have seen that himself and done something about it. As it was, he was giving Aurora two weeks off, starting immediately.

206

"Cosmo was overwhelmed," Aurora said. "If she'd told him to jump out the window, he would have. Too bad she didn't."

Their next stop had been Beeble Productions. Kathy had probably called ahead and warned Horatio because he didn't seem surprised to see them. Surprised or not, he didn't fare any better than Cosmo. "Marci shredded him. Told him he should be ashamed of himself for letting me destroy myself trying to make his business viable. That's his job, and when was he going to get off his ass, quit feeling sorry for himself, and do it? Marci's awesome."

"Your hero."

"Yeah, sort of, but I've changed my mind about wanting to be her lover. She's too damn controlling."

"She's a lot like you that way."

"Thanks, but I've got a long way to go to get to her level. In her way Marci¬-Freyja--is as intimidating as Firman."

"She'd be delighted by the comparison."

"She might be. I'll tell you one thing I've figured out, Christian. I'm glad she's on my side, and I'm not going to compete with her. Until I'm sure how you two fit together you'll have to make do with verbal thanks from me."

"That's all I want."

"You don't know what you want."

Christian showed Aurora the little she needed to know about the apartment, and set up his computer so she could use it for her e-mail. "Sorry, my TV doesn't work very well."

"Don't need one. I'm on vacation. For me, TV is work. Okay, where's the nearest grocery store? Your fridge is empty."

"It doesn't work very well either." They went out, and he showed her where she could get food. The neighbourhood made her nervous, so on the walk back, he offered to do deliveries. If she emailed her food order, he'd bring it the next day.

"Could you do me another favour? I may be dropping you, again--at least for the time being--but I won't give up on Judy. I'm beginning to think she may be the one, the woman of my dreams, and I want her to know what's going on. Take her out to dinner and explain it to her, please? Call her now?"

Christian said didn't understand the situation himself, so he didn't see how he could explain anything to Judy, but he'd try. He reserved a table at Chez Celeste, and phoned her. Judy accepted and asked if she could speak with Aurora.

When Christian left, Aurora was telling Judy about the previous night at The Second Circle. If she was going to do that, why he was taking Judy out? It didn't make sense. Christian didn't care. After Aurora and Marci, Judy promised to be light, delightful company. He needed a break himself--maybe that was the idea behind it--Aurora was doing something nice for him. It didn't seem likely.

Chapter Twenty-Three

Forty-five minutes after leaving Aurora, Christian walked into the lobby of The Factory. Kathy had just handed her reception duties over to the next shift and was still there. Uncharacteristically, she was dressed in dark grey, the first time he'd seen her in anything other than black. The smile she shot him put him in mind of a sleek, sensuous shark. She was glad to see him, especially at mealtime.

"Well, if it isn't the man on a mission." And he'd thought he'd been about to get a break from difficult women. As he had the first time he saw her, Christian detected echoes of Lucy in Kathy. Physically, they didn't look at all the same-¬Lucy was all angles, and Kathy, lush plains.

"Good to see you, Kathy."

"Good to see my breasts, maybe." Christian had been trying to avoid her eyes. That was where one similarity with Lucy lay. If Lucy wore grey-blue contacts, their eyes would be the same.

"Seems I was wrong about your friend," Kathy continued. "He's stupid. What's worse, he's a lousy lay."

So Horatio had got that far with her. "You'll have to be patient. He's going through some rough times."

"Who isn't? I just heard I'm supposed to let my roomie go for dinner with you. I suppose that's better than having her hang around with Medici herself. The bitch give you any other instructions?"

"Just to be nice."

"Make sure you don't try to be any nicer to Judy than she wants." If Kathy had been his height, they'd have been nose-to-nose. Her complexion was perfect, and her hair smelled like spring.

"What kind of a man do you think I am?"

"Male. Isn't that bad enough?"

"You'd get along with Marci."

Kathy laughed, and seemed to relax a little. "Freyja? Yeah, I expect so. I wish I could have heard her tear into Cosmo. It must have been beautiful; he hasn't stopped trembling since she left. Judy's getting dressed. Sit and wait."

Christian sat on the couch where he'd waited for Aurora the previous evening, feeling like a student who had just written a difficult exam, and thought he had passed--just. Kathy returned in a few minutes, with Judy. Judy had on a tiny, clinging cream-white dress, almost certainly the one Aurora'd worn home the day Christian met her. It evoked interesting memories, and what's more, suited Judy. Against it, her hair looked flame-red, and her blue eyes even darker.

"Aurora said you liked this dress. We're the same size, you know. We could be twins."

Kathy made a choking sound.

"Kathy doesn't like Aurora," Judy said to Christian, as if confiding a great secret. "I think she's jealous because Aurora's well-known and she's a nobody."

Kathy left without responding.

"I think that hurt her," Christian said.

Judy sighed. "I'm afraid so. She's got to quit treating me like I'm still nineteen. I'm twenty-two now. Sure, she's helped me grow up, but I wish she could see I've done it. I know you can."

"Yes, I can." He most certainly could. "Give her time."

"I have. More than enough." She asked the receptionist to call a taxi. It arrived almost immediately.

"So, how did you meet Kathy?" Christian asked after he'd told the driver where they were going. Then he sat back and listened. Judy talked non-stop, her pique with her apartment-mate seemingly put aside. Kathy had been right. Judy heated up and cooled down quickly.

Judy had met Kathy three years previously. After she finished high school, at seventeen, she'd taken a college diploma in broadcasting. As a recent graduate, she came to Noronto for an interview at COSMO-TV. She'd been nervous. When the receptionist quizzed her, she'd answered, thinking it part of the process.

It might have been. Cosmo had put her in front of a camera, had her read off the teleprompter for a couple of minutes, and then thanked her, saying he'd let her know the next day. She should see the receptionist on her way out.

Kathy had taken her for lunch. "I was so excited, I was talking on a mile a minute, wondering if I'd get the job, what my family would say if I did, and if they'd let me live in Noronto on my own. They live on a farm outside Kitchener and

211

think Noronto is evil and ugly. They don't understand why I like living here."

Judy paused for a breath. "Oh! We're here already? Aurora sounded envious when she told me you were bringing me here. You've never brought her."

Christian paid the driver. "It's hard to take Aurora anywhere. She's the one who does the taking."

Judy smiled. "You sound as cynical as Kathy. I hope I never get as old as either of you."

As had happened in the Westshire, with Aurora, Christian felt everyone in Chez Celeste watching as Judy and he were conducted to their table. Again, he knew it was nothing to do with him... it was his companion. It was a much more comfortable experience, and quite different. This room was all smiles; people took note of Aurora, but they liked Judy. For her part, Judy seemed oblivious to the attention she was drawing.

At the table, Judy continued her story. Christian sat back and looked forward to a dinner at which he could eat and savour his food.

At their lunch, three years previously, Kathy had told Judy that the woman she'd been sharing her apartment with had just moved out. She was looking for someone new to help with the rent. Kathy had already told Cosmo that Judy seemed ideal, as an apartment-mate and as a TV personality. Since Cosmo liked to keep Kathy happy, Judy could consider the job at The Factory hers. And no, whether or not Judy agreed to move in with Kathy didn't factor into that. The job was hers. Period.

"What's Kathy's hold on Cosmo?" Christian asked.

"Her body? You think that might be it?" Judy speared her last snail from its pool of butter and popped it in her mouth. Her eyes twinkled. "He certainly would like it to be, but I guarantee she isn't sleeping with him--never has and never will. She despises him. I think he knows it, but Cosmo relies on Kathy--a lot. She knows what's going on, where everyone is and what they're doing. Getting on her bad side is dangerous. Do that, and you'll find all the nasty little things you'd like to hide becoming public knowledge. Nobody messes with Kathy, not even the boss."

"Aurora does."

"Oh, they snipe at each other, but that's where it stays. In some ways they're too similar to get along. And they always compete when it comes to men. Sometimes I think the only reason Aurora goes after men at all is to annoy Kathy. Aurora much prefers women."

"I knew that. I wondered if you did."

Their entrees arrived. Judy sampled her salmon. "I love fish. I think I could eat it forever." She grinned. The room brightened. "Now don't you go making a 'Kathy' mistake, Christian. I'm not an innocent little girl. Treat me like one, and I'll burst into tears. Then everyone in the room will hate you."

Christian didn't doubt it. She'd put a slightly sharp tone in her voice, and already a couple of

213

people had started to glare. The entire world seemed as protective of Judy as he knew Kathy to be. At the moment she was just playing, but Judy wasn't as unaware of the effect she had on people as he'd thought.

"Of course I know Aurora is courting me." Judy waved her fork in the air. "I've never been interested in women, not that way. I'm open-minded though; I might give her a chance to convince me."

"You're interested in men, that way?"

"Very. But unlike Kathy and Aurora. I'm picky."

"You're looking for a longer term relationship than they are?"

"Why Christian! Is that an offer?"

"No, no... Although..."

"Leave it there," Judy said, interrupting. "I want to concentrate on this lovely fish."

Christian's tenderloin was also worth fuller attention. He didn't ask Judy anything more until dessert. He needed time to readjust his view of her. Like Aurora, on TV Judy played a part. Hers was that of innocence. Again, he'd confused the role with the actor.

They both ordered chocolate cheesecake. "So," Judy's fork hung poised in front of her mouth with the first piece. "Aurora tells me you and Marci aren't an item after all."

"You're asking if I'm available?" Christian asked, attempting to match Judy's teasing. An expression of pure delight came over her face as she tasted Chez Celeste's dessert offering, ignoring Christian's admittedly feeble effort at banter. "I

214

can't speak for Marci," Christian continued. "But to me, Marci's starting to feel more like family, almost like another sister."

"I never would have guessed," Judy glanced at her watch. "Will you look at the time? I hate to eat and run, Christian, but I do need to get to bed. I shouldn't eat this anyway, and I wake up early to be bright for the morning show. If I don't have enough sleep, I sound cranky. Can't have that. Cosmo doesn't pay me to be a bitch."

Christian flagged the waiter and asked for the bill. He winced as he handed over his personal credit card. This had been much more pleasure than business though. It wouldn't be right to charge it to Grace.

In the taxi on the way to Judy's (and Kathy's) apartment, Christian asked Judy a question that had started bothering him somewhere between the appetiser and tenderloin. "If you don't mind my asking, Judy, why are you still doing the weather? You're capable of so much more." Like, for instance, becoming the hostess for Ovation Christian was supposed to be looking for.

"I know. I've had a lot of offers from other stations, including the major networks. I'm biding my time, Christian... waiting for the right offer. I'm aiming for the top. I'm going to get there, but on my terms. I'm certainly not looking to move up at The Factory. That would involve making compromises I just won't make." She shot a meaningful look at the driver. She didn't want to say anything more with someone else around.

Christian dismissed the cab and walked Judy to her (and Kathy's) door. Outside it he asked, "Compromises?"

"You should understand, Christian. I'm like you--I've got principles. If I was willing to spend an hour a week on Cosmo's couch, or under his desk... No thank you. I think it must run in their family-- Aurora thought she could bribe you with her body, didn't she? I could have told her it wouldn't work. I knew the instant I saw you that you were special, a man who couldn't be bought with money, or sex, or anything. You're not for sale. Well, neither am I."

Judy had inched closer as she spoke. A glow that came from more than her body heat spread though Christian. Despite it, he did his best to process what she'd told him. While Judy liked Aurora, even admired her, she saw the flaws. Aurora wasn't her idol.

Christian had a bad feeling he might be though, and knew himself unworthy of that honour. He hadn't so much refused Aurora's offer as changed its terms, delivering Lucy and Horatio instead of Ovation. And while Judy might think he hadn't slept with Marci out of principle, it was, in truth, more a matter of fear and self-preservation.

"Yoo-hoo… Christian?"

"Sorry, I was thinking."

"That's not what you should be doing. Do you want to come in for a while?"

He did, and didn't. He wasn't the man Judy thought him to be. Also, Kathy might be there, or might come back before he left. "I probably shouldn't."

216

Judy stuck out her hand to be shaken. "Then this is good night. Thank you for a lovely dinner, and a most interesting conversation."

When Christian got back to Grace's apartment, he found Marci was already awake--and ready to leave. Inspiration for a painting had come to her in a dream and she wanted to start it before the vision faded. She did stay long enough to hear a quick report of how Christian had helped Aurora settle in, and his dinner with Judy. She stayed, but Christian wasn't sure she paid attention.

Her eyes were turned inward.

The next day, when Christian checked his email, he found Aurora had requested not only food, but also a wide range of toiletries... and Judy. Judy had called Aurora that morning and said she'd like to visit. Considering the neighbourhood, Aurora thought an escort was in order. Christian agreed, and soon found himself making daily visits to his own apartment, with Judy. Aurora claimed to be writing her memoirs in the daytime, and she and Judy would chat about Aurora's storied life while Christian cooked dinner. After dinner he and Aurora would play chess while Judy washed up.

Christian's days were also full. When Marci wasn't busy with her painting, she continued to expose him to culture. In addition to setting reading and listening assignments, she took him to art galleries, the occasional concert, and gave him dancing lessons.

In the two weeks leading up to the big Halloween bash, Christian's life settled into a comfortable routine. Grace remained incommunicado, and Lucy Firman unseen, at least by Christian. Horatio, Christian did see once in a while, but not often. With Aurora away, Horatio was busy learning all he could about Beeble Productions, in an effort to ensure he'd be able to hold his own when Aurora came back. At night, Kathy claimed Horatio's time. Christian avoided Kathy as much as possible.

Chapter Twenty-Four

The afternoon of the Halloween party, Christian was on the couch, reading, when he heard a key in the door. Grace had said she would be back for Cosmo's gala, and Marci was coming over to finally show him his costume and get ready to go. They were the two other people who had keys. This could be either.

Christian hoped it was Grace. He needed to talk to her. Since Judy's revelations regarding Cosmo, Christian had put work-related activities on hold. Finding a hostess for the man felt too much like pimping. He hadn't done much before Judy told him, but for the last two weeks, he hadn't looked at all. He didn't anticipate Grace would be pleased.

It was Marci, not Grace. She put a small suitcase down and turned in the direction of the elevators. "Thanks, Fred. You're a sweetheart."

Christian couldn't see Fred. Marci leaned forward and down, her head and hands leaving Christian's field of view. From the distance she'd bent, Christian assumed she'd kissed the security guard on the forehead. When her hands reappeared, they held two large clothing bags. "Fred gave me a hand with my things." She closed the door. "He insisted."

"I'll bet he did." Marci's coat was unbuttoned. Under it, she had on a thin, form-hugging body suit. "I'm sure he wanted to keep an eye on you."

"I'm perfectly decent, and this is what I'm wearing under my costume." She handed the bags to Christian and hung up her coat. "Well? Open them. You've been bugging me for weeks to show you yours. Today's the big day."

"Like Fred, my mind is on other things." Since the charity ball, Marci had worn only loose clothing. She was all he'd remembered, all he'd dreamed of, whether he wanted to or not--voluptuous, with muscles that rippled--lavish and solid. He also knew that from experience, from having her in his arms during his dance lessons, but seeing--as it was said--was believing. Christian believed.

"Idiot." His forehead got kissed as she went past and took the bags back from him. She draped them over a chair and unzipped one. "This is mine." The contents were long, black, and formless. "And this is yours." Long and brown. "Turn around. I'll put it on you. It goes over your head." The world went dark. It was a robe of some sort. "There. Now pull up the cowl."

"I thought the whole thing was a cowl." He was going to the party as a monk.

"Either way, and don't try to be difficult. You're good enough at that without trying. The hood, if you prefer, pull up the hood." Behind him, her voice sounded muffled. Her costume evidently went over her head as well. His hood was stiff. It came over his head and out well beyond his face on both sides. With it up, his face would be entirely in shadow.

"If I wear it like this, no one will see who I am."

"Yes, that's rather the idea. More for me than for you. You can wear the hood down, if you'd like." Christian would like; with it up, he could only see the world through a tunnel. "I borrowed these from a theatrical company in London, Marci continued. "Cosmo can televise me to his little heart's content now, and no one will know who I am."

Christian turned around. Marci was adjusting a wimple as generous in size as his hood. She was going to the party as a nun. "You think that's why he invited you?"

"I suspect so. In Europe, Freyja Van Deer is well known in the circles Cosmo wants to be accepted in. She's a woman of mystery and a figure of some note."

Marci had handed him a couple of straight lines. Christian decided to leave the 'well known' part alone. "I'd say it's more that she has a figure of some note."

"And you'd be wrong. You forget. I'm a goddess." Marci took off her wimple. "Come here." She flipped back his hood and kissed him, full on the lips. She'd never kissed him like that before. No one had. Fire rushed through his body. Marci became the world.

She pulled back. "We'll take care of you after the party," she said. Her brown eyes were unfathomable. "Aurora tells me you told Judy you think of me as your sister."

Christian took some time processing that. Not only was it was confusing, he couldn't remember quite what he'd said to Judy. He also had no idea how Judy would have translated his words to Aurora. The subject of Marci, or Freyja Van Deer, hadn't been discussed while he'd been with Aurora and Judy at his apartment, so they must have been talking on the phone as well.

"I think I said you were becoming family..." he finally ventured. "Almost as if you were another sister. Almost. You've been talking with Aurora?" If she had, Christian hadn't been aware of that either.

"Every night. After you and Judy are long gone. And if you said 'almost', either Aurora or Judy didn't hear it. It could have been Aurora. She was in rough shape. I'm not a bad therapist, for an amateur. She needed me." Marci paused. Her eyes challenged Christian to ask for details on Aurora's needs.

He didn't need to know. "Well, I do think of you as family," Christian said. "I'm not sure about the sister part."

Marci snorted. "Considering you haven't talked to your real sister since last December, I hope not."

Chapter Twenty-Five

Judy greeted them at the door of The Factory. "Hi, Christian. Thought I'd wait for you here; Aurora said you'd be early. And you must be Freyja. We haven't met, but Aurora's told me all about you." Not while Christian had been present, Aurora hadn't. Most evenings at his apartment Aurora had kept their conversations on her favourite topic... Aurora.

Marci and Judy shook hands and made noises of approval regarding each other's costumes. Judy got the point of Marci's immediately. "Cosmo's going to hate this. He told the cameras to look for a tall, stacked blonde."

For her part, Judy was a convincing vampire. She hadn't worn her usual make-up--without it her skin was pallid, making her deep blue eyes stand out even more. Two long teeth protruded over her lower lip and a black cloak tapered to flatter her figure. That was all the costume she needed. "Aurora's inside, fussing about the broadcast. Come on, you've got to see her!" She skipped ahead in most unvampirelike manner. Marci and Christian followed in more serene style, as befitted their vestments.

The area normally partitioned into the Bull's Eye newsroom and several other studios had been opened into one large room and decorated for Halloween. Since they were among the first to arrive, the few people present looked lost in the space. Marci and Christian caught up to Judy.

"Now where is she? How could she possibly hide in that getup? Aha! There she is. Hey, Bo-peep!" What had been a flash of white in the middle of a cluster of black-clad, cable-laden technicians became Aurora.

She stopped, turned to give last minute instructions, and then continued towards them. Christian admired the way her short, frilly frock bounced, alternately revealing and hiding her toned thighs. "Ah yes, the Brother and Sister act. Judy, would you take over for me? All they need to do now is set the mike to the right height for me and check sound levels. Cosmo wants a word with these two."

"That's an interesting costume." Unmistakably, she was Little Bo-Peep, the schoolgirl shepherdess, complete with lacy cap.

"Don't think it was my choice. I was away, so someone picked it for me." She glared at Judy. "Someone my size--who has a perverted sense of humour."

"You love it, Aurora. Admit it. Pardon me folks, I've got to go and pretend to be Aurora." Judy sucked in her cheeks and affected a sour look. "What's the matter? You stupid? It goes there! Where's my spotlight? Not bright enough. Another!" She had Aurora's voice down pat. Christian doubted it was the first time she'd done it. She swaggered away with an exaggerated swinging motion.

"I think I liked it better when she was scared of me," Aurora said as she and Christian watched Judy's exit with interest.

Marci coughed behind her wimple. "Cosmo wants to see us?"

"In his office. He's waiting to make a grand entrance later on. And before you see his costume, no... I didn't tell him how you were coming dressed. As luck would have it, you'll fit right in with him--in a way."

Cosmo was in magnificent red and white robes, topped by a tall hat. As they entered his office, he hung up the phone and rose. "By the authority vested in me, I release you both from your vows."

Marci moved to the couch, sat, and stretched lazily. "You can't. You're only a Cardinal."

Cosmo sighed. "I know. I hoped you didn't. I couldn't find papal robes my size." He turned to Christian and Aurora, who were still standing by the door. "Christian, I have a new task for you. My problem child is leaving The Factory."

"Damn right I am." Aurora put her hands on her hips. "I'm tired of you pushing me down. It'll be a pleasure not seeing your fat little face every day."

"She thinks she's going to be a rock star." Cosmo sighed. "At her age, one would think she'd have more sense. She doesn't, so I'll need someone to cover her beat. At least she's responsible enough to say she won't leave until I find a replacement."

"You managed without me for two weeks."

"And missed some big stories."

"Nonsense, Cosmo dear. We don't cover events, we create them. Anyway, we had this argument this morning." Aurora hadn't made any move to sit. Christian thought he would so he could watch the fight from the sidelines rather than the

225

ring. He started towards the couch. Aurora grabbed his hand.

Marci produced a demonstrative yawn and shifted position, revealing a shapely ankle. Cosmo's eyes fastened to it.

"You already have the perfect person on staff." Since no one else was talking, he should. Cosmo didn't respond. Christian waited.

Aurora cleared her throat. Cosmo tore his eyes from Marci. "Well? I do? Out with it, man. I can't see who it is."

"Judy."

"Judy? Nice girl. Too nice to fit into Aurora's shoes."

"Screw off, Unc." Aurora dragged Christian towards Cosmo. "You're wrong, as usual. Judy can handle herself, and she's smart. She's been smart enough to avoid you, isn't she? Isn't that the real problem?"

"No, it isn't. It's that Judy's good for fluff, nothing more. A cute little thing like that? How could anyone take her seriously?"

Aurora tensed. Christian prepared to hold her back. Cosmo either didn't see how angry Bo-Peep was, or trusted Christian to protect him, because he continued--and pushed it too far. "Bet you're suggesting her just so you can seduce her yourself, aren't you?"

Christian released Aurora's hand. Slap! Cosmo's Cardinal hat went flying.

"Enough!" A flurry of black sailed between them... Marci. "Cosmo, they're right, sort of, and you're wrong." She ran a hand down Cosmo's cheek

226

and rested it on his neck. "I think we should discuss your attitude towards women. Christian, you take care of Aurora. I'll take care of Cosmo."

Christian scooped Aurora from the floor and carried her out of her uncle's office, into the hall. She didn't struggle. He took her to the elevators and pushed the button.

"I'm okay. You'll notice I didn't hit him, just his stupid hat. You can put me down."

Christian set her on her feet, careful to stay between her and her uncle's office. The elevator arrived.

"I hadn't thought of Judy for hostess." Aurora sounded thoughtful. "But you're right. I hope you know I'd never try and bribe Judy to get her into bed."

"Wouldn't work, would it?"

The elevator left. "Not a chance. If she only looked at me like she looks at you."

"The way she looks at me?"

Aurora reached behind and pushed the elevator button. "She's in love with you. Don't tell me you didn't know."

Okay, he wouldn't, but he hadn't--until that moment. Love? Maybe Judy thought so... he didn't. "She's infatuated, maybe?" The elevator arrived.

Aurora smiled. "It's a subtle difference. Go for it. Worry about that later."

Christian had never seen Aurora's eyes shine such a verdant green. "No. It wouldn't be fair." The elevator left.

"Why? She wants you, and you want her." Aurora pushed the button again. The elevator

arrived. "And life isn't fair. Or hadn't you noticed?"
This time they got in.

Chapter Twenty-Six

The party room had filled to about half its capacity: ghosts, ersatz film stars, witches, cartoon characters and assorted other beings stood in clusters. Aurora had to get back to work. Perhaps it was only that she wanted to make sure things were set up to make her look good on the air, but Christian thought for someone so eager to leave The Factory Aurora sounded amazingly concerned with its well-being. Left on his own, he roamed deeper into the room, looking for someone he knew.

Horatio and Kathy were in a corner, dressed as vagabonds in tatters of black and grey. Kathy's costume suited her, but if Horatio was a bum, he was the King of Bums. Such was his curse. Even in rags he couldn't help looking elegant.

"Hi, Kathy, Horatio."

Horatio mumbled a response. Kathy was more eloquent. "Having a good time? I'm not."

"It's early. At any rate, I'm glad I found you, Kathy. Aurora's too busy to be a good liaison. You're right though, this is dull. Who are these people?"

"Christian, meet the great, unwashed public. Public, Christian. They're waiting to be entertained. So far, pretty much all that's showed up are contest winners, viewers who were promised a chance to rub shoulders with the great. The great, such as they are, will condescend to appear in their own good time. Of course, now you've brought Aurora back, she's the main draw." Kathy's eyes travelled in the direction Aurora had gone. A crowd had formed around her. "If you'll both excuse me, I'm going to go and spread vicious rumours."

"She likes you," Horatio said as Kathy went towards where the drinks were being served. "That's more than she's said to me all night." On the other side of the room, Aurora took the stage with an impressive flash of legs. She talked to the disc jockey and the music became louder and livelier. She left the stage, wading back into her admirers.

"So, how are things with you?" Horatio continued. Christian moved closer so he could hear. "Haven't seen much of you lately."

"I've been busy. Figured you were too. How are things at Beeble Productions?"

That got Horatio going. He'd been busy too. He outlined all he had done, all he had learned about his new business. Much of what he said got lost in the music. The gist was that it was going better and that was enough to know. Christian wasn't interested in the details.

The music went up another notch and shifted to a throbbing, dance beat. Horatio and Christian moved nearer the door where it was quieter and Horatio continued to talk. Christian continued to pretend to listen while he watched the people. Marci returned, with Cosmo. Immediately, Cosmo drifted away from her, deeper into the room. He seemed so dazed, Christian almost felt sorry for the man. He remembered being on the receiving end of a blast from Marci, and Cosmo looked like she'd given him both barrels. Marci saw them and came over.

"It's settled. He'll give Judy a chance. Good evening, Horatio. Christian, you should find Judy and give her the news. Horatio and I need to talk about Aurora." She'd put Cosmo in his place, now it was Horatio's turn.

Christian suspected Aurora was the last thing Horatio wanted to talk about, or perhaps the second last. Neither her name nor Kathy's had passed Horatio's lips in ten minutes of monologue. Or, if they had, Christian hadn't heard. That was possible.

As far as Christian knew, the only time Marci and Horatio had met was when Marci had chewed him out for allowing Aurora to push herself too hard. The nervous way Horatio shuffled from foot to foot in front of the stern nun Marci had become confirmed that he expected the worst. Or perhaps childhood memories were haunting him; Christian remembered Horatio's family was Roman Catholic. Christian attempted a reassuring smile before leaving to look for Judy.

More people had arrived and vampires were a popular item. Christian figured that was due to The Factory being close to the financial district--there were probably a lot of stockbrokers present, and lawyers. As the morning weather personality, Judy should have a considerable following of her own. She was short though and would be hard to spot, despite her red hair. Christian concentrated on the larger swarms and found the evening news anchor, a faded country and western diva, Aurora's scruffy guitar-playing friend, and near the stage, Aurora.

Aurora pushed her way to Christian. "Come on, Cosmo's talking to someone you should see." She led him past a couple of security guards protecting a roped-off area beside the stage. Behind the speakers, it was much quieter. Cosmo was there, with a man dressed as Julius Caesar. Beside them stood Cleopatra, Cleo Wong, his (or formally his) Cleo.

Christian had seen her Cleopatra of the Nile costume before, in fact he'd seen it every Halloween they'd been together. She'd had it specially made, tailored to hug her figure, saying when one had the name and body, one should flaunt them. Christian's first impression was that Cleo looked exactly as always; his second was that she was no Aurora, much less a Marci. She didn't wear her body as well--it was just another costume. She and Cosmo were talking, with Caesar standing silently by. Cosmo's eyes were on Cleo's scant cleavage; hers were on Cosmo's eyes, watching him watch her.

Aurora tapped Cleo's arm, gave Christian a peck on the cheek and left. Cleo swivelled. "Christian! It's been far too long." She slithered towards him, stopped short and blew him an air kiss. "I'd like you to meet Irving Spratt."

They shook hands. "I understand congratulations are in order," Christian said.

"Yes, it was difficult, but I finally got the development resolution passed. I hope I can count on your support when I run for mayor." Irving pumped Christian's hand enthusiastically.

232

Christian had a vague idea what Irving was talking about. He was a member of city council, and there had recently been a long debate regarding whether a block of historic buildings should be torn down and replaced by skyscrapers. It had got the go-ahead by a one-vote margin.

"I was congratulating you on your marriage," Christian said. "I don't care about politics." Irving dropped Christian's hand. "You're a lucky man," Christian continued. He wasn't so sure about that, but it was what one said.

"I thought he was somebody important," Irving said to Cleo.

"He is." Cleo closed the gap between herself and Christian. "Among other things, he's the best lover I've ever had." She put her hands on Christian's hips and tilted her head up for a kiss.

Christian removed Cleo's hands and stepped back, holding them. "That was years ago. You're married. Besides, you don't do a thing for me anymore." It was only a small lie.

"I'm sorry, Christian. I can understand you'd still feel hurt. I was wrong about you."

"And I was wrong about you. We all make mistakes." He offered Irving one of Cleo's hands. "Here. She's your mistake now."

To Christian's surprise, Irving laughed. "It's an open marriage, lad. People like their politicians married and she'll help me win the ethnic vote. Go ahead, if you're interested."

"I'm not, but I think Cosmo is. Good to see you again, Cleo." It had been. Any vague thought of getting back with her that had remained was gone.

Christian went back through the security cordon and into the crowd. He didn't continue looking for Judy, heading for the door instead. He needed air.

Since he wasn't looking now, he did find Judy, in the lobby by the reception desk, signing autographs and chatting with fans. "Hi again, Christian. Pardon me, folks. Business calls." She dealt with half a dozen more people before breaking free. "Let's go somewhere quiet." That proved to be the well of a staircase on the far side of the elevators.

The door closed behind them. "Freyja told me about my new duties. Then she and Kathy went back to the party. They're so much like each other. I just know they're going to be friends." Marci and Kathy similar? Christian hadn't considered it, but Judy had a point. Both were unforgiving and had a vicious streak. "I'm so happy," Judy continued. "Now, finally, I understand why you didn't come in with me after our date."

"Date?"

"When you took me for dinner, silly. You were working on winning me a higher profile here and getting involved with me would compromise your integrity."

Christian looked up the stairs, and then down. Help didn't come from either direction. He hadn't gone in largely because he'd been scared of Kathy. Now he had another reason. He didn't want to hurt Judy. Aurora had said that he should go for it... she would. But she'd also said she thought Judy might

234

be the love of her life. Christian liked Judy, but didn't think she could be the love of his.

"Yes, it wouldn't look right." Agreeing with Judy's theory was the easiest way out.

"No, it wouldn't. That's why I'm going to turn the offer down." She removed her false vampire teeth. "There. Now there isn't any reason you shouldn't kiss me."

Except Kathy, and his conscience. Christian was tempted, but in his crude way, Cosmo had been right. "Fluff" was too harsh, but while the real Judy wasn't as innocent as her TV persona, she wouldn't hold his interest for long. She waited, lips pursed.

"I think we should get to know each other better." He knew that wouldn't work.

It didn't. "That's the idea, Christian. The instant I saw you, I knew you were the one... and I've noticed the way you look at me."

With lust. "Yes, but I'm still involved with Aurora." It was the best he could do on the spur of the moment. There was some truth to it. Aurora had felt good in his arms earlier--her hard body encased in lace and silk.

"Aurora?" Judy's laugh echoed in the stairway hollows. "I thought you understood. Lover, you just don't have what it takes to keep her happy--wrong genitals. I'll talk to her. Come on, we can get this settled tonight."

Judy put her fangs back in. It was a respite for Christian, nothing more.

It took ten minutes to cross the lobby. Judy kept getting stopped and wouldn't brush people off--she smiled, chatted and signed her name. Finally, they arrived at the door in to the party. The room was packed, which muffled the music where they were, but Christian could tell that deeper in it would be deafening. He stepped inside ahead of Judy.

"There you are. We've been waiting for you." Marci's voice cut through the racket. "We sent Horatio to search the room, in case you'd slipped by." She pushed Christian back into the lobby. Out of the corner of his eye, Christian saw Kathy give Judy the same treatment.

"You have no idea how happy I am to see you."

"Bet I do. Kathy filled me in on Judy's fantasies. Don't worry, you're safe from her, for now. I've got other plans for you tonight. Oh shit, no time to talk." Marci was looking behind Christian, at the door to The Street. "Lucy and entourage have arrived. Kiss me."

The kiss wasn't the least bit like the one at Grace's apartment. There was no passion--this was stagecraft. This time Marci was working on Lucy's illusions, not his. Lucy had assumed Marci was functioning in her professional capacity as Freyja Van Deer and been hired by Grace to be Christian's companion. That explained the skilful hand in the pocket of his robe.

"Oh ho, and ho ho ho. Elf, get out the naughty-or-nice list." Lucy was directly behind Christian. From her words, he could only assume she'd come dressed as Santa.

He turned, his arm around Marci's waist. This wasn't a Santa for children. Lucy wore the stocking cap and curly white hair to her shoulders. Her suit was a loose red tunic that hung over her ample breasts, leaving their bottoms visible. Her tights were also red, but her eyes were burnished gold. This Santa would be rated X.

"Evening, Lucy. I must say red is your colour." Christian felt Marci quake on his arm--with laughter, not fear.

"I've always favoured it. Your companion's name please? Can't keep the elf waiting."

Eunice had a pen poised over a little black book. Her elf costume was brown, and heavily padded. Apparently, she was boiling in it--a sheen of sweat covered her face.

"I'm Freyja Van Deer. I know who you are."

"Of course you do. And have you been naughty, or nice?"

"I've always considered that a false dichotomy."

"Put her on both sides, elf. Christian, might I have a word with your friend in private?"

Marci squeezed Christian's waist to tell him that was fine. He moved back a couple of steps.

Lucy's entourage, as Marci had called it, seemed to consist of Eunice and Patsy, who was probably supposed to be Rudolph, judging from the antlers and nose. He was carrying a large sack.

Two others might be with Lucy--Christian wasn't sure. Several feet back, on either side of the door, stood two spies... each in the traditional trench coat, wide-brimmed hat and sunglasses. Apart from that, they were far from a matched pair. The one on the left was a hulk, built like Horatio but several inches taller. His trench coat was buttoned up. It barely fit, and was stained and greasy.

His partner was a spy with style. Her crisp coat hung open, displaying a figure as impressive as Lucy's. More so--the spy's shoulders and rib cage seemed designed to support her magnificent breasts--Christian had always thought Lucy's looked like they'd been glued on, even though he'd seen firsthand that they weren't. The smaller spy slipped designer sunglasses down an aristocratic nose, winked at Christian, and pushed them back up. Her eyes were so pale as to be colourless. When she grinned, her face was a study in mischief. She knew she'd hooked Christian. He did too and hoped against hope that she would decide to reel him in.

"So, is she another candidate to become your sister?" Judy asked. There were tears running down her face.

"Never seen her before."

"But I bet you will. And that you'll break her heart too, you... you cad!"

Christian closed his eyes and braced for a slap. It never came. He opened them in time to see Judy disappearing in the direction of the stairwell. He started after her.

"Don't." Kathy caught his arm. "Freyja tells me you're not as dumb as you come across. Prove it by not following."

"But she's wrong about Marci and me." There was no need to complicate matters further by mentioning the smaller spy.

"So? She's wrong about you and herself too, isn't she? See… two wrongs can make a right."

238

"But someone should make sure she's okay."

"Not you. I'll go talk to her."

"I'll go with you." Marci was back from her meeting with Lucy.

"Sure that's a good idea?" From her tone, Kathy didn't think so.

"Yes. It might help her to know she's not the only one who hasn't had any luck with him. I've given up, for now. She should too. By the end of the night, she'll see Christian and Aurora still have something going. He'll be leaving with her."

"I will?" That was news to Christian.

"He will?" Kathy asked. News to her too, evidently.

"Reindeer! Why are you standing around? Give out the gifts!" Lucy's voice filled the lobby. "A handful for Christian's other blonde."

Patsy scuttled over, and shoved a fistful of tickets into Kathy's hands. She glanced at them. "Free passes to The Second Circle. Good. Horatio never takes me anywhere interesting."

"Sure that's a good idea?" Marci asked, gravely.

"Tell you what. I'll live my life my way, you live yours... yours, okay?"

Christian took a step backward, away from Kathy and Marci. Judy had misjudged another relationship, and been right about it at the same time. Yes, Kathy and Marci were similar--far too similar. They were two piranha who had agreed, for the time being, to pretend there was a sheet of glass between them. Christian didn't want to be in the middle when they changed their mind about the glass.

Eunice tugged his robe. "Pardon me? Boss wants another word with you."

That would get him further from the stare-down. Christian turned and saw Lucy had moved to a couch. She was watching Kathy and Marci with evident interest.

"Don't you want to sit on Santa's lap?" Lucy asked when Christian stayed well away from her. "Or would you rather she sit on yours?"

"I think I've got enough problems at the moment, thanks."

"Yes, having all these women in love with you must be such a trial. You can't help it, you know. Any woman you want is bound to love you. Even Freyja, it would seem. I'm impressed."

"Are you in love with me?" She'd made an outrageous statement. It only seemed fair to ask an unreasonable question in return.

"Of course, but then, I love everybody."

"And everybody loves you in return. It's been pleasant, as always, but I really should get back..."

He'd been about to say to Marci and Kathy, but they were gone. The only ones left in the lobby were Lucy and himself, Eunice and the smaller spy. Patsy was by the door to the party, handing out coupons to people inside while keeping a nervous eye on Lucy.

"I should get back to the party." That was an even better idea. Grace might have slipped in while he was busy elsewhere; he needed to see her, now more than ever. He got up from the couch.

"And I should get to it." Lucy also stood. "Don't bother looking for Grace though. She's not here yet."

"You're sure?" Christian asked.

"Oh yes, I always know where Grace isn't."

Chapter Twenty-Seven

Christian threaded though the press of bodies, aiming for the stage. If Grace wasn't at the party yet, he had other business. Marci had said he was going to leave with Aurora. If so, Little Bo-Peep should have told him. Or at the very least, given him a hint. She hadn't. It was becoming clear that there was a great deal he didn't know.

Until earlier that day, he hadn't known Aurora and Marci had seen anything of each other since two weeks earlier, when Marci set up Aurora's vacation at his apartment. He'd talked with both of them every day in-between, and neither had mentioned the other's name, except in passing. Now, it seemed that not only had they been spending late evenings and perhaps nights together, they also were in cahoots.

He was only a few feet away from breaking through onto the dance floor when the music stopped. There was silence, and then a squeal of feedback. Aurora stepped onto the stage.

"Thank you for your patience. Our technical problems have been ironed out, and the news starts in fifteen minutes. You all know The Barely Cool Laddies." She waved her hand at the musicians filtering onto the stage behind her. The scattered applause was mixed with jeers. "They'll be playing through the news, and after. When we're live from here, the volume will go down. Please, just keep on dancing. Be cool. Tonight, you're all insiders.

Welcome to show business!" The crowd cheered for itself.

A man darted from offstage and whispered in Aurora's ear. "Oh yes, and please remember Bull's Eye News is a family show. Which means blood and gore is okay, but those of you in the X-rated costumes, especially the giant penises and tampons and the like--you know who you are--will be expected to keep out of camera range. Dance at the back, okay?"

The man who had whispered made circular motions with his hand. Aurora gave him a friendly wave. "I'm being told I'm hogging the stage. You all know I wouldn't do that." There was laughter, mixed with hooting and wolf whistles. "Thank you, thank you. But I already have a date." More laughter, some booing. "Okay, one last thing. After Bull's Eye, the cameras will be on for occasional bits broadcast on VideoView, but big dancing dicks are okay there. Have a great party!"

Aurora had shouted her last words. Before their echo died, the band cut loose. Aurora tossed the microphone to the singer and walked off. If the news was that close, Christian probably should wait until after to talk with her. He glanced around to see if anyone he knew was in sight. Cleo was coming towards him, a knowing smile on her face. She hadn't taken no for an answer, and wanted to dance with him, like they had in the old days.

Christian had sudden, uncomfortable memories of things Cleo liked to do at parties while in her Cleopatra costume. She'd had hidden slits specially built. It was amazing what two people could do on a dance floor while everyone pretended not to notice. Christian looked around again, frantically. There had to be someone else he knew in the vicinity. Anyone.

The shapely spy was behind him, to one side. Her partner wasn't in sight. Christian tried to catch where her eyes would be behind the sunglasses, and then glanced at the dance floor. He attempted an inquisitive Marci eyebrow lift.

The spy touched her hat in salute, grinned and accepted. The band was playing a fast number and she danced with enthusiasm. Her glasses slipped down her nose and her eyes met his. Christian still couldn't decide what colour they were, other than pale. Her eyebrows were almost white. The song ended and the singer announced a slow tune to lead into the news. Christian stepped towards her, but she held up a hand in a stop sign and, twitching her head, used the brim of her hat to point behind him.

Christian turned to look. Marci. He looked back. His former dance partner was nowhere to be seen. Hat and all, she'd disappeared.

Marci danced the slow number with him. She was the perfect height to dance and talk with-- holding each other close, both their heads could rest on a shoulder.

"Who is she?"

"No idea."

"Her partner followed Kathy and me." Marci led, and danced them to the corner furthest from the stage. "Maybe she's keeping an eye on you."

"Worse things could happen." Christian felt Marci chuckle. "How's Judy?" he asked.

"She'll survive. I convinced her you and I aren't an item--as if it's any of her business. I left her with Kathy. They're welcome to each other."

"What happened with Lucy?" That seemed a safer topic, and he did want to know.

They arrived at the outer edge of the dance floor. Even in her nun costume, Marci was keeping well away from the cameras. Christian had long since thrown back the cowl on his. "She offered me a job. Triple what Grace pays me, with a big bonus if I keep you around."

"What did you tell her?"

"That three times nothing is nothing, and I don't work for anyone but myself."

The slow song ended and a faster one began. Marci and Christian separated. Over the heads, Christian saw Aurora in a small clear patch of floor, microphone in hand. Horatio and Kathy, and Cleo and Irving, were dancing near her broadcast location. Aurora moved to Cleo and Irving and started to talk to them. Marci bumped into him and Christian switched his attention back to her.

Marci's eyes flickered to one side as she twitched a brow. Christian casually turned his head the indicated direction--the voluptuous spy and her associate were dancing on very edge of the floor. They looked like a couple on a blind date that couldn't be over too soon

Marci guided their course towards them as another slow number started. Christian moved to take Marci into his arms once more, but she slipped away and turned to face the hulk. She put a hand on the huge man's shoulder and gave him a look that was pure promiscuity. Without waiting for an answer, she glided into his arms. He co-operated. That she seemed small and delicate in his grasp gave Christian further appreciation of the man's size--and Marci's acting ability.

He felt sudden, stinging pain in his right shin and, looking down, met light eyes over pushed down sunglasses. Her hands were on her generous hips, and her expression said she wouldn't be ignored. As she drew her foot back for another kick, Christian bowed in acknowledgement, asking her to dance.

Her hat hit his chest as she moved into his arms. She removed it, revealing a puff of platinum blond curls, and nestled her head sideways on his chest, her ear just below his heart. She wasn't as short as she'd seemed next to her spying partner-- Aurora's height, perhaps. Christian had no difficulty dancing with her. She fit, although in a quite different manner than Marci, with no question of them talking. That didn't bother him. The way she pressed against him communicated all he wanted to know for the moment.

The band shifted to an upbeat tempo. Christian tried to let her go, but she didn't release him. They danced three fast numbers with a rhythm independent of that set from the stage.

A hand clamped onto his shoulder. "The newscast has been over for five minutes," Marci said in his ear. "Judy talked to Aurora, saw you, and headed for the exit. I wouldn't blame you if you didn't go after her."

246

Christian reluctantly pried himself loose. Marci might not blame him, but he would. The spy jammed her hat back onto her head and stood rigid, her face a study in fury, then turned and stalked into the crowd.

As Christian manoeuvred towards the lobby, dodging drunken witches and partying ghosts, his regret at leaving his mystery woman increased. Judy had a head start. He probably wouldn't catch up with her, and even if he did, why did he want to? It wasn't his fault she was upset; he hadn't encouraged her, had he? He bumped a ghoul and almost spilled its drink, made the ritual motions of apology, and then looked around to see if he could spot his spy.

After a few minutes, he gave up. Even if he did find her, she'd made her displeasure clear. And he couldn't have stayed with her--he knew that--not after Marci had told him about Judy. No, it wasn't his fault, but still, Judy felt hurt. Maybe if he explained again that he did like her, but not in the way she wanted him to, it might sink in. No, probably not, but he had to try, if he found her. He looked back at the ghoul. It shrugged and downed its drink.

Christian wound a desultory path towards the lobby. Unless fans had caught her again, Judy would be long gone. He pushed through a phalanx bunched by the door and into the lobby. Judy was there--with a clown.

"Grace?" Christian asked. No one else carried a purse that colour and size. Her face was painted white with grotesque wide red lips, and she was

247

wearing a traditional polka-dot clown suit, with a drooping hat, white gloves and floppy shoes. No unpainted skin showed. She was unrecognisable--except for the purse.

"She was waiting here." Judy enunciated each word carefully like someone who was borderline drunk and pretending otherwise. "She knew who I am and introduced herself. How can a rat like you have such a nice mother?"

"She's not... I mean, I'm not sure--just lucky, I guess." Grace gave him a thumbs-up for a quick recovery. Encouraged, he continued. "Mom's always let me make my own mistakes. Then she patches them up." Grace's clown lips frowned. Yeah, that had been a little much. "Most of the time she can't, of course."

"Well I should think not. You were almost having sex with that tramp, right in front of me!" Judy advanced on him. Tramp? Kathy was the tramp. Oh, the spy. Behind Judy, Grace grinned in a manner reminiscent of said spy.

"You talked to Aurora?" When you can't defend, deflect.

"Oh yes, she said you got turned on by the way I look on television, but once you met me, you didn't want me anymore."

"But I do like you." Had Aurora said that, or was this Judy's interpretation? Not that it wasn't true--in some ways.

"So, what you're saying is that if you weren't so terribly fond of me, then you'd screw me?"

Grace was having a great time. Safely out of Judy's line of sight, her painted grin was off the sides of her face and she was doing a clown soft-shoe shuffle. Thanks, Mom. Now what? Everything he said got him in deeper.

"No, Judy." Aurora's voice came from behind him. "I was interrupted and you left before I finished. His problem with you is that you think you love him. Me, I think he's a rat's ass, but he's a good lay." She came up beside Christian and wrapped an arm around his waist. "Of course, it could also be that he knows that after having me, you'd be a real disappointment."

Judy swung a roundhouse. Aurora let go of Christian, caught Judy's arm and ended up behind her, half hugging and half restraining her. "You've got a long way to go, little girl."

Judy went slack and Aurora let go. Judy spun. Slap! "Not as far as you think, bitch." She turned and marched out of The Factory.

Aurora shook her head to clear it. "Well, at least she used an open hand the second time. Should someone go after her?"

"Neither of you, that's for sure." Grace shuffled up to Aurora. "Even if she did pull both her punches. She likes you, Aurora. Don't worry, she'll be fine, now she's heard the truth--or a reasonable approximation." Grace started for the door in to the party. "Come on, kids. I've got to see Lucy and Cosmo, and meet Marci. No time to waste."

They caught up with her at the door. "I miscalculated," Grace lifted a size twenty-five foot. "I'll never make it through the crowd with these shoes."

249

"Cosmo and Marci were both near the front, last I saw of them." Aurora was in 'all-business' mode. "We can take a back route. Follow me." She started for a side door.

Grace flopped along beside Christian. She reached into her purse. "Here. Stick this in your robe. You should have an inside pocket." She handed him a thick envelope. "That's a bonus for finding Marci, and another for pointing out the redhead to Cosmo. If he's too slow to see her quality, it'll be his loss. Some extra expense money too... and your credit card slip from when you took our little flame to Chez Celeste. Uri rightly refused to send it in. You got everyone started talking about you again that night. It was good work. So it was pleasure too... so what? What did I tell you your job was?"

"To find a hostess for Cosmo's new channel?" There was indeed a pocket in the robe. The envelope barely fit.

"Oh, quit playing stupid," Grace said, as close to anger as Christian had ever heard her. Aurora looked back, either to check that they were still behind her in the maze of corridors she was leading them through, or in response to Grace's raised voice.

"Sorry. You want me to get known around Noronto."

"And tonight should help too. You should have seen the ears at the door bending to hear that little scene. It'll be all over town tomorrow. By the time tongues finish wagging, they'll have it that the redhead knocked Aurora out cold." Aurora looked

250

back again. "We're fine, dear," Grace called. "Just having a private word or two."

"Can I trust Aurora?" Christian asked quietly.

"Can she trust you? You have to make up your own mind about people, son. You will anyway. Offhand, I'd say you can trust Aurora to be Aurora."

Aurora came back to them. "Okay, we're here. The next door is to the backstage dressing rooms. Finished talking behind my back, or do you need another minute?"

"I was just telling Grace I may be falling in love with you." Okay, it was a lie, but it was also the truth.

"Yeah, you might be that stupid. Come on. Grace said she was in a hurry."

"I'll wait here," Grace said. She hopped onto a desk. "You can bring the people to me." She pulled out some balls from her purse and started to juggle. "Marci first. Go get her, Christian."

Chapter Twenty-Eight

Christian made his way through the dressing room area and rejoined the party. Cosmo's VIP sanctuary had filled. Anyone who was someone seemed to find it preferable to the crush of the room.

Cosmo was there, of course, talking with Horatio and Irving Spratt. His eyes, however, were fixed on where Lucy stood with Cleo and an assortment of other scantily clad females.

A number of the celebrities were signing autographs at a table that bordered the public area. Patsy stood beside it, still handing out free passes to The Second Circle. Eunice was there too, apparently noting names in the "naughty-and-nice" book. Kathy was behind the bar, helping out and helping herself. But Marci was the one Grace wanted to see, and she wasn't in sight. Christian went to look for her; he had a feeling where she'd be.

He found her where he'd expected... at the back of the dance floor, again wrapped in the leviathan's arms. Christian grabbed her shoulder, much as she had his earlier. "Grace would like to talk with you," he said into her ear. She broke away, and flowed into Christian's arms. Her former dance partner stood for a moment, glared at Christian, turned and walked away.

"I see you've still got your tail." Marci had rested her head on his neck. Christian felt as much as heard her voice.

He swung them around in time to glimpse a short, hatted figure vanishing into the crowd. "She found me again," he said to Marci's ear.

"Bet she never lost you. Grace would be backstage?" Marci pulled away from him as easily as she had from the oversized spy, making any answer other than a nod impossible.

Behind the security cordon, the sound level was more tolerable. Kathy had seen Christian and Marci approaching, and confronted Christian as soon as they were clear of the guards. "I hear you think Judy would be no damn good in bed." Kathy's breath was rye whisky.

The rumour was already garbled, as was Kathy. Christian grasped her shoulders to steady her. "I didn't say any such thing. Aurora did, sort of."

"You're drunk, Kathy."

"And you're a goddamn whore, so what?"

"Half right, I hope," Marci said, almost to herself. Then louder, "Christian, maybe we should bring Kathy. Get her out of public before she embarrasses herself."

It might be a little late for that, but Marci had a point. "Maybe Horatio will take care of her," Marci added. Christian wasn't sure of that. When Horatio had seen Christian and Marci coming off the dance floor, he also had started in their direction. By the time he'd noticed Kathy join them, it had been too late for him to pretend he'd been going elsewhere. He stayed an arm's length away. No, things weren't going well with those two.

"I'd rather go with you." Kathy leaned heavily on Christian as the four of them made their way to the door. Maybe he'd find a chance to pass her off.

Aurora met them inside. "Grace sent me to get Cosmo. Nice lady--never really talked with her before. What's with Kathy?"

"I'm drunk." She had the slur back in her voice.

"Not half as much as you're making out. Forget it. He's going home with me."

"Stupid dyke bitch."

"Slut," Aurora answered, pleasantly. "Horatio, she's all yours, you poor beggar." She held out a hand to Christian; he disengaged from Kathy and took it.

"I'm a hobo," Horatio answered. "Not a beggar... oh, you weren't referring to the costume." He took a half step towards Kathy and stopped. Christian thought that wise, if a tad cowardly. Kathy wasn't having any trouble standing on her own, and was clearly unhappy with Horatio, Aurora, and the world in general.

***

Grace was juggling seven balls when they walked through the door. She looked at her visitors through the blur of her swiftly moving orbs without missing a beat. "Now, who have we here? You're Marci, no doubt about that. Take off that foolish costume, child."

"Thank you, Grace. It's far too hot." Marci pulled off the wimple and shook out her cascade of golden hair. She pulled her habit over her head. Her black body suit was everything Christian remembered. Horatio hadn't seen it before, or seen

254

Marci in anything that wasn't severe. His jaw dropped to the ground. Kathy quickly moved to him and clamped onto his arm.

"And who else do we have here?" Grace seemed to be paying full attention to the people... without missing a catch or throw. "Kathy, I recognize you. After all, you're the heart of poor Cosmo's operation, and a fair bit of the brains. You should set your sights higher. You're far too good to let yourself be used the way you do."

"Thank you, oh mighty wizard." No, Kathy wasn't as drunk as she made out.

Grace grinned. "You certainly don't need any more courage."

"She'd be a good candidate for the heart," Aurora commented. She didn't sound particularly angry with Kathy. "Even more than me."

"And you'd be Horatio." Grace managed a slight bow without losing her rhythm. "Christian has mentioned you."

"Give him the courage," Marci said.

"I'd have said 'brains'," Aurora put in.

"A couple of your balls and something to put between them." Kathy gave an indication of size with her hands--no one was built like that.

Grace laughed. "Horatio, I'll see you at your studio tomorrow. Christian, would you please leave Marci with me and see your other friends out? Invite Lucy back if you will. And, if you meet Cosmo, tell him I'll see him tomorrow as well. No time tonight." Grace turned to Marci. "Now, child, do you juggle? You should learn."

255

They met Aurora and Cosmo halfway to the door back into the party. "She doesn't want to see you, you little turd" Kathy sounded even more drunk than before. "So haw, haw, haw."

"I think you're forgetting who's the boss around here." Cosmo rearranged his robes and straightened his Cardinal's hat. Even so, he was shorter than anyone there, except Aurora. He tilted his head up to look into Christian's face. "Is she right?"

"Of course I am. Everyone knows you're a turd." Kathy batted the hat, knocking it off Cosmo's head.

"Grace wants to spend some time with Marci," Christian explained.

"And not with you, faecal face," Kathy added.

"I think you've pushed this drunk routine about as far as you should, Kathy," Aurora said, letting go of Christian's hand and moving between her uncle and Kathy.

"Not yet, I haven't." Kathy skipped away from Aurora. "Kiss me," she grabbed Christian and tried to bend him over. As they'd all discovered, Kathy's tongue wasn't in the least incapacitated. As she started to grind against him, Christian forced her head back. He had her bent over almost double when he felt her start to go limp and broke it off.

Kathy straightened instantly. "Whew! Why don't I keep him, Aurora? You can have Horatio. You might enjoy him. You like girls; he likes pretending he's a girl--a match made in heaven."

"That does it!" Horatio yanked Kathy away from Christian. "We're leaving!" He picked her up

256

and carried her away. At the end of the hall, he kicked the door open.

Cosmo broke the silence. "Grace really doesn't want to see me?"

"Not tonight, Unc." Aurora picked up his fallen Cardinal hat and put it on for him. "Tomorrow. Run along now. Christian and I need to talk." Cosmo turned, and slowly went in the direction Horatio had taken Kathy, back towards the party.

"Strange," Aurora said, when Cosmo was out of earshot. "Usually I'll kick him when he's down. Do we really need to talk?"

"I think so. Marci and you have both said I'm leaving with you tonight. I am? Why?"

"Because the two of you made me look bad at the charity ball, admittedly with some help from me. Tonight, I'm going to take you back from her-- good for the image, what? Of course, you don't have to stay with me after we're out of sight of The Factory... unless you want to."

Christian answered her with a kiss. It seemed the wisest response. Aurora proved tender and teasing, aggressive and submissive in turn. In the middle of a passive phase, she suddenly bit his lip. Christian yanked his head back. "So, as good as Kathy?" Aurora's own answer was obvious.

"Yes." No... Kathy hadn't been acting.

"Good, then let's get this show back on the road. Lucy next. I'm looking forward to that." He could hear she wasn't.

All was much as before in the VIP area of the party. As Christian and Aurora approached, Lucy was holding court in her Santa guise, with Eunice

257

by her side noting names as Patsy handed out coupons for The Second Circle. He must have had an endless supply.

Lucy turned to face them. "I've been summoned?"

"Grace would like to see you," Christian answered. "Backstage."

"Backstage. Where else? So, what happened to poor Cosmo? He came back looking ever so unhappy."

"Ms Machina changed her mind about wanting to receive him," Aurora said. "Maybe she'll change her mind about you too."

"My, aren't we bold? I think I've misjudged you, my girl. First things first-¬Eunice, go and console Cosmo." Eunice gave her notebook to Patsy, and left. "I do apologize for that contretemps last time you were in The Second Circle, Aurora. It was nothing to do with you... I was angry with our friend here. Is there anything Santa can give you to make amends?"

"My apartment." Aurora didn't need to think about it. "I want my place back."

"Done. Patsy!" Patsy's nod was almost a bow. "You're moving. Tonight.

Have all your things out of Ms Medici's by sunrise."

Patsy's head bobbed twice. "Can I use the limo?"

"What was that?"

"Can I use the limo, please, Mistress Firman, ma'am?"

258

"I suppose. Grace will give me a ride. Give me the ledger and get out of here." Patsy passed Eunice's book to Lucy and darted away. "Now, you're sure there's nothing else you want, Aurora? New bedmates, perhaps? I know a set of twins I'm sure would worship you--blondes, models--very flexible..."

"I'm happy with Christian, thanks."

"I doubt that," Lucy answered with a smile. "And even if you are, I'm sure he'll never be happy with you."

Christian felt Aurora tense. He waited. "Excuse me," Aurora finally said. "I have things to do. I'll see you later, Christian. Ms Firman, Santa, thank you for the lovely gift." She walked stiffly away.

"Not bad," Lucy commented. "She's beginning to learn the wisdom of self-control."

"I can think of others who need it more."

"Me?"

"No, you're always in control of yourself. And anyone you can coerce."

"Well, you certainly couldn't mean Kathy. She knows exactly what she's doing. I was meaning to thank you for drawing her to my attention. I don't know how I missed her all these years."

***

Grace had a dozen balls in the air when Christian and Lucy arrived. Marci was having trouble juggling four.

Lucy didn't spare Marci a glance. "Still playing games, Grace? I like the clown suit. Much better than that moth-ridden judge getup you used to favour."

"It was old. Speaking of old, I see you're still doing the same routine, Santa my love."

"What can I say? It's me."

Grace and Lucy both laughed.

"Catch." A ball whizzed towards Lucy. She caught it and tossed it back into Grace's pattern. "Give us fifteen minutes," Grace said to Marci. "Lucy and I should be finished by then."

"Twenty." Lucy caught another ball and throwing it back. "And then there's a few things the three of us need to discuss."

Marci let her balls fall, caught Christian's eye and nodded towards the door. "What did I tell you?" she asked once they were out of the room. "They're two peas in a pod."

"I don't see it."

"You don't want to." She touched Christian's arm. He turned to face her. "To them, life's just a game. But after meeting Firman, I'm not as frightened by her. Thank you." She opened her arms and moved closer.

"Stop." Marci froze. "Please?" Christian asked. "The way the evening's gone and with you dressed like that, if you kiss me, I'm afraid I'll lose control."

"That's what I had in mind. We've got fifteen minutes to spare. I can make it seem a long and happy lifetime."

"But you and Aurora have a deal." And you're exaggerating.

"That she'll be seen leaving with you." She caressed his cheek. Her eyes threatened to absorb him.

260

"Still. To make the deal work properly, you and I should be seen dancing." He started for the door.

"Coward."

***

The music was fast and Marci put on a show, her hair flying in a wild, aureate corona, and her midnight-clad body writhing with the throbbing beat. Within five minutes, she'd drawn a large audience. Christian felt Marci's eyes on him, but didn't dare meet them. The music slowed--the singer announced the last song, a waltz. Marci drifted towards Christian.

Aurora moved between them, a wisp of white Bo-peep facing Marci. "That's enough. I'll take over." Marci leaned over, kissed Aurora lightly on the lips and with a laugh, turned to go backstage once more.

"I wish she hadn't done that," Aurora whispered. "Should we dance?"

"I don't think so."

"Neither do I."

The murmuring crowd let them through.

Aurora and Christian didn't touch in the taxi, or until they were inside his apartment. Soon after her Little Bo-peep costume was in shreds. In the morning Christian dropped the monk's robes off at a dry-cleaners. Aurora packed all her clothing. She wouldn't be coming back, ever, she said.

"We're through again?"

Aurora laughed. "I'm going to be busy, and you'd just wander off and make me look bad again. Besides, you enjoyed it more than I did. I'm afraid we both prefer women, and pretty much the same

261

ones. You were thinking of her weren't you? It's okay--I did too, and Judy."

They didn't talk on the way to Aurora's apartment. If it was over, it was over, but Christian hadn't thought about Marci, or any woman but Aurora. In truth, he hadn't spent much time thinking.

However, there was something he did want to ask Aurora. He waited until they'd paid off the cab. "How could you be with me and think about a woman?"

"See. That's another reason we're not compatible. The brain is the only sex organ that counts. Every woman knows that."

Christian doubted that, and what's more, didn't believe her. She always demanded a lot of attention be paid to places far from her brain.

Aurora's apartment looked exactly the same to Christian, no sign of Patsy having moved out. "Everything he had here, was in his bedroom," Aurora said. "And until I met you, he hadn't slept here for years."

"You're blaming me for your problems with him?"

"Boy, are you touchy this morning. I won't miss those male post coital blues either."

Patsy's former bedroom was empty, and spotless. "I'm surprised." Aurora moved to inspect a corner. "I thought he'd leave a mess. Guess I'll have to give him back his half of the damage deposit after all. I thought I'd need to use it to get someone in to clean."

"Maybe he didn't want you complaining to Lucy."

"Understandable. Would you do me a favour? Drop by The Second Circle and see he gets his money… today? I'll write you a cheque. I don't want to owe Patsy anything. I'd do it myself, but I've got to get someone to change the locks and then it's off to rehearsal, and a recording session."

"You don't want to see Lucy?"

"It's okay… don't do it if you don't want to."

She didn't mean that. "Sure, I'll take care of it. So, looking for another apartment-mate?"

"No, Christian. I told you… we're history."

"Not me… Judy. I don't think she and Kathy are getting along."

"At the moment, Judy isn't happy with me either."

"You didn't leave her much choice, and remember, like Grace said, Judy pulled her punches. I'll bet she'd be willing to make up."

Aurora's answer didn't come immediately. "You're probably right. And what you're saying is that I should point out there are several ways she can make amends."

That wasn't what Christian had meant at all.

Chapter Twenty-Nine

It was a glorious first day of November, sunny and unseasonably warm. Christian felt full of life and wide-awake, despite not having slept. He considered pinching himself, but didn't. If this was a dream, he didn't want to wake up. He would go by The Second Circle immediately. It might be too early, but if he got lucky and Lucy or Patsy were there, he could get the task of refunding Patsy's damage deposit over with. If neither of them was, he'd go to The Factory and check out the aftermath of the party, and see who'd made it in to work... and who was speaking still on speaking terms.

He stopped short. Grace was in town. He'd intended to go by her place first thing that morning, but first thing, he'd been otherwise occupied.

There weren't any taxis on Aurora's street; the only car moving at all was a clunker, meandering along in fits and starts as if searching for an address. Christian started to sprint towards the nearest main street and stopped immediately, wincing. The night had been a triumph of mind over matter, but now morning had arrived and matter was taking its toll. His spirit might be soaring, but his body was chafed, abraded and bruised.

He limped on. Eventually, he convinced a taxi to stop. In the driver's mirror Christian saw a wild-eyed, unkempt reflection. No wonder he'd been asked to pay in advance. He wouldn't trust himself either, looking like he did.

Finally, they arrived in front of Casa del Carlos. The driver had succeeded in finding every traffic jam, and every road under construction in the city. Christian didn't get any change from his advance payment.

Fred, the security guard, glared at Christian as he entered the lobby. For once, Christian didn't wonder why. The way he looked, even the proverbial cat wouldn't drag him in.

"Grace!" Christian called, the moment he opened the door.

"I'm in here, Christian." Marci's voice answered, from the computer room. "Get yourself a coffee. I'll be right with you."

There were the remnants of a breakfast for two in the kitchen. He poured a coffee and went into the living room. A couple of suitcases sat by the couch. He was certain they belonged to Marci. He was equally certain Grace was gone.

Still, he asked the question when Marci appeared. "Grace?" Marci was dressed as she had been when he first met her at the concert, in the same baggy blouse and flowing skirt. She was even wearing the totally unnecessary glasses.

"Should be taking off right now. She emailed me from the airport just before boarding."

"You're leaving too?"

"I've got a few minutes, and then I should head for the airport too. Where's your costume? I'll be going to London at some point. I should take it back when I'm there."

"It needs to be cleaned. Did Grace leave me a message?"

"Only that she's accepted Horatio as a client. And that I should be sure to thank you for turning Freyja down last night."

"You're Freyja."

"Grace says I'm not. Freyja's going out of business, Christian. That's why I'm off to Europe. Grace's associate in Paris, Gabby, is going to give me a hand, and then I'm going to Zurich so some guy named Peter can help me get my finances in order. What's the matter? You look upset. I'll stay, if you want me to."

"I think what you're seeing is confusion and lack of sleep. You're going to work for Grace?"

Marci shook her head. "No, she's commissioned a painting from me as payment."

"And this is what you want to do."

"I think so."

"And I think Grace is wrong about you, just like she's wrong about Aurora, Cosmo, Lucy and me. I'd hoped I'd have a chance to talk to Grace some more. Frankly, I don't think she knows what she's doing. You are Freyja."

Marci took a long time to respond. "I certainly agree with some of that, but Grace has more faith in you than you have in her. She said the main reason she's leaving is so her opinions won't overly influence your actions."

"Which is probably why you're leaving too."

Marci leaned forward and kissed his forehead. "See, and you think you're stupid. Walk me downstairs, please? My cab should be here soon. So, how was your night with Aurora? Looks like it was a success."

On the way downstairs, Christian dodged questions. All Marci got out of him was that Aurora had her apartment back, and that Aurora and Christian were no longer an item. They stepped outside. Marci's cab wasn't there yet.

"I'm glad to hear you two have split, Christian," Marci said. "I may or may not be Freyja, but neither Freyja nor I is your sister. Until I see you settled with someone who suits you, I'm not going to give up. And about your real sister... get in touch with her. Grace agrees you should. Oh yes, and she said to tell you to apply for a passport. You may need it soon." A taxi pulled up. Christian put Marci's bags in the trunk. She got in. "The robes," she said after rolling down the window. "Mail them to me care of Gabby in Paris. The address is in the computer. Bye."

Christian went inside and asked Fred to order a cab for him as well.

"I told you before, Plowman. That's not my job."

Christian walked to the subway. It was faster than going back upstairs and calling his own. He was too wound up to sleep, much as he might need it, and he wanted to get his business with Lucy out of the way. He arrived at The Second Circle a bit after noon.

The door was open. Immediately inside he was greeted by one of the bouncers. Unfortunately, it wasn't one he remembered seeing before. "Not open. Go away."

"I'm here to see your boss."

Tiny eyes considered him from between folds of flesh. "Right." He picked a telephone and fumbled with the buttons. "It's me. Me, Rico, at the door. Another guy here to see you. Yeah. Okay." He hung up. "Boy, has she got some short memory. You wait."

Christian moved to sit on a nearby chair. The guard cleared his throat. "What'sa matter, you stupid? Wanna get hurt? Don't move." Christian shifted from foot to foot, wondering if he could get out the door and away. He decided not to risk it.

Five long minutes later, Eunice ambled up, adjusting her blouse. "Rico, you idiot. He's not here for an interview. Why didn't you tell me it was Mr. Plowman?"

"You never asked. All you said was keep him here."

Eunice sighed. "Go ahead, Christian. She's in her office."

Christian went across The Second Circle and through the door behind the bar. Before he could press the buzzer, Lucy's voice came from the small speaker beside her door. "Come in, Christian." Christian paused to look for a camera in the hall, but couldn't see one.

Lucy was wearing a black business suit and short black hair. Her eyes were still the deep gold of the night before, but today no one would mistake her for Santa. "Good afternoon, Christian. This is a pleasant surprise." She put down her pen, stood, and came around her desk.

"Aurora asked me to return Patsy's damage deposit." He took out the four hundred dollars he had ready, and gave it to her.

She took it. "Oh dear, and here I was hoping you'd come for your gift. I didn't have the opportunity to give it to you last night. I suppose you'd like a receipt?"

"Please." Lucy went back to her desk. "My gift?" He knew he shouldn't ask, but he was curious. "What were you thinking of giving me?"

Lucy picked up a pad and scribbled on it quickly. She came back and handed him the receipt. "What do you long for more than anything?" She was standing close to him. "A beautiful woman who won't abandon you. Someone to guide you through life."

"Such as yourself."

"Is there anyone else around?" She brushed his lips with hers. A hand stroked his hair. The aftermath of his night with Aurora fell from him. Christian looked in Lucy's eyes and as before, saw himself reflected. Now he was golden. "I wouldn't ever leave you. I promise that." Her breath was warm and invigorating.

"Not even when I wanted you to?"

Lucy moved away from him. "See? When you get offered your heart's desire, you change your mind. I'll give you your gift, Christian, when you can name it." She smiled. "Any time you're interested in sampling possibilities, come by the club. For you, the smorgasbord is always open."

Chapter Thirty

Christian nodded to the new guard as he left, receiving a blank look in return. He stepped outside and shivered. A cold front had moved in. He hurried down The Street towards The Factory. A quick stop there, and he could go back to Grace's and relax.

Someone coming from the side bumped into him. "Sorry." Any polite Norontonian would apologize in the circumstances. It hadn't been his fault, at least he didn't think so, but when in doubt, say you're sorry.

"Not so fucking fast, buddy." A hand the size of a construction crane bucket clamped onto him. "You go when I fucking say you can."

"Behave, Justin." The husky voice that interceded was commanding. Christian was released instantly.

Christian looked in the direction of the voice, rather than the hand. The curvaceous blonde he'd been dancing with the previous night stood posed against the fender of an old, dented car. She was wearing sunglasses again, a different pair. Today her hat was a stylish grey beret that made her platinum hair seem white. Her severely belted coat enhanced a figure that needed no help. When he managed to notice the car, Christian recognized it as the one that had been poking along outside Aurora's apartment earlier.

With a certain reluctance, Christian then checked the source of the hand. At expected, it

270

belonged to the blonde's hulking partner. He was in the same greasy brown trench coat he had worn at the party. It matched his hair in colour, and cleanliness.

"Oh yes, the spies," Christian said to the blonde. "I certainly couldn't forget you... beauty and the beast. You've been following me?"

"How did you know we're spies, smart mouth? Talk, or I'll beat the crap outta you."

"Justin, I said behave. Now you've blown our cover--for no reason at all. That's what I'll put in my report too. He was referring to our costumes from the party last night." Her growl sent a shiver down Christian's spine, even though it hadn't been directed at him. "Mr. Plowman, we would like to ask you a few questions. Would you mind if we sat in the car? It's warmer."

Christian got in the front on the passenger side. She scooted around front to the driver's seat. The car sagged when Justin got in the back, and shuddered when he slammed the door.

The blonde reached into her purse, pulled out a wallet-sized folder and handed it to Christian. It was stiff vinyl and creaked as it opened. The bottom half held a gold badge and the top a document covered with seals, stamps and numbers around and over a picture. Interpreting the clutter, Christian determined it identified her as Vanna Fairchild, special agent, Canadian Federal Investigation Bureau.

"CANFIB, you're with CANFIB? I thought you were with Lucy."

"What did you show him that one for, you fucking tramp? You're not fucking supposed to show that to anyone but the cops."

Vanna ignored Justin. "We're investigating irregularities in international currency flow, Mr. Plowman. At one time we were a team of six, but with cutbacks it's down to me and Mr. Diplomacy. Once upon a time, he was the team's muscle."

"Yeah, and you were the bimbo. And now you think you're some kind of brain, not fucking over-rated tail."

"One more comment like that, and I'll recommend you be suspended without pay. One. And for your information, I'm top-notch tail... not that you'll ever find out. And I am in charge. Let's hear you say it."

"You're in charge, Vanna."

"What? I didn't hear you."

"I said, you're fucking in charge, Vanna, but don't fucking push it."

"That's better, I guess." Vanna sighed. "I don't know how Ottawa expects us to work so short-staffed. If we had a full team, you wouldn't have noticed us.

But changing times call for new strategies, and I've decided, on my authority as chief investigator..." Vanna directed that comment towards the back seat. "...to approach you directly and ask you to co-operate."

"I suppose it depends. Who are you hoping to charge, and with what?"

"You. Your fucking ass is open meat in a crowded cell if you don't tell us fucking everything."

"Justin." Vanna looked at her partner. Her voice had become deadly quiet.

"Sorry."

Vanna turned to Christian and took off her sunglasses. In the low light of The Factory, Christian had thought her eyes colourless. Of course they weren't, but they were close... wisps of grey that complemented her platinum hair. Christian had thought Vanna's hair colour originated in a bottle, but now he wasn't so sure. The eyes fit the hair, and Vanna wasn't wearing contact lenses. He'd practised spotting those since he'd met Lucy.

Vanna met his scrutiny with her own, and grinned. Her elfin face spoke of mischief, but her voice remained all business. "Unfortunately, Justin may be right. We can't touch Firman; she owns too much of everything, and everyone. Machina's more subtle, but it's every bit as unlikely the government would charge, much less convict her of anything. No, if anyone's going to get hurt, it's going to be someone small, someone who isn't important and who can be set up to take a fall. Someone like you, Mr. Plowman."

"Or Marci."

"No. It was computers poking into databases asking about her that woke up the half-wit bureaucrats and put us on the job. They ran a full check--and even they are bright enough to see she can't be touched. She's careful and pays tax-¬far more than she could get away with. She may be a prostitute, but in itself, that isn't a crime."

"Good fucking thing for you, it isn't."

Vanna sighed, but otherwise ignored Justin. "Anyway, she also has contacts near or at the top of important European governments and citizenship or legal residency in several places. No one knows quite what influence she has, but her involvement tripped a lot of red flags. The balance between Machina and Firman is delicate and with Van Deer involved, things could change. If there is one thing bureaucrats hate, it's change. So, here we are... checking things out."

"My tax dollar at work." It was Christian's turn to sigh. "No wonder Ottawa ran us so far into the hole. I don't think anyone would mind me telling you that Marci, or Freyja, if you prefer, is working on a commission basis for Grace. She's going to contact Grace's associates in Paris and Zurich."

Marci's trip to Europe would be a matter of record--if the agents hadn't known, they could have found out. The rest was all true, if somewhat deceptive. His grandmother had taught Christian it was a citizen's duty to mislead the government, just as it is the government's to mislead the public.

Vanna's ash-grey eyes lit. "Wow! Ottawa will think that's major information. They'll stay up all night analysing that." She turned to her partner in the back seat. "And you thought this was a mistake. Hope you've got your bags packed, 'cause you're on your way to France." She opened her door. "Excuse me, Mr. Plowman. I'll be right back. I've got to

274

make a call. Him..." She hooked a thumb towards Justin. "Him, you won't see for a while."

She leapt out. A passing taxi screeched to a halt to avoid hitting her door. Vanna gave the cursing driver the finger as she dashed around to the sidewalk and a payphone. Justin wrestled himself from the back seat. A relieved groan came from the old car's springs as his weight was removed. He hammered the door shut, and trudged over to the phone booth.

Vanna's call didn't take long, but it was entertaining. As she relayed her news, she hopped and skipped with glee. Christian wondered if he should have said anything; Justin might cause trouble for Marci. He doubted that, but Marci might be angry with him for reporting her activities to CANFIB. But Grace had told Christian she operated in the open, and Christian worked for Grace, and no one else. Besides which, Christian wanted Vanna to like him.

After finishing her call, Vanna turned to Justin, and with a few words and a wave of an arm, dismissed him. He lumbered down The Street. She ran back around the front of her car, checking for traffic this time, and jumped back in behind the wheel. "What a coup! In one swoop, we've put the staple counters in a tizzy, and rid me of my liability." She bounced on the seat. Christian's knees slammed against the dashboard.

He squirmed his legs sideways in case her excitement continued. "You told me you weren't after Marci, and now you've sent your charming comrade after her. You lied."

Vanna put a deliberately serious look on her face. "Well, I did say it was questions about her that put us on the case and I'm justified in sending Captain Beefhead after her. Even if he does find her, I can't see him being smart enough to cause her any grief. Besides..." She switched the look from serious to smug. "...besides, I know your background. You're holding back on me, for sure. I don't care. It gets the oaf off my back. Anyway, if you're really with Machina, you know she'd tell us everything--if we could find her."

For Christian, that last was the winning argument. Still, he wasn't tempted to tell Vanna the whole truth. In his opinion, Grace wasn't in tune with the modern world. She was guilty of bad judgement. Most of the people she'd more or less implied were on her side were really on their own, not hers. Christian could adapt her morality to his circumstances. Time to change the topic. "So--I'm curious. Why did you use a payphone? I'd have thought these days, CANFIB would have gone cellular."

"Payphones are more secure. And cheaper. Bigwigs gotta afford their mistresses and junkets even in tough times, you know?" Vanna put the key in the ignition and rammed the accelerator to the floor. The car roared and the radio blared. "So, where do you want to go?" she shouted. "I'll give you a ride. It's easier than trying to follow."

Christian turned off the radio. "I was going to The Factory, but I've changed my mind. I'm starving, so I thought I'd grab some lunch and head back to Grace's."

276

"So, where are you taking me?"

"You're presuming a fair bit, aren't you?" he said for the sake of form. He'd hoped she'd keep him company. There had been something between them when they had danced the night before. Or rather, nothing. She'd fit his arms perfectly.

"Hey, I'm a fact of your life, Mr. Plowman, so you'd better get used to me. If you get real lucky, the mission might call for me to finish seducing you, but don't count on any more feels if it doesn't. Our relationship will remain totally professional. You're not my type."

"And what is your type?"

"Rich." Vanna gunned the motor, and grinned. "Filthy, stinking rich and breathing. And so smitten by my charms they wouldn't dream of asking me to sign a prenuptial. Hey, let's go to that Westshire dining room you and Medici go to. It must be okay. Your treat."

"Okay. You seem to know a lot about me."

"Probably more than you'd like, Mr. Plowman." Vanna put the car in gear and did a quick U-turn across the oncoming traffic.

"Then since you must know my first name, please use it." Christian frantically scrambled to find his seatbelt. "That Mr. Plowman stuff makes it sound like you watch too many cop shows."

"Okay Christian. Whatever." She sped up to shoot through an intersection before the light turned completely red, and swerved to avoid a jaywalker. Christian dug out the belt from the crack in the seat. He doubted it would protect him from much, but it was the thought that counted.

Chapter Thirty-One

Vanna stopped her car directly in front of The Westshire and got out. The doorman rushed over, explaining she couldn't park there. She whipped out some identification--it wasn't what she'd shown Christian earlier.

"Official business," she said with a snap. "We're in a hurry. Don't move it unless you have to. We may be a couple of hours." She slapped a bill and the keys into the doorman's hand and sailed into the lobby.

Christian caught up with her outside the dining room. "You watch too much TV. I think I saw that episode. Wouldn't it have been easier to use their valet parking?"

"Bribes are an allowable expense--valet parking, isn't. Don't ask me, ask headquarters. Of course, you should see what they drive. No junk heaps for the honchos and their handmaidens, no siree. Be a gentleman and relieve me of my coat."

It was Christian's pleasure. He was treated to a gentle waft of expensive perfume. His fingers brushed her wine-coloured top. It was the softest silk imaginable. As he stepped back his eyes feasted on her tight but tasteful grey slacks.

She turned and handed him her beret, running her other hand through artful platinum curls. She grinned. "Work hard and maybe someday you'll be able to afford a body like this. Not that you're doing too bad for a pauper. Van Deer and Medici have charms beyond the physical."

278

Christian filed Vanna's remark as he put away her coat and hat, and his jacket. It sounded like she was willing to exchange information. Maybe he had done the right thing in telling her about Marci's arrangements; he needed all the help he could get, even from a source as unlikely as CANFIB. His advisors and friends hadn't given him much... maybe the other side would prove more useful.

The waiter showed them to their table. Heads turned and the low buzz of the room intensified. Christian was getting used to it. "I expect people to check me out, but this seems extreme," Vanna said as she straightened and, in a redundant display, thrust her full front further forward.

"With respect, it's got more to do with me than you. This is a hangout for the society crowd. They've seen me shift from Aurora to Freyja Van Deer, and then last night, back to Aurora. Today, I'm here with you."

"Make the most of it." Vanna's strut intensified, and as she put her purse on the table, she bent far more than necessary. Christian idly wondered why her designer blouse had buttons at the top. No one who could carry off wearing it would ever do them up--it wasn't that kind of blouse. She caressed her hair. Her smile was that of a woman well satisfied with a night's activities. Another actor. "Hope this won't muck up your chances with Medici."

"It couldn't. Last night was a face-saving exercise. By now I'm sure Aurora has made it known we're no longer an item." Christian hoped Aurora had done that first thing. She might not have; she certainly wouldn't have expected him to

279

show up in public the next day with anyone... let alone someone as flamboyant as Vanna Fairchild.

"I didn't know that." Vanna settled softly back into her chair and regarded him with pensive eyes. "That's a pity, but I suppose it may work out for you. Van Deer's probably a better bet--if you can actually land her. Even we can't unravel how much she has hidden in Liechtenstein."

The waiter brought their order. No free seafood appetiser today--that was an honour the Westshire bestowed exclusively on Aurora. Vanna had ordered a large salad with no oil, and a mineral water. Christian got the prime rib. He was hungry, and with all the expense money Grace had given him, he certainly could afford it.

When the waiter left, Christian addressed Vanna's preceding remark. "What do you mean, if I can land Freyja?" He only dreamed of doing that when he was asleep. Awake, he knew better.

"Oh, I've no doubt you can. Guess I'm just envious. My fondest wish would be to have two wealthy suitors bidding for my hand, like you do."

"Huh?" Inarticulate, but it got the point across.

She leaned forward. His eyes dropped from hers to her décolletage. "Nice isn't it?" she asked.

Her remark snapped his eyes back up, but the grin on her face took any sting from her words. "Come on, Christian. I'm just a poor kid like you and I'm on your side. Hook whichever you can. They're both loaded. Play it right, and you may even end up being able to afford an expensive lover on the side. Knowing Medici's tastes, she probably would consider a threesome. I'd sleep with anyone for the right price... even her."

Vanna thought he shared her goal of marrying money. He didn't... his baser interests were based on bodies, not bankbooks. He could understand that, as Freyja, Marci had probably done well for herself, but Aurora? "I suppose Aurora makes a decent salary, but I'd hardly call her rich."

"You don't know?" Amazement showed in Vanna's hazy eyes. "I mean, it's a private company and all, but Sharpe and Medici's old man were equal partners. Medici's mother holds the shares, but Medici represents her. And as long as Sharpe doesn't have any legitimate kids, Medici stands to get his as well when he kicks. I thought you were playing with Machina's ten-percent to squeeze Sharpe. You mean you're not?"

"No. I didn't even know Aurora had a mother."

Vanna laughed and again sat back. "You thought she sprang from the bowels of the earth? Her old lady hangs out in Florence and Milan. After the old man checked out, she buggered off back to the homeland. Mama considers Canada a society of barbarians, and Sharpe its crowning glory. God knows why she married his brother--must have been thinking with her gonads instead of her brains. Medici Junior's got brains though--it was after she showed up that Sharpe really took off. Aurora should inherit the empire... she built it."

"Is this generally known?"

"Not unless you can access tax returns and legal stuff. Medici's weird. She doesn't flaunt her cash, or her roots--like anyone cares if you make it on your own, long as you've got it made. I figured Machina had told you. Guess you're not as with it as I thought you were." She'd been picking at her salad, casually flicking croutons onto the table with a long, pink fingernail. She aimed one at Christian, but missed.

"A lot of people give me too much credit," Christian said, between bites. He was ravenous, not surprising after his busy night. "I can understand why Aurora doesn't tell anyone. If she did, she'd figure that was all people were interested in, her money. She wants to be lusted after for herself."

"Guess I can see that. I kind of enjoy it too. If I had the bucks, I might indulge myself as well." Vanna ate a mouthful of lettuce and then directed some bacon bits towards the same general region her croutons had landed. "So, want to know stuff about Van Deer as well? She tell you she's French-Canadian on daddy dearest's side? I could tell you her birth name, who her plastic surgeon in Switzerland was, how much her paintings have sold for, or more or less who she's serviced and her price range."

It seemed a perfect opportunity to find out how much of what Marci had told him about her past was true. Christian found he didn't care as much as he'd thought he would. Marci was the person she'd made herself into, and his friend… he hoped.

There was also no guarantee Vanna knew more than he did. The official government version could be pure fiction. The information regarding Aurora was likely a matter of record, but Vanna's interpretation of Marci's history would be based on

282

hearsay. And if Lucy Firman didn't know everything about Marci, the chances the authorities would were slim.

Christian was more interested learning more about Vanna. "No thanks. I know as much about Marci as I need to. You can quit showing off now."

"Aw, but showing off is what I do best. And I don't want you to think of me as just another unforgettable face stuck on top of an incredible body. I'm a fabulous brain too. I'm sure I know things about Van Deer even she doesn't."

"Okay, I'm impressed. But no more dirt unless I ask, please?"

"If you say so." A stubborn bacon bit was stuck to her fingernail. "I can see this was a mistake anyway."

"The salad?"

"Well, that too, but I meant coming here. People are paying way too much attention. You'd think I was sitting here naked."

"Well, maybe if you quit playing with your food..."

She surreptitiously wiped her finger on a napkin. "No, it's more than that. I hadn't figured on how much attention you'd grab after last night's performances. I should have. You were damn good. And here I'm supposed to be undercover. I know I'm no good at it--I was trained to be noticed, and basically, I'm too hot to hide, but I'm supposed to try. Guess I shouldn't be seen with you. Too bad. You're kind of fun." Vanna looked around the room nervously, "Hey, you gonna finish soon? That guy over there making a phone call from his table is a reporter."

Christian had intended to order dessert, but he popped the last piece of meat into his mouth and signalled for the bill. "Okay, but this will just make it look like we're in a hurry to go someplace private."

"Yeah, well that's okay--long as I don't get my picture in the paper. He was probably calling a photographer." As Christian piled bills onto the cheque, Vanna got up and headed for the door.

By the time Christian arrived at the restaurant's entrance, she had her coat and hat on, and was trying to dissolve into the wall. "I'd better not be seen with you again," she said, in a low voice. "If you notice me around, and you're with people, pretend you're just checking out my tits, okay? Anyone would buy that. And don't tell anyone about the investigation. It's classified. I don't need to tell you what that means--you watch movies."

***

Back at Grace's apartment, Christian opened a pint of premium ice cream to compensate for his missed dessert. Spoon in hand, he checked his e-mail. Nothing. He went to the table where he'd left the envelope with his bonus cheques and the bulk of the expense money. There was a lot of cash. He didn't know how much--he didn't even know the current exchange rate for the American currency, let alone the Euro. There were a lot of zeros on the bills.

Expense money he supposed he could accept. The cheques were a different matter. Bonuses? For

284

what? Finding a friend, and pointing out to Cosmo that he had talented people on staff? He wouldn't cash them--Grace was already paying him too much.

He spooned out the last of the ice cream, and considered the cash again. What did Grace expect him to do, rent a helicopter? He hadn't seen a safe in Grace's apartment, so he deposited it in a file drawer... after peeling off a few hundred.

Deciding the previous night finally had caught up with him, Christian headed upstairs, to bed. When he looked in the mirror, he got a surprise. When he'd been in the cab after leaving Aurora's, he'd looked horrible--wild-eyed and dishevelled. While he did feel exhausted now, he looked almost respectable. He didn't know how, but he knew when it had happened... when he'd been with Lucy. He'd felt a weight fall away when she touched him. He didn't want to think about it, or her. He didn't. Christian slept well.

Chapter Thirty-Two

The next morning, there was e-mail from Grace. "If you don't want the bonus money, give it to charity." That was it. As always, she signed as "Mom." Christian could have used more counsel than that, but it was better than nothing... just. He consulted the off-line computer for Gabby's address in Paris so he could send his costume back to Marci. As promised, it was there... just. Gabby's last name wasn't given, and there were no other details, except an e-mail address. He printed the information.

Christian left Grace's apartment at the height of rush hour. He'd be travelling in the opposite direction from the subway crowd, so it wouldn't be too bad. The early November weather had remained cool and he walked briskly to the nearest stop. Halfway, he noticed Vanna's junker, puttering along behind him.

He waited on the platform for a train to go by. Vanna would need time to park. She appeared, and when the train came, she got on the other end of the same car. He'd hoped she'd changed her mind, and they could travel together. No such luck. Fine.

At the station where he transferred to the other line, Christian wove through the throng in a manner only one who often travelled the subway could manage. He moved as far down the platform as he could before a train arrived. Maybe she'd make it on, and maybe she wouldn't. It would be close. Four stops later, an out-of-breath Vanna dashed into his car, and seeing him, tried to regain her poise. Normally oblivious Norontonians variously scowled or ogled as Vanna fell onto a bench, her ample chest heaving. Christian smiled at her. She continued to ignore him.

At his stop, Christian waited until the last minute, then spurted through the closing door. He didn't look back to see if Vanna made it out. She knew his address; she'd catch up with him. He knew he was being petty, but it was fun.

Christian's apartment reeked of sweat and sex... leftovers from Aurora's visit. He stripped the sheets. He had to wash them. As he was locking his door, the one across the hall opened.

"So you're the one she was calling Jesus the other night. Funny, I've always thought of Him as shorter and kind of swarthy." Aurora had been loud, profane and had demonstrated her usual fine grasp of cursing. At her place, the walls were thick. Here, they were paper-thin. And even if she hadn't been thinking of Christian, she'd enjoyed herself. Aurora might be more interested in women, but she knew how to use a man.

"Sorry."

"Oh, it didn't bother me. It was so much more interesting than anything on TV. I was impressed." She stepped closer and sniffed. The bag hid the sheets, but not their aroma. "Very impressed."

Christian didn't know what to say. He'd never seen this neighbour before. He'd have remembered. She was tall, and willowy... Marci's height or more. Her figure was model-thin like Lucy's, but more normally proportioned. She was rich ebony. Next to

287

her, Horatio would look pale. Her face was all her own, and incomparable. To Christian's eyes, she didn't belong in this dive of a building or even on this Earth. She was young, but even in the pantheon of beauty he'd been surrounded by since he'd met Grace, she was extraordinary. Christian was awed, and speechless.

She was amused. "I'm Liza. When you get up the nerve to ask me for a date, drop over. Any time." She swung her long black braid to her back. "Unfortunately, I can't stay and chat any longer. I've got to get to my terribly important job. Bye now." At the end of the hall, she blew him a kiss. For the first time, Christian noticed her uniform. It was brown and yellow, the study in ugliness that was the corporate colours of a large fast-food chain. Christian pulled out of his trance and waved back, but she'd already turned the corner.

When he recovered, Christian continued to the laundry room, and put his sheets in a washer. He left them unattended and went to get the costume from the dry-cleaner. He wanted to ship it to Marci as soon as possible. If anyone stole his sheets while he was away, he could afford new ones. These were in threadbare anyway.

The robe was ready. He hurried over to the courier's office across from his building's lobby and packed it into a box, conveniently available for an exorbitant price. He paid cash for that, and to send the package overnight to Freyja Van Deer, care of Gabby's address. Marci might not be there long, and Christian wanted to be certain she got the costume before she left for London, or Zurich, or wherever.

As he left, Christian saw Vanna, pretending to window-shop at a discount hardware store between two deserted storefronts. She wasn't convincing.

When he got back to his building, he stood in the dimly lit lobby and took his turn watching Vanna. She was at the courier's, showing the clerk an identification folder. Evidently, that didn't produce the desired result. She reached into her purse for something else. Christian didn't wait to see what happened. He was certain Vanna would get her way, coercing or buying access to his shipment. She was dogged, if not subtle. He hoped what she discovered would be worth the effort, but doubted it.

His sheets were finished and still there, which meant Christian needed to dry them. As they tumbled, he read a tattered romance novel someone had left behind. It was better than watching the sheets, but not by much. Could people believe such things happened? That an allegorical knight would implausibly sweep a fair maiden from her dreary life and into a wonderful new world? Only in third-rate fiction were such things possible. When the dryer's buzzed sounded, Christian abandoned the book in mid-sentence.

Upstairs, he made his sofa bed and tidied the room. Aurora had left food in the refrigerator so he ate a leisurely lunch. If Vanna wanted to keep an eye on him, she could hang around. He didn't owe her any favours. He wasted some more time playing computer games. When he got bored with that, he turned the computer off and left. He should visit Beeble Productions. He wanted to see how Horatio was doing. At the party, it had seemed the answer was "not all that well."

Vanna was pacing in front of his building. She followed him to the subway, and once more got on the other end of the same car. Christian decided this game was boring too, and at the transfer point again managed to get on different cars. One stop later, he got out. Marci had said Grace suggested he get a passport, and there was an office nearby. He saw Vanna's face pressed to the window, watching him, as the train carried her away.

After filling out the application, Christian discovered he couldn't submit it until he got the signatures of two upstanding citizens who knew him. That should be easy--he was on his way to see one. The stalwart owner of Beeble Productions should qualify.

***

Christian was surprised to find Horatio the only one there. "You're lucky I came in early to catch up on things." Howard looked tired. "These days, the action here doesn't start until after sunset."

He ushered Christian into his office. Christian glanced at the hole in the wall, and Horatio laughed. "I'm leaving it as a reminder to not to take things quite as seriously. Sure, I've been pushing myself, but everything is under control."

"Is it? You and Aurora are getting along now? Really?" That wasn't Christian's primary concern, but it wasn't a bad lead-in.

"Much better. Thanks to you and your friend Grace, there's no doubt who is in charge. Cosmo bought a half interest but then Grace took her ten-

290

percent... for an outrageously high price I must say. She said you'd vote it. I know you'll back me, not Aurora and Cosmo. Won't you?"

"I'd rather not have to decide." The arrangement was news to Christian. Damn Grace-- she should tell him these things. "I'd much prefer to have you guys talk things out, and not force me to take sides."

Horatio nodded. "Grace said that's what you'd say. No problem. I've figured out the key to Aurora. Make her look good, and she'll let you do anything you want. I can handle her."

Christian had his doubts; he thought it more likely Aurora would lead Horatio by the nose, perhaps without him knowing it. Speaking of which... "It didn't look like you're getting along very well with Kathy. Why are you two still together?"

The answer was a long time coming. "You can look at her, see her with me, and still ask?" Horatio paused, as if waiting for Christian to comment, then continued. "Christian, for my part, it's that she's just so incredibly beautiful." He gave a deep sigh. "Did you know she's a model part-time? She could have made it in New York, if she'd wanted. To have her on my arm shows the world I'm a man to be reckoned with, a success despite my setbacks. But I suppose you think that shallow."

"You're right, and there has to be more to it than that."

"Yes, it's also very much how Kathy is in bed. I never believed a woman could teach me so much about sex." Horatio stopped. "But you're probably laughing, considering the women you have."

"Trust me, I'm not. And I don't have any women, as you put it. Mind you, in your case it sounds more like the woman has you."

"Utterly. I admit it--in private. I'll stay until she pushes me out. But you I don't believe. I know Aurora and you are in the past, but I've heard much about you and Freyja--not to mention you and some other mysterious blonde."

"Marci's in Europe and the other blonde isn't talking to me. Could you sign this?" He handed the passport application to Horatio. "And would you be interested in going out on the town with me Friday night?" He could ask Liza.

Horatio signed the form and gave it back. "I'd like that. Of course, we would have to include Kathy."

"Of course." Christian's spur-of-the-moment plan was to provide concrete proof to Horatio, in the person of Liza, that there were women other than Kathy in the world. Next to Liza, she'd fade... anyone would.

Horatio smiled. "Kathy's really not as bad as you think, Christian. Come on, I was just going up to The Factory to take her for dinner. I'll need to clear our plans with her anyway. Also, you can get the second signature you need while you are there."

At The Factory, they found Kathy handing over her desk to the evening shift. "You're late. I thought you were going to stand me up."

"Never. Christian has something he'd like to ask you."

292

"Looks like he expected you to do the asking. Guess he hasn't figured out what a coward you are."

Christian was learning. "I'm inviting the two of you out for a tour of the clubs Friday night. You can make the plans, if you'd like. I'm paying. The sky's the limit."

"You're sure of that? Got someone lined up for yourself?"

"Not yet." He hadn't asked Liza. She might be busy. On such short notice, it was hard to imagine that she wouldn't be. He'd ask her as soon as he got home.

"Good. Then you can take Judy."

"I'm not sure she'd want to go out with me."

"She'll drop her pants for the opportunity, or any time you ask. She's all buddy buddy with Aurora again and doing her damnedest to be just like the bitch, now you've got her trying out the bitch's job. Go ask her. She's doing a segment from VideoView."

Christian went through the door he'd got to know so well at the party. The area had been walled off into sections again. He didn't see Judy, so he asked a woman with a clipboard.

"Ah yes, Christian, isn't it? Judy's two partitions over, and to the left. The broadcast starts in three minutes, but she's not on for seventeen after that. Now scoot, or I'll get you to read the sports instead of the usual loser," she added loudly, neatly ducking the resulting basketball.

Judy was perched on a desk, joking with the woman operating the camera. Her skirt and blouse were pure Aurora, tight and revealing. She saw

293

Christian, slipped off and sauntered over. "Well look who's here. Looking for me, I presume?"

Not by choice. "I'm taking Horatio and Kathy wining and dining on Friday. Kathy suggested you might like to balance the group."

Judy crossed her arms. "That's not a very romantic proposal."

"It wasn't meant to be. I'll understand if you say no." And I'll thank you.

"I thought you'd ask your blonde trash."

"Vanna?"

"Hah! I thought you didn't know her name."

"I didn't until I ran into her again yesterday." Actually, he'd run into Justin, or rather, Justin had run into him. "She's busy Friday night." Watching him. "Look, if you're going to be difficult, I'll ask someone else. Maybe the lady with the clipboard would be interested." Or Liza, but Christian wasn't going to give Judy another name to pounce on.

"Rani? You'd go out with an old woman like that--instead of me?"

That stopped Christian short. "Old? She's closer to my age than you are. And better company I suspect." He started to leave.

"Christian? I'd love to go. I promise to behave. And just in case you're really interested in her, I'd better tell you Rani's a rarity around here... she's happily married. So, where are you taking me?"

Christian hoped he hadn't articulated his sigh. So much for Liza and Friday. "Couldn't tell you. Kathy's making the plans. I'll see you then. I've got to find Cosmo before he leaves."

As usual, Cosmo was on the phone. He raised an eyebrow as Christian walked in. Cosmo wasn't as eloquent as Marci, but the question was obvious. Christian shook his head; he didn't want to talk about anything. He put the form in front of Cosmo and handed him a pen. Cosmo glanced at it, and signed. Christian mouthed his thank-you. At least something at The Factory had gone as planned.

Chapter Thirty-Three

Thursday afternoon Christian found himself tired of sitting around Grace's apartment, reading her books and eating her food... essentially, doing nothing. He decided to walk to the government offices to file his passport application. He needed the exercise.

When he stepped out of Casa del Carlos, he heard an immediate squeal of tires. Vanna was on the job. She inched along behind him as he walked towards Yonge Street. Christian debated whether he should make her life easier by using the side streets, but decided against it. One of them should work to earn their pay. He wasn't, ergo...

He walked down Yonge. Horns blared. On the main drag, crawling along and blocking a lane wasn't acceptable. Soon Vanna's car zoomed past him and into a donut shop parking lot. Christian pretended he hadn't noticed. He heard a door slam. Vanna evidently had decided to follow him on foot. He considered that a wise choice. She probably needed the exercise too.

At the passport office he took a number and sat to wait. Out of the corner of his eye, he saw Vanna pacing and glancing at her watch, pretending to be there to meet someone, someone who was late. A couple of men offered to be the friend she was looking for, only to be rebuffed. Christian imagined she'd had a great deal of practice fending off unwanted advances. How unwanted they were might be debatable. She'd probably feel hurt if she weren't constantly propositioned.

When his number was called, Christian took his application to be checked. That wasn't strictly necessary... he could have dumped it in a box and left, but he wasn't in a hurry and did want to make sure he'd done everything properly. It might also give Vanna an extra sentence or two for her report. Keeping tabs on Christian Plowman must be tedious. These days, being Christian Plowman wasn't much better. The clerk informed him everything was in order and that in ten days or so his passport would be sent by registered mail.

Outside the office Christian stopped at a bank of payphones. Vanna checked where he was and barged over to the clerk, shoving the next person out of her way while flashing one of her identification folders. The clerk picked up a telephone. Christian did the same and, still watching the action, put a quarter in the slot and called The Factory.

Kathy answered. "It's all set. Be prepared to drop a bundle. Dress up, but not in a tux--a suit would be better. Be here at seven. Three other lines are lit-¬I've got to go." She hung up without asking if he wanted to talk to anyone else. Really, he hadn't. Still, it would have been nice if she'd asked.

Inside the passport office, the person the clerk had called arrived and pulled Vanna aside. She was literally hopping with rage and, at the same time, twisting her head to keep an eye on Christian. He waved good-bye and walked back to the donut shop where she'd abandoned her car. He went in, ordered a cup of coffee and sat by the window. Vanna soon came running up Yonge Street full tilt, her chest heaving. Christian admired the sight, as did others-- a minor fender-bender in the southbound lanes was, beyond any doubt, directly attributable to Vanna's exertions. She was as much of a hazard on foot as in her car.

In the interests of public safety and his stomach, Christian left his coffee unfinished. He stepped outside, stood still until she saw him and then walked slowly back to Grace's apartment, this time taking the side streets. He almost felt ashamed of himself for teasing Vanna, for making an expensive woman a source of cheap entertainment. Almost, but not quite.

Chapter Thirty-Four

Christian next ventured into the world Friday evening, as planned. A little after six, he called a taxi. Eternally optimistic, he went downstairs immediately and, for once, was rewarded. His cab was there. As the driver pulled away, Vanna roared into action.

"We're being followed, mister," the driver said as they pulled on to Yonge. "Want I should lose 'em?"

"Like in the movies? Nah, slow down. There's an extra ten in it for you if you really crawl."

The driver shrugged and complied. They arrived at The Factory with Vanna riding their bumper. As he pulled up, the driver took a good look in the rear-view mirror. "Love a duck! She's a doll, isn't she? I wouldn't run from her either, guy. Thanks, have a good one." He remained there, staring longingly into the mirror.

Horatio was in the lobby, pacing. "Ah, you're early too."

"Didn't want to keep the ladies waiting."

"No chance of that. Kathy's dressing, and Judy's still working. Since you're here, shall we go watch her?"

Judy was in the VideoView studio again, perched on the same ledge as on Christian's previous visit. She had on an elegant, low-cut evening gown. It was black, long and slit to the waist on one side. She sat showing a full length of leg. The camera's red light was on as they approached--Judy was talking, plugging COSMO-TV's weekend fashion showcase. The red light winked out. Judy slipped off the ledge and into her heels.

Judy might not be the woman he wanted to go out with, but Christian didn't see any reason they shouldn't be on good terms. She'd had a crush on him; one he hoped she was over. It was obvious she'd put a lot of work into dressing up, and the least he could do was acknowledge that.

"Noronto sure is getting an eyeful on Bull's Eye tonight. You look sophisticated, like Aurora in a refined mood. I'd say you're ready to step into her shoes."

"Hottest I've ever seen her." The camera operator grabbed his crotch. "Like this! I couldn't decide if I should stay long for the leg or go in tight for the cleavage."

"So which did you do?" Trust Horatio to ask.

"Panned in and out a lot."

"I'd focus on her eyes. They're so soft, so exciting." Horatio was making moves on Judy? That would end poorly.

"Bad TV."

"Not to mention a bad idea, for you, once Kathy shows up." Judy smiled at Horatio. "Pay too much attention to my eyes, and she'll poke out yours."

"If you were the last thing I saw, it might be worth it."

"You're full of it, know that?" Judy moved to Horatio and gazed up at him. "But I'll bet you've sweet-talked your way into a lot of beds." She touched his arm. "Not that a big, virile man like you would need to try all that hard."

"Thirty seconds," the operator said. "Give it all you've got--this is your finale."

Judy squeezed Horatio's arm before going back. The light winked on. "And tomorrow, you can catch the second Thong's concert at the Dome. Tonight's is sold out. Or, if you're looking for a walk on the wild side, try Shaft and the Chocolate Bunnies at Dance Dance Dance. Hope your night will be as exciting as mine." She winked at the camera. "But I doubt it... over to you, Bob." The light went out.

"You're that thrilled about tonight?" Christian asked.

"I'm going to make something happen. If you're not interested, I'm sure I can find someone. Wouldn't you say so, Horatio?" Judy started in Horatio's direction. Horatio took a step towards her.

"Horatio seems to." Kathy's voice came from behind Christian. Horatio froze.

"Kathy, I didn't notice you come in." Judy was facing the door. If she hadn't seen Kathy, she needed her eyes checked.

"I'm sure Horatio didn't. Easy to get going, isn't he? Too bad he doesn't know where to go once he's started... so, like my outfit?"

She pivoted slowly. Her blouse was translucent white, opaque enough to satisfy public decency statutes but transparent enough to make it obvious she wasn't wearing a bra and didn't need to. The long skirt that went with it was a solid white, but the fabric was cut in inch-wide ribbons that swirled as she moved, showing glimpses of leg and thigh. What, if anything, she was wearing under the skirt wasn't clear.

"It's impressive." It was the politest word Christian could find on the spur of the moment. "Not many women could wear that."

"Or would want to." Judy flinched at the look her remark earned. "I wouldn't have the... nerve."

"Oh, I don't know. You seem to have a lot of nerve of late. Glad you like it, Christian. It's an original by Rory at Maison de Fade. He's bringing out a new line, and asked me to show it off for him." She went past Christian to the motionless Horatio. "Like it, lover?" she asked, a playful note in her voice.

"It's very... interesting." Horatio had the look of a man being led to the gallows.

"Does it make you feel... virile?" Kathy smiled at Judy. "I was in the control room. You weren't on the air, but your microphone was live. It's okay, I'm not jealous. If I was going to poke the poor man's eyes out for gawking at you, I'd have done it the other night when you pranced through the living room in that nightie. Come over here, come on..."

Judy reluctantly went to Kathy. Kathy took her hand and one of Horatio's, and joined them. She left her victims and moved to beside Christian. "Don't they make a lovely couple?" She slipped an arm around Christian's waist. "Why don't we try it this way for a bit and see how we all like it?"

302

Chapter Thirty-Five

The limousine was waiting in front. Inside, Kathy sat beside Christian and explained the facts of life in Noronto's fast lane. "Okay, I arranged tonight on short notice. That means I had to play my contacts for all they're worth and that we're going to need to grease palms even more than usual. If you'll trust me with your bankroll, I'll do that. I know the prices."

Christian'd left the Euros currency Grace had provided as expense money but brought all the Canadian and American. He handed it to Kathy.

"Nothing smaller?" she asked. Without waiting for an answer she opened her purse and changed two of his hundreds into twenties. She kept that and a number of fifties and gave the rest back. "This is Noronto. You came prepared for Manhattan or maybe Paris. Musn't over-bribe. Looks pretentious."

At the restaurant, Kathy swept onto Christian's arm and they led the way in, leaving Horatio and Judy behind. "I'm sure you're wondering what's going on. Like I said, Aurora apologised to Judy the day after the party and they're pals again. In the two days since you asked her out, Judy's been vamping Horatio, acting as if she was trying to take him away from me."

"You think Aurora put her up to it."

"I'm sure. Aurora would... if I were dumb enough to hang around with her. If I push Judy and Horatio together it'll take all the fun out of it. Don't worry, I'll let them off the hook after they've squirmed a bit." They waited for Judy and Horatio to catch up. "Good evening, Alphonse." Kathy shook hands with a man in shiny tails, slipping him a couple of bills. With a flourish and show of teeth he conducted them to a table in the middle of the room.

"Horatio and I have been here before, of course. They're overpriced, and the food is atrocious."

"Kathy! You're talking too loud." Horatio twisted in his chair. Their arrival and passage to the table had been widely watched.

Kathy smiled, and shifting closer to Christian, leaned against him and continued in a whisper. "But if you want to be seen, this is the place. Look at all the attention we're getting." They were, from the room and more particularly, Horatio and Judy.

"You're hard to ignore."

"To date, you've done a good job."

"Oh, I've noticed. But I was involved with Aurora before. I'm afraid I'm a one-woman man."

"That's fine in itself, I suppose." Kathy sat back again. "Long as you choose the right one."

The meal progressed. Kathy was right; the food was dreadful. Once she moved to a less intimate distance from Christian, Horatio and Judy had relaxed and started talking with each other. They had a fair bit in common. Both had been brought up in a rural setting by deeply religious parents and they also shared an interest in contemporary music. Since Christian didn't know much about livestock, crops or prayer meetings, and didn't care at all for

304

rap or hip-hop, he found himself talking with Kathy.

She wouldn't say much about her upbringing, other than it was urban and he gathered, unhappy. He did discover she was well read, and had a degree in Philosophy. She'd taken it part-time while working at The Factory.

"Never studied it myself. But my mother had a PhD."

"I know." Kathy smiled. "Her speciality was Ethics. Mine too. I've read everything she wrote."

Christian hadn't. He tried several times when he was younger and found it far beyond him. Or boring. He'd never decided which.

They didn't linger. Kathy had scheduled a full night. When the bill arrived, Christian paid immediately, in cash. The sight of as much legal tender as he was carrying seemed to attract as much attention and lust as Kathy's outfit.

As they rose to leave, Judy installed herself on Christian's arm. "Kathy may be a friend, but my patience does have limits."

Left together, Horatio and Kathy started arguing, quietly at first. At the entrance, Christian looked back to see them still at the table, nose to nose. Horatio raised his voice. Kathy turned to leave. Horatio put a hand firmly on her shoulder. Slowly, she turned back, menace in her motion. Horatio took her into his arms and kissed her. There was a smattering of applause. As she began to respond, the applause became an ovation. It was a scene from a bad film and suited the ambience of the restaurant perfectly.

"Good." Judy moved a bit closer. "That's settled. Now you're mine."

"You're assuming a fair bit, aren't you?"

"Oh, I don't think so. Aurora told me how to handle you. I can manage it."

"You're not Aurora. Besides, I doubt Kathy's going to let you two off the hook that easy."

On the way to the limo, Christian saw Vanna's car parked near a hotdog vendor. He suspected she might have dined as well as he had and at a much more reasonable price. He wondered if a hotdog was an allowable expense and if Vanna got paid overtime. She'd been putting in a lot of dull hours keeping tabs on him. Good thing he was giving her a night out.

Chapter Thirty-Six

At each of a series of dance clubs, they whisked past the line, Kathy paid the appropriate bribe and they were ushered into a crowded room where a table always waited. They would dance to a beat that was to Christian's ears largely devoid of music--all four on the floor together and separate-- and leave again, their drinks untouched. Christian hadn't heard of any of the clubs before, and didn't consider their names worth remembering.

After the fourth such stop, Kathy needed to replenish her bankroll. "They're all poor imitations of The Second Circle," Christian said, handing her bills. "Dull, duller and dullest. Are we going to give Dance Dance Dance a try?" He didn't think they'd been there. He remembered the name from the end of Judy's broadcast.

Kathy laughed. "You'd hate it. The band playing there couldn't hum a tune if they tried. Christian, you've just been at four of Noronto's top nightspots and I'm sure everyone noticed how bored you looked. They'll be wondering who you are-- ¬everyone knows me and most recognize Judy--a few might even recognize fat boy. People will figure you must be a someone to be moving in such fast company. But you're right, of course, those places are for folks who don't have the balls to go to The Second Circle."

Horatio took that personally. "It's an evil place."

"Bah and humbug. The Second Circle's a business, supplying a needed product."

"I didn't appreciate it at the time," Christian said. "But at least the clientele there is interesting." And so was the company... well... Lucy at any rate.

"Exactly. I was a regular there once upon a time, long before the latest change in management. Not that I don't appreciate all the free passes-- before, I always had to pay to get in. But no, we're not going there tonight."

"Why not?"

"Any number of reasons. Not the least of which is, whether she appreciates me or not, I still look out for Judy. Remember what happened last time you took a date there, Christian?" Kathy tilted her head towards Judy. "The new owner of The Second Circle has the hots for Christian. He went there with Aurora and there was a frightful scene. Christian had to step in, or it would have come to blows."

Judy shrank against Christian. "No, I don't think we want to go there."

Christian couldn't tell from Kathy's account whether or not she knew what had happened. Lucy had been rude, quite true, but Christian was reasonably certain that had been personal and to do with Aurora as herself, not as his date. As for it almost coming to blows, well... yes and no. Aurora had taken a swing she'd intended him to stop, and they'd left. Still, Christian was just as happy not to go to The Second Circle. The only time he'd been there since had been to return Patsy's damage deposit.

"So where are we going? Another dump like the last four?"

"I like those clubs," Judy said quietly. Horatio mumbled agreement.

"No, and this is our last stop. It's one of Noronto's true meat markets, a place where successful men meet young, available flesh. Horatio knows it well, from back when he had money. They play real music there, quiet enough to talk over and suitable for romantic dancing."

The club was as promised. Christian and Horatio were among the youngest men. Kathy might have been the oldest woman but dressed as she almost wasn't, by far the most eye-catching. She made a substantial gift to the doorman and they were directed to a table on the far side of the room.

Judy clung to Christian like a limpet. "Oh my, now this... this is decadent. I feel so old. That girl there... she doesn't look over sixteen. He could be her grandfather."

"Her rich and overly affectionate grandfather." Christian thought of Vanna. From what she'd said, this would be her kind of place. Maybe she'd come in.

Judy waited for Christian to pull out a chair. When he did, she didn't sit.

Instead, she turned to him. "This is where I make you mine. Let's dance."

"I think I'm going to barf." Kathy was beside them. "That is, if Christian doesn't beat me to it," she continued. "Like I said, Judy, I'm going to look out for you... whether you like it or not. Can't you see the man's not interested? Go dance with

Horatio. He can gaze into your soft, exciting eyes and you can check out his virility." Kathy had Judy and Horatio's earlier endearments at The Factory down pat, mimicking and exaggerating the key words with deadly accuracy.

Judy moved a hurt expression from Kathy to Christian. "I did tell you she hadn't let you two off the hook, didn't I?" Christian asked, thankful he'd been right. "Better do as she suggests."

Christian danced with Kathy. She felt silky smooth. "Not that I don't appreciate getting away from her, but that wasn't very nice."

"I'm not nice, I'm good. Anyway, sometimes you have to be cruel to be kind."

"I remember that song. Nick Lowe, one of his best."

"I know. Judy wouldn't. I doubt Aurora would either. Lowe never made it big enough for her to notice."

Christian stopped dancing and gently pushed Kathy away. "Okay, I think you've made your point. Time to have mercy." Horatio and Judy were dancing, awkwardly. Neither looked happy.

There was ice in Kathy's steel blue eyes. "Don't think so. The merciful thing would be to keep you and Judy apart. Otherwise, people are going to get hurt."

"People are getting hurt right now." Christian conducted Kathy to Judy and Horatio. "Time to switch partners." The smug smile that spread on Judy's face caused him to instantly regret his words, and his decision.

"I knew I was going to win," Judy said once they were away from Kathy and Horatio. "It had to be. It's our destiny to be together."

Christian's stomach grumbled. The dinner had been appalling, and this wasn't helping. "You haven't won anything. I figured Horatio'd suffered enough for letting you come on to him."

Judy didn't answer, but instead jammed herself solidly against him. Over her shoulder Christian saw Vanna enter the club. Even dressed modestly her slender waist, platinum blonde curls and well-developed upper half made her an immediate target. She caught Christian's eye, winked, and settled on a bar stool to consider offers.

"You're coming around. I can feel you're interested." Judy's hand started to wander. Christian blocked it. "My feelings won't be hurt if you call me Aurora by mistake."

"Why would I do that?"

"Oh, I don't know... maybe in a moment of passion. After all, I'm so much like her."

Judy was the same height as Aurora and approximately the same build. All similarity ended there. Aurora was diamond and Judy... butter. Christian separated from her, quit dancing and held her at arms' length. "We'd better sit. We need to talk."

Judy went quietly. If Christian had used the same tone with Aurora, he'd have been in big trouble. Kathy and Horatio also returned to the table. Judy ignored them. Her eyes remained riveted on Christian.

311

"You're not at all like Aurora," he continued. "And if you try to operate like her, it won't work. Sure, you can do the job she was doing, but as Judy... not as a redheaded Medici clone. Try that, and you're going to screw up. Aurora's one of a kind, thank God. I think you're going to become someone special, but you still need to grow into yourself. You're not there yet."

"Okay, so I'm not her. I'm me, and I think I'm pretty special. You said you used to get up early just to see me on television. Come home with me tonight. Tomorrow morning you can see me live, on you."

"You'd take it too seriously."

"Don't be so damn condescending. If that happens, it's my problem, isn't it now?"

"Only half. It's not a good idea."

Judy turned to Kathy. "Can we get out of here? I'd rather continue this in the limo." She stood and left. Kathy caught up with her a few tables away.

"You're nuts, Christian," Horatio said as he stood. "Never turn down free tail." He lumbered after Kathy and Judy without waiting for an answer.

A philosophy to live for, Christian thought as he got up. He didn't see much point in continuing anything in the limo but there was even less in staying in the bar by himself. He passed Vanna at the bar. Her pale eyes asked him a question.

He went over. "I'll be going back to Grace's, so you don't need to follow. Stick around and enjoy yourself. You've been working hard lately from what I've seen."

"You bastard!" Judy was back. "I saw her earlier. Making a date, are you? Well, if you'd rather sleep with this trash than the woman who wants to have your children, well then... I say go to hell, Christian Plowman!" Judy further punctuated his name by picking up the vile pink concoction in front of Vanna and throwing it in Christian's face. She stormed away, past Horatio who was by the door, doubled over laughing.

Vanna slipped off her stool. "Thanks, but it's time I was going too. This guy's a loser. I was just killing time."

Horatio had more or less composed himself by the time Christian reached the door. "Thank you, Christian, for a most entertaining night. And, if you're riding with us and not your blonde friend, I strongly suggest you remain silent. Explanations would be wasted effort."

"No kidding."

In the limo, Judy sat as far from Christian as she could. Horatio had a big, silly grin he couldn't seem to lose, and even Kathy was having a hard time keeping a smirk hidden. "I told you so" was written on her face.

Judy saw all. "I'm going to Aurora's. She's not at the studio tonight. She's waiting there for... for me."

Silence reigned until they pulled to a stop in front of Aurora's building. "You should walk Judy in, Horatio," Kathy said. Horatio got out before Judy. Judy slammed the door.

"Are you really?" Kathy finished her sentence by jerking a thumb towards the back window. A

313

now familiar old sedan was behind them, Vanna, still on the job.

"No, but I'm not going to try to explain her to you either."

"Fair enough. Then, since you just turned down a two girls and one guy scene, could I interest you in two guys and one girl?"

"Kathy! I couldn't do that to Horatio."

"I'm not suggesting that... you can both do it to me. Of course, if you did him as well it'd be the biggest thrill of his life. Come on, Christian, grow up. There's nothing wrong with it. I can handle two, and it's not like you guys haven't shared a woman before. Only difference is, this time you'll both be in the same bed at the same time."

"I suspected he had an affair with Cleo at some time, but..." Except he hadn't suspected, not consciously. A lot suddenly made sense to Christian.

"That stupid..." Kathy couldn't find a word to fit. "The way he talks about the good old days, I didn't even consider you might not know." The door opened. Kathy quickly moved beside Christian. "Horatio Beeble, you're an even bigger jerk than I thought. He didn't know about you and Cleo!" The limo moved off.

Horatio slumped. "For a long time I was convinced he did and then I decided it was just he didn't want to see. It was so obvious." Horatio's voice was flat. "Right from the beginning, after she had been with him, the earth moved for me every time."

"And you play at being his friend. Some friend." Kathy picked up the phone to the driver. "Stop the car, please. Someone's getting out." The car pulled to the side of the road.

Horatio opened the door. "Sorry, Christian."

"Like hell you are. After Christian has me, I promise you'll never touch me again. Get out!"

The door clicked shut and the limo started moving again. "The earth moved indeed. It should swallow that piece of walking shit." She put a hand on Christian's knee. "So, if I've got you read right, you're going to turn down the best piece of ass you've ever been offered again, aren't you?"

"I have to. If I don't, then you and Horatio are really through and I'd be responsible."

"Yes, you would consider that honourable. Would it help if I told you your mother would say to screw my ass off, and then laugh in Horatio's face?"

"My mother isn't with us anymore. I have to make my own decisions. I hope you know this one's hard."

Kathy's hand strayed upward. Hers, he didn't block. "Yes, I can tell." She kissed him lightly and moved away.

After Kathy got out, and the limo was on its way to Grace's, Christian looked out the back window. Vanna was still there.

Chapter Thirty-Seven

The hangover Christian had Saturday afternoon puzzled him. He didn't remember drinking much. Even when he did, he seldom felt this bad. He stared at a cup of thick, old, reheated coffee. It sneered back at him.

He sipped it. It was as vile as it'd promised. It suited the day. Maybe he should have stayed with Kathy. Physically, she was exactly the woman he'd have pinned on his wall when he was younger. He still might, if he had an appropriate picture. He'd enjoyed her company far more than he'd expected. Kathy was tough, cynical and witty in addition to being beautiful. And surprisingly easy to talk to.

Christian downed the remainder of the lukewarm coffee and shuddered. Okay, Kathy was beautiful but she was a man-eater. His stomach churned. Maybe fresh air would help. He needed groceries anyway. He'd almost eaten his way through Grace's freezer.

He grabbed a jacket and the drink-splattered suit from the night before, went downstairs. He dropped off the suit at the dry-cleaner next to the bank. As he came out, he saw the other pin-up in his life sitting in her ramshackle car. She waved him over.

"You look like warmed-over shit," she said after Christian got in the passenger side.

He twisted his legs to fit the pushed-forward seat. "Thanks, Vanna. It's a package deal. I feel like shit too."

"Any plans for the rest of the weekend?"

"Why? And why are you talking to me? I thought you were trying to be inconspicuous."

"Yeah, like I've had much success doing that. Anyway, I figure our cover's blown. Freyja beat the crap out of dear Justin in a Paris alley and then lost him. I need to take some time off... get my hair done, buy some clothes--you know, girl stuff. So I figured if you'd be a nice guy again and tell me what you're planning, I can fit all that in and not miss anything important."

"Might as well take the whole weekend off. I'm going for groceries, and then I'm going to hole up."

"Really? Far out! I'll drive you to the store." The car lurched forward, and Christian's coffee considered a return visit to the world.

"So..." Vanna shifted gears. Christian's insides lurched with the car. "You're going to pass up Kathy, I guess. Good move. She may have it upstairs and up front, but she doesn't have it in the bank. Hangs out with a rough crowd too. Say, where'd she get that outfit? I'd look good in it, wouldn't I?"

"Try not to jerk the car, please? That outfit? Maison de Fade. But you don't need anything like that. Neither does she, but with your figure, you'd overwhelm it. You'd do better in something understated. Why gild the lily? You should dress to bring out your character."

Vanna brought the car to an abrupt halt in front of a supermarket. Christian's knees slammed into the dash. "Oops, sorry," Vanna said. "You think I'm that good looking?" She preened in the rear-view

317

mirror. "Compared to Kathy? How about next to Aurora, or Freyja?"

Christian took a moment to see if his stomach would settle. The coffee decided the world was boring after all and the trip up not worth the effort. "On the surface you cut them to shreds. But think of the difference between Judy and Aurora. Realistically, Aurora's unexceptional except for her eyes. But it doesn't matter--she is Aurora Medici. And sure, Marci and especially Kathy are beautiful, but that isn't what draws people, not after the first look. It's their presence, style and character. I don't know quite what to call it, but they've got something most people only have in flashes, like say, Judy does. Most of the time, she's bland... pleasant and bland maybe, but bland all the same. Now you, you do have character, and for my money you're so spectacular physically that you could do well for yourself with just that. But..."

"Yeah." Vanna interrupted Christian's ramble. "Your money. That's the problem. If you had any... go get your stuff. I'll wait here."

When Christian returned with his groceries, Vanna pulled away smoothly. They returned to Casa del Carlos in silence.

"You're okay, you know that?" Vanna said as Christian got out. "Hope you feel better soon."

The car glided away. In the lobby, Fred, the security guard, scrutinised Christian closely as he passed, but didn't say a word.

318

Chapter Thirty-Eight

Christian kept to his stated plan, and didn't go out again that weekend. He played computer games, slaying virtual monsters by the thousand. Once in a while he took a break and tried to read, but he couldn't concentrate on a book. He turned on the TV dozens of times, flicking through the channels and then turning it off. Thoughts flickered though his mind on occasion, then flickered out as well. The stereo was on all the time, but it was background noise. He didn't check for e-mail or phone messages.

Sunday blended into Monday and then Tuesday. He ordered in food. The delivery people were the only ones he talked to and their conversational interests were limited.

Wednesday, in the early afternoon, Christian was confronting the latest evil tyrant, when he heard the apartment door open. He didn't get up.

"So there you are."

Christian shot a nuclear missile at the overlord of darkness. Missed. He adjusted his aim. Marci reached over and turned the computer off.

"I was winning!"

"You're disgusting." She turned him around in his chair and lifted him by his shirt. "What the hell are you doing? You're a mess. I come back to Noronto, hoping to get some painting done and then Aurora calls, asking if I'd seen you. She says Horatio's impossible and she's so busy consoling Judy she can't deal with him too. I head to The

319

Factory to check things out and Kathy starts to cry on my shoulder. Kathy? Get upstairs. Shave. Clean up. Now!"

Christian didn't have much choice. Marci had carried him to the bottom of the stairs.

By the time he returned, Marci had thrown away his litter of fast food boxes and the dishwasher was running. "That's better. Slightly. You still look like walking scum but that may just be me. Get a coat. It's cold outside."

"How was Europe?" Christian asked as he moved to obey.

"Still there." Marci put on her own coat. "Most of Grace's associates are decent... helpful, responsible... everything you aren't."

Christian didn't risk any more conversational gambits on the way downstairs. Outside, Marci turned away from Yonge Street and the subway, and towards Vanna's car. "I noticed this on the way in."

Justin was back with Vanna. Marci walked up to the passenger door and yanked it open. "Get out. Now. Both of you."

As Justin pried himself out, Vanna circled around the front to stand beside Christian. Marci ignored her. Her focus was on Justin, who towered over even her. "Yeah? You fucking got something to fucking say? Woman?" To him that was probably the ultimate insult.

"I saw you skulking around my house last night. I don't want that to happen again."

"So fucking invite me in and I'll show you what it feel like to have a real man fucking you."

Christian wasn't sure if he was more surprised at Justin's nerve, or at his finally using his favourite word in proper, if unwise, context.

"A real man? Where? Remember Paris? One tap on your thick head and you were out cold--long enough for me to check all the phoney ID you carry. I'd say you're with the government. No one else would be dumb enough to hire you."

"I'll quote that line in my report," Vanna said to Christian, quietly. "You can bet on that."

"You didn't fucking play fair. You sneaked up and used a fucking pipe or something. It won't happen again, cunt. Come on, admit it--you fucking want me--you want what you were feeling up at the fucking dance." He grabbed his crotch to make sure Marci understood exactly what he meant.

"I hit you with my bare hand--and somehow I except you're as bad at fucking as you are at fighting, you big pussy."

"I'll fucking show you what!" Justin reached out to put Marci in a bear hug.

She shot a kick where it did the most good... the place Justin claimed he had a big target. As he folded, she landed an elbow on the back of his neck. Justin's head bounced once on the curb. He stayed down.

"I can't tell you how much I enjoyed that!" Vanna started to applaud.

Marci turned. "You're next," she said, advancing.

Vanna huddled close to Christian and he put an arm around her. His hand landed in an interesting spot, but then again, Vanna didn't have many spots that weren't interesting.

"Oh, so it's like that, is it? Well, she's been stalking Aurora and Judy, and Fred says security wants this eyesore of a car gone. I suspect calling the cops wouldn't do any good, but if she's yours, Christian, tell her to lay off or else."

Justin started writhing and moaning on the pavement. Marci stepped over him and taking a handful of coat, hoisted and shoved him towards the still open passenger door. "I went easy on you, wimp. You shouldn't need to go to a hospital, but bother me again and I'll boot your balls into your brains--not that I think you have either."

"Another quote," Vanna said, quietly this time as Justin staggered onto the seat and tried to fit his body in. Vanna gave Christian a final squeeze before running around to her door. She got in and adjusted the seat back a notch. For Justin? Marci must have done a lot of damage.

Marci had left the scene. She stood in front of Casa del Carlos, hands on hips, waiting for Christian. As he approached, her scowl darkened. "And I didn't believe Judy about you and that baggage. You filthy, miserable..." She searched for a suitably vicious word. "Man!"

Christian winced. Of all the epitaphs she could write, that was, for her, the ultimate. "Marci, I'm not..."

"Oh shut up! You're not anything. But you're going to The Factory anyway. Let's see if you can manage one decent action."

The trip downtown was accomplished in hostile silence.

As Marci crashed through the front door of The Factory, Christian in tow, Kathy looked up from the switchboard. "Christian!" She ripped off her headset and sped to him, into his arms. "Play along and I'll get you out of this," she whispered in his ear.

"Kathy! All the lines are lighting up." Marci was at the desk.

"Who cares?" Kathy kissed Christian.

"Kathy!"

Kathy held the kiss and got all four of their hands involved. She reclaimed her tongue from his throat as he began to struggle for breath. Christian felt much better. His hangover was gone. "I'll be off soon," Kathy whispered. "Wait for me. We need to talk."

"Yes, we do." Christian removed his hands from two intimate locations.

Kathy wafted her way back to her post, ignoring Marci. She put her headset back on and flipped a switch down. All the lights went out. She turned the switchboard back on. "There... all taken care of. See? There was no need to panic. See you later, Christian."

If the mood had been unfriendly before, on the way to Cosmo's office it was glacial. Cosmo hung up the phone when he saw them. Marci left Christian and threw herself onto the couch.

"I've written Grace, complaining about you." Cosmo didn't stand, much less offer a hand to be shaken.

"That's interesting." Christian sat in the most comfortable armchair and made a show of relaxing. "What did you tell her?"

"Everything! I told her everything... how you seduced my niece and then poor, innocent Judy, and not content with that, stole your best friend's fiancée. And you haven't done a thing you've were contracted to do. Grace made a huge mistake hiring you, that's what I told her. You've destroyed me. The Factory is chaos, thanks to you--I don't want to see you here again--you're anathema. Get out of my sight." Cosmo collapsed in his chair, panting. His bald spot was as livid a red as his face.

Christian went and crouched beside Marci. "I know you're furious, but for God's sake, calm him down. I seduced Aurora? Sure I did. He's lost his grip. I'll do what I can to clear things up, but not because I've done anything wrong. It's just... someone has to."

Christian stood. Cosmo waved a wild hand and tried to stand also, but failed, falling back into his chair, gurgling invective.

Kathy was still at her desk when Christian got back to the lobby. "I'd better go. Cardinal Cosmo excommunicated me so I'm persona non grata here at The Factory. You know where Aurora is? I need to tell her Cosmo's fallen apart."

"I'm gone too." Kathy again tore off her headset.

"No. Don't do it that way, please. Get someone to cover. I'll wait outside."

Kathy's eyes shifted from steel to titanium for an instant, and then softened again to steel. "Only because you said 'please'." She sat.

She was with Christian, outside on The Street, within two minutes. "Good thing I'm owed so many favours. I gave notice though--two weeks and I'm history. What a bunch of idiots... speaking of which, Aurora's at Beeble Productions."

As they travelled, Christian filled Kathy in on what had happened since Marci had arrived at Grace's earlier that afternoon. "She claimed you were crying on her shoulder? Hard to believe."

"Good. I sucked her in. You haven't been answering your phone or your e-mail, and I figured she'd manage to dig you out. Sorry... didn't think she'd do it so emphatically but after Friday night, my life's a mess. The Factory really is falling apart and Judy's moving out--says it's my fault she didn't bag your ass. Horatio told Aurora what happened after Judy split, and now they all figure we did the deed."

"So you want me to tell them nothing happened."

"No, I don't want you to lie. Something happened... just say we didn't screw. Until Horatio's convinced of that, I can't take him back."

Kathy had told Horatio after Christian had her, Horatio never would again. Christian hadn't, therefore Horatio still could. Christian waited until they were outside Beeble Productions before asking the obvious question. "You want to get back together with Horatio?"

325

"I want it to end for the right reasons... reasons which have nothing to do with you."

Once again, there was no one in the outer areas of Beeble Productions. Progress, however, had been made. The equipment that had been piled in boxes was set up and ready to go. The entire place was spotless. Christian and Kathy went through to the first studio. Horatio was at the control board, fiddling with knobs and levers. Faint music came from his headphones. Inside the glass booth, Aurora was arguing with an assortment of musicians and a man Christian recognized as the regular soundboard technician. None of them looked happy.

Aurora noticed the new arrivals and came out. "You showed up just in time." Her back was to Horatio. "He thinks he's an expert. Unless he smartens up, the guys say they're out of here. Deal with it." Aurora's face was flushed the same colour Cosmo's had been earlier.

Kathy made a wide circle around Aurora, went to Horatio and took his headphones off. "Christian wants to talk to you. In your office. Now." She had to grab Horatio's arm to steady him. The whites of his eyes were solid red. Christian followed them down the hall.

In Horatio's office, Kathy pushed Horatio onto the couch and stood back. "Should I stay?" she asked Christian.

"Please," he answered. He sat beside Horatio and wished he hadn't. Along with sixteen hours sleep, the man desperately needed a shower. "Horatio. You make me sick." It wasn't far from the truth. Horatio mumbled something that contained the words "Cleo" and "sorry", and hung his head.

Christian reached out and lifted it back up. "I can forgive you for Cleo. That's easy. It's in the past. But right now you're making a fool of me all over again. I told everyone you could make a success of this place. If you feel you need to do something to patch things up, then make Beeble Productions work. You're a salesman. What you're best at is creating a positive atmosphere, and convincing people to take chances. Concentrate on that. You can't do everything. Quit trying. Let others do what they do best as well."

Christian let Horatio's head sag again and got up. "Think any of that got through?" he asked Kathy.

"Gee, I hope so. They certainly were words to live by. Now, about me?"

"Oh yes." Christian sat again. "Horatio, I was too smart to sleep with Kathy."

"Huh?" Horatio's head lifted on its own.

"That's right. She's still all yours, you poor bastard." Christian got up again. "Happy now, Kathy?"

"Overjoyed. I love you too." She hugged him. "I do owe you one, sort of. I'll find a way to pay you back. Count on it."

Aurora was waiting for Christian in the control room. "So, all cleared up?" Her face was a more normal colour, but he heard the anger in her voice.

"I tried. I'm sure you'll tell me if it isn't."

"Damn right."

"I was just at The Factory. Cosmo kicked me out and told me not to come back."

Aurora shrugged. "Worse things could happen. Now, if you'll excuse me, I'm working. Other than for the recording, things are going very well for me, thank you ever so much. I'm planning a guest set at a club soon."

Maybe if they talked about her for a few minutes she'd calm down enough to listen. "You're ready to perform in public?"

"It's not brain surgery, Christian. I wrote the stuff at your place and have professional backing. Stardom's about image, not music. VideoView'll be taping me for broadcast too. Everything is coming together. My album will go gold before I finish it. Anything else you want to know?"

"Maybe why you're angry with me?"

Aurora laughed. "With you? I was ready to throttle Horatio, but I couldn't be angry with you... not after all you've done for me. Come on, I'll walk you out."

They walked out into the empty but neat space that was the outer office of Beeble Productions. Aurora shook her head. "I sure hope he does something about this soon. The recording business is ninety percent promotion, like all show biz."

"Tell him... after he's had some sleep. You sure sounded angry with me."

"You're so self-centred, Christian. The damn world doesn't revolve around you. Speaking of sleep, I haven't been getting much." Aurora punched his arm lightly. "Now if you want to see someone who's pissed at you, see Judy. Hell hath no fury like a woman scorned, and all that crap."

"Maybe she's the one who's been filling Cosmo's ears with lies about me." He again tried to shift the conversation the direction he wanted it to go.

Aurora stopped by the door out. "Maybe, but what's the problem? Your job there is done. Judy gets Ovation."

"Why? Because she's sleeping with you? Cosmo would love that, proof positive he was right. And even if she does, what about your old job? Who gets that? I don't think I'm finished with The Factory any more than I think you are." Christian watched Aurora digest his logic. Her expression became wide-eyed dismay.

Christian pressed his advantage. "The place is crumbling without you. Kathy's put in her notice. If you're going to look after your mother's interests, and your inheritance, I think you'd better get back there... pronto."

"You do, do you? And who told you about our family arrangements? I'll bet it was that blonde... Vanna, Judy said her name is. Freyja told me she's some sort of government investigator. I don't care. She's dead meat if she doesn't back off."

"Freyja, I mean Marci, already delivered that message."

"Good. As for the rest of it... no. I'm not going back unless Cosmo gives me full control. And if he did, Kathy would be out the door within the hour."

He should have left well enough alone, and not mentioned Aurora's stake in The Factory, but since he hadn't, he had one last question. "But you told me the day we met, you didn't want to be an administrator... you wanted to stay in the limelight."

"He was trying to turn me into a flunky, Christian. You helped me escape that. Would I go back if he turned things over to me? Of course. Then I could have both the power and the glory. Who wouldn't want that?"

Chapter Thirty-Nine

Thursday morning there was e-mail from Grace, sent to both Marci and Christian. "Cosmo doesn't sound happy?"

Marci's response. "Don't worry. He's been pacified."

Grace's answer. "Did I say I was worried?"

That exchange seemed over and didn't require any input from him. After breakfast he took up the task of tidying the apartment where Marci had left it. She'd been right; he'd let himself go. Christian didn't understand why the revelation about Horatio and Cleo had affected him so deeply. It probably hadn't. More likely it had just been the last bit of the accumulated chaos needed to tip him over. In some ways he'd been better off before he met Grace. Life had been simpler then, more certain.

He was in the kitchen when the apartment door opened. "Hi, Marci. Here to chew me out again?"

"No, to apologize."

"Why? You were right. I needed a kick."

"You did. And the goon begged for one in the nuts, and your girlfriend needed to be told to clean up her act."

Vanna wasn't his girlfriend, but Christian didn't think it wise to break Marci's flow. "But I didn't have any business threatening her..." Marci continued "You'd think I was jealous! When I cooled down, I realized you're naive, but a pretty good judge of character. If you like her, she must be okay."

"You don't believe I led Judy on?"

"Not any more. I talked to her. I'd say your mistake was not running away fast enough, or sooner. She's a real troublemaker I'm sorry, Christian."

"Apology accepted. Have you checked your e-mail recently?"

"Grace?" Marci asked, and went to the computer. "Not worthy of another reply," she said after reading Grace's quip. "And she should have been worried. Grace relies far too much on others to clean up after her." She stood. "Is the coffee fresh?" She headed off to find out for herself.

"So how is Cosmo, really?"

"Okay. He's a solid man, if a bit vain. And he's under control for the moment." The answer drifted back to him.

Christian caught up with Marci in the kitchen. "Your control?"

She paused, coffee pot in hand. "For now. You asked me to intervene, and I did. I've got a confession to make." She put the pot down, her cup still empty. "I was jealous." She shrugged. "Seeing Kathy crawl over you made me see it. I've no right to feel possessive. I'm no better than Judy."

Christian poured Marci's coffee for her. "I disagree. And to make amends, you're with Cosmo?"

Marci sipped. "Like I said, he's okay. Besides, it gives me something to do."

"The painting isn't going well?" Christian didn't even want to think about Marci and Cosmo together, much less discuss it.

332

"No. Now I've got the time and opportunity to create, the muse has left me." She took her coffee, sat at the table and stared out the window.

Christian moved between her and the world. "What did you do in Europe? Exactly?"

"In Paris, Gabby helped me close off Freyja's affairs and clean out her apartment. Then I went to Zurich and Peter put Freyja's finances in order. She's piled up a bundle over the years, I hadn't realized how much. In terms of money, she did well by me."

"You turned her off like she was a light. Was that what Grace suggested?"

"She told me I needed to sort myself out. I decided making a clean break from Freyja was the only way."

"So you gave yourself a lobotomy. No wonder you can't paint."

Marci's eyes were deep, brown, and blank. Christian tried again. "I remember you telling me Freyja frightened you--you thought she might be stronger than Marci. All I can do is say again what I told you then... you are Freyja, and Freyja is Marci. The demon you exorcised is yourself."

Silence. On cue, the sun burst through the clouds and into Marci's eyes. She turned her head away from it, and away from Christian. He stood, and went to put a hand on her shoulder. She wouldn't meet his eyes. "I never thought I'd use this phrase literally," Christian said, "But for God's sake, woman... pull yourself together!"

She rewarded him with a wan smile, more than Christian thought his attempted joke deserved. But at least something had registered. Finally, she looked up at him. Christian glanced into the living room. Marci stood and let Christian lead her out of the sunlight. He sat beside her on the couch.

"It's interesting," he continued. "One of the few things Grace told me is that image is everything. And she wanted me to work on mine. I thought she meant my public image, but I've realized that's worthless until my self-image improves. When I think about the people I've met since Grace hired me, I see the two go together. People with a high opinion of themselves are seen as being of consequence by others... very often for no other reason. When it's someone like you, like Freyja, whose complete confidence has a basis, the effect is overwhelming. Grace and Lucy are the only two I've met who are like that all the time. When you're yourself, Freyja, you're in their class." Christian stopped and waited.

"You do have your moments," she finally said, softly.

When she didn't continue, Christian did. "Thank you. I'm not sure I do. See? That's my problem. I'm always surprised when someone says I'm worth knowing. I figure they're making a mistake and to protect them, I back off. No more. I'm going to go with the flow, trust what I'm feeling and take my chances. If I'm wrong, at least my mistakes will be different... and maybe more fun. I'm going to interpret what Grace told me the way I want to. I think you need to as well. Okay, so Grace said you needed to sort yourself out. Maybe she meant you should pull your selves together, not slice off a third, then toss it out."

"I don't give a shit what she meant. Grace is an interfering hag. She butts in and then buggers off. You're right. I never should have listened to her."

Was that what he'd said? It didn't matter. Christian was looking into the eyes of Freyja. "Good to have you back. I love you... like a sister."

"An older, wiser sister, I hope." Christian knew she was younger than him, but it wasn't a time to argue. "Speaking of which?" Freyja added, "Talked to your younger one?"

"No, I haven't got in touch with Aster."

"Do it. So... now that you've paid me back and booted my ass in return, what are your plans? What's the new, improved Christian going to do now?"

He hadn't thought about it. His response surprised him. "Right now, I'm moving back to my apartment. Grace's place is just too damn comfortable. No wonder I got lazy."

"Don't blame your surroundings, but thank-you, Christian. You've given me a lot to mull over, a lot to do. I'm going to go do it." Her kiss was platonic. He felt mildly disappointed by that.

Chapter Forty

Christian didn't waste time packing. He watered the plants and sent e-mail notification of his move to all who might be concerned: Grace, Cosmo, Aurora, Freyja (even though she already knew), and as an afterthought, Lucy. At the dry cleaner, he picked up the suit Judy had soaked with Vanna's pink, sticky drink. The stain had come out, but at a price. He paid it with Grace's credit card. He exited and walked towards the subway.

A short way down the block a candy-red sports car screeched to a halt beside him, honking its horn. Vanna? Evidently she'd chosen to interpret Marci's warning about not letting her old car be seen on Grace's street again to her advantage. She had new wheels.

She touched a button and the passenger window rolled down. "Like it? Hey, where are you going?"

"Home. You have the address."

"Ah shit, you would. Leave this baby on the street in that part of town, and it'll be stolen or stripped bare in minutes. What happened? Grace side with crazy Cosmo and toss you out?" Vanna got out of her growling auto and came around the front. Her tight jeans fit perfectly, short jacket unbuttoned--it couldn't have done up--and she wore a beret at a rakish angle. She'd cut her platinum hair closer to her head. All in all she looked like a woman who belonged in a fast car.

"No, I decided home is where the heart is."

"Then you're the crazy one. What could you miss about that dump? The leaking lobby, the garbage in the halls, or is it the losers, deadbeats and junkies you have for neighbours? You like the beret, eh? I saw you checking out the one I had on when we met on The Street. I decided it's my quirk. Like it?"

"It's you. You're wrong about my neighbours though. Sure, some of them are like you say. But most of them are good people." And a few, fascinating... like Liza. Christian had almost forgotten about her. She was the best reason he'd thought of so far for moving back. Vanna wouldn't appreciate that. Liza was undoubtedly poor.

"So, want a ride?"

Christian took another look at her car and remembering Vanna's driving habits, saw a red fibreglass coffin. "I'll pass, thanks anyway. After all, I am trying to get back to the simple life."

Vanna looked hurt. Christian hadn't intended that, he did like her, a lot. He just didn't like her driving. And, from what he'd seen, she was only trying to do her job, however impossible the government tried to make it. "I think I'll go to The Second Circle later," he decided on the spur of the moment. He was tired of only himself for company. "Maybe I'll see you there."

"Count on it." Vanna beamed. "I like that place. I'll pump my esteemed colleague full of pain killers and we'll be there."

"So, how's the investigation going?" Might as well see if she'd tell him anything.

337

"It's entered a new phase." It sounded like she was reciting a line from a document.

"Which means?"

"That what we were doing was pointless, so now we've been told to do something equally pointless, but different. The paperweights in Ottawa like calling that 'entering a new phase'. Weather's getting cold." She shivered to make her point, which also called attention to her scenic wonders. "See you later." Vanna made her way back to the driver's seat, put the car in gear, and left a patch of rubber half a block long. Christian congratulated himself on the wisdom of turning down a ride. Vanna was undoubtedly smart, breathtakingly beautiful and attractively sarcastic, but it wasn't worth his life to ride with her again. The subway ride was uneventful.

As Christian walked into the dim lobby of his building, he saw a figure coming the other direction. Fate was on his side. "Hi, Liza."

"Well hi there..."

That was right. He'd been so tongue-tied he hadn't given her his name.

"Christian."

"Well hi there, Christian. Glad to hear that laryngitis has cleared up. If you're going to ask me out, do it soon. I'm moving on at the end of the month."

"Tonight?"

"Sorry, I'm going to work. You didn't think I dress like this for fun, did you?"

"I didn't notice the uniform," Christian answered. He'd been noticing her, and comparing her to Vanna. Physically, they were complete opposites. In contrast to Vanna's blonde extravagance, Liza was tall, lean and dark. Her beauty was almost understated, but every bit as overwhelming in its way. Her eyes were black, and Vanna's without colour but Christian saw much the same thing in them, a sparkling sense of delight at being alive. That wasn't anything he'd been used to seeing. He found it attractive.

"You should notice it." She pinched a fold of the sleeve with her fingers. "It's cheap polyester. Makes you sweat, and no matter how often you wash it, it holds the smell of stale grease." And like Vanna, her words made her sound world-worn, but her eyes always said that was a lie. "Speaking of which. I hear a rack of burgers calling. Tell you what, Christian... after tonight, I'm off until Monday. Drop over anytime. I'll be there. Bye now."

When he stepped into his apartment, Christian realized it wasn't home... it was just where he'd lived for the past three plus years. Still, he thought he would be better off here than at Grace's, if only because he wouldn't be tempted to stay in. He had before, but couldn't any more. He'd changed.

He went out to buy groceries. When he returned, he stood in the hall for a moment, staring at Liza's door. Why was she living here? Vanna's opinion of the building's occupants hadn't been fair but it hadn't been totally inaccurate. This was the outer edge of desperation. Some here had given up and were still hanging on. Others were struggling to get out. Christian had been in the first group but didn't fit it any more. Liza certainly didn't either. She might belong in the second category, except she didn't give any sense of struggling. Liza was just passing through.

It was still too early to go downtown. Christian looked around his box again. His eyes came to rest on his old, soundless, black-and-white television. It had to go. He could afford a new one; he'd been paid. He took it downstairs, and left it in the lobby. Someone would pick it up, probably thinking they were stealing the set. Christian rather hoped so, and that it would bring them joy. The television wouldn't.

The nearest electronics store was a block away. Christian managed to convince the sales clerk that in a one-room apartment, a forty-inch screen wasn't needed. He bought the best twenty-inch portable available, and a good antenna. After unpacking his purchases at the store, Christian lugged them back. Predictably, his old TV had vanished.

Christian hooked everything up. The picture was clear, and there was sound. COSMO-TV was showing a talk show that seemed to be about blonde housewives who had affairs with priests. Christian turned the television off.

It was still too early to go to The Second Circle but he felt restless. He put on the nightclubbing outfit he'd bought from Eunice at The Black Hole. It felt uncomfortable. He pinched the fabric. Polyester--slick against his skin like it hadn't been cleaned. He looked in the mirror, and decided that while he still looked like himself, this clothing didn't suit him at all. He left it on. If he hurried, he

340

might still have time to get to The Street and find something better before the stores closed.

***

Once on The Street, Christian window-shopped. Everything looked pretty much like what he was wearing. Nothing caught his eye. He passed a building for the second time and noticed a small sign, "Maison de Fade--upstairs". He went up. They might not have anything for him, but he did want to meet the person who had designed Kathy's sensational white outfit.

The door at the top opened into a small room, packed with racks of dresses, skirts and blouses. An unshaven man in tattered jeans looked up from a magazine. "Hello. We were gearing up to leave, but we certainly won't turn down business."

"I'm not sure I am business. You're Rory?"

"Indeed, and the advantage is yours," he said, closing the magazine.

"I'm a friend of Kathy's." Christian fumbled with his wallet, trying to find a business card. He hadn't used them in ages. "I wanted to tell you how much I enjoyed that remarkable white ribboned creation." He handed Rory his card.

"Then you must be Christian." Rory glanced at the card. "And, of course, you are. Kathy's description of you was letter perfect. Thanks for the guarded compliment. Remarkable is the perfect word. Kathy said she wanted to be noticed. I'd gather you did."

"Everyone did. Men lusted after her and women hated her with even greater passion."

341

"And Kathy loved every minute. Now. If I may ask, where are you going? With respect, you look like a refugee from a bad punk fashion show."

"The Second Circle." Christian looked around again. All he saw were women's clothes, but the room was so crowded it was hard to see much of anything. "I was hoping to find something to replace this first. Do you do men?"

"Nope. I don't swing that way. I do design for them though. Dee!" A door, one almost completely hidden behind a rack opened further and a tall woman in a bright silver sari slipped through it. "Unfortunately, she doesn't swing that way either. Christian, meet Dee, my junior partner and overage model... the light of my life."

"You wish, child, you wish." Dee had the same willow build as Liza, perhaps an inch or so shorter. Her short hair was grey, her bronze features wrinkled and animated. "Rory gets a kick out that 'junior partner' routine. I was listening in, of course--this place is too small for secrets, and besides, I am nosy."

"Rory is a callous youth." Christian took Dee's hand and kissed it. "Some day he'll know thirty-nine isn't old. But there's too much wisdom in those eyes for me to believe you ever modelled."

"See Rory? This is what a gentleman is." Dee smiled, rearranging furrows into new patterns. "If not for that nasty little prejudice, he would be perfection."

"Oh oh," Rory said, almost to himself.

"Some models do have more than air in their craniums, you know," Dee continued, to Christian.

342

"Of course, some don't. Models are just like other people. Kathy, for instance. I would hope you agree she is nobody's fool."

"Dee likes you. You got off easy. She has five and ten minute versions of that lecture. Now, to business. Get out of that dreadful clothing. You've got a good male model build. If you were in shape, you'd be ideal. We can probably fit you off the rack."

"I wouldn't want to keep you from dinner."

"Then if you'll buy us take-out, you won't have to."

"Rory!"

"Aw, come on, Dee. Kathy said Christian's loaded."

"That is no excuse." Dee shook her hear. "But take-out sounds good. I'll get something and we can split it. After all, Christian is a friend of the family, so to speak."

"It's okay." Christian got out his wallet again. "It's on me." He had brought some of Grace's cash. Once again it was all in fifties and hundreds. He handed Dee a hundred… it was on top. "This will do?"

"All of it?"

"It's expense money. But please, no hamburgers." After listening to Liza he'd probably never eat one again.

While Dee was out, Christian tried on a pair of straight black pants and a black vest worn over an off-white turtleneck, all in natural fabrics. He didn't even check in a mirror. The clothing was comfortable and he wasn't going to take it off.

Rory talked about his business. He wasn't as young as he looked, or sounded, and been in fashion in Noronto for about ten years, with limited success. A few years earlier, in one of the down times, Dee had happened by. She'd invested a little money and added her expertise to his. She was much better at sales than Rory and they were making enough to live on. Rory loved his work and couldn't imagine doing anything else.

"From Gourmet-to-Go," Dee said when she came back in with a large brown bag. "Since you insisted on splurging, Christian. It's getting chilly. You'll need a good coat this evening." She put the bag down on the counter and went to the back of a series of racks. "Here, try this on for size." It was knee-length black leather and fit perfectly. Christian did look in the mirror this time. Christian Plowman, with style, looked back. Aurora might consider leather a cliché, but then again, what wasn't? He'd keep it.

They sat around the counter to eat. Christian asked how they knew Kathy.

"She's been a small time model for as long as I've been in Noronto." Rory used the time he talked to reload his plate. "Right now, she's our promotional budget. We get a walking ad, and she gets to show off. It works. Business has picked up."

Christian knew where some of the business had come from, or thought he did. What Vanna had been wearing the last time he'd seen her could well have been from Maison de Fade.

"Kathy could have gone to the bigs if she'd wanted," Dee said. "Still could, even in her thirties.

344

You might think she's a bit short, but when I was in New York with her last year, the agencies were over her like flies. Even in Noronto she could make a living modelling full time."

"Why doesn't she?"

"I've always wondered," Rory said. "But I'm not about to encourage her. I couldn't afford her if she went pro."

"Kathy's happy with her life." Dee put down her fork. "Or so she says. And 'all over her like flies' was her phrasing. She's not particularly fond of flies."

"Once Kathy makes her mind up, she won't change it." Rory sighed. "I don't know how many times I've asked her out."

"Every time you see her, I'd gather." Dee glanced at Christian, her fork hovering over the last escargot. He shook his head--no thank you--one had been more than enough. "She says you're a drooler."

"Never told me that. Anyway, I'm in good company. She hasn't given you a tumble either."

Dee bounced a roll off Rory's forehead. "But she'll go places with me.

When you get older, you may learn when to admire someone from afar."

After dinner, Christian haggled with Dee regarding the price of designer clothing. When he explained he was charging it to his expense account she permitted him to pay more than she'd initially asked, but less than Christian thought he should. Rory told him to drop by again. He had Christian's measurements and would alter some other items he thought Christian would like.

"What should we do with those?" Dee indicated the clothing from The Black Whole.

"Give it to charity, if you know one that would accept it."

"Oh, she would. When she's not here or sleeping, Dee can usually be found volunteering somewhere or other."

Christian felt a sudden stab of guilt. He still had the bonus cheques Grace had given him for finding Marci and pointing out Judy to Cosmo. He'd meant to give the money away, and hadn't.

He took out his wallet again, and unfolded the cheques. "Would you know a place that could use these?" He handed them to Dee.

She looked at the amounts. "Seriously?"

"It's money I couldn't ever spend." Accepting money for meeting Marci didn't seem right, and he hadn't done anything regarding Judy that deserved a bonus. He didn't understand why Grace had insisted on rewarding him for things he hadn't done. Christian signed the cheques over to Dee. "I'll pick up the receipts sometime. I suppose I should declare it on my tax."

Chapter Forty-One

There was a short line-up at The Second Circle. Heads turned as Christian walked to the door. Eunice was there. She peered behind him.

"I'm solo, Eunice. I don't want a table. I'll hang around and mix."

Eunice shrugged, almost falling out of her dress. She took his coat, saying she'd store it in Lucy's office.

The Second Circle wasn't full; the line was due only to the checking and paying processes at the door. Christian stopped to lean on the rail one level above the dance floor. A distance away, he saw Vanna, sitting with Justin. She appeared to have taken his fashion advice to heart. Her loose black outfit flattered without being blatant and her beret added a jaunty European touch.

He'd found a good spot. He didn't see anyone else he knew, but got a good sampling of the crowd as it paraded past. A bottleneck developed below him, as women stopped, posed, and idly looked around before being jostled on their way. Two leaned on the rail beside him and began a loud discussion of their plans for whatever lucky fellow they chose that night. Christian glanced at them. Neither was a Liza or a Vanna, not even close--a bottled blonde and a bottled redhead. Both would look better brunette. He looked around the club again. If this was the cream of young, beautiful Noronto, Liza would float effortlessly on top. It was a shame she'd had to work.

The press of the crowd started to make Christian uncomfortable. He continued to the bar and chose a seat on an empty stretch, well away from the dance floor. By the time his beer arrived, the adjoining stools were occupied--by a leggy natural blonde who had a major investment in the cosmetic and perfume industries, and an Eunice-in-training who looked far too young to be in a bar. She ran her tongue around her lips and licked a flagrant finger. Christian turned away. The blonde smiled, cracking her make-up. Christian picked up his beer and made his way towards where he'd seen Vanna. Around him, the crowd surged.

After bumping and rubbing half the people in the room, Christian reached Vanna and Justin's table. He leaned over to talk to Vanna. "Congratulations. You look very sexy, and very much you." She was by far the most attractive woman in The Second Circle, one of the few who really seemed to belong there.

Vanna smiled. "You look like a million bucks yourself." High praise from Vanna.

Before Christian could reply, a familiar hand, half the size of the SkyDome, came to rest on his shoulder. Christian wasn't sure if Justin was trying to intimidate him, or had stood and suddenly felt the need to steady himself. With a slight twist, Christian straightened.

Justin tottered. He looked like a stuffed bear, his eyes duller and more glassy than most. "You fucking keep away from her. I don't fucking like you talking to her."

"I'm sorry to hear that. Maybe you should sit down before you fall over."

"I can still fucking outfight, out-fuck and outsmart the likes of you, runt. I'm a man! I'll fucking give that bitch of yours a lesson soon too. She fucking sucker punched me."

"Want we should toss 'em out, Mr. Plowman?" The voice in Christian's ear made him jump. He turned to see two bouncers. One was nearly as large as Justin... and much steadier on his feet. The other was smaller, only Christian's six foot four. It was Percy, one of the few employees of the club Christian knew by name.

"No, Percy. My fault. I was trying to pick up his girl." Vanna gave Christian a withering look. "Can't say I blame him, but I couldn't help myself. He's a lucky guy. His date is the sexiest woman in the room, wouldn't you say?" Vanna showed Christian an indignant finger as Justin slumped into his chair.

Percy informed Christian his presence had been requested in the owner's office. Between two large men with no misgivings about shoving and pushing, the trip back to the bar took no time at all. Christian felt every eye in The Second Circle track his progress. He was conducted around the end of the bar and through the door, into the hall to Lucy's office.

Lucy was working at her desk. She had on short black hair and a black top. Her glance revealed a pair of contacts almost as dark.

"Evening, Lucy. So, how are you and Grace doing with the chess game?" It was something to say.

"It's a normal middle game position. I have more pawns and she may have an advantage in position. But enough of that. What are you doing here tonight, other than trying to start a riot? I don't mind you coming by, quite the opposite, but you'd be wise to call ahead so we can lay on the special services." Percy and friend, Christian assumed.

"Sorry, I guess. It was a whim. I wanted to hang around and watch the crowd, but tonight it seems all too mutual."

"Of course. They recognize you are Someone." Christian heard a capital letter. "I'm busy, Christian, but if watching is your kick tonight, go to the stairs at the end of the hall, up, and back this way to the last door. Open it, and say hello to Sibyl." Lucy bent her head back to her papers.

Christian followed Lucy's directions. The room at the end of the upstairs hall was dimly lit; the front wall was a window. Through it, The Second Circle could be seen. From below, Christian had seen no hint of such a window--it must be one-way glass. He completed Lucy's instructions. "Hello, Sibyl."

A chair by the window swivelled. A dark figure rose from it and moved towards him. Christian's first impression was that Sibyl was a scaled-down Lucy--close to a foot shorter. Like Lucy, she was lean, her figure perhaps more normal, but not by much. Her short black hair and coal eyes were identical to those Lucy had on. That couldn't be coincidence. Sibyl's face was similar, except a more generous nose made her look like a hawk, rather than the fox that was Lucy. If Lucy's skin was cream, Sibyl's was caramel cream. She looked like Lucy's sister, or perhaps, half-sister.

Sibyl waited until Christian's assessment was complete. "Welcome to the upper reaches, Mr. Christian." Her voice reverberated. "Let me introduce myself." She handed him a business card, "Sibyl D. Jinnah, LLB etc.-- International Promotional and Media Law". A long list of countries her credentials were accepted in followed, with an e-mail address and toll-free phone numbers at the bottom. It was the most crowded card Christian had ever seen. It also didn't tell him much.

"You're a lawyer." When in doubt, state the obvious. "You work for Lucy?"

"Yes and no."

"That answer proves you're a lawyer more than this does." Christian pocketed the card.

"I'm a mercenary, Mr. Christian. I work for the highest bidder. Lucy has contracted me to handle her media relations for a time." She waved a hand. "Along with certain other matters."

"Her media relations? But I've never seen her name mentioned anywhere. I'm sure most people have no idea she exists."

"Correct. I do good work, no?" Sibyl moved back towards the chair she'd risen from. "Get yourself something from the bar. Should you fancy something other than booze, check the cabinet on the end. I'm fine for now, thanks."

Behind the padded, waist-high ledge that was the bar, Christian served himself a beer. He took it to a chair at the other end of a deep leather couch from Sibyl and put his feet up on the wide windowsill. The chair moulded to his body. "If Lucy prefers anonymity, why has she been out in public so much recently?"

"Perhaps she enjoys paying my invoices. I don't ask. I bill." Sibyl paused to sip from her glass. "So, Mr. Christian, how do you enjoy being a celebrity?"

"I'm not one."

"From what I saw down there, you most certainly are. The people have raised you above their paltry selves. You have something they want and for a chance to partake, they offer themselves, bodies and souls... if any." Sibyl took a remote control from the windowsill. In front of the couch, a large television descended from the ceiling. She pressed a button. Views of The Second Circle flickered on the screen. Sibyl settled on one that showed the bar, and zoomed in on the Eunice-in-training who had been beside Christian. "She would fall on her knees and consume your manhood, if you permitted--at the bar, in the middle of the dance floor, anywhere. If you don't believe me, test it."

"I'll take your word. I found her pathetic, almost grotesque."

"How nasty, Mr. Christian. I do like you. Yes, she is ever so average... but if you chose her, she would embody sexual allure thereafter... to others of her ilk." Sibyl tossed the remote control onto the couch next to Christian and went to the bar.

"Tonight you have come into yourself. You walked in, confident and with charisma seeping out every pore, dressed in what all can see are designer originals and looking for action. Whomsoever you grant the privilege of rendering the services you seek, will gain great acclaim, and far more. Opportunities such as you, are what those come to The Second Circle pray they'll find. It's all they live for, to be with someone like you, Mr. Christian."

Christian played with the control, zooming out from the bar and looking around. A cabinet door opened behind him. He heard a gurgle of liquid. He found Vanna's table and moved in on her.

"Ah, the pest." Sibyl returned with two tumblers of amber liquid. She handed one to Christian, put a couple of pills in her mouth and washed them down with half the contents of hers. "Do try the Scotch. It's a private label."

Christian sipped. It was good, excellent, smooth with a bite.

Sibyl smiled at him and looked at the screen again. "She senses she's uncovered too much, and that her present masters will leave her in the lurch." Sibyl drained her glass and put it on the couch. Christian took another, longer, sip. "She's chosen to overplay her role when she could have kept it small. As it has been for others before, ambition will prove her downfall."

"I wouldn't want to see her get hurt, Sibyl."

"Your concern is doubly misplaced. Herself, she should be of little interest. Me, I simply say what I see coming. Move in closer, if you would."

353

Christian zoomed in. Vanna's face filled the screen. Yes, she had a beauty all her own. Christian put down the control and took a longer drink. It was the best Scotch he had ever tasted.

"Interesting. Her fortune is other than I saw before." Sibyl's voice sounded increasingly distant and dreamy. The alcohol and pills were kicking in, or in Christian's case, just the alcohol. "Her undoing is fully in place, but it won't be her end. She will discover a powerful friend."

Christian didn't know what to make of Sibyl's doggerel. He didn't know what to make of much, other than his drink. He took another gulp. "So what do you see for me, Sibyl?"

Her laughter came from everywhere. "For you, Mr. Christian? Now you have become a luminary, your future will be what you will it to be." She moved behind him. Christian spun to face her and stood. She put her hands on his shoulders and stared into his eyes. "You tell me. What do you see?"

He saw Sibyl's resemblance to Lucy was uncanny, far greater than he'd first thought. She even seemed taller. "Tell me, what do you see?" she repeated. She'd stolen Lucy's voice as well. Christian's vision blurred. Aurora's face flickered in front of him, then Kathy, Judy, Marci, Liza. Christian shook his head to clear his eyes. They didn't clear. He inched forward to get a better look. Sibyl still looked like Liza. Her body brushed his, and then he met her lips with his. He wanted her, then and there, whoever she was.

"Hey Christian, wanna boogie?" He knew who that was... Eunice. He moved away from the

354

woman he'd been about to kiss. Eunice stood frozen by the door.

"Oh shit! Ms Jinnah. I'm so sorry. I didn't know." Eunice started to back out.

"Stop!" Sibyl was most decidedly herself as she whirled towards Eunice. Eunice cowered in front of her. "You do know. You know you're not to enter this room. There is no excuse. Wait outside." Eunice backed out and closed the door.

Sibyl marched to the bar and washed down more pills with another tumbler of Scotch. Christian watched her closely, but his vision had returned to normal.

"Sibyl?" She didn't look at all like Liza.

"Please, don't intercede for her as well. She is of The Second Circle."

"No, I was going to ask how you did that."

"The prophecies? I hope I didn't upset your world-view, Mr. Christian, but such things have been since time began. The other? That was you, not me, but I wasn't about to stop anything you'd care to start. You were he whom I want most and I assume I was the same for you. Think of it as mutual hypnosis, if you will. We were about to live as each other's dream when that nothing burst in. That moment is gone forever... for now." She walked to the door. "If you'll excuse me, the bottle is on the bar. Make yourself at home."

Chapter Forty-Two

Christian looked out over The Second Circle. Sibyl had told him to make himself at home, but home was the place you belonged, a place that was known and secure--or so Christian had heard, somewhere. He didn't have a home and hadn't since his parents died. Nothing was secure... nothing known. He sipped his Scotch. He didn't believe Sibyl's explanation of what had happened between them, but didn't suspect that the drink was drugged anymore. It seemed fine, more than fine. It was excellent Scotch.

On the big screen TV, he saw Vanna stand. A breast filled the screen. Christian moved the view out in time to see her slap Justin awake. Justin stood and staggered beside her in the direction of the door. Exit one fair maiden and one bleary beast.

Vanna hadn't been one of the panoply of women Sibyl had become. Christian wondered what that meant and if the order they had appeared had been meaningful. Right, Plowman, like there was any logic in having seen them at all.

He drank some more Scotch and fiddled with the remote, changing cameras and perspectives. He didn't feel any more odd effects so he replenished his drink and continued to survey the world below. Horatio appeared. He seemed ill at ease. Kathy must have brought him. So, where was she?

Christian pulled the picture back and saw her. Resplendent in a black fishnet dress, Kathy had made herself into a sensual icon, a catalyst for lust.

She was in her glory. Moving out further, Christian saw Horatio was merely the nearest of her admirers. Percy and two of his brutes were nearby, keeping the others away. That confirmed for Christian what Lucy had meant by "special services". He could see they were needed for Kathy. Most people probably considered Horatio fortunate to be with her. From the haunted look on the man's face, Christian knew Horatio wasn't as convinced.

Christian adjusted the picture so Kathy filled the screen. The mesh of her dress stood up to that close an inspection. Christian allowed decorum to prevail and didn't move in closer. He put down the control and admired the view.

"Exquisite, isn't she?" Sibyl asked. He hadn't heard her come back. "And yours for the asking," she continued.

"She's with Horatio."

"What was between them is over. Before a week is done, she'll find and lose another," Sibyl answered. "You could change that." She shrugged. "Do as you will. At any rate, Lucy will be with us when she finishes disciplining her hireling. In the meantime, maybe you'd like to wrestle me? Best two out of three? You might find it inspiring."

"I'd rather talk."

"Believe me, you'll never discover anything about yourself that way. I suppose you'll take notes?"

"I'd appreciate some explanations, that's all. What's happening to me?"

"How would I know? I'm not you. You'd learn more far wrestling me. And have much more fun.

No? Oh well, I'll try… but words are useless tools. I'm a lawyer, Mr. Christian, so I know that. More Scotch? I assure you it's not drugged¬-except, of course, with alcohol."

Christian sat and Sibyl refilled their glasses. As she handed him his, she took the remote and turned off the TV. It glided back up into the ceiling.

"Technology, isn't it wonderful?" She stretched out on the couch. "Okay, since you ask, I'll try to teach you something, using words. The keyword to the puzzle of Christian is probably 'charisma'. I said you came in tonight oozing it, and you didn't argue."

"I took it as a figure of speech."

"And so it is, and why it explains nothing at all. Those are words, a meaningless phrase, as are all. But whatever that which I call charisma is, you've got a great deal, Mr. Christian. Everyone has their quantum, but with most humans the amount is small. Yours is overpowering. Until that sorry excuse for a manager tore the spell, I was about to share your essence."

"And what would have shared? Other than the obvious." He sipped his drink.

"How crude, Mr. Christian. What you term the obvious is a powerful symbolic act replete with arcane power. You're mistaking the symbol with its actuality. Language is inadequate, but what we would have been sharing is life force, if you will-- and we would both have become stronger."

"Usually, after a night with someone, I feel exhausted--drained." Christian reached to refill his glass. He fumbled with the bottle.

358

"Allow me." Sibyl slid to the end of the couch by him. "I hate to see precious fluids wasted." She handed him a full glass. "Your problem, Mr. Christian, is that you haven't been keeping company with suitable females."

"Yes, but I've spent nights with the same woman, and one time felt burned out after and then fantastic a later time. That screws up what you're telling me, doesn't it?" Christian gulped a triumphant drink. Let her answer that.

Sibyl was silent for a time. Christian felt proud; he might be drunk, but it hadn't made him stupid like it did most people. He finished the glass to celebrate his coup.

"No, you're right, that shouldn't happen," Sibyl sounded disturbed. "Who was that with? And when?"

"Aurora... recently, of course. With Cleo I always felt exhausted after, like I have after every one-night stand." Not that there had been many of those. He must be in worse shape than he'd thought. This wasn't something one discussed with a stranger--or even a friend.

"After which time with Aurora did you feel tired?"

Might as well see it through, now he'd started. "The first. The day I met her. The day I met her, Lucy and Grace. A big day." Christian suppressed a hiccough by drinking.

"That explains everything. Aurora wasn't intended. She insinuated herself into the framework unexpectedly and only subsequently received her

359

benediction, after she was acknowledged as an unavoidable complication."

"Huh?"

"Words, Mr. Christian... just words. To put it crudely, as you seem to prefer--given the options you were presented with, no one thought you'd want to screw her once, let alone a second time. Now Aurora may do well; she's among the immortals, who can tell?"

"Aurora was born a star."

"Yes... and no. She had a certain glamour, but now she has more. Intimates exchange some charisma, as we've been calling it, every time they join with each other. Of course, as most people have next to none, that's what they pass to one like you. You end up sapped while they get augmented. Now you've awoken, women who have a measure of what you possess will come your way."

"Like Aurora." What Sibyl was telling him didn't make sense, but as Grace had once suggested, he'd go with the flow. It took less effort than arguing.

"Like Aurora now. You'd still be better off renouncing her limited charms. She remains a primitive and may never be self-aware. I'd be much better with you, Mr. Christian and I regret to say, so would your Marci. Lucy and Grace were very excited when you revealed her as Freyja Van Deer."

"Anyone else?" Might as well keep playing along.

"There are always others. The trick is discovering who they are. Those who are easily found are the minor players, like Aurora and Kathy.

360

They will do, if you're willing to settle for less than you can have. Most who are aware and powerful prefer to remain hidden."

"I can understand why." Christian drank down half his latest tumbler of Scotch. He was surprised he was still rational, or was he? Not judging from the conversation.

"No, you don't. But you will. That I can see even without the aid of prophecy. Concealment is forbidden for you. Grace and Lucy agree you shall remain in view. That makes you unique."

"I'm a one in a million kind of guy, all right." Christian added as much sarcasm as the Scotch could muster.

"Oh no. For once a word fits my meaning precisely. You're unique. If you were one in a million, there would be many more like you in the world... thousands. Do your math, Mr. Christian. Do your math."

"No thanks. Where were we? Oh yeah, you were telling me you're the only woman for me." It was the Scotch speaking. Christian drained his glass.

"No, I would never dare tell you that. There are five I know of."

"Five?" Christian took his right hand in his left. "Okay, that would be you and Freyja." He folded over two fingers. "Lucy." Another. "And Grace?"

Sibyl pushed down his thumb. "Yes, but I understand Grace and you have adopted each other as mother and child, so by your archaic moral code, Grace is off the roster."

"Freyja is too. She's my sister now."

"I'm sure she'll never agree, but if you feel that way, it's true. Of the five, that leaves only Lucy and myself."

Christian looked at his right hand. There was one finger still standing. "And?"

"Your real sister. But not only is that forbidden, I understand you've already pushed her from your life. A wise decision. She's a brat, spoiled rotten and manipulative. You're better off forgetting her."

"I'm not sure I've quite done that." Christian opened his hand again.

"But think how she's treated you. Has she shown you any respect? Do you think she cares for you? But that's your choice, as is the other matter. You're left with Lucy, me or a minor talent such as Kathy. She would be much better for you than Aurora. Kathy is more sophisticated, and at least partially aware of her other side."

"But she's with Horatio, and therefore also out of it. My archaic moral code again." As far as this night went, Christian knew he was the one who was out of it. Too much Scotch.

"You'd be doing him a favour. Again. You made him what he was. She may yet destroy what is left."

Christian sighed. "I hear another fairy tale starting." He reached for the bottle.

Sibyl beat him to it. "Tired of words already, Mr. Christian?" She poured the drinks. "Alas, poor Horatio. He and Cleo are demonstrable proof of your power. When you met them, they were mere meat... Horatio a tawdry hustler and Cleo, the Eunice of her day. Due to all the time she spent

362

draining you, Cleo's become a small-time epicentre in her own right. As long as she stays within her limits, and she will, she'll be an influential woman. Especially now Lucy has taken advantage of her skills. Horatio is far less perceptive. What he gained from you, through her, he's squandered. He overreached and was brought down. Now he may be raised again, but only because you name him friend."

"You're saying I people I sleep with become successful, maybe even famous?" He wasn't drunk enough to believe that.

"No, what you do is more substantial. Fame and success are ephemeral. They come, and they go. Anyone can be made famous, Mr. Christian. The media rules minds and I rule the media, when I choose. Select anyone out there. I'll make them an overnight success." Sibyl waved her hand to indicate The Second Circle.

Christian looked out. The room was empty. He started to laugh.

Sibyl waited for him to finish. "No matter, my point stands. Thrust anyone forward, say they are worthy of notice with the proper voice, and the masses will agree. Take away the hype and the person disappears. What you did with Cleo and in a lesser way, Horatio, is pass on some of your essence, your charisma, as we've been calling it. By being with you they became more than they were."

"Sorry, Sibyl. I may be drunk, but I'm not drunk enough to buy that." He wasn't drunk either.

"So test it. Bring me an unknown... any 'no one' you know. I'll supply the media blitz. If you'd like, you can give them some staying power by making them yours. Either way, you'll see. And if you don't want to bed them, I might do it myself. I have before, many times. I'm less particular than you."

"Should I feel insulted, Sibyl, my sweet?" Lucy's voice came from behind them.

"I couldn't insult you if I tried. Mere words are incapable of conveying how truly vile and contemptible you are."

Lucy laughed. "Thank you. Flattery will get you everywhere. How do you stand it so bright in here?" The room went from dim to murky. Christian turned. A filmy black negligee swirled around Lucy like smoke as she moved to the bar. "Come along now, Sibyl dear. Mama needs a massage. I'm leaving for Orlando in the morning, Christian, so I'm very glad you dropped in after all. Sibyl's been keeping you entertained?"

"It's as good a word as any." If nothing else, Sibyl had half-convinced him words were useless. Hers most certainly were.

Lucy laughed again. "So, are you going take her bet? Or are you afraid?"

"When?" He wasn't going to back down from a challenge from Lucy.

"Tomorrow. Like she said, it doesn't matter who you bring, as long as they don't inspire you to loathing or hatred."

"Why is that?"

"Sibyl, I'm disappointed. You didn't tell him the dark side."

"I tried. He didn't listen."

"Yes, he can be like that. A little higher, if you would. My neck is all knotted."

Sibyl complied. Christian retreated to the couch where he could hear but not see.

"What's the matter, Christian?" Lucy asked. "Shy?"

"I figure I can watch, or listen... not both." Despite all the Scotch, his body had been responding to Lucy. "You were saying something about 'the dark side'?" To prove he could function without Sibyl's help, Christian poured himself another drink. No problem.

"Yes. Passion is the key, Christian, the key to all power. Our lust or love-¬whatever you want to call it, builds people up. So what would our fury do?"

"Destroy." It was first-rate Scotch.

"Very good. A little lower, Sibyl. Yes, that's very nice. Yes, Christian, our wrath is dangerous. You do remember how your former employer's company collapsed? The man reneged on a contract with me. If I allow anyone to do that, everyone will think they can too. For a lesser example consider how all at The Factory fear Aurora. Even before being with you, her anger brought misery to people, not just at work, but also in their lives... illness, financial misfortune, accidents. Now, thanks to you, she's even more dangerous. You've done good work for me, Christian my lad."

"But I work for Grace."

"Do you? Whatever. It doesn't matter. Everything is interconnected. Grace knows that.

365

Come closer, Christian. Talking like this is awkward."

Christian finished his Scotch and went towards the bar. Lucy was face down on it. In the low light, she seemed suspended waist high in the air, naked. She was an awesome sight; everything a woman could be. He didn't know how he could have thought otherwise.

"Maybe you could take over from Sibyl, Christian. She tries, but she doesn't have the strength to work the tension out of me."

"I think I'm too drunk to do you much good."

"Could you give it a try, please? It won't be for long. I have only one more thing I must tell you. I know you're tired... and Sibyl and I have much to do before morning."

Lucy's muscles yielded to Christian's touch. Her skin was lustrous and slick with oil. His hands slid lower. "You have one more thing to tell me?"

"Yes." Her body swelled as she took a deep breath. "I am required, by solemn agreement with Grace X Machina, to state that not everything I, or my agents, may have told you or implied, is necessarily true in the sense you understand truth, assuming you do at all, although it may so be; and that no knowledge, gift or other consideration you may or may not receive, now or at any time, shall in any way obligate or bind you, whether or not you remain in association with any person named, not named, or unnameable in this statement, and that in turn I am under no obligation to you and am not required, now or ever, to reveal any matter that may jeopardise my interests or those of anyone who may

366

or may not be under contract to me, directly or by proxy." She let out what was left of her breath and took another. "How did I do, Sibyl?"

"Very well, but I think I still need to work out some of the punctuation with Grace's lawyer."

"Things were much simpler in the good old days."

"Seems clear enough to me." That was far from the truth. Lucy's voice had lulled him deeper into his Scotch stupor. His hands were on one body, but his eyes saw several.

Lucy turned her face to him. Her six eyes were red smouldering coals, flickering flame. He felt their heat and started to sweat. "Move lower." Her voice shook his bones. "You've always liked my ass. Tonight, it's yours."

Haze finally enveloped Christian.

Chapter Forty-Three

Christian woke up in his apartment, horny and alone. All things considered--particularly a bottle of Scotch--he was amazed how good he felt. He didn't remember coming home. He didn't remember anything after Lucy's invitation to use her nether parts as he would. And he couldn't have. It was impossible... he'd been far too drunk.

He took an extended, icy shower. At the hour he'd woken up, there was no choice, all the hot water was gone, but it was what he would have chosen, given a choice. He checked in the mirror while towelling himself dry. He didn't look like himself; his eyes weren't right. They had an unfamiliar predatory gleam.

On the kitchen counter Christian found evidence he'd had help getting home--the bottle of Scotch, empty, with a note hung around its neck. The side facing him read, "Thanks for a wonderful night (over)?". He flipped it. The other side asked, "What is truth? (PS Check your e-mail.)"

Christian laughed. Lucy's mind games couldn't affect him today. One truth was that if she'd been in bed with him this morning, he wouldn't have resisted. Last night? Wonderful? Impossible.

He turned on the coffee maker, and then checked for the promised e-mail. There were two messages. One from Lucy. "A most productive encounter. I'll be out of town for some time. Feel free to treat Sibyl exactly as you would Me. - ¬Love, Lucy." It sounded like her (with a small h).

The second message was from Sibyl. "Assuming you're a man of honour, I'll see you with your mystery companion tonight at The Second Circle. Be there at nine sharp, and be prepared to have your eyes opened further. Regards, your Sibyl." His Sibyl?

Christian replied to Lucy. "It was a memorable experience, what I remember of it. I look forward to seeing you when you get back." He used small Y's.

To Sibyl he wrote: "I'll be there. Companion still a mystery to me too." He hoped that was half a lie. Christian knew who he wanted to go with, but he hadn't asked.

He put on a tracksuit and, coffee in hand, stepped into the hall. The sound of a TV was coming from Liza's apartment. He knocked lightly. The volume went down and the door opened.

Liza was wearing pink flannel pyjamas. Somehow, he'd never pictured her that way. Her apartment was furnished with one chair, a dresser and a mattress on the floor in front of the TV. She was tuned to VideoView. "Well hello, Christian! Do come in."

"Maybe I should come back later."

"Not a chance. I'm as dressed as you are." Liza left the door and sat on the mattress, cross-legged, leaving him the chair. "Well?"

Christian stepped inside and closed the door. "I'd like to ask you for a date. Tonight." He sat.

"Good, I'm available. What did you have in mind?" Her voice bounced with life.

"Nothing terribly original. Dinner and dancing."

"And?"

"That's it."

"No way. I'll make a counter offer. No dinner, no dancing and we don't say 'so long' at least until the weekend is over. We can start now."

"Counter offer? You expect me to negotiate? What would you do if I agreed to those terms?"

Liza quickly unbuttoned two of the five buttons on her top, paused to see if he was going to say anything, and reached for the next.

"I think you'd do it, wouldn't you?"

"I hope to." She kept her hands on the third button. "Why? You're going to ask me why. I'll save you the trouble. I'm at the beginning of my travels, and there's something I need to get out of the way. You can help me." She grinned. "I'm sure of that. I've heard your references echoing across the hall."

Earlier Christian would have had sex with a goat, if he'd woken up with one. Now, he felt like running. "How old are you?"

"Twenty, well... almost. I graduated from high-school last June. That bothers you?"

"Yes. And you're telling me you're a virgin?"

"Might as well be. I suppose I have to count the time in that Ford but I didn't enjoy it. The girls in school all told me I'm too choosy. I don't think I was choosy enough… until I chose you." Her hand remained poised to unbutton.

This wasn't what Christian had expected, or hoped for. He'd thought she was five years older. "You don't expect to find love this way, do you?"

"I'm young, Christian, not stupid. I'm ready experience life. Right now, I want to get laid... by someone who knows what they're doing. You don't have to feed me or take me anywhere at all."

"Well... I'm flattered... I guess, but I do need a date for tonight. Last night I was drinking with a woman who bills herself as a media expert. She claims she can make absolutely anyone an overnight sensation. When I expressed doubt, she told me to bring someone with me tonight, and she'd demonstrate." That was as much of the story as Christian thought he should tell Liza.

"Sounds like a bet to me. If you're going to win, you should take a real loser. Sorry, I don't see myself that way. If you do, I'd like you to leave, now."

"I don't see it as a bet. I see it as her playing games. I've decided I'll play my own."

"And decided I'm a perfect playmate!" Liza broke in. Christian wouldn't have phrased it that way. "Okay, I'll go. But I'm warning you--you don't feel you have to play by her rules? Well, don't count on me playing by yours."

"Meaning?"

"Among other things, that after tonight I'm going to spend rest of the weekend in bed with someone. I want it to be you, but if you turn me down, I'll go with the person it will upset you the most to know I'm with. I don't care who they are. Understood?"

"Understood." He didn't believe her. He had the date he wanted, even if she was far too young. Later would be soon enough to worry about later.

"So, where are we going?"

"For dinner, and then to The Second Circle."

"Tonight? You can get in there tonight?" Christian found new understanding of the expression 'youthful enthusiasm'. "They've been talking about it all week." She waved at the TV where VideoView was promoting the beer for all the moments of your life, Hops To It. "You're sure? There?"

"Personal invitation from the management. Be there at nine for the red-carpet treatment. Why? What's happening?"

"Only the biggest band ever doing a special taping as thank-you performance. They started their tour with a show at The Second Circle--you must have heard about that. Since then their tour has sold out and their album is the fastest selling of all time."

"I was there the first time. I hadn't heard about this though." No one had mentioned it to him. He wondered what the band owed Lucy. But that was their problem. His was that he'd been set up and would be taking Liza into the middle of a prearranged media nightmare. She was nineteen, innocent.

"Christian? Something's wrong?"

"You can back out if you want." He knew she wouldn't.

"Not a chance. This is going to be so fun." Liza unfolded her legs, bounded off the mattress and past him to the closet. "I should have known you were there. I saw all Aurora's stuff on VideoView. Now, what can I wear that will really upset her?"

372

"You know Aurora?"

"Been watching her on TV all my life." Yes, Liza was that young.

"My bet isn't with her."

"I didn't think it was. I figure this is the best I've got." She held up a short dress covered with silver sequins. "It's nothing special, but it shows off my legs."

"Why do you think she'll be upset to see you?"

"Because she was your girlfriend, and now she'll think I am. It'll drive her nuts."

'Girlfriend' wasn't the right word for either of them, but it wasn't worth arguing. There were other things bothering him. Sibyl had manipulated him with ease. He wondered if Liza had as well. "Why? How did you know she was my girlfriend?"

Liza hung up the dress and came over to him. He stood. She looked into his eyes for a long time. The light slowly left hers and a long time passed before she answered. "I don't like what you're thinking, Christian. I'll repeat this one more time. I'm nineteen, not stupid. How did I know? First of all, I saw you with her on VideoView one night, having sex up against the window. The video jockey made a big joke about it." Christian had forgotten that incident. They hadn't actually been having sex, but it had been close.

"Second, I saw her skulking through the halls a few times, acting like she didn't want to be noticed but hoping it would happen anyway. Guess she was disappointed. Most people probably figured she was only someone trying to look like Aurora Medici. After all, what would someone like her be

373

doing in this cockroach hotel? Anyway, the second time I saw her, she was going in to your place and I did say hi. She cut me cold. She doesn't like black people, Christian. Did you know that about Aurora?"

"Aurora's like that with everyone."

Liza shook her head. "I know the look. That's something else I've seen all my life. Do you believe me?"

"I think I have to." He'd better.

"Good, because now I know where we're going, I've got another reason to want to be with you. She'll be there for sure." Liza's smile wasn't one of innocence. "I'm going to enjoy myself big time."

"Do I owe you an apology?"

"Depends exactly what you were thinking earlier."

"I was wondering if you wanted to know me because I had contacts, like Aurora for instance."

Another long time passed. "I suppose I shouldn't blame you. You don't know me, and there are enough people like that in the world. No, I don't want to go anywhere, like in becoming famous or anything. Okay, if it happens, it happens--and maybe I am sort of curious to see if this media expert can do what she says, but I don't care much one way or the other. I only want to go places like in travelling and seeing the world, that's all. Do you believe me?"

"Yes. And I do owe you that apology, Liza."

"So how are you going to make it?" She undid the next button on her top.

374

"By seeing if I can find you a dress that will bowl Aurora over. I know a designer." He did, although only since the previous night.

"You know, I might like that almost as much." The fourth button, one left. Christian had never realised how sexy pink flannel could be.

He reached out and did the fourth button up once more. "If we start that now, we won't get to The Second Circle at all."

Liza laughed. "That might not be so bad, but you may have a point--as well as a hard-on."

***

When Christian called Maison de Fade, Dee answered the phone. Christian asked if she could find a dress for his date, one suitable for a big night at The Second Circle.

"Tonight? It's almost afternoon. What are her measurements?"

"I don't know." 'Perfect' wouldn't be an adequate answer.

Christian asked her to hang on and went to get Liza, who now was dressed in jeans and a top. She described herself in centimetres, numbers meaningless to Christian, laughed and hung up. "She said to get there as soon as possible, but you shouldn't worry and that you should have just told her you were dating a model. Do you think I could model, Christian?"

"I think you could do anything you want."

"Play football? Dad always wanted one of his kids to do that."

"But do you want to?"

375

"Good point. Come on, we'd better get moving." She didn't offer to unbutton anything.

They stopped in the lobby because Liza wanted to see if there was anything from her family. Nothing from hers, but Christian's sister, Aster, had sent him a change-of-address card. He put it in his pocket and they went outside to flag a cab. The first one that passed, stopped. As it pulled away, a bright red sports-car fell in behind. As usual Vanna was on the job.

Chapter Forty-Four

"You're black!" Dee's reaction on seeing Liza was immediate.

"She's aware of that." Christian prepared to leave.

"I don't mean it that way and she knows it."

Lisa smiled, at Christian first and then Dee. "It's okay, Christian."

"The dress I had in mind would be wrong." Dee shook her head as she looked around, searching. "One of you should have thought to mention Liza's colour... and I should have asked. You have such a rich skin tone, child, I can do things with it. By the way, this is Rory."

Rory had his own concern. "Dee said we're to dress you for The Second Circle. Tonight's a big night. What's really going on? If we're going to get this right, we have to know."

"Christian's got a bet with some woman. She told him she can make a star out of a nobody. He didn't believe her, so she said she'd show him what for."

All eyes went to Christian. He'd been wondering if he'd become invisible. The looks he got from Dee and Rory made him wish he was. "I'm trying to lose."

"I should say so." Dee put an arm around Liza. "Have you ever considered modelling? "

"Not until now, not really. Models travel, don't they?"

"More than they'd like, most times." Rory looked at Christian. "Okay, who's the bet with?"

"I'd never heard of her before." And couldn't remember her last name. He dug for her business card. "Her name is Sibyl..."

"Jinnah." Dee and Rory chorused.

Christian found the card. "That's right. You've heard of her?"

"I've have too, Christian," Liza answered. Dee and Rory were busy exchanging meaningful looks. "They call her The Pawnbroker. She's got quite the reputation."

Dee's arm had remained around Liza. She turned Liza to face her. "Yes, but you don't have anything to worry about. You're not a pawn... you're a queen."

"People claim Jinnah's motto is 'I make them. I break them'," Rory said to Christian.

"Far too trite." Christian responded. "She'd come up with something better. She's good with words." Especially for someone who didn't think they meant anything.

"The point is, Christian, she's not anyone you should cross. You don't want her as your enemy."

"Better that than to think she's your friend." Dee sounded sure. "We're in, of course. Now, Christian, you have, of course, ordered a limo and made dinner reservations?"

"No."

"And I won't let you wear the same thing two nights in a row," Rory added. "But dressing you is a minor concern. Get lost for an hour. Put the 'Closed' sign on the door on your way out."

Christian didn't leave until he'd hired a limo. The first four he called were already booked. He succeeded only when he contacted the firm Kathy had used for their night on the town and mentioned her name. To get reservations at Chez Celeste his own name did the trick.

It was Friday afternoon, and the weather was excellent for November in Noronto; it wasn't raining or snowing, and the temperature was well above the freezing point. The Street was busy. Since he was in the neighbourhood Christian thought he should drop in to The Factory and see if he was welcome. On the way, a few people greeted him by name. He didn't know any of them. Outside The Factory a cluster of teenage girls stopped him to ask if he was still seeing Aurora. When he told them he wasn't, they were delighted. He told them he had a new girlfriend and their faces fell.

Kathy was behind her desk. "Hi, Christian. What brings you here?" Even her eyes smiled. Christian couldn't imagine how he'd ever thought them cold.

"I brought my date down to Maison de Fade to get a dress for tonight. Big night at The Second Circle."

"I know." Christian felt a sudden stab of icicles. Kathy flipped a switch. "Mr. Sharpe? Mr. Plowman is here. You'd like to see him."

For once Cosmo wasn't on the phone. He apologised profusely for his behaviour on Christian's previous visit, blaming it on increased sunspot activity, a low point in his biorhythms and general executive stress.

"I thought it might be more that Aurora isn't around."

"Nonsense. I'm glad she's gone. Running a business is a man's job. Women should stick to what they're good at, like Kathy and Freyja do. Freyja's good at what she does, isn't she?" Cosmo winked at Christian and grinned.

Marci had told Christian she'd retired her Freyja personality, and he'd believed her. Who was involved with Cosmo? Freyja? Marci? Certainly not the painter.

"But Kathy put in her resignation, didn't she?"

"I talked her out of it. You have to know how to handle women, Christian. Be firm. Don't let them get away with a thing."

Christian managed to extract himself from Cosmo's office gracefully. It was time for him to get back to Maison de Fade. And time for him to get far away from Cosmo. Evidently, the sunspots were still flaring.

***

Rory was the only one at Maison de Fade when Christian arrived. "They went out looking for the perfect purse and shoes. Okay, let's see what I can do with you."

Like the previous night's outfit, what Rory chose was simple--dark grey pants and jacket, and a black turtleneck. The cut was different, to Christian's eye halfway between what would be normally seen on The Street and something more suited to the financial district. Christian wasn't sure he liked it. "It makes me look older. World-worn, almost but not quite totally dissolute, don't you think?"

"You've got a good eye. That's exactly what I'm going for... a total contrast to Liza. She's young, fresh and exciting."

"Which makes me?"

"A man who makes things happen for girls like her. The male equivalent of Sibyl Jinnah."

"Except nicer?"

"That's up to you, Christian. We can set a basic image using clothing but the rest comes from the person who wears them. Dee taught me that. Now, if you'll excuse me, I need to work on Liza's dress." He went into the back room.

Liza and Dee returned before long, bags in hand. Christian was still looking at himself in the mirror, trying to decide if he liked what he saw. This wasn't a Christian Plowman he knew.

"Oh yes!" Liza dropped everything, came up behind and wrapped her arms around Christian. "You're awesome, wonderful, marvellous..." Suddenly, his opinion didn't matter... even to him.

"Liza!" Rory called from the back.

"And you are wanted for a fitting," Dee said. "Off you go."

Liza left, taking the bags with her. Dee met Christian's eyes in the mirror. "I hope you have long range plans for her."

"She may be the woman I've been waiting for all my life."

Dee's reflection grimaced. "Please. This isn't a fairy tale. Or if it is--not that one... please... it isn't."

Christian turned to face Dee. "What do you mean?"

"You've got as much hope of keeping her around as I do of sleeping with Kathy. Kathy isn't interested in me that way, and Liza is not looking for anything permanent."

"She'll change her mind."

"No. The question is more whether or not she is going to end up with Jinnah after her weekend with you. I've been around modelling for over forty years, Christian. Liza will go to the top… assuming she wants to. Right now, she does."

"You told Liza she didn't have to worry about Sibyl."

"No, because we'll do that for her. If you don't have some good contacts, I'll spend the night on the phone to Paris and Milan trying to scare up mine."

Paris? Christian got out his wallet. When he'd mailed the costume to Marci in Paris, he'd written down the street and e-mail addresses for Gabby, Grace's associate. He still had it. But since he had his wallet out, there was one other matter. "How much do I owe you?"

"Nothing. If Jinnah is pulling out the stops then Liza, you, and our designs are going to be seen everywhere tomorrow."

Christian handed Dee the card. "Okay. If you say so. Here… she's the only contact I have in Paris."

Dee took the card. "Gabby… from the e-mail address, I'd say that's Gabrielle Lange. Well, if you're only going to know one person in Paris, she may be the best. Write her."

382

"Could you? I've never met her, and I'm not sure what I should say."

"That Liza exists. And Jinnah is about to break her onto the scene."

"If it's urgent, I think you should write. Not me. I expect I'm going to be busy tonight."

"Dee!" Rory's voice came from the back. "Which shoes?" Dee hurried off. She kept the card.

Liza came out less than a minute later. Her dress was a sheath in the same grey as Christian's pants and jacket and it hugged her contours like a second skin. Christian hadn't seen her hair loose before. It was thick and luxuriant, jet-black against the dress. With heels she was a scant inch shorter than him.

"It's one of Dee's designs. I like the way it plays up the colour of my skin, don't you?"

"Anything would look good on you. You're the most beautiful woman I've ever seen."

"How painfully original." Kathy. Behind him. Ice on his spine. Christian slowly turned.

Kathy walked past him, to Liza. "He says that to everyone. In your case, it may be true." She addressed Dee. "I got someone to take over for me after Christian came by. After all, his last surprise date was Freyja." She put her hands on Liza's shoulders. "Yup, you're as real as she is. Okay, where did he find you? Milan? I'm sorry, I'm forgetting my manners... I'm Kathy Romanova."

"Liza Little. I'm the girl next door--well, across the hall, really--but you must be a real model. You look like Elle does when she's blonde, except you've got a much better figure." The comparison was lost on Christian, but it cracked the ice. Kathy beamed.

"Kathy is four inches shorter," Rory said. "Elle's six foot. But otherwise, yes. See, Kathy? I've told you that."

"But you'd say anything to get into my pants. Except the right things, of course."

Dee coughed. "I hate to break this up. But I want to try some more outfits on Liza before she goes." She whisked Liza away, leaving Christian with Kathy and Rory.

"Aurora will be furious." Kathy sounded delighted. "She's launching her new career in the second set tonight. Liza's going steal the show."

Maybe he could cheer Kathy up a bit more. "Tell Liza that and she'll try extra hard. You've got something in common with Liza--a passionate dislike for Aurora. You're going to be there? I saw you at The Second Circle last night, but I didn't get a chance to say hello. I loved the black mesh..."

Rory broke in. "The mesh? You wore the mesh? So what are you intending to wear tonight?"

"A bathrobe." She turned to Christian. "Horatio and I called it quits. I was hoping you'd heard and had come to ask me out, but now I've met Liza..." She shrugged. "When I was her age, I could have held a candle to her, but now? Not a chance. Across the hall? Really? And why are you taking her tonight? It's for more than the obvious reason, isn't it now my friend?"

"Sit. Please." Christian ran through the story of the previous night one more time, again leaving out the juicy or possibly juicy bits.

384

Kathy was spellbound. "Now I wish I was going. Cosmo's got a table, but since I've resigned, I don't think I'd be welcome."

"You can go anyway... you've got all those free passes. At any rate, Cosmo thinks he's talked you out of leaving. He said he was firm with you, and you gave in."

"Hah! The turd couldn't talk me out of or into anything. He's as big a pest as Rory that way. But now I have another dilemma. Do I hold off flattening Cosmo or hope my passes will be honoured tonight?"

"They'll be honoured. For you, if for no one else."

"I'd say your problem is what you're going to wear." Rory moved between them. "You've done the ribbons, wasted the mesh--I don't have anything else ready that's you."

"I'll find something. Later. Right now I want to see what Dee and Liza are up to." She disappeared into the back.

"Dumb broad." Rory said it quietly. "I'd better dig something up. She's got absolutely no taste."

"Who's Elle?" Christian asked. He didn't agree on who lacked taste. Rory's garish creations worked on Kathy only because anything would.

"Check the magazine on the desk. The cover and an inside spread." He started picking through the racks.

Christian leafed through the indicated magazine. He could see why Liza had made the comparison. The biggest difference between the two women wasn't in either the figure or the height.

385

It was Elle's smile. She enjoyed life and what she did. Kathy didn't, and it showed.

Dee came out from the back room. "You left those two alone?" Christian was only half joking. He wasn't sure Liza was safe with Kathy.

"I couldn't take it. They're bonding. Liza assured Kathy she only wants you for the weekend, they exchanged notes on Aurora's less endearing qualities, and now they're gushing over each other like teenagers. I can excuse Liza, but not Kathy." Dee didn't sound all that displeased. "Find anything, Rory?"

Rory muttered something incomprehensible.

"How about what Liza is wearing, but in black?" Christian asked Dee.

"That way they'd play off against each other."

"I could manage that. What's better, I think I can sell the idea to Kathy. It'll take me a couple of hours, but I can fit her into this one." She took a dress from the nearest rack. "Maybe I can convince her to go for a more innocent look with her make-up too, to match Liza."

"Kathy?" Rory dug through a rack. "Look innocent? Impossible. I was thinking maybe this." He held up several bright red straps, sewn together. To Christian's eye it was as blatantly carnal as anything he'd seen in Aurora's 'Toy Closet'.

"Why don't we let Kathy decide?" Dee asked. The partners went into the back, competing outfits in hand.

Liza re-emerged soon after, in the grey sheath but wearing lower heels. She was carrying a cream yellow dress and a red pantsuit. "Dee says the high

386

heels are only for entrances and exits, and I'm to dance in these. These outfits are for me too... this is all so ridiculous, but I am enjoying myself. I'm ever so lucky... Kathy's awesome, and if you weren't so shy, you and she would be dating and none of this with me would ever have happened. I invited her to spend the weekend with us if she wants."

"What... what did she say?" Christian wasn't sure what answer he wanted.

"To tell you she'll think about it and that I should kiss you now, and ask her again later, if I still want to." Liza hung her clothing on the nearest rack.

Christian put everything into the kiss. A moan moved from Liza's mouth to his and back as they started to grind against each other. Christian didn't want to go to dinner, or The Second Circle. Liza's original agenda of spending the weekend alone and together sounded good.

"So, still want to share him?" Kathy's voice cut Christian's mood a little but hardly enough. Liza disengaged and went over to Kathy. Their eyes were on his crotch, which wasn't the least bit bashful--it grew in response to the attention. On the other hand, Christian didn't need to look in the mirror to know his face was beet red.

"I'm not sure he's the one I was thinking of sharing." Liza kissed Kathy.

Kathy responded more slowly than Christian had but didn't pull away. They looked good together. If Kathy agreed... he didn't know what he'd do.

Liza's hands started to roam. Kathy caught them and broke off the kiss. "Thanks, but I don't think so. No hard feelings?"

"Not from me. I'm not so sure about Christian." Kathy and Liza laughed, and Christian wilted. No, Liza wasn't innocent, merely inexperienced. And determined to change that as quickly as she could.

"Guess I'm being too greedy, trying to get another first in this weekend," Liza continued.

"Well, that I can help you with." Kathy whispered in Liza's ear. Liza's eyes went wide. "Try it. And do let me know how it goes." She gave Liza a friendly hug. "Right now, you should let poor Christian take you to dinner, and I should go get sewn into a dress."

Chapter Forty-Five

The driver of the limousine waiting outside Maison de Fade was the same man who'd driven Christian the disastrous night that had ended with Judy throwing a pink drink in Christian's face. "George, isn't it? This is a coincidence."

"Not at all, sir." He opened the door. "I insisted I be called in if you ever requested a limo. Driving you was, shall we say, entertaining."

"I'm afraid you may be disappointed tonight."

"I doubt that, sir. I saw the itinerary and now I've seen the lady. I'm sure it will be far from dull. If you'll allow me, I'll hang her clothing."

Halfway to Chez Celeste, Liza asked if she could talk to the driver. Christian turned on the intercom.

"George?"

"Yes, ma'am?"

"I'm curious. What do drivers do while they're waiting?"

"I can't speak for others, ma'am, but I'll be working on my thesis. A laptop and books fit nicely under my seat."

"I'm impressed. What's your thesis in, George?"

"Cultural anthropology. My doctorate, ma'am."

"Thank you, George. And please, I'm Liza." She turned off the intercom. "Interesting. On TV they never tell you anything about drivers. I wonder if this job is field research?"

At Chez Celeste, Liza didn't interrogate the waiters, contenting herself with admiring the room and its patrons. "It's like a movie set, almost too perfect to be real." Her interest and sentiments were reciprocated... by the customers. The room withheld comment.

Liza proved to have as healthy an appetite as Marci, except she didn't drink. Although he hadn't felt any ill effects from his previous night's overindulgence, at least not in the sense of feeling hung-over, Christian decided to abstain as well. He'd need a clear head for The Second Circle and he didn't want to lessen his physical capability to handle whatever Liza had planned. He wasn't going to be able to avoid sleeping with her now, not that he wanted to avoid it now.

In response to her request, Christian once again related the story of his life. Liza listened as well as Grace and Marci had, and with as little comment. He could see from her face that the thought of losing one's family so suddenly affected her.

As he continued, relating how his young sister, Aster, (three plus years older than Liza, a reality Christian found unsettling) had gone to live with Grandma Weeks in British Columbia, Liza finally interrupted. "So, Aster Weeks is your sister. You must be proud of her."

Christian didn't know how to respond. It must have shown. "Guess we don't watch the same TV and movies. She's had some really good parts. Sort of cult following with people my age. I'd also guess you don't talk to her. You two have a fight?"

390

"I guess we did. But I suppose it's more a matter of distance and age. And now, habit."

"You should get back in touch with her, Christian. Family is important. I'd hate to think you still can't connect with her because of the age difference. Promise me you'll try."

Christian sensed the evening would screech to an abrupt halt if he didn't. "I promise." He resumed his story, and struggled to put a more positive spin on the past.

He paid for dinner with the expense account credit card. Yes, this was pleasure but it was also business, Grace's business. She'd told him to improve his image and acquire a high profile. If what Dee had told him was true, he was about to do one of those things. He wasn't sure how his image would fare, being seen dating someone so young, but he didn't doubt this was the night he would leap into full view of the public. He suspected he was more nervous about it than Liza.

George was waiting in the limo. Vanna was waiting behind. His turn to tease a bit more. "I was told to get to The Second Circle at nine sharp. Drive around in circles if you need to kill time. If nothing else, it'll make our tail work for her money."

"I had assumed you'd noticed her, sir. Reporter? Would you like me to lose her?"

"It's not necessary--and she's not a reporter, she's a spy." George and Liza both laughed. They didn't believe him.

Chapter Forty-Six

When they arrived at The Second Circle, precisely at nine, the line-up was in place, winding down The Street. The less ambitious were being held at bay around the entrance. They were there to see their idols as they came in, nothing more. Reporters, photographers and video-camera operators were clustered inside a ring of security. As the limo pulled up, the crowd and the media tensed in anticipation.

George's voice came over the intercom. "Haven't seen anything like this in a while, folks. Sit tight, and wait for me to open the door and help you out. That looks better on the news, more professional."

As they stepped out, camera lights flared and flashes strobed. Between the spots in front of his eyes, Christian saw reporters charging towards them, microphones thrust forward.

"Is it true that? Are you? Have you? Do you? Who? Will you? Would you? What?" Liza and Christian smiled and made their way towards the entrance. It was all they could do. Christian was certain one of the blurs he half saw standing there was Sibyl Jinnah.

It was. They reached her, and she held up a hand. The media quieted, but a murmur could still be heard from the crowd. "There's no time for this now. The band will be starting soon." Sibyl's voice carried well. "There also will be a photo opportunity when they leave. In the meantime, those of you who are allowed inside know enough to be discreet. Anyone who interferes with the taping or The Second Circle's special guests will be tossed out on their ear."

"And only their ear, if they're lucky."

"You shouldn't complain, Rufus. You recovered." With that, Sibyl spirited Liza and Christian inside and with a wedge of bodyguards, pushed through the clamour and into the office.

"You set me up, you bleeding son-of-a-bitch! You damn well knew who you were bringing." Sibyl turned from Christian to an unruffled Liza and examined her from head to toe. "Exquisite. I couldn't have done better myself."

"Are you talking to me?" Christian asked. The last comment seemed to be for Liza but that didn't make sense.

Evidently Liza thought the same. "Thank you. I think. I'm Liza Little."

"If you say so. Sibyl Jinnah." She stuck out her hand. "I do apologise for that scene. Mr. Christian double-crossed me. I asked him to bring a nobody and he brought you."

"But I am a nobody. I'm Liza Little," Liza answered, repeating her name slowly, as if she thought Sibyl dense. "I'm nineteen and I work in the fast-food industry, although I suspect the last won't be true after tonight."

"If it was before. Okay, if that's your story, that's your story. I've put the machinery in motion to make Mr. Christian and his companion of the night into a major presence... like you need my help. Sure that's what you want?"

393

"With all my heart. Christian decided he should share me with the world. He could have had me to himself for at least the weekend, but he wanted me to be seen." She stepped closer to Sibyl and cradled Sibyl's face with her hands. "It's too late to stop things anyway, isn't it? I'm going to be famous. I'm sure you're going to do your best to make that happen."

"I will," Sibyl said. "I hope you know what you've got yourself into, Mr. Christian."

"I haven't a clue."

"Truer words were never spoken. Very well. Your table awaits, and the show is about to commence. If I'm right, it will be a memorable night."

When, after her doggerel prophecy, Sibyl didn't make any move towards the door, Christian led Liza from the office. He stopped in the hall. "At least the weekend?"

"At least. Who knows? I might have fallen hopelessly in love with you and stayed with you forever. Instead, I love you and am going to leave."

"Forever?" Christian wasn't sure if he was asking whether she would have stayed forever or if, after the weekend, she wouldn't come back.

"Enjoy the moment, Christian. Follow the flow." She was handling matters much better than he was. Their encounter outside had disturbed him and exhilarated her. Light seemed to radiate from every pore of her perfect body.

The owner's table was unoccupied, the only empty seats visible in the room. Patsy and Eunice were at the bar, or at least were until Sibyl rushed out behind Liza and Christian, plucked them from their stools and headed for the stage area. Closer to the stage, but down a level from the owner's table, Kathy sat at a table with Cosmo, Marci, Horatio and Judy. Horatio and Judy were sitting close together, as were Cosmo and Marci. Kathy was the odd person out.

Liza dashed down the stairs. By the time Christian arrived, everyone was on their feet with Liza and Kathy hugging like they hadn't seen each other in years. They did look good together. Christian moved between Horatio and Judy as Kathy broke off from Liza and took her around to introduce her to Cosmo and Marci.

"So, Horatio. What's new?"

"Other than your date, Kathy... it would appear," Horatio answered, with a laugh. "Breaking up has been good for her. She looks happier, and much younger."

Christian agreed, but thought it more a matter of cosmetics. "You're taking it well."

"Oh, it was past time, as you know. There are other fish." His eyes flickered to Judy and away.

Liza and Marci were getting along famously. Cosmo looked from Liza to Christian and back in disbelief. Marci embraced Liza a second time and sat.

A voice came from the stage. "Thank you for being so patient. It'll be a few minutes more." There were scattered boos.

Kathy brought Liza around to their side of the table. "My ex-roomie, Judy, who despite the fact

395

she's not talking to me, is still okay." Kathy said to Liza. "Judy, meet Liza Little."

"Hi. And I am talking to you again, I guess--if you want to talk to me that is. I'm sorry."

Liza moved on to stand beside Christian, allowing Kathy and Judy some privacy to make up. "I guess the last introduction is up to me then," Christian said. "Liza, this is Horatio Beeble, an old and dear friend."

"Not as old as you, you lecher. It's so unlike Christian to rob the cradle, but even the strongest man would succumb to you, sister." Christian stood back as Horatio reached to take Liza's hand for a kiss.

"Oh cut the crap." Liza's words jerked Horatio to attention. "Gallantry is one thing, but that's bigoted sexist, ageist trash."

"Right on." Yes, Kathy was a fan. "You tell him!"

There was no need to encourage Liza. "Okay so I'm young, female, and yes, as they say, black like you--but I won't be condescended to on any account... brother. Care to try again?"

"I think I should. I'm as impressed by the spirit within as I am the body surrounding it. I do hope you know how overwhelming you are. Better?"

"A bit--apology accepted. Incidentally, if you touched up your attitude and your gut, you'd be a hunk. Think about it."

"I probably will," Horatio replied, and added in a loud aside to Christian. "Damn. Close my eyes and I'd think I was talking to Kathy."

396

"Thank you, Horatio." Liza gave him a quick squeeze. "Now that's a compliment that means something." Over Liza's shoulder, Horatio winked at Christian. Christian gave an inward sigh. The sound of a guitar drifted around the room.

The voice from the stage spoke again. "Okay, it's show time!" There was a roar. "But before I introduce the band, let me remind you this is being taped for broadcast on VideoView, so be careful around the cameras. Now, without further ado, here they are..." Cheers and shouts drowned out everything else. The stage lit, and people surged onto the dance floor.

With a wave to Kathy, Liza took Christian's hand and dragged him back to the owner's table. He had time to order two bottles of mineral water while Liza changed into her dancing shoes. Before they arrived, they were on their way. Liza wanted to dance.

She snagged Kathy as they passed and swept to a position directly in front of the band. The crowd parted to let her through. With abandon and a style that suited the world-beat music and herself--long hair flying, lithe body coiling and uncoiling in a dress that faithfully and flawlessly flowed with her, Liza danced. The music consumed her, and in turn, she made it hers.

Once in a while, Liza emerged from her trance to note Christian remained in her orbit. He was glad she had hauled Kathy up with them. It gave him someone to dance with... Liza was in her own dimension, one the musicians were also beginning to touch. Kathy danced with ease and style but remained aware of the world. Christian felt like a rhino stuck in the middle of cavorting gazelles. The only consolation was that between them, no one would notice him at all.

A circle formed as people moved into shuffle-and-watch mode. The band had all eyes on Liza and blended one song into the next without missing a beat. For the first time, Christian heard their sound as more than mere rhythm, as actual music. The guitarist Christian remembered from the 60's rock band looked away from Liza long enough to catch Christian's eye, grin, and stick in a riff from his best-known hit of that era. It worked. Everything worked. The Second Circle was sizzling.

Chapter Forty-Seven

Liza floated back to earth when the set was over. Skin glistening, she wilted in Christian's arms. Kathy waited close by for Liza to recover, and to forestall anyone who might want to intrude. No one did. A few people returned to their tables but most milled around, reluctant to leave the source of a departed magic.

Sibyl came from behind the stage, talked to Kathy and Kathy came over. "The band would like to meet Liza. I think it's a good idea. They'll have refreshments, and after that, we all need fluids."

Backstage, Christian stayed by Liza while they both downed a couple of bottles of water. Liza attacked the buffet and soon was surrounded by members of the band. They posed with her for instant photos they signed and then for more, which she signed for them. Christian moved to the corner where Kathy was talking with the guitarist who was keeping one eye on the action and the other on Kathy.

She smiled and waved Christian to the spot beside her. "Sit and relax. We were just renewing our acquaintance and catching up on news."

"You know each other?"

"Couldn't forget Kathy. I remember you too, although not the same way." Both he and Kathy laughed, and she punched his arm lightly. "Last time we were through, I noted you as Aurora's latest. Must say you've improved the company you're keeping. Before we went on, Ms Jinnah came back to talk with Aurora. The dear girl went through the roof." He chuckled and looked over at Liza. "I can certainly see why."

"I heard you had a run-in with Aurora yourself," Kathy said to the guitarist. "Heard you turned down her favours when she did the interviews in New York last month."

"That story got out? I shouldn't be surprised. If anyone was going to hear it, you would."

"Lipstick obscenities on your dressing room mirror are mild. She's mellowed."

"Her spelling and penmanship were impeccable. But enough about Aurora. You're looking good. If it wasn't for the ingénue, you'd be by far the sexiest woman in the room."

"Are you trying to pick me up? Again?"

"Would I have any luck?"

Negotiations were brought to a halt by Liza's arrival. She had a sandwich in one hand and another bottle of water in the other. "Boy, it's hard to get away from those guys, but I had to meet you. Your blues recordings have been played around me since before I can remember."

"I'm glad you found time to tell that to this suddenly old man. One of your parents is a fan?"

"My father--and you're not that old. Dad's always said for an Englishman, you have an amazing feel for the blues."

"Bet he doesn't call me an Englishman, though. You know, blues is all this white boy ever wanted to play. This stuff, well, until tonight I didn't care for it."

"Then why do you do it? For the money?" Christian asked.

"Don't need more, thanks, but once you get on the merry-go-round, it's hard to get off. I love performing, but can't play small clubs any more. Word gets around, and there are riots. I know, I've tried. Once the public makes you theirs, they won't let go. After tonight, you folks are going to find that out for themselves."

"Why?" Christian didn't want to believe that, but did.

"I was watching the cameras. Liza upstaged us. That first set will be as much her show as ours. It's going out on satellite. By tomorrow, she'll be known worldwide. As she should be. We don't mind--it's good for us too." He smiled at Liza. "Get ready for fame. What do you think, Kathy?"

"That you're the expert." Kathy patted Christian's hand. "Come on, let him fill Liza in on how to be a legend while we see what's left on the buffet."

The guitarist took Kathy's hand and held it for an instant. "If you're not too busy later, drop by the hotel."

Kathy took Christian to the buffet but neither wanted anything except water. "So, Kathy. If he's right... if beauty and vitality are what it takes, I'll ask what Liza did earlier. How did you miss out?"

"Maybe I didn't want it... and maybe he's feeding her a line. There's more to making it big than that, Christian. Like the desire and connections, and luck."

"I get the feeling you have the connections."

Kathy smiled. "Yes, and if I took scalps, I'd have more on my belt than Aurora. But I'm too old now. Liza's young; she's the future."

"You're younger than me, I think."

"But you're a man. It makes a difference."

"You're making excuses. I'd say you've always wanted it--you've just been afraid."

"And I'd say, 'fuck off, Christian--you're a fine one to talk'." Kathy's voice remained warm. Strangely, so did her eyes. "Come on. It's time to get out of here."

Liza joined them at the door. "He gave me his addresses in London and Monte Carlo. I like him-- he knows who he is." Her smile bathed Christian and Kathy in sunshine. "And how are you two doing?"

"Okay." Kathy answered for both of them. "Better."

They met Sibyl in the hall. "Heading back? Good. Aurora will be on soon. Could I prevail on your good will and ask you three to stay off the dance floor for her set?"

"I wouldn't dance to her if you paid me. Good enough?" Kathy's question was a challenge. "Oh, I guess I'd dance on her grave, but that's it."

Liza grabbed Kathy's arm. "Sibyl? We've got empty chairs at our table. Will anyone else be joining us?"

"No. Fill or leave them empty as you see fit. Of course, everything's on the house for you and your guests."

They passed the COSMO table. Horatio and Judy were sitting even closer together. Liza had already said Kathy was going to sit with them. That left four empty places at the owner's table. Christian sensed Liza was determined to fill them.

Liza scanned the standing-room only crowd then, much to the consternation of Percy and the special services crew, dashed into it. Almost immediately, she emerged with an arm around a short but sturdy, dreadlocked woman. With them, was a study in purple--her tights, top and hair matched. Against her fair skin the effect was remarkably pleasing. Purple suited her.

Liza stopped and said something to her newly acquired companions. They slipped back into the crowd. Liza beckoned to Christian and Kathy and they went to the owner's table. "Ti worked with me until she had a fight with the manager. At work we said Ti was short for Tiger. Violet's her friend. I told them to find some guys."

Ti and Violet soon appeared with a pair of pleasantly bewildered young men. As introductions were taking place the voice from the stage boomed out, announcing the beginning of the second set, featuring Aurora. Her band started to play. A spotlight hovered on the edge. Aurora leapt into it and then to centre stage.

If she truly considered leather as much a cliché as she'd once claimed, Aurora was all cliché. Dressed in black, her pants seemed sprayed on and her studded jacket was open as far as the law would permit.

The music was equally obvious. A guitar screamed, doing a passable imitation of the man Christian had been talking with backstage, the bass

403

growled and the keyboards wrapped around the melody, filling out Aurora's voice. It was well done, but wasn't music that would sell itself. It needed to be sold by the performance.

Aurora tried. She played provocative games with microphones and necks of instruments, leaned over so eyes glued to her jacket, hoping it wouldn't hold... stroked her hair and thighs suggestively.

At the owner's table her efforts went unnoticed by all but Christian. Liza had given out the signed instant pictures she had collected backstage and they had been handed back for her signature to be added. Even with the noise she also managed to visit with Ti, her former workmate, displaying an ability Christian had never mastered. As far as he was concerned, when the music started, spoken communication ended. On his other side, Kathy and the aptly named Violet were also talking.

Kathy and Violet got up and went to the washroom. Shortly afterward, Marci came up the stairs and collected Liza. Evidently feeling left out, Ti, the only woman left at the table, trailed after them. Christian decided it sounded like a good idea and went to the Men's Room. He wasn't surprised to get back before the female contingent.

Ti's date was watching the stage, drumming his fingers to the familiar new songs. The man Violet had selected caught Christian's eye and used his green Mohawk to point at the seats Kathy and Liza had been occupying. He gave Christian a thumbs-up of approval. Christian shrugged… it wasn't true, but he knew no one wanted to believe that.

404

Violet and Ti returned and took their men to the dance floor. Liza and Kathy came back and sat beside each other. Marci didn't sit--she caught Christian's eye and hooked her thumb towards the back of the room. Once there, she shouted into his ear. Christian shook his head. He couldn't hear a word. He led her around the bar, and through the door to the office and upstairs areas. The sound level went down. Christian knocked on the office door.

"Yes." Sibyl was there. Christian had hoped she wasn't.

She wasn't for long. Christian introduced Marci as Freyja, and Sibyl as herself. They said the things people who profoundly dislike each other say when being polite and then Sibyl excused herself.

Marci glared holes into the closing door.

"You were trying to tell me something?" Christian asked.

"I could tell you a few things." The glare switched to him but instantly softened. "I hope you know what you've got yourself into."

"Of course I don't. Tell me."

"I'll stick to my most immediate concern." Sibyl had cranked the publicity machine into overdrive; Christian, and especially Liza, were being anointed as media idols. Since Christian was listed in the phone book, not only would his phone keep ringing, but reporters would also camp in his lobby, lurk in the halls with cameras and probably listen at his door with tape recorders. They were sure to discover Liza lived across the hall from him. Security in their building was nonexistent.

"I got Liza's keys from her. She won't be able to go back there for a long time, if ever. All she wants are her letters, photos and underwear. For tonight, you two should get a hotel room, or maybe go to Grace's. Not many people know about that, and the security is good."

"Aurora's been there. Her name is at the desk."

"Not anymore." Marci flashed her teeth. "I had Fred strike her off. She's recovered--if there ever was anything for her to recover from."

"Then we'll go there. You won't drop over?"

"Only if you promise to call me in the morning. Well, let's say before noon. You're going to need help to survive this."

Marci was exaggerating again but Christian agreed to call her. They returned to The Second Circle proper as Aurora was effusively thanking a mildly applauding crowd. Liza exchanged looks with Marci, smiled, and gave Christian a quick kiss. The applause swelled.

Aurora hopped off the stage and made her way towards Cosmo's table. A few young males who wanted an autograph or a peek into her jacket stopped her.

"I should talk to Aurora." Christian felt sorry for her.

"Why?" Liza didn't seem to.

"It's not a bad idea," Kathy said. "You've rattled her cage--give her an opening to bite back. It'll be a good photo op."

Aurora was being interviewed by a man with a VideoView camera on his shoulder--a clump of other reporters were clustered around. As

406

Christian's party approached, the attention shifted to them. Aurora turned, took a step towards them and stopped.

Christian gently freed himself from Liza and Kathy, and went to Aurora. Cameras flashed and whirred madly. "Can't stay away from me, can you?" Aurora asked in a loud rasping voice. She jumped into his arms and wrapped her legs around him, puckering for a kiss. The area lit.

Christian's hands had instinctively gone around her to support the sudden, unexpected burden. He didn't kiss her before he put her down. "We're history. Remember?"

It was only what she had said to him. Cameras rollicked. Aurora wheeled away, and immediately bumped into Sibyl Jinnah. Sibyl hugged Aurora and whispered something into her ear. Aurora stiffened, relaxed, let go and stomped in the direction of the office, elbowing an eager photographer and sending his camera crashing to the floor. Sibyl followed her and kicked the shattered equipment as she passed. The rest of the media buzzed.

"That was brilliant." Marci's words didn't have the sarcastic tone that usually accompanied her statements. She kissed him. It wasn't at all sisterly, but an assertive Freyja Van Deer kiss that got his body's full attention. She broke it off and shuffled him over to Liza. "All yours." As she slipped out of his arms, Liza slid in.

Liza took over the kiss where Freyja had left it. She came up for breath, eventually. "Let's get out of here."

Christian wasn't about to argue.

407

"I'll call for the limo. Don't leave without me." Kathy rushed towards the backstage area.

"Don't be gentle with him, Liza." Marci encircled both Liza and Christian with her powerful arms. "And remember, Christian--call me before noon. I'm sure you'll be up." She left them, chuckling as if she'd said something original or clever.

Christian and Liza went back to the owner's table to say their goodbyes. Christian called over the ever-watchful Percy, and asked him to take care of Liza's guests, and to see them safely to taxis if they overindulged in the free booze. Liza hugged everyone. Christian contented himself with handshakes, except for Ti, who had pursed for a kiss. She slipped a piece of paper into his pocket as he bent over and brushed her lips.

Arm in arm in arm, Liza, Christian and Kathy left The Second Circle as the third set began. The band had jelled and sounded as good as they had with Liza dancing. Darkness ignited as the trio stepped outside. They made their way to George and the limo, a throng of jabbering reporters surrounding them. Liza was the only one who answered any of the questions--she was Liza Little, nineteen, and thrilled Christian had discovered her.

When the door closed, peace reigned... for an instant. Then Liza and Kathy whooped and hugged. "Perfect. As planned. She fell for it."

"Explain. Please." The women exchanged self-satisfied smirks.

"Certainly." Liza took charge. "One. You decided I was born to live in the limelight; I decided the same for you. Mission accomplished." She and Kathy slapped hands in a high five. "Two. We'd done that, so it was time to get to the rest of the weekend. I can tell you're ready."

"Three." Kathy took over. "Aurora slit her own throat and then you jabbed the knife in. As you said, she's history--I love it."

That hadn't been how Christian had intended or even said it, but yes, it probably would be taken that way. Kathy was too pleased with herself. "Four," Christian fixed her with his eyes as if pinning her to the seat. "You've stepped up and shown yourself to the world, in our company. If we've hit big, so have you."

"Shit. You're right." Kathy shifted away from Liza and fell into a dark study.

"What did Ti give you, Christian? Her phone number? Liza asked"

Christian looked at the piece of paper in his pocket. "And her address."

"I'll keep it for you, for now. You can have it back after the weekend. You'd like her." After taking it Liza closed the gap between herself and Kathy, and took Kathy into her arms. "I love you, Kathy. About tonight?"

"I love you too, but I already told you... no, I'm totally straight. I'll keep the car and go back. I need to have a few words with Cosmo, and I don't trust a certain guitarist to make it to his hotel room without other company." The light on the car phone had been flashing for some time. Kathy picked it up and listened.

"We've lost the swarm. George thinks we'd better get to where we're going before they find us again."

Chapter Forty-Eight

"Discovery time," Liza said as Christian locked the apartment door. She wiggled out of her dress. He took off his jacket and reached for her. She ripped his shirt open.

"Not here." She stepped back. "In the nearest bed."

They went up the stairs, arms entwined. Liza opened Grace's door. "Yes. This is the place." Christian hesitated. Grace's room? It didn't seem right. Liza undid her bra, let it fall and went in. Christian followed, struggling to drop his pants. Grace's bed was as firm and lush as Liza. Christian poised himself.

Liza had other thoughts. "Condom. If I were her, I'd keep them here."

She reached out an arm and opened a drawer in the bedside table. Condoms. She fumbled and finally slipped it over the head. Christian came.

"Oops."

Christian could have found stronger words.

"I'm sorry, Christian. My fault. I shouldn't have insisted."

"No. You were right." He'd had unprotected sex with Aurora, and there was no telling who else Aurora had slept with.

"We'll just try again." She tried. Christian tried. Nothing worked.

"In the morning," Liza said at last. "You likely need some rest."

Christian wasn't sure what he needed... to be ten years younger, to be the man she thought he was, to be somewhere else, anywhere at all. He rolled over and she nestled into his back.

He woke up alone, smelling bacon. Hadn't this happened before? Almost? After visiting the bathroom, he went downstairs.

Liza appeared from the kitchen with a large mug of coffee, black and strong, the way he drank it. "Here you go. Your breakfast will be ready soon. I already ate."

"I'm sorry."

Liza laughed. "For what? You've had a busy couple of days, and you hardly ate last night. You've had a good night's sleep. I need to build you up. Sit and relax."

Christian had been about to kiss her and try again. Instead, he sat.

Along with the bacon, Liza had cooked eggs and a pile of toast. "I'm going to check in with Kathy. She'll be at the hotel. It's okay, I found the phone--what a funny place to keep it!"

As Christian ate, Liza's voice was a murmur from the kitchen. He couldn't make out what she was saying no matter how hard he tried. When he took his plate into the kitchen, she was sitting cross-legged on the floor. She looked up. "We'll be another few minutes."

They could be much longer. Christian hated to think what Liza was telling Kathy, or what Kathy was saying in return. He went to check his e-mail. There were three messages--from Dee, Gabby and Grace, in that order.

Dee's was a copy of what she had sent Gabby. It described Liza physically and in terms of character. Properly handled, Dee said, Liza could become a household name, worldwide. After the previous night, Christian wondered if Liza already was.

The e-mail from Gabby included Dee's and was copied to Grace. Gabby's actual reply was short. She agreed Liza sounded special and said she felt privileged to be the one Dee would write--along with the rest of European fashion world, she had been wondering when Dee would come out of exile.

Grace had written to Christian only. "Liza should go to Paris--the sooner the better. Call my lawyer, Daniel Webster. He's already got the paperwork moving. And yes, he'll be in the office Saturday. Keep in touch. Love, Mom."

Christian found the lawyer's address and phone number and went to see Liza. "Sorry to interrupt, but I need to make a call."

Liza relayed the information and hung up. "Kathy sends her love, and says to remind you to phone Freyja. What's happening?"

Christian told her. Liza refused to surrender the phone. "I'll handle the lawyer." The call was quick. Liza's end consisted of the word 'yes', repeated several times. "He's sending the documents over. Now, call Freyja." She handed him the phone.

Marci answered on the first ring. "It's about time. Have you seen the papers? No? Put Liza on and go get them."

"Good morning, Freyja. Nice to talk to you. Liza?" He returned the receiver to her.

The guard in the lobby greeted Christian by name; he'd thought Fred was the only one who knew him. He understood the instant he saw the newspaper boxes. The tabloid had a full-length shot of Liza on the front, making her look all leg. He was on a different front page, leaving The Second Circle with Kathy and Liza. The third paper didn't feature any of them. That was no surprise… it was the sombre, grey paper of business. Christian bought a copy anyway, along with the other two.

Liza was still on the phone. He went to the table to look over the papers.

Inside the tabloid the story was spread over two pages, chiefly more pictures. One sequence featured him. Under the headline "Lucky Man!" were shots of him kissing Marci (identified as Freyja Van Deer), Liza, Ti and Aurora (not actually kissing, but with her legs wrapped around him). The picture of him leaving The Second Circle with Liza and Kathy, captioned, "Talent scout Christian Plowman knows his talent."

There was also a large picture of Liza dancing. She was referred to as a supermodel. Aurora, his "former flame", did have her singing debut mentioned… in unflattering terms. It was reported Sibyl Jinnah was going to manage Aurora from now on, instead of Christian (he wasn't aware he had been) and he was quoted (misquoted) as saying "Aurora is history".

The band got an excellent review. Sibyl was quoted as saying Liza was destined for the top and that caught between the next modelling superstar and the hottest band on the planet, Aurora had suffered. Sibyl was sure Christian would regret what he'd said and agree Aurora had a solid career ahead.

Christian didn't like any of what he read in the tabloid. While they were pretending to feature Liza, the real focus was on him. He detected Sibyl's hand in that... this was her revenge. If she knew what had happened after they left, Christian was sure she'd be jubilant. She'd probably find out. Liza was certain to have told Kathy, and Kathy was a clearinghouse for gossip.

In the paper that featured Christian with Liza and Kathy on the front, the story inside was short. There was one other picture, a leggy shot of Liza. The text mentioned Christian and the first band in glowing terms, and called Liza and Kathy "top local models". In this paper, Christian was an "agent". Aurora didn't get mentioned.

Surprisingly, the business paper did have a story and even they hadn't resisted Liza's legs. According to them, Noronto was on the verge becoming a "hotbed of the modelling business", thanks to Christian. He had introduced Liza's "fresh face" and was behind Kathy's "revitalised career". The Second Circle and the first band were a "backdrop Mr. Plowman used". Christian thought this Mr. Plowman sounded clever. He admired the man's business acumen. Again, Aurora wasn't mentioned. All three papers did say the concert was to be shown that night on VideoView.

There was a knock on the apartment door. Liza rushed out of the kitchen to answer it and came into the living room with a brown manila envelope in hand. The papers were spread on the table, showing all the relevant pages. Liza gave them a cursory examination. "They like my legs, don't they? Isn't Kathy stunning! Nice shot of Ti. What do they say about me?"

"That you're a model, a supermodel, the greatest discovery of all time."

"Then I guess I'm off to Paris."

"What did Freyja and Kathy have to say about last night?" Christian didn't want to know, but figured he might as well hear it sooner than later.

"What would you expect them to say?"

The worst, and he couldn't imagine what that would be. Liza studied his face, and then smiled. "Oh, you mean about that? Nothing. I told them our sex lives were none of their damn business." She sat across from him and opened the envelope. He moved around to look over her shoulder. She turned the papers upside down. "No thanks. I'll read these over myself. After all, it's my future, not yours."

"But I'm your agent. It says so in the newspaper."

"Don't believe everything you read and no, this has nothing to do with anything else. Mr. Webster told me you didn't even read your own contract... and you want to read mine?"

She had a point. Christian retreated to the other side of the table and read the newspaper articles again. He took some time to look at the pictures

416

properly. No, Liza hadn't eclipsed Kathy, well, not totally. "Finished yet?"

"No. Maybe you should go get dressed. We're meeting Kathy and Freyja for lunch at the Westshire. Well, I am and you're invited."

"We're going out?" Christian didn't want to get dressed, and didn't want to go anywhere other than back to bed. "We just ate." That should settle it.

"We're coming back as well. And I'm always ready to eat. Come over here, you."

Christian went to her side of the table. She stood. "We could do something else first. Look what I have here." A condom. She kissed him and her hand explored. It didn't find anything that would make them late.

Chapter Forty-Nine

Liza didn't speak to Christian on the way to the Westshire. He wouldn't have blamed her if she were angry but that didn't seem to be the case. She turned her head towards him, a half-smile on her face. Her eyes were deep and calm. Christian returned her smile but couldn't find anything to say. She turned her head away. This wasn't the coltish woman he'd asked for a date.

The doorman at the hotel offered Liza a hand out of the cab and a slight bow. Christian might as well have been invisible... he slipped through the lobby door behind her. A clerk at the front desk noted their arrival and picked up his telephone. The door beside the desk opened. A suit appeared, three pieces of lavish black fabric with a brass nameplate, 'Andre Rathbone, Manager.'

"May I be of assistance, madam and sir?" Andre Rathbone's face was impeccably tailored, its skin stretched in a smile.

"We're meeting a friend in your dining room." Christian knew the way.

"But of course, the delightful Ms Romanova. She suggested I be on hand to conduct you. May I?" He offered Liza his arm. She glanced at Christian. For once, he knew what she wanted; her touch was light, but firm. "Then, if you will follow me," the manager continued, smoothly transforming his spurned offer into a turn.

The restaurant was moderately busy but Kathy had a table for six to herself. An impatient tug on

418

his arm told Christian that Liza had seen her. Christian took the time to thank Andre Rathbone for his assistance before starting across the room.

"It's her!" A squeal.

"And him! Mother! Look!" Another teenaged girl shoved a copy of the morning tabloid in her mother's face as she leapt to her feet.

The first was already beside them. "Liza! I'm your biggest fan ever! Can I have your autograph? Please?"

"Young lady, sit down. We don't allow this sort of behaviour." Andre Rathbone to the rescue.

Liza didn't want rescuing. "Why? What harm can it do? Certainly," she said to the girl. Girl? Christian looked again... she might be a year younger than Liza, or a year older.

"You're even hotter than you look in the paper. Please?" The other girl. Girl? Not with those knowing eyes... shoved her paper into Christian's hands and stood, too close, gazing up at him. Others were headed their way... and did everyone own a cell phone?

"Liza, we're going to cause a riot." That was the harm it could do.

"Please?" He was being asking for more than an autograph. Christian retreated a step.

"You're exaggerating." Liza signed her name again. "Hi there." She cut between Christian and his admirer. "I'll autograph this." She took the paper from Christian. "And then we had better sit down. Sorry," she added to Andre Rathbone. "This is all new to me."

"It's quite all right. We have it under control." Waiters and security guards had intercepted most of the other fans and were herding them back to their tables. "Reinforcements are on their way. We're quite accustomed to hosting stars." This time Liza didn't resist when he took her arm.

"So, how are you two taking to fame?" Kathy asked when they arrived at the table. "Thanks, Andre. You're a prince."

"Your humble servant, Miss Romanova."

Kathy was wearing the dress she'd had on the night before. It and her hair were uncharacteristically dishevelled and her arctic eyes were sparkling. One of them winked at Christian. He wasn't sure he knew this Kathy. Overnight everyone had seemingly changed. "Who else are we expecting, your boyfriend, the guitarist?" he asked, quickly looking away from her.

"Him? No way, they left early this morning. I didn't get out of bed to see them off." She smiled.

"The chairs are for Marci and Ti," Liza said while Christian was still searching for an appropriate response. "They went to get my papers and stuff from my old apartment," she added. "Marci didn't think it would be safe for me to do it."

"She has to be right about something once in a while." Kathy hadn't changed her opinion of Marci.

"Can we risk the buffet?" Liza looked longingly at the food.

Kathy got to her feet. "We can. Andre's troops are in place."

They had the buffet to themselves... a ring of uniforms insured that. Liza loaded up her plate.

420

Christian didn't feel hungry and evidently neither did Kathy; all she took were a few pieces of cantaloupe and a slice of melon.

"Okay Liza, let's see this contract you were telling me about," Kathy said as she sat. "You didn't read me the fine print over the phone."

Liza's arm disappeared into her purse and emerged with a thin sheaf of paper. She gave it to Kathy and then attacked her food.

Kathy put the contract in front of her and devoured it quickly, running her finger down each page and then turning to the next. She finished. "It's more than fair. I recommend you sign it as is. One thing though... just what is this Plowman Talent Agency a finder's fee is to be paid to?"

Liza sighed and put down her fork. "I just knew you were going to ask that... troublemaker." She took another, thicker, document out of her purse and gave it to Christian. "I was going to show this to you later."

Christian skimmed it. "I've been fired."

"Not true."

"This is my termination pay." A cheque for a hundred thousand dollars was clipped to the second page. It was ridiculously generous, but fired was fired.

Kathy shuffled to the chair beside him. "Let me see." A wave of musk wafted over Christian; his hand trembled as he gave her the papers.

She read for a minute. "No, Liza's right. According to this you've fulfilled the terms of your contract and are being paid the agreed-upon bonus, that's all. You were a freelancer, not an employee, so you couldn't be fired."

"Christian didn't read the contract before he signed," Liza said through a mouthful.

"Figures. The original is attached to the back." Kathy flipped to it.

Fulfilled the terms of the contract? Christian tried to think, and tried to ignore the pheromones Kathy was sending to attack his brain. What had Grace hired him to do? Or, more to the point, what had Grace said she'd hired him to do? Maybe Kathy actually had showered… who knew what that dress had been through overnight? Okay, Grace had wanted him to find a hostess for Ovation's flagship show and yes, according to her, he'd done that, whether Cosmo accepted Judy was the right person or not. And he was to improve his image and become known to the public. Okay, he had become known, if only last night. He wasn't sure his new image was an improvement but then again, his opinion didn't matter.

"It doesn't say what you were actually hired to do." Kathy's eyes asked another question or two. She didn't give the papers back.

"I guess I have to accept I've done it."

"Then this is yours." Kathy handed him the cheque. "Free and clear, if you want it that way." Her breath was sweet and warm. Couldn't she move back a little? Should he? Had Liza noticed what was going on across from her? No, she was intent on her plate.

"And welcome to the world of the unemployed."

"You've lost your job at The Factory?" Maybe Liza was paying attention after all.

"Cosmo booted my ass. Last night. Said he wouldn't put up with me peddling it out of his lobby anymore." She smiled. "Told him it wasn't my fault I like sex and rich men like giving me jewellery." She put a hand on Christian's arm. Was she flirting with him?

"I've never seen you wear jewellery." He hoped he hadn't.

"I don't." Kathy moved closer to Christian. "It's funny how men will give you what you don't ask for instead of what they think you want--like I'd want them to stick around--hah! Freyja actually backed me up." Amazement filled Kathy's voice. "Told Cosmo he was being a fool."

"She would," Liza said. Christian glanced at her again. How much did she know about Freyja... about Marci?

Liza met his eyes. "Kathy told me all about Freyja this morning. Then when I talked with Marci she told me what Kathy had got wrong."

"I don't get things wrong."

Liza ignored Kathy and continued. "Marci says she's retired her Freyja persona."

"Her? Retire? I doubt that."

"Can we get back to my problem?" Christian asked.

Kathy and Liza both laughed. "What problem?" Kathy stroked his arm. "You're rich, famous, and you could get any woman you want into bed by just asking."

"He'd better not! Not until I leave for Paris! Unless you've changed your mind."

"You were serious last night?"

"Christian, you wouldn't know an opportunity if it broke down your door. Case in point." Kathy slammed the papers she'd been holding onto the table in front of him, barely missing his plate. "Here you're being handed one of the greatest gifts I've ever seen and all you can say is that you've been fired. Read the damn thing--oh hell, forget it... even I know better than to ask that."

Kathy took the papers back. "That cheque you did nothing to earn is earmarked to be your initial investment in The Plowman Talent Agency-¬charming name--with you and one Freyja van Deer as equal partners. Hah! At least Grace knows who the woman is." She flipped a page. "All start-up costs to be paid by the aforementioned Grace in exchange for ten-percent of the net profits--net, mind you. Offices provided at 88 The Street, rent-free for three years--blah, blah, blah--if anyone handed me something like this I'd jump on it before you could blink."

"What does this theoretical Plowman Talent Agency do?"

"Good question, for once." Kathy flipped pages. "Blah, blah--and I quote 'locate and/or develop hitherto unrecognised and/or underappreciated talent.

Talent to mean the needs, present or potential, of the fashion and/or entertainment industries.'" She put the document down again, more gently this time. "In other words, you and Freyja can do pretty much what you damn well want. Or rather, you can. It also says she intends to be a silent partner."

"Silent? Her? That, I don't believe."

From their laughter Liza and Kathy agreed.

"Seriously, Christian." Kathy took a pen from her purse. "Sign it. What have you got to lose, other than a hundred thousand bucks you earned, in essence, by sleeping with Liza?"

Put that way, Christian didn't see he had much choice. He didn't want to but he had to accept. However… "I don't know a thing about running something like that. I don't think I can. Do you want a job, Kathy?"

"Don't you hate it when he whines?" Kathy asked Liza. "No, Christian--no way I'm going to work for you, and I certainly won't for Freyja van Deer."

"Would you like to be a partner then? You could invest the proceeds of the jewellery you earned, in essence, by sleeping with all and sundry."

"That's nasty, Christian, turning my words back on me that way. Didn't know you had it in you." Kathy furrowed her brow. "Yeah, I will if Freyja agrees--fat chance of that. Yes, Andre?"

"Pardon me, Miss Romanova, I'm terribly sorry to bother you but there are two female persons in the lobby who seem to be in possession of property belonging to Miss Liza. The police insisted I check their story with you. If you can believe it, one of them claims her name is Tiger."

"They're with us. Could you bring them through the back to avoid the crowd?" The main entrance to the dining room was jammed solid.

"If you insist." The manager wheeled and marched away.

"Dumb bitch." Kathy was sounding more like herself. "If she'd use her proper name she wouldn't have any trouble."

"Ti?" Liza's innocence sounded forced.

Kathy went for it though. "No, Freyja van Stupid--when you've earned a name that opens doors, you should be bright enough to use it."

Ti arrived in jeans and a shirt with torn-off sleeves, Marci in a pair of her paint-stained overalls. Andre Rathbone and two police officers accompanied them.

"Thank you, Andre." Kathy shook her head in disbelief. "Hard as it might be to believe, these are Liza and Christian's friends. Look at you two! No wonder you had problems."

"Any world class hotel knows not to judge people by their appearance." Marci didn't sound bothered by Kathy's criticism. "Hi, Christian, Liza. Ti, give Liza her stuff and go attack the buffet. It's probably safe--no one here seems to be suffering from ptomaine yet... that was last month."

"Is there anything else, ma'am?" Andre bowed again... to Kathy only.

"I don't think so." Was Kathy suppressing a smile? The manager bowed once more and stepped back to just barely out of earshot. "I hate to admit it, Freyja, but you're right. I only use the Westshire because it's convenient."

426

"And because they'll let you in and kiss your butt to boot. Don't try to be pleasant, Kathy. It doesn't suit you." Marci sat. "So, Christian... are we in business?"

"I want Kathy to work with us." No use avoiding the matter.

"Sorry, I told Ti she could be the receptionist."

"With us, not for us. I want her to be a partner... or I don't sign."

Marci's eyebrows didn't believe what they were hearing.

"Kathy knows showbiz, modelling and fashion and has good contacts. And Grace likes her. Says she's the brains of Cosmo's operation."

Kathy laughed. "Scant praise that is. Freyja, why are you sleeping with the little jerk?"

"Be quiet. You're not helping your cause." Kathy looked as surprised by his words as Christian felt. "And Cosmo's an okay guy." He had to be. Grace and Marci both liked him.

Marci met his eyes and smiled. "Okay, this agency is your toy. She's in if you want her."

"I suppose I've just been insulted." Kathy didn't sound hurt. "But if I can get what I want, I don't really care what anyone thinks. However, before I agree to your generous offer I have a condition."

One of Marci's eyebrows told Kathy to continue, and that she had a lot of nerve.

"You're Freyja van Deer on the contract."

"The money is still in that name. It's going to change."

"No it isn't, not if I'm along for the ride. Grace knows marketing and she signed a contract with

427

Freyja, not some colourless Marci creature. Freyja's a name, a force... if you'd come here today as yourself dear Andre would have used a bazooka to blow open a route to the dining room. And I assure you Cosmo's not boasting he's got Marci Nobody crawling at his feet. No way. He's promoting himself as Freyja van Deer's true love, the one man she wants so much she'll do it for free."

"I doubt he is. But, other than trying to get him in trouble, your point is?"

Kathy took a deep breath. "That maybe you don't want to sell Freyja any more, but I do. Christian and Liza are overnight sensations; you're a legend, a ten thousand night sensation."

"Hardly that many."

Kathy ignored the interruption. "Besides which, I've been watching you. Maybe you're on a mental vacation, but inside you're still Freyja: arrogant, conceited and unbelievably narcissistic. When you regain your sanity you'll regret most of the decisions you've made the past couple of months. Don't compound them by giving away your name."

"Are we supposed to applaud now?" Ti asked.

"You're supposed to be seen and not heard." Marci said and ignored the rude gesture Ti made in response to that comment. "Okay Kathy, I'm Freyja and you're in... to something that doesn't exist. Christian hasn't signed, has he? I doubted he would."

"He damn well better now."

Christian agreed. There was no way out. Marci was Freyja, Kathy was a partner and he was going to have to deal with both of them on a daily basis, as the head of a business he didn't want. If he'd been thinking, he would have taken the money and run.

"Should I read the contract?"

"Yes, but you won't. Don't bother pretending." Kathy scribbled a line at the bottom, crossed out a few things, added some and inserted her name wherever Christian and Freyja's appeared. "Initial the changes. The lawyer should be able to accept it as it," Kathy added to Freyja.

"Now I am impressed. Grace and Christian are right. There is a brain behind that trashy exterior." Freyja took the contract as she stood.

"I can arrange for a courier. We have a full range of business services, Ms. van Deer." Andre Rathbone, re-entering the conversation from where he'd been hovering.

Freyja's glared moved him back a step. "And you can lip-read and have been eavesdropping on everything we've said. No thanks. Ti and I will hand deliver it. We have a limo waiting--didn't notice that earlier, did you?"

"Very well... madam. The Westshire is pleased to have been of service. Naturally, lunch is on the house."

"Then this is for tips." Freyja tossed enough on the table to pay for their meal twice over. Andre bowed his way backwards, spun on one heel and stalked away.

Freyja watched him go. "Kathy, from now on, this hotel is out of bounds. We can't afford to be associated with scum." She waited for Kathy's nod of agreement. "Okay Ti, lead us out of here."

The crowd parted as Ti approached, dreadlocks swinging. The Westshire's security force scurried to catch up as Liza and Christian strode directly behind Ti. Kathy and Freyja brought up the rear. In the lobby Liza stopped to sign autographs and talk to the reporters--she was leaving for Paris soon--excited--nineteen, almost twenty--oh, and a hundred eighty centimetres and circa 65 kilos--which sent everyone hunting for a calculator.

Kathy broke it up. "Ms Little will be available again before she leaves. We'll let you know."

Their party forged to the limousine and piled into the back. There was plenty of room but Christian found himself sandwiched between Liza and Kathy, their clasped hands resting in his lap.

Freyja and Ti were on the facing seat. Freyja's eyes were on Christian's lap. "We get out first. Give me a call when you have time, Kathy."

She and Ti discussed what they would do after the lawyers' and what a jerk Andre Rathbone was. The limo slowed and stopped. "No, don't get up, Christian," Freyja said as she opened the door. Very funny. Again. The door closed.

Chapter Fifty

"Guess I'm next," Kathy said. "To get out, that is."

Christian wasn't sure if that was a statement or a question and if it was a question, how he should respond. He paused to give Liza an opportunity to intervene. She didn't. "Guess so,"

Liza squeezed Kathy's hand, and Christian. "We can't expect to change everything about him overnight."

Christian pried the women's hands apart. "I don't intend to change at all." He sensed that if he let go of either one, the former status quo would be re¬established, so he didn't.

"You already have changed, Christian." Liza sounded certain.

"I could add that you haven't any choice." Kathy was quickly regaining the icy edge. Christian let her hand go. "But I think you'll decide you like the way things are going, after you get over the shock." She gave his cheek a gentle kiss. "After Liza's gone, you'll be at my mercy." She picked up the phone to the driver. "Pull over so I can get out, please and thank you." She hung up. "And before you head off to Paris, Liza, feel welcome to stay with me when you've had enough of him." The limo pulled to a halt. "Bye guys, have fun."

Upon arriving back at Grace's apartment, Christian's most pressing need was to visit the bathroom... maybe Freyja had been right about the quality of the Westshire's buffet. Liza was going to be disappointed again, but he couldn't help that, a man didn't have control over his stomach. When he felt better he cleaned up and took a shower.

He found Liza in Grace's bed, reading Shakespeare. "Love's Labour Lost?" he asked.

"Oh please! Much Ado About Nothing." Liza closed the volume and put it on the bedside table. She opened a drawer and pulled out half a dozen condoms. "Now, since you've lived up to your end of our bargain so brilliantly, it's my turn. I promise I won't disappoint you."

"You're remembering things backwards."

"Really? I told you I wanted experience and you've given me the world. And what did you want the first time you saw me, Christian? What attracted you? Can you admit it? Oh, you're so cute when you blush... no, it wasn't my firm, young body. You find any number of women more attractive than me, particularly Kathy... don't think I didn't notice." She pulled the covers halfway down, swung her legs to the floor and started towards him.

"You're right. I'm sorry."

"Sorry? You're pathetic." Liza's laugh took the sting from her words. "Look at me, not my feet... no, not my legs either, me!" She lifted his head with both her hands. Her eyes were impossibly dark, wide and friendly. "Innocence seduced you. Enjoy it, Christian, it's all yours."

"Your innocence seems to have been an illusion."

"Then enjoy an illusion, Christian. That's how to handle this world."

An infinitesimal forever later Christian found himself floating in a dense fog of dream. It closed

432

in, surrounding him with breathless pressure, and then burst into clear sky. His eyes unlocked to the vision of Liza looming impossibly large above him. Her eyes were raised to the heavens as she started moving, creating a pain that spread deliciously from his middle, bunched and then leapt with a voiceless scream. She collapsed onto him, sunk into him and joined him in darkness.

Christian woke up alone in Grace's bed. It was dark outside. He went downstairs. Liza was at the table, wearing the red pantsuit Dee had given her the day before, sipping coffee. Another cup, steaming hot, sat across from her.

"Time for me to be on my way, Christian. I borrowed one of Grace's purses. My stuff fit in it better and it's more elegant than the paper bags Freyja and Ti brought me." The purse matched her suit and looked like the one Grace had been carrying the first time Christian met her.

"You can't stay longer?"

"I'm not going to. You need your rest. Starting tomorrow, you have a business to run."

"One I don't want. I'd rather go with you."

"I don't think so." Liza finished her coffee and stood. The cut of the suit flattered perfection. Christian couldn't believe he'd slept with her, couldn't believe she was leaving. "You know your place is here. Here where you've set change in motion. Freyja, Kathy, Horatio, Ti and yes, Aurora--and hundreds, maybe thousands of people you haven't met--are all counting on you to follow through on what you've begun. You would never forgive yourself if you left now."

433

"I'm not the man they see."

"Haven't you learned anything, Christian?" Liza took Grace's purse from the table. Her inviolate eyes caressed him as she approached. "If I was your illusion, consider yourself theirs. Don't try to bring them down to earth. You might succeed and then, you'd have failed."

"I love you." Christian couldn't control his tears.

"And I love you." Liza leaned forward. He felt a flicker of tongue as she took a drop of salt water from his face. "Good-bye."

Christian watched her walk to the door. Her long hair swung hypnotically. Grace's purse hung heavily in her hand. "Good-bye?" He got the answer he expected. None. As the door closed behind her, Christian returned to the table, sat, and drank the cup she'd poured.